THE
DEVIL'S
FORTRESS

BOOKS BY DALE BROWN

THE

DEVIL'S

FORTRESS

DALE
BROWN

**BLACK
STONE**
PUBLISHING

The characters and events in this book are fictitious.
Any similarity to real persons, living or dead, is coincidental
and not intended by the author.

Printed in the United States of America

First edition: 2024
ISBN 979-8-212-18840-1
Fiction / Thrillers / Military

Version 1

Blackstone Publishing
31 Mistletoe Rd.
Ashland, OR 97520

www.BlackstonePublishing.com

*This novel is dedicated to the people
of both Ukraine and Israel, especially those killed
or wounded by the brutality and cruelty of others.
America needs to stand firmly in support of these two nations.*

"Freely they stood who stood, and fell who fell."
—John Milton, *Paradise Lost*

"Out of intense complexities, intense simplicities emerge."
—Winston Churchill

PROLOGUE

SPECIAL RESEARCH INSTITUTE FOR PLANT GENETICS,
NEAR KAMESHKOVO, EAST OF MOSCOW, RUSSIA

LATE SPRING

Silhouetted against the fiery orange-red glow of the setting sun, three
twin-engine Kazan Ansat helicopters flew east in a V-formation above
a dense green forest of pine and birch trees. The lead machine was a
black-and-scarlet Aurus VIP luxury transport model. The two helicopters
trailing it were far more utilitarian and lethal designs in olive-green-
and-gray camouflage—equipped to carry troops and armed with
door-mounted 12.7mm KORD heavy machine guns. Their stubby fuselage wings bristled with antimissile flare and chaff dispensers.

Not far ahead, the woods gave way to an extensive complex of
modern-looking steel-and-glass buildings encircling an inner core of
large, solidly built greenhouses. A double row of tall wire fences ringed
this top-secret installation. Heavily armed guards manned a fortified
checkpoint, securing the sole entry point.

Rotors whirling, the three helicopters swung low over the complex,
and then flared in, landing one after another on a wide concrete helipad.
The moment their skids touched down, uniformed men carrying submachine guns jumped out of each helicopter—fanning out across the

pad to form a protective screen. For a long, tense moment, they scanned their surroundings, plainly ready to open fire at the slightest sign of any threat. At length, their leader spoke into his throat mike, "All clear, sir. The local security environment is Code Green."

Immediately, Pavel Voronin swung down out of one of the two armed helicopters. Trim and physically fit, he straightened up easily. A slight frown crossed his face as he noted the now-dusty and wrinkled sleeves of his perfectly tailored Savile Row suit. Compared to the plush leather passenger seating of the Ansat Aurus VIP transport grounded nearby, the gunship's fold-down canvas seats had been dirty, cramped, and uncomfortable.

But then Voronin shrugged, discarding his brief moment of irritation. It had been a sensible precaution to fly here crammed into the back of one of the escort helicopters, using the brightly painted Aurus as a decoy in case of a surprise missile attack. After all, he had dozens of handmade suits—but only one life. And there were a great many people, both inside and outside of Russia, who would be happy to see him dead.

For several years, his shadowy company—Sindikat Vorona, the Raven Syndicate—had provided advanced intelligence and military expertise, equipment, and black ops services to many of the world's most unsavory regimes, all close allies of Moscow. Along the way, he had amassed tremendous power and personal wealth, climbing ever higher in the circles of Russia's ruling elites. In fact, until very recently, his influence over the nation's authoritarian president, Piotr Zhdanov, had made him effectively the second most powerful man in Russia.

Voronin had used this influence to orchestrate two back-to-back covert operations aimed at destroying the United States and completely upending the world's balance of power in Moscow's favor. The success of either plan would have left him perfectly positioned to elbow the aging Zhdanov aside and seize the reins of authority for himself. His frown deepened. Instead, both operations had failed, the last catastrophically so. As a result, he now teetered on a precipice, still enormously powerful and dangerous, but with an increasing number of foreign and domestic enemies eager to hurl him over the edge.

All of which made the secret research and development work being carried out at this relatively remote and highly guarded scientific complex that much more vital.

"An impressive-looking facility," a quiet, self-assured voice said from behind him. "At least from the outside looking in. I only hope these supposed scientific breakthroughs justify the enormous sums you've invested here."

Voronin turned to face the man who'd followed him out of the helicopter. Lean and long-faced, with short-cropped gray hair, his companion was the most visible sign of his weakened status.

Kiril Rodin was the Raven Syndicate's new chief of Special Operations. But unlike the rest of Voronin's personnel—mostly veterans of Russia's foreign intelligence services, the SVR and GRU, and its armed forces—who were personally loyal to him and to the high salaries he paid, Rodin was wholly Zhdanov's man. He was the Russian leader's personal agent inside the Syndicate, and he had explicit orders to keep Voronin on a tight leash going forward.

That would have been bad enough, but Rodin was actually something considerably more dangerous. He was not simply Zhdanov's spy; he was also a trained assassin. In effect, Rodin was the cocked pistol held ready at the base of Voronin's skull—poised to liquidate him the moment the increasingly paranoid president lost patience with the younger man's perceived failures or began to see him as a serious threat.

"You'll be able to judge the strategic significance of these technical advances soon enough," Voronin promised, holding his temper in check. He turned back to watch as the Institute's director and chief scientist, Dr. Georgii Neminsky, hurried across the landing pad to greet them. A curt signal from his senior bodyguard sent two men to intercept the short, balding scientist before he got too close. Swiftly and efficiently, they patted him down for concealed weapons before passing him through.

Now somewhat flustered and disheveled, Neminsky was still straightening his tie when he reached them. "Welcome back, Mr. Voronin. We're honored, as always." He turned to Rodin. "You must be—"

"Rodin. Chief of Special Operations," the gray-haired man said simply.

"And also my resident skeptic," Voronin told Neminsky with a slight, humorless smile.

Obviously unsure of how to react, the scientist merely bobbed his head in acknowledgment and gestured toward the central building. "All right then, gentlemen. If you'll follow me, I can brief you fully on our extraordinary progress."

While the hallways and administrative workspaces the scientist guided them through wouldn't have looked out of place in any ordinary modern office building, the Institute's primary laboratory control center was eye-opening—a technological marvel that might have been the bridge of some enormous science fiction starship. Consoles topped by keyboards, multiple UHD displays, and virtual reality goggles paired with controllers of varying types were slotted along stepped, curving tiers—all facing a wall-sized screen. White-coated technicians and scientists manned these consoles, wholly intent on monitoring what appeared to be a bewildering array of brightly color-coded graphs and streams of ever-changing alphanumerical data.

Watching his subordinate/minder, Voronin hid a cynical smile. Despite his earlier skepticism, it was obvious that Rodin could not help being impressed. That was one hurdle down. Now it was time to discover if the other man could think strategically—on a global scale—or if he was just another unimaginative trained killer fit only to follow orders from his superiors.

Voronin glanced at Neminsky. "You may proceed."

Obeying, the scientist touched a control at one of the consoles. Immediately, the large central wall display blinked to life. It showed the view from a camera covering the complex's inner core. Fortress-like windowless structures ringed multiple greenhouses. Another tap highlighted them in red. "These are our key research labs," he explained. "They are accessible only through a series of 'clean' rooms of steadily increasing rigor. To kill surface bacteria and reduce the odds of potential contaminants entering from the outside world, we use high-intensity ultraviolet lighting and keep them under positive air pressure. We also recirculate the air inside through a series of ultra-efficient particulate filters, while maintaining consistent temperature and humidity levels."

Voronin saw Rodin nod his understanding of the need for such precautions. Advanced genetic manipulation and selective breeding research being carried out by the Institute's scientists required near-total control over the laboratory environment. The slightest unwanted infection or impurity could create havoc, wrecking whole experimental strains and causing weeks or even months of delay.

Neminsky selected another control. The camera view zoomed in on the greenhouses sited at the very heart of the sprawling facility. Lights glowed brightly inside some of them. Others were dark. "Entering these greenhouses themselves requires an even more demanding set of precautions," he continued. "No one goes inside unless they're wearing a full biohazard suit, complete with sterile gloves, boots, and air-displacer helmets—and then only after completing a series of intense decontamination protocols. And, naturally, those same rigorous decontamination protocols apply to anyone leaving the greenhouses—which are also held under negative air pressure to help prevent the escape of any of our genetically altered organisms."

Rodin frowned. "That seems remarkably cumbersome."

"It is," Neminsky agreed, "which is why all but the most delicate work inside these areas is conducted remotely—using special, purpose-built robots and other machines controlled or supervised from this control center." He indicated the virtual reality gear equipping many of the room's consoles. "In effect, we operate our test sites as if they were their own, entirely separate alien worlds."

"At a tremendous expense," Rodin observed, "according to the figures I've been shown."

"Dr. Neminsky's precautions are quite necessary," Voronin assured Rodin. He signaled the scientist. "Show him your results, Georgii."

With a tight nod, Neminsky brought up a series of new images—this time from cameras sited inside several of the greenhouses themselves. They showed row upon row of dead and dying plants. Brown and yellowish patches discolored their leaves, stalks, or stems. He switched from camera to camera, naming the different crops as they were shown.

"What you see are wheat, corn, barley, rye, potatoes, rice, soybeans, and sorghum, among others—"

"The world's most important food sources for both humans and livestock," Voronin pointed out.

Neminsky nodded. "Exactly."

"And your creations are what's killing them?" Rodin said slowly. "These plant diseases you've manipulated?"

Again, the scientist nodded. "Most of our work here is focused on fungi, the chief destroyers of plants in the natural world. Our most recent tests confirm that the organisms we have successfully engineered are now resistant to all currently available fungicides."

Rodin stared at the screens. "Which means what, exactly?"

"Already nearly a quarter of the world's food crops fall prey to naturally occurring fungal infections," Neminsky told him. He indicated the imagery of dead and dying plants. "But we estimate that our modified organisms are lethal enough to wipe out between 95 and 98 percent of any infected crop. And we have also successfully modified these fungal spores to survive extremes of temperature, humidity, and UV radiation . . . all while being so small that they are easily dispersed by the wind."

Rodin looked at him. "So, in effect, you've created a new class of doomsday weapons." He shook his head dismissively. "Weapons that cannot have any practical use in the real world. Who would seriously contemplate releasing diseases that would effectively destroy the entire world's food supply? No one." He glanced sidelong at Voronin. "Except, I suppose, a suicidal madman determined to pull the whole human race down into the grave with him." His bemused expression hardened. "And I can assure you that President Zhdanov is neither suicidal nor insane, which means this costly research and development effort—scientifically impressive though it may be—is nothing but a dead end. And a total waste of the Syndicate's resources."

Voronin merely smiled. "Ah, Rodin. I fear you've committed the cardinal error of jumping to a flawed conclusion on the basis of incomplete data." He turned to Neminsky. "Perhaps you can explain the situation more fully to our friend?"

The scientist nodded. "We have been conducting another extensive research program—one that runs parallel with our development of these more infectious and lethal plant diseases." He brought up new imagery on the central wall display. These showed video captured inside other greenhouses. Greenhouses that were full of lush, vibrant plants. "The fields you see here have also been exposed to our weaponized plant diseases," he explained. "But we sowed them using seeds genetically modified to resist the effects of our deadlier creations. In addition, we've developed high-efficiency fungicides tailored specifically to these altered fungal spores. This means we can extract normal crop yields even from the worst-infected agricultural zones."

"So we have both a sword and a shield," Rodin realized.

"Aptly put." Voronin looked at Neminsky. "Can your Western counterparts develop the same kinds of new fungicides and genetically altered crops?"

The scientist shrugged. "Certainly. But neither quickly nor easily. Replicating our work would take them several months at the very least, and more probably, well over a year."

"A year without sufficient food for man or beast?" Rodin said thoughtfully. "The political, social, and economic effects on the United States would be—"

"Devastating," Voronin said. "Tens of millions dead of starvation and disease at a minimum. Perhaps more. And the survivors would inhabit a bankrupted, anarchy-riddled land."

All three men smiled, inwardly contemplating the benefits Russia would accrue from crippling its most powerful and dangerous rival. The fall of the old Soviet Union had weakened their country—robbing it of its status as one of the world's two superpowers. Now, saddled with an aging population in decline and a moribund economy, Russia was, at best, only a second-rate power. Without its enormous oil, gas, and coal reserves, and its massive nuclear arsenal, most dispassionate observers would rank it as just another Third World nation on the brink of an inevitable collapse into geopolitical irrelevance. In one blow, destroying American agriculture could reverse that equation, especially if the rest of the world ultimately found itself reliant on Russian-supplied, disease-resistant crop strains and advanced fungicides.

Then Rodin frowned. "All of this assumes that these new weapons can somehow be effectively employed without being immediately traced back to us. Given the probable consequences, Russia cannot risk being identified as the culprit. The chances of triggering overwhelming retaliation would be far too high."

"And if I can demonstrate this is possible?" Voronin asked coolly.

"Then I believe President Zhdanov would be quite interested in this project you call—"

"VELES," Voronin replied with a predatory smile, giving the president's man the operational code name he had selected for this effort. Veles was the ancient Slavic god of the earth, the underworld, magic, trickery, and wealth—a counterpart to the old Norse gods Loki and Odin, if they were combined into one deity. Given the devastation he planned to inflict on the Americans and their allies, with the resulting profits—both for Russia, and, equally importantly, for himself personally—the association seemed entirely fitting.

ONE

NEAR THE RAVEN'S NEST, SOUTHWEST OF MOSCOW

LATER THAT NIGHT

Under the light of a quarter-moon high overhead, patches of silver light and dark shadow dappled the mile-wide, heavily guarded private forest surrounding Pavel Voronin's imposing country estate. Staying low, sticking to those shadows wherever possible, and taking infinite pains to avoid making unnecessary noise, Nick Flynn slowly worked his way through the tall trees and dense undergrowth. A few yards ahead, the brush thinned a bit, revealing what appeared to be a trail cut through the woods. It ran southeast, toward the low hill topped by the Russian oligarch's sprawling, two-story ultramodern villa, which he called the Raven's Nest.

Cautiously, Flynn dropped to one knee and glanced over his shoulder to check on the man behind him, a member of his Quartet Directorate action team. Even at close range and using his night vision goggles, he had a hard time making out Tadeusz Kossak as more than a vague shape, almost invisible among the tangle of pine tree trunks, low-hanging branches, ferns, and other underbrush. Like him, the Pole wore camouflage fatigues and a Special Forces–pattern tactical assault vest made with advanced, innovative materials that made him difficult to detect— either visually or with sophisticated thermal sensors.

Kossak, a veteran of his own country's Special Troops Command, moved up to join him and flashed an interrogatory signal. Which way now? Should they risk taking that trail?

Thinking quickly, Flynn considered their options. Moving along the trail would be much faster, but also far too dangerous. Paths through these woods would be focal points for any sensors and patrols. He decided to move parallel to the trail instead, using it as a guide toward Voronin's dacha while staying in as much cover as possible. One flick of his hand communicated this to Kossak. The other man nodded.

They went on, threading their way carefully and deliberately between pines and clumps of bushes.

Flynn carried a compact, Russian-made PP-2000 submachine gun in the low ready position, with the stock lightly pressed against his right shoulder and its short barrel pointed down. Both the weapon and its special 9mm armor-piercing ammunition had been acquired on the international arms black market by Quartet Directorate operatives.

Besides a 9mm MP-443 Grach pistol holstered on his vest, Kossak had an equipment bag slung across his back, containing the ready-to-assemble components of a powerful Lobaev DXL-5 Havoc sniper rifle chambered for 12.7mm rounds. Fully assembled, the weapon would be more than five feet long. It had also been covertly bought for this mission. Using "sanitized" Russian-made weapons was a necessary precaution since they were operating so deep in hostile territory.

Contemplating the firepower they were carrying, Flynn felt a tight smile cross his face. He'd done his time as a Boy Scout while growing up in Central Texas, and their motto, "Be Prepared," was a good one. Tonight's sneak-and-peek effort to penetrate the security zone around Voronin's estate was primarily intended to scout workable routes for his full, six-member action team. With better knowledge of the ground in hand, they hoped to assassinate the Russian oligarch the next night. But neither Flynn nor Kossak planned to pass up the chance for an immediate kill shot on Voronin if one presented itself.

Flynn pushed down a momentary pang of conscience. Killing in the heat of battle was one thing. Going in with the cold-blooded intent to assassinate a specific human target was quite another. But this was the operation he'd chosen. In fact, he reminded himself, this was the operation he'd pushed hard for—even over the objections of some of the Quartet Directorate's senior heads of station. Because, if there ever were a textbook case of "someone who needed killing," it was Pavel Voronin. Over the past several years, the mercenary Raven Syndicate headed by the Russian oligarch had spread death and destruction around the world. And twice Voronin had come close—far too close for comfort—to successfully carrying out covert attacks on the United States that would have killed tens of millions of innocents.

In both cases, Flynn and his team had been lucky enough to stop him, but the cost had been high, and their margin for error frighteningly slim. Given the Raven Syndicate's vast resources and Voronin's utter ruthlessness, it was only a matter of time before one of its plans to cripple the U.S. bore lethal fruit, which made playing defense ultimately a sucker's game.

Taking the Russian oligarch permanently off the board, Flynn had argued, was the only way for the Quartet Directorate to continue carrying out its long-standing mission—to act decisively against serious threats to the free world. The Directorate, commonly referred to as Four by its members, had been organized by veterans of America's OSS (the Office of Strategic Services), Britain's SOE (the Special Operations Executive), and the anti-Nazi resistance movements of Poland, France, Norway, and other allied countries at the outset of the Cold War against the old Soviet Union.

Even then it was obvious that the West's official intelligence agencies were increasingly mired in bureaucratic caution and politics, as well as being deeply penetrated by Soviet spies and moles. Unwilling to see the wartime sacrifices they had made for the free world wasted, Four's founders had created a top-secret private intelligence and covert action force—one able and willing to operate outside the bounds imposed by risk-averse government officials and politicians.

Over the following decades, Four's highly trained operatives had waged a clandestine war—fighting in the shadows against the West's enemies without the sanction or protection of any government. Near-absolute secrecy was the key to their survival and success given the odds they faced. Flynn knew the imperative to maintain that cloak of secrecy had been one of the most serious arguments against his proposal to kill Voronin on his home turf. This far inside Russia, the risks of being caught, interrogated, and either imprisoned or executed were extraordinarily high. Which was why Rule Number One for this operation was to avoid detection at all reasonable costs.

Just then Flynn caught the faint sounds of movement. Someone was coming up the trail behind them. He froze and then slowly went prone, avoiding the sort of quick, flickering motion that might draw attention, even in darkness. Close behind him, Kossak did the same thing.

Boots crunched across the dried pine needles littering the trail, accompanied by the faint squelch of a radio and a murmured exchange in Russian. "*Pyatyy patrul' priblizhayetsya k oranzhevomu markeru. Net kontaktov.* Patrol Five is coming up to orange marker. No contacts."

"*Ponyatno, Pyatyy*. Understood, Five."

Flynn pressed his face to the ground to hide the betraying gleam of his eyes as two Raven Syndicate guards ambled by no more than a few yards away. Breathing shallowly, he waited until the sounds faded away in the distance and silence descended again across the nearby woods. Cautiously, he lifted his head. They needed to press on. This late in the spring, nights were relatively short, and he and Kossak had a lot of ground to scout before the rising sun robbed them of the cover of darkness. He shifted to get back to his feet . . . and then froze again at the warning touch of Kossak's gloved hand on his leg.

Just in time.

A third Russian, moving far more quietly than his two comrades, came ghosting up the trail they were paralleling—with a KORD 7.62mm assault rifle up and at the ready. Flynn narrowed his eyes. This man was acting as a rearguard for the first patrol, sweeping up from behind to catch any unwary intruders who might have been fooled into believing they'd just been missed. *Good tactics*, he thought dispassionately. And a useful reminder that the Raven Syndicate troops guarding Voronin's

estate weren't just cannon fodder. That fit the available intel, which suggested the oligarch recruited heavily from Russia's Spetsnaz, its special
forces units.

He and Kossak lay motionless, waiting until this Russian, too, vanished ahead of them among the trees and undergrowth. Then Flynn
curled back toward the Pole and signaled a change of course. Now that
they knew for sure the nearby trail was a patrol route, staying so close
to it was a bad bet. Kossak nodded in agreement.

Together, they low crawled off to their left, heading deeper into
the woods. Several dozen yards farther on, they came face to face with
a dense hedge of thorn bushes and other brush extending across their
line of travel for as far as they could see in the darkness under the trees.
Coils of razor wire were laced into this natural barrier, rendering it virtually impassable. For a long moment, both men studied the obstacle.

At length, Kossak edged even more to the left, pointing out what
appeared to be a narrow opening near the base of this interwoven wall
of thorns and wire. Tunnel-like, it led deeper into the brush, apparently heading roughly in the direction they wanted to go. It could be
a trail broken through the surrounding vegetation by rabbits or foxes,
Flynn theorized. Worming their way along it without getting snagged
by the overhanging brambles and branches would be challenging, but
it should be doable.

That was mighty convenient. Then he frowned. Maybe too convenient.

Before Kossak could wriggle forward, Flynn stopped him. Carefully,
he scanned the surface of the trail through his goggles, looking closely
for any signs that the soil had been disturbed by something other than
paws. His jaw tightened. Not more than a foot or two down the path, a
patch of earth in the center seemed slightly mounded, rising a fraction
of an inch higher than the ground to either side.

Flynn reached into one of the pockets of his tactical vest and pulled
out a thin, extendible, stainless-steel prod. Gingerly, he probed the earth
ahead and stopped the instant he felt the tip of the prod contact a solid
object buried just a couple of inches down. *Well, shit*, he thought, it

was a damned good thing Mama Flynn's dark-haired boy was paranoid after all. If he had to guess, that was some variant of the Russian PMN antipersonnel mine, containing enough high explosives to rip a man to shreds. The old military adage, "the easy way is always mined," was dead accurate in this case—with the emphasis on *dead*. A small animal wouldn't have the weight to trigger the mine. A man would. Gently, he retracted the prod and stowed it away.

Then he tapped Kossak on the shoulder and used the hand signals for "danger" and "mine." The other man's eyes widened slightly. "I'm beginning to think visitors are not welcome here, Nick," the Pole murmured in a barely perceptible tone.

"Seems so," Flynn agreed quietly.

Together they slithered back from the hedge of thorns. Putting some distance between themselves and that newly discovered land mine seemed sensible while they considered their next move. Using their wire-cutters could be a possibility, Flynn thought, although the work would be painfully slow and exhausting.

Closer study of the barrier, however, foreclosed even that option. There, tied in among the tangle of thorns and razor wire, they could make out the leads for what were likely to be other sensors and alarms of some kind.

Flynn shook his head in disbelief. They'd suspected that the defenses around Voronin's country estate were tight. But this was a level of security beyond anything they'd originally envisioned. He sat back for a moment on his haunches. Dangerous as it was, the only practical way to get closer to Voronin's villa would involve paralleling those forest trails so regularly patrolled by Raven Syndicate guards.

Abruptly, three helicopters flew over them, racing just above the tree-tops—howling past with an earsplitting clatter of whirling rotor blades. Pine branches overhead whipped back and forth in a sudden frenzied dance, tugged and torn by the powerful down blast.

Flynn breathed out. Those helicopters were heading straight for the low rise at the center of this fenced-in estate. And he was pretty sure that they were the same three birds they'd seen departing several

hours ago—not long before he and Kossak began this difficult attempt
to scout Voronin's lair.

If so, the chances were good that the Russian oligarch was returning from wherever he'd flown. Which meant he and Kossak might really
be able to take him out this same night. Assuming, of course, that they
could somehow thread their way safely through this intricate and deadly
web of sensors, wire, mines, and roving patrols. There were a hell of a
lot of "ifs" in there, Flynn reminded himself. And even more when he
considered their need for a solid escape plan in all the resulting confusion if they did manage to nail Voronin. After all, neither he nor Tadeusz
Kossak was the suicidal type.

TWO

Constructed to Pavel Voronin's own exacting design, the above-ground elements of his large modernist dacha testified to his enormous wealth and power. Floor-to-ceiling windows looked out across a spacious lawn and a helicopter landing pad. At the far edge of sight off to the west, beyond the dark expanse of his private forest, moonlight gleamed on the Moskva River. Inside the brightly lit mansion, expensive furnishings from the most exclusive designers filled nearly every room, along with original paintings and sculptures by Kandinsky, Rothko, and other renowned abstract artists. And at the dacha's center, a spacious, glass-roofed atrium held a heated swimming pool and sauna.

Below ground, everything was far more utilitarian. Down a long concrete corridor twenty meters below the surface, the estate's security control center occupied a medium-sized chamber protected by an armored, vault-style door. Under cool, blue-tinted overhead lights, desks topped by monitors and computer consoles were arranged in a half-circle around a workstation set aside for the senior Raven Syndicate officer on duty. Half a dozen personnel, veterans of the GRU or Russia's internal security service, the FSB, operated the computer consoles. Each monitored the camera feeds and motion sensor readouts from specific, sixty-degree arcs around the compound's outer perimeter.

The senior officer, a former GRU major named Vladimir Annenkov, kept his own jaundiced eye on the watchers. By its very nature, guard duty was monotonous. That was especially true for the men assigned to watch video screens in this air-conditioned artificial environment. At least the troops patrolling the woods and exterior of the dacha were in the natural world—fully immersed in everything their own senses of sight, hearing, and even smell were telling them about the local environment. They could react instantly to the faintest crack of a dead branch or to the slightest hint of movement when everything should otherwise be still. But the men under his immediate supervision had no such stimulus as they paged repetitively through the various digital images and graphs transmitted by the multitude of cameras and sensors sited in their designated sectors. Under these conditions, it would be all too easy for one or more of them to "zone out"—seeing only what they expected to see on their different feeds.

Annenkov's mouth turned down in a scowl. Others inside the Syndicate, including Voronin himself, knew this tendency. That was why they'd recently installed a brand-new piece of advanced software to backstop the fallible human observers watching the estate's perimeter. *Too bad the enormously expensive and highly sophisticated program was an absolute piece of crap*, he thought dourly.

Movement on one of his own video feeds caught his attention. The three Kazan Ansat helicopters had just landed. He watched Voronin and Rodin disembark and head inside, surrounded by the security team that had accompanied them to the scientific facility at Kameshkovo. Maintenance crews were already hurrying across the pad to refuel and check over the grounded helicopters.

Abruptly, a red-flagged alert message flashed across Annenkov's screen. "What the hell?" he growled. He leaned forward, scanning the text box blinking on the monitor. His heavy brows furrowed.

"Sir?" one of his subordinates asked. "Is there a problem?"

"Only that our *brilliant* new robot overlord claims it has spotted a significant anomaly at the outer perimeter fence," Annenkov said with heavy sarcasm. "Again."

The artificial intelligence piggybacked onto the Raven Syndicate's security systems was called POSPETSNA, short for "*Pomoshchnik po spetsial'nomu nablyudeniyu*," "Special Surveillance Assistant." Its assigned mission was to analyze the huge amounts of video and other data gathered by the compound's dozens of surveillance cameras and motion sensors—acting as a sort of all-seeing eye to spot problems that mere humans might otherwise miss. However, although installed with great fanfare, the AI system was now about as popular with Voronin's security troops and their commanders as a puritan scold at a bachelor party in a bordello. Initial efforts to allow it to monitor the camera and sensor feeds in real time had led to complete chaos. POSPETSNA had triggered multiple alerts—sending guards rushing wildly from point to point around the estate's perimeter to respond to perceived incursions—only to cancel those alerts as false alarms just as rapidly.

Realizing the situation was untenable, but unwilling to scrap the expensive program entirely, Voronin had instead ordered the AI tasked to examine imagery and motion sensor data on a one-hour delay—to enable POSPETSNA to teach itself to operate more efficiently over time. In this instance, it was only allowed to contact the Raven's Nest senior duty officer, Annenkov, if it detected threats or sensor anomalies that it assessed as extremely serious and for which there had been no sign of any human reaction earlier.

But while shifting the AI out of real-time mode significantly reduced the number of false alarms it generated, POSPETSNA had not yet issued a single warning that proved worth following up.

"I wonder what terrible threat we're facing this time?" the same subordinate asked, not bothering to hide his cynicism. "Maybe a windblown tree branch banging into the perimeter fence? Or perhaps another deadly pile of leaves drifting over a motion sensor?"

Annenkov snorted. Both sets of natural phenomena had triggered POSPETSNA alerts in the recent past. He shrugged and tapped the text box on his screen. "According to this, our software 'genius' claims to have detected something 'anomalous' about the feed from Perimeter Camera Twenty-Four."

His fingers jabbed ferociously at his own keyboard as he cued up the AI-flagged footage and sent it to his team for their review. It was undoubtedly a waste of their time and energy, but, if nothing else, shooting down yet another POSPETSNA-generated false alarm should provide more ammunition to those who wanted to rip the idiotic software out by its digital roots.

Still scowling, Annenkov tapped a key to play back the video stream recorded an hour ago. He stared closely at his monitor. The enhanced night vision imagery showed a section of the three-meter-high chain-link fence topped by tight coils of razor wire that would strip the flesh off anyone trying to climb over. Nothing at all seemed wrong or out of place. According to the digital time stamp at the bottom of the screen, seconds passed in a steady procession. Abruptly, from the right of the screen, a gray-brown feathered shape swooped low across the fence, gliding just above the coiled wire and settling onto a tree branch in camera view. Disconcerting yellow eyes shone brightly as a large, rounded head swiveled through almost a complete circle—scanning for nocturnal prey in an eerie simulacrum of the surveillance camera filming it. And then, barely half a minute later, with another fluttering explosion of its wings, the bird darted into the darkness and vanished off the left side of the screen.

"*Der'mo*," Annenkov muttered to himself. "Another bloody owl." The birds were a relatively common nightly sight in the skies over the local woods as they hunted small rodents. Early on in POSPETSNA's ill-starred career, the AI had mistakenly tagged several of these owls as unmanned aerial vehicles, drones—and then triggered a full-scale alert against a possible air attack. If this were a similar occurrence, he'd be tempted to find whatever piece of computer hardware contained the idiot AI and personally slash through every connecting cable.

But the flagged video footage kept running. For another minute or so, nothing stirred. And then another big owl glided in from the right, flying low above the knife-sharp wire. It landed on the same branch vacated by the first bird and followed suit, swiveling to look for possible prey. Moments later, it fluttered away and disappeared off to the left. Again, the video kept running, showing nothing onscreen that was unusual.

Until, an owl suddenly swooped in from right to left across the fence following the exact same trajectory . . . until it too landed on the identical tree branch—

"Mother of God," Annenkov snapped, jolting upright in his seat as he finally grasped what he'd been seeing. "That's the same damned owl! We've been watching a loop of footage played over and over. Someone hacked that surveillance camera."

He felt a sudden, cold shiver down his spine. Because of the time delay imposed on the POSPETSNA AI's analysis, the events they were just now seeing had occurred well over sixty minutes ago. This meant the human watcher responsible for that perimeter arc, an officer under his direct command, had somehow completely missed seeing what was happening. Worst of all, Annenkov knew that whoever hacked the security camera had to have been operating inside the Raven's Nest security perimeter—freely and utterly undetected by any patrols or the compound's other sensors—for most of those same sixty minutes. That was a recipe for potential disaster.

He stabbed down on a key control that opened encrypted emergency radio links to all the Raven Syndicate security troops stationed on site. "All units, this is Annenkov. Intruder alert! I repeat, intruder alert! This is not a drill." More orders followed in rapid succession. The first sent a patrol hurrying toward the section of perimeter fence covered by the surveillance camera that somebody had hacked. The second directed the former Spetsnaz captain commanding Voronin's bodyguards to immediately rush the oligarch and Kiril Rodin to an armored safe room deep inside the building.

"Understood, Annenkov," the bodyguard commander assured him. "We're moving them now." Then he warned, "Mr. Voronin isn't happy about this situation. So whatever shit's hit the fan had better be real."

"Tell me something I don't know!" Annenkov growled back. He

switched frequencies, summoning all personnel—off-shift or not—into action. Some guards would deploy to protect every entrance to the villa itself. The rest, armed to the teeth, would start sweeping the surrounding woods, hunting for the intruders who'd spoofed that camera and then penetrated the Raven's Nest's security perimeter.

THREE

THAT SAME TIME

A wide expanse of cleared ground stretched beyond the security fence. At the far end, it was fringed by another thin patch of woods. A cursory look would have suggested this open, grassy field was as flat and featureless as a pancake. In reality, many shallow dips and hollows and low hummocks offered modest cover and concealment for anyone willing to hug the ground and crawl.

Close to the far edge of the clearing, Quartet Directorate field agent Laura Van Horn lay prone at the lip of one of those little depressions. There was more cover in the fringe of woods behind her, but she wanted a clear line of sight to the outer perimeter of Voronin's estate.

She had a small, hand-held controller on the ground beside her. A faint red light indicated it was on standby, ready to power up at the push of a button. Her eyes narrowed slightly as she scanned the forest behind the line of razor-wire-topped fence. Everything seemed quiet. She glanced down, pulling back the sleeve of her jacket to check her watch. So far, so good. But they were on a tight schedule here. Flynn and Kossak had a limited window of darkness remaining to complete their planned reconnaissance and slip back out of Voronin's compound without being spotted.

"Ah . . . shit," the tall, wiry man to her left murmured.

Van Horn turned her head. "Trouble?"

Wade Vucovich, their team's surveillance expert, nodded. He had his head down, intently studying the faintly glowing bar-graph displays on a compact piece of electronic equipment. Combining an electro-magnetic signal detector with a frequency-hopping scanner allowed him to monitor a wide band of channels used for tactical communi-cations. "Yeah. The level of radio chatter from inside the compound just spiked through the roof. It's all highly encrypted, so I can't get a firm read on what the hell the bad guys are talking about, but I figure it can't be good."

Van Horn frowned and keyed her mike. "Lynx Ears to Eyes One," she radioed. "See anything?"

"*I've got movement near the entry point*," Shannon Cooke replied. Like her, the tough, forceful, ex–U.S. Special Forces operator spoke in perfect, idiomatic Russian, without even a trace of his usual soft Virginia drawl. Although their own radio transmissions were also encrypted, no one on the team wanted to take the risk of being immediately identi-fied as a foreign agent. "*I have three goons in sight. And they're poking around the fence.*"

Not good, Van Horn decided. She switched frequencies to the one allocated to Flynn and Kossak. "Ears to Lynx Prowler. Bad news, guys. You're busted."

"*Copy that*," Flynn said a heartbeat later. "*Heading toward the alter-nate extraction point now.*"

Van Horn nodded. Now to find out the hard way if all their care-ful contingency planning would pay off. She picked up the hand-held controller and tapped a Cyrillic alphabet–inscribed button to power it up. A tiny, green-tinged screen glowed in the darkness, showing the view from a quadcopter-mounted drone. Gently, she tweaked the twin sticks on her controller, maneuvering carefully and watching as the remote camera picture changed in response to her command inputs.

"Quick as you can, Prowler," she told Flynn. "Things are going to get very loud real soon."

AT THE FENCE, NEAR CAMERA 24
THAT SAME TIME

Fyodor Malov held his KORD assault rifle at the ready. Using his night vision gear, the one-time Spetsnaz warrant officer kept watch on the grassy field beyond the perimeter fence. At the same time, the other two Raven Syndicate guards in his patrol moved down the fence line—periodically pausing to tug hard at the metal links. "Anything?" he asked.

"Not yet," one of his subordinates called back. "Think this is just another of those AI screwups?"

Still scanning the expanse of open ground, Malov shrugged his shoulders. "Who the fuck knows?" His voice hardened. "But keep checking, anyway, Sergei. If the stupid machine fouled up, that's on it. If we miss something, that's on us. And I sure as hell don't want any mistakes pinned on us, do you?"

"No, sir," the other man said devoutly. The duty security chief, Annenkov, was widely known as a hard case whose preferred approach to discipline was all stick, without a single carrot ever in sight. Sergei moved a meter farther down the fence and again yanked hard at a section of the woven metal mesh. To his amazement, it peeled back in his hands. Wire-cutters had snipped enough strands loose to make an opening that was just big enough for a man to crawl under. "Son of a bitch!" he said in disbelief. "We've got a real breach here!"

At that exact moment, Malov caught a quick flutter of motion out in the open field beyond the fence. Something small was headed toward them across the grass—moving fast at about chest height. Reacting instinctively, he tucked his assault rifle tighter into his shoulder and opened fire, squeezing off two-round bursts in rapid succession.

He missed.

The tiny shape jinked left and right, dodging his fire as it zigzagged closer and accelerated.

Malov's eyes widened as he suddenly recognized what they were facing. "Drone! Take cover!" he screamed.

But it was too late.

With a blinding orange flash, the explosives-carrying quadcopter remotely piloted by Laura Van Horn detonated only meters away. Ball bearings embedded in the explosives sleeted outward at more than a thousand meters per second—shredding the three Raven Syndicate guards and hurling them aside like tattered rag dolls.

INSIDE THE PERIMETER
THAT SAME TIME

Nick Flynn loped through the forest with Kossak close beside him. They were hurrying back toward the perimeter fence, aiming for a section far from their original entry point. Together, they darted between trees and bulled straight through clumps of undergrowth.

With the Russians alerted to their presence, stealth was out in favor of speed, quick reflexes, and camouflage. At a distance and in the dark, their tactical gear and clothing might be mistaken for that worn by the Raven Syndicate patrols they'd observed on the way in. *Given a bit of luck anyway*, Flynn thought. But he kept a tight grip on his Russian-made submachine gun, remembering a caution from one of his Air Force Special Operations tactics instructors long before he'd been recruited into the Quartet Directorate. "Luck is nice," the veteran NCO had told him dryly. "Superior firepower is more reliable."

Suddenly, a couple of hundred yards away, an orange ball of fire lit up the surrounding woods and night sky with an echoing *WHAMM*.

"At least Laura's having fun," Kossak said matter-of-factly with a quick, fleeting grin. The Pole's bright white teeth contrasted sharply with the blotches of tan, green, and black camouflage paint streaking his face.

"She *does* love a good explosion," Flynn agreed with a tight smile of his own. He detected an abrupt blur of motion off among the trees and shadows on their right flank. Men were moving there, coming fast in this direction. He spun to the side and dropped to one knee with his weapon up and ready. "Action right!" he snapped.

Kossak dove for cover—just as another three-man Raven Syndicate patrol group loomed up out of the darkness. Without hesitating, Flynn flipped the submachine gun's fire mode selector to full auto and opened up at point-blank range. The PP-2000 hammered back against his shoulder as he swept its muzzle across the knot of stupefied enemy troops, burning through most of a forty-four-round box magazine in seconds. Hit repeatedly by 9mm armor-piercing rounds, the guards folded over and tumbled to the ground, already dead or dying.

Flynn breathed out raggedly, feeling the adrenaline still flooding his system. That had been way too close. Then he swore under his breath as whistles blew shrilly in the woods somewhere behind them.

The two Quartet Directorate agents scrambled back to their feet and hurried onward. While on the move, Flynn dropped out his mostly empty magazine and slid another into place, shaking his head in frustration. So much for what was supposed to have been a nice, quiet, and above all, undetected, scouting mission. Instead, this had quickly turned into a deadly combination of a pell-mell race and an all-out pitched battle.

Through the trees ahead, Flynn caught a glimpse of moonlight glinting off metal. That had to be the razor wire–topped fence, he realized. And it was only about fifty yards away. Maybe they were going to make it after all.

But then he skidded to a stop as Kossak suddenly held out a clenched fist, signaling danger. They both threw themselves prone again.

Swiftly, Flynn eyeballed the situation through his night vision goggles. He grimaced. There were more Raven Syndicate guards by the fence, already settling into firing positions behind the cover of trees growing just inside the perimeter.

He gritted his teeth. They were boxed in—with enemies on the alert ahead and more closing in from behind. This screwed-up situation was starting to resemble the Alamo or Thermopylae much too closely for his comfort. Heroic last stands looked great in the movies, but they sucked in real life. Which meant it was time for more fireworks. "Eyes Two, this is Prowler," he whispered over his radio. "We're in position at the alternate extraction point, but it's blocked."

Through his headset, he heard the voice of another member of his Quartet Directorate action team, Cole Hynes. "*I see 'em, sir,*" the former soldier said. "*Keep your heads down. Way down. I got this.*"

FOUR

OUTSIDE THE PERIMETER

THAT SAME TIME

Cole Hynes lay prone in the grassy field roughly thirty yards outside the security fence surrounding Voronin's estate. Carefully, he turned to ready a piece of gear that looked oddly like a carry-on-sized suitcase with a small, blunt-nosed rocket attached to the front. The rocket was attached to a length of gray nylon tubing coiled inside the case—a flexible tube stuffed full of connected fragmentation grenades to make an explosive line charge.

This variant of the U.S. military's antipersonnel obstacle breaching system was initially designed for deployment by a two-man team. The standard two-case device was utilized to blow a path through minefields and other barriers several feet wide and up to fifty yards long. Since that was far more capability than they needed for this mission, Hynes had modified it for his own solo use by cutting the length of the line charge in half and using grenades and a miniature booster rocket manufactured in Russia.

Tight-lipped with concentration, he aligned the head of the rocket, rotating it a degree or so until it was aimed squarely at the distant, moonlit perimeter fence. He took one more quick look to verify that he was on target, and then reached into the back of the open case. Gently, he pulled the pin on a green metal cylinder at the far end of the coiled line. That armed a tiny explosive charge intended to pop open a small drogue parachute. One more careful movement took out the pin on a similar black cylinder fastened at the front of the line charge. Now the rocket itself was armed and ready to fire.

Showtime, Hynes thought. His fingers curled around the base of the rocket and tugged out a third pin, the final safety. All set, he pulled down sharply on a black retainer ring dangling below the rocket assembly—activating its ignition timer.

Aware that he had just fifteen seconds to get clear, Hynes rolled off to the side and wriggled backward through the tall grass. *Four . . . three . . . two . . . one . . .* he counted down silently. *Now!*

With a loud, crackling *hiss* and a pulse of flame, the little rocket soared into the night sky—trailing the swiftly uncoiling line charge behind it. A fraction of a second later, the drogue chute snapped open at the rear of the rippling nylon tube, braking the whole assembly so that it arced down to drape across the top of the razor wire–topped metal fence.

That drew startled shouts from the Raven Syndicate troops on guard there.

WHUMMP.

As the dozen or so grenades in the line charge detonated simultaneously, thousands of fragments ripped outward, slicing apart the chain-link fence and razor wire in the blink of an eye. A dense pall of black smoke, blast-thrown dust, and whirling shards of shredded bark and splintered tree limbs billowed high into the air.

INSIDE THE PERIMETER
THAT SAME TIME

Faces pressed hard against the dirt, Flynn and Kossak clung to the ground as it heaved, jolted by the enormous nearby explosion. Bits and pieces of debris hurled skyward by the colossal blast pattered down all around them.

Cautiously, Flynn opened his eyes. A roiling cloud of smoke and dust cut visibility to only a few feet. And his ears were ringing, temporarily deafened by the shattering sound of Hynes's breaching charge. He shook his head to clear it, clapped Kossak on the shoulder, and then rolled to his feet. Nodding, the Pole scrambled upright himself. It was time to go.

Together, they charged forward into the thick haze of swirling dust and smoke. Trees and clumps of underbrush appeared out of the darkness and then disappeared just as suddenly behind them. Brambles and thorns tore at their clothing and gear.

Flynn ran past a Raven Syndicate guard writhing in agony on the ground and kept going. The injured Russian's torn, smoking, and blood-spattered clothing and empty, weaponless hands made it clear that he no longer posed a threat. Faced by an armed enemy, Flynn would kill without hesitation, but he drew the line at shooting people if he didn't need to.

Still running, they reached the area where Hynes's breaching charge had detonated. Where a ten-foot-high fence festooned with razor wire had once barred the way, there was now only a blast-torn gap. Blackened and twisted pieces of metal littered the ground.

Flynn and Kossak leaped over the tangled heaps of smoldering debris and sprinted out into the cleared ground beyond the perimeter. They high-tailed it north through tall grass toward another stretch of woods that separated Voronin's compound from the nearest village, a tiny farming hamlet. Hynes arrowed over to join up with them.

"Prowlers are out!" Flynn radioed. "All Lynx elements fall back to the rally point. We're bugging out of here ASAP."

"*Wait one,*" he heard Shannon Cooke reply. "*We've got company coming. There's a helo headed your way. Altitude very low at my one o'clock.*"

Oh, fricking joy, Flynn thought darkly. He glanced back over his shoulder . . . and saw the unwelcome shape of a Kazan Ansat helicopter lifting off the pad near the Russian oligarch's sprawling country home. Its nose swung toward them as it leveled off just above the treetops. "Crap. I really, *really* hate it when the enemy does smart shit," he muttered to himself.

OVER THE RAVEN'S NEST
THAT SAME TIME

Pilot Valentin Khutakov worked the cyclic, collective, and foot pedals in combination—transitioning his Kazan Ansat gunship from near-vertical takeoff mode to level flight. He dropped the nose slightly as the helicopter slid forward across the pine forest below. They weren't moving especially fast yet, no more than thirty kilometers per hour. His left hand shifted toward the throttle grip on the collective, ready to feed more power to the helicopter's twin engines, but then he stopped. After all, what was the hurry? They were chasing down enemies fleeing on foot, right? So accelerating now would only make it easier to accidentally overshoot their targets. Better to do the job right and show his employer, Pavel Voronin, the superiority of combat aviation over Annenkov's glorified, gun-toting security guards—the morons who'd already so singularly failed to stop the intruders who'd broken into the Raven's Nest.

"Three faint IR contacts moving north across the open ground ahead of us," his copilot reported. "Approximately nine hundred meters out."

Khutakov nodded. He could see the same, wavering images through his own night vision gear. He blinked rapidly, but they remained stubbornly out of focus. Ah, he understood, those fleeing enemy commandos must be wearing sophisticated camouflage cloth that blurred their heat signatures.

A wolfish smile creased his broad face. High-tech camouflage or not, the result would be the same when his door-mounted 12.7mm machine guns opened fire—hosing the whole area down with hundreds of rounds moving at nearly a thousand meters per second. Those intruders scrambling to get away would be chopped into mincemeat. "Stand by, Misha," he instructed his right-door gunner, who was crouched and ready in the crew compartment behind him. "I'll veer off in a moment and come around to give you a steady gun platform to light up those targets."

"Copy that, sir," the gunner replied.

But then the situation all went to shit.

From his position, the Ansat's left-door gunner saw a blindingly bright flash erupt from the ground. A dazzling spark slashed through the night sky—climbing fast on a rippling plume of gray-white smoke, curling around to head straight for them. "Missile! Missile!" he yelled in horror. "At our nine o'clock!"

"Fuck," Khutakov grunted, slamming all his flight controls over in a desperate bid to hurl the helicopter into a tight, evasive turn away from the oncoming missile. Out of the corner of his eye, he saw his copilot frantically stabbing at icons on his defense control panel in an effort to trigger a burst of anti-missile flares and chaff.

But the Ansat was far too low and far too slow. Before more than a handful of incandescent flares had rippled outward from the helicopter's wing-mounted pods, the Russian-made 9K333 Verba surface-to-air missile streaked across the intervening distance and detonated only meters away. Hundreds of fragments ripped through the helicopter—killing and wounding its crew and smashing vital electronics and flight control systems.

Trailing smoke and fire, the Kazan Ansat gunship rolled over and slammed into the forest. A huge orange-white flash starkly outlined the shapes of trees for a millisecond. When it vanished, all that remained was a thickening pillar of oily black smoke curling away on the light wind—a pillar lit at its base by a few, dully flickering red-tinged flames.

WEST OF THE PERIMETER FENCE
THAT SAME TIME

"Nailed the son of a bitch," Shannon Cooke reported. "Bugging out now." He tossed the spent SAM launch tube aside and sprinted across the field toward the fringe of trees.

He wasn't worried that anyone could trace the anti-air weapon he'd just fired. Like the rest of the military hardware for this operation, Quartet Directorate operatives had snagged the missile system on the international arms black market. The Russians themselves had originally sold it to their Syrian client state. And using a Russian-manufactured missile to knock a Russian-made helicopter out of the sky added a nice touch of irony. *Around and around the weapons you sell go, and where they'll eventually be used, nobody knows*, the ex-Special Forces operator mused. Since it was the only one their team had been able to smuggle this deep into hostile territory, he was glad the shoulder-launched SAM had worked as advertised. Many supposedly sophisticated Russian weapons looked great on paper but turned out to be garbage in the real world.

Once in the cover of the woods, Cooke headed straight for the rally point they'd mapped out earlier. Flynn and the rest of the team were there ahead of him. Van Horn and Vucovich were busy stripping away leaf-and-branch-studded camouflage netting that concealed three battered-looking Ural motorcycles, each with its own attached sidecar. Meanwhile, Flynn, Kossak, and Hynes were all hurriedly shrugging out of their military-style fatigues and assault vests and changing into civilian clothes. The others, including Cooke, already wore jeans, T-shirts, hoodies, and dark jackets. All of their gear and weapons, except for small, easily concealable pistols, disappeared into zippered duffel bags.

"Any more signs of trouble?" Flynn asked quietly, looking up at his arrival.

Cooke shook his head. "Not so far. Not from the air, at least. My bet is those other two Syndicate helicopter pilots aren't exactly in a hurry to commit what could be suicide."

Flynn nodded. The combination of total surprise, darkness, and drone- and rocket-delivered high explosives had acted as force multipliers—making it virtually impossible for Voronin's security forces to get an accurate read on the actual numbers of those attacking them. That should make them cautious, unwilling to risk their remaining helicopters in case more missile teams were waiting to ambush them.

But their self-imposed paralysis wouldn't last long, Flynn recognized, which made it imperative that his team get moving again and break contact before the Raven Syndicate forces recovered their nerve.

Flynn finished pulling a plain gray hoodie over his head and then glanced around. "Everyone set?"

Heads nodded. "Just waiting on you, cowboy," Van Horn said with a grin. She and Cooke were already astride two Ural motorcycles, with Hynes and Vucovich seated in their sidecars. "We figured there was no point sticking around until the bad guys come calling. They seem a little pissed off at us."

Flynn matched her smile. "Shooting things up does have that effect on people, I guess." He swung his leg over the remaining motorcycle and waited while Kossak scrambled aboard. He hit the ignition switch, and the bike's 650 cc engine rumbled quietly to life. Special mufflers were fitted to reduce the motor's noise, especially in low gear.

One by one, they took off slowly, bumping along a narrow dirt track that meandered generally west through a patchwork of woods, darkened farms, and rocky, brush-covered ground. They were headed toward Voskresensk, a small city on the banks of the Moskva River only a few kilometers away.

FIVE

A SHORT TIME LATER

Pavel Voronin stalked into the blue-lit control center. Kiril Rodin and four bodyguards trailed in his wake. Startled, Annenkov and his security team scrambled to their feet and snapped to attention.

"Well?" Voronin demanded. "What's the situation? How many troops are pursuing these intruders?"

There was an awkward silence.

Voronin's eyes narrowed. He marched closer to the heavyset security chief. "I asked you a question, did I not?"

"I've ordered our surviving guards to stay inside the perimeter for now," Annenkov admitted. "At least until we obtain a clearer picture of the threat we're facing."

Voronin stared back at him for a long, painful moment. His mouth compressed. "Is it possible, Vladimir Ivanovich, that you did not understand my orders?" he asked finally.

"No, sir."

"Then, why," Voronin continued carefully, "are your men sitting here safe on their cowardly asses . . . instead of going out there to track down, capture, interrogate, and then eliminate the insolent bastards

who just tried to kill me?" Every word came out of his mouth with the
icy precision of a serpent coiling to strike.

Annenkov stiffened. "Sir, we've already suffered thirteen casualties—
all of them veteran combat soldiers or air crew and all of them dead or
dying. Plus, we've had a helicopter gunship downed by a surface-to-air
missile. These losses were inflicted in a matter of minutes in separate attacks staged at several points inside and outside our perimeter. Attacks
carried out by enemy forces of unknown strength." He gestured at the
screens, which showed green-tinged night vision imagery from the surviving cameras along the outer fence. "Right now, we cannot know how
many of them may still be out there, waiting to ambush any reaction
force we send out. But we do know that these attackers seem liberally
equipped with missiles and explosives."

Voronin stared at him. "Are you suggesting they may plan to hit
us again?"

The other man nodded. "It's possible, though perhaps not likely. But
the enemy has already significantly attrited our security forces. Given
that, risking more troops in action beyond the perimeter could easily
weaken our defenses to the breaking point."

Voronin felt a hand on his elbow. He turned. It was Rodin.

"Annenkov is right," the gray-haired man said. "In the circumstances,
pushing more men out into the darkness would be a fool's game."

Voronin eyed him coldly. "So you agree that we should simply
huddle here in terror? Leaving these would-be assassins free to strike
again or to escape unscathed?"

Rodin shook his head. "Not at all. We've been attacked. The sensible move is to call for reinforcements." He indicated the secure
communications links at Annenkov's workstation. "You have the president's direct line. And those of the security services and the Ministry
of Defense. We're only ninety kilometers from Moscow. An airborne
reaction force from *Spetsgruppa* 'A,' for example, could be here in less
than an hour."

Voronin kept a tight rein on his expression. *Spetsgruppa* "A" was
a highly trained anti-terrorist commando unit. It operated under the

authority of the FSB, Russia's internal security service. On the surface, Rodin's suggestion made good sense. But only on the surface.

There were two reasons why Voronin knew he could not risk relying on assistance from the FSB—or from any of the other anti-terrorist troops controlled by the government, for that matter. First, because he had spent several years and tens of billions of rubles building the Raven Syndicate into an independent special intelligence and military force within the Russian state. In matters of politics and government, power fed perception and perception fed power. His power rested primarily on President Zhdanov's continuing belief that the Syndicate was more capable and more effective than its official counterparts: the military, the GRU, the SVR, and the FSB, whose near-universal record of defeat, failure, and humiliation over the past decades was infamous. Begging for help from the security and defense ministries would puncture this carefully nurtured image of strength. Given the current tenuous state of his relationship with President Zhdanov, it would be an admission of weakness he simply could not afford.

But there was another, even darker, reason Voronin believed calling for help from Moscow would be too dangerous. And that was the strong possibility that this attempt to kill him was actually the work of some of Russia's own special forces units. Not on direct orders from the president himself. After all, if Zhdanov wanted him dead, Rodin was already in place to pull the trigger. But there was a chance—a significant chance—that one of his many jealous rivals inside the nation's military and intelligence elites had secretly orchestrated tonight's bloody attack. What if someone inside the FSB, the GRU, the SVR, or the military had decided to take him out now and seek forgiveness from Zhdanov later? If so, summoning more troops from Moscow might well be the equivalent of handing his would-be murderer a sword and then baring his own breast for the fatal blow.

His decision made, Voronin shook his head. "No," he said. "If it's too hazardous to chase after these attackers ourselves, we'll handle this another way." He stabbed a finger at Annenkov. "Contact the police commanders in Voskresensk, Yegoryevsk, Kolomna—" Swiftly, he rattled off the names of half a dozen towns and cities in a wide radius around the Raven's Nest. "I want checkpoints set up on all roads and transit stations in and out of this region. Their officers are to be on the lookout for suspicious groups of men attempting to leave the area. Warn them these men are suspected terrorists and likely to be desperate and heavily armed."

Annenkov nodded his understanding. From the moment he'd started building this fortified country estate, Voronin had worked hard and successfully to buy the loyalty of all the local law enforcement authorities. The "special pay supplements" he authorized more than tripled their official salaries. With that much money on the line, the police would be only too happy to obey his instructions. And since it was well after midnight, anyone trying to escape the immediate area—whether headed toward Moscow or somewhere else—should stand out like a sore thumb.

ON THE OUTSKIRTS OF VOSKRESENSK, SOUTHEAST OF MOSCOW
THAT SAME TIME

Voskresensk was an industrial city of about ninety thousand people stretching along the Moskva River's east bank. Manufacturing plants producing concrete, rolled steel, and fertilizer were the major employers. Like many of the other small localities of the region, it had largely been missed by the waves of economic prosperity that occasionally washed across Moscow itself. None of Russia's government-owned megacorporations saw the value in pouring significant amounts of time or money into Voskresensk or its neighboring towns. As a result, anyone scooped up by a time machine at the tail end of Stalin's dictatorship and plopped down again eight decades later would have seen nothing alien or unexpected in their surroundings. There were the same drab brick and concrete low-rise apartments, factories, schools, and stores. The same trash-littered empty lots and rusting metal fences. The same sense of impoverished stasis.

Nick Flynn swung off a narrow, badly paved street near the city's

eastern rim and continued south on another dirt road. Tangled thickets
of scrub trees and underbrush lined one edge. Along the other were row
after row of small, one-story cinder-block buildings. They were nearly
identical—all gray with low, flat roofs. Most of them were covered in
spray-painted graffiti and looked abandoned. Amateurishly lettered signs
above others showed they were in commercial use, either as storage sheds
or as car and motorcycle repair shops. This late at night, none of them were
open. Darkness shrouded the whole area, with only a few dim yellow lights
glowing behind the windows of neighboring utilitarian apartment blocks.

Flynn counted openings under his breath as he rode past them. Four.
Five. Six. *There it was*, he thought, spotting a rusting metal stake silhouetted in the beam of his headlight. With the Ural's engine barely turning
over, he swung into the sign-posted alley and slowly puttered between
heaps of old trash bags and worn-out tires. There was just enough room
for his bike and its attached sidecar.

Roughly halfway down the alley, he stopped in front of one of the
small cinder-block buildings and switched off his engine. Crude graffiti scrawled across its dented, rust-flecked, metal roll-up door suggested
it was among those long ago left to rot. Only a relatively new padlock
securing the door hinted otherwise. Van Horn and Cooke pulled their
motorcycles in right behind him. They both dismounted, followed by
Hynes and Vucovich.

Stiffly, Flynn climbed off his bike and stretched, rotating his hips
first in one direction and then the other. Muscles and joints popped.
He felt like he'd been hit by a refrigerator-sized linebacker, stomped into
the astroturf, and then trampled by a whole marching band at halftime.
He appreciated that avoiding those kinds of outcomes was exactly why
he'd decided to run track in school and not play football. High school
football in Texas was played for keeps.

And judging by how awkwardly Kossak levered himself out of the
Ural's cramped sidecar, Flynn guessed the other man was feeling pretty
much the same way.

"You guys getting old on us?" Van Horn teased.

Flynn resisted the temptation to quote the old *Raiders of the Lost Ark* line about it being the mileage, not the years. "I think maybe the whole crawling, running, jumping, almost getting blown up, and narrowly dodging bullets thing might be wearing us down some," he said instead.

Kossak nodded. "This evening was . . . somewhat stressful."

"Fair point," Van Horn allowed. "The next time we try to pull off a mission like this, you should give the rest of us a chance at all the fun stuff."

Hynes turned from where he'd been unloading equipment bags from one of the motorcycle sidecars. "Uh, ma'am, not to be disrespectful or anything, but your idea of fun just might be a tiny bit skewed," he said carefully.

She shrugged. "Hey, Nick's never complained."

"Now, Ms. Van Horn," Cooke said slowly, with more than a hint of laughter. "Are you really telling us that your private outings with our esteemed and glorious leader typically involve gunbattles and explosions?"

"Well, not yet," she admitted. "I've been going easy on him up to now."

"Ah, so that explains it," Flynn said to her with a half-smile of his own. Their personal relationship wasn't a secret from the rest of the team, but he was still glad it was dark enough to hide his face's slight, embarrassed redness.

"Sir," Vucovich interrupted suddenly. "I'm starting to pick up a whole lot of new radio traffic."

Flynn turned toward him. The surveillance expert still had his headset on. He'd continued monitoring the enemy's communications while they slipped away from Voronin's compound. "Can you make anything out?"

The other man nodded. He paused momentarily, listening to the signals intercepted by his handheld scanner, and then looked back up. "From what I'm hearing, the local Russian cops are setting up a whole bunch of checkpoints all over the place. And based on the locations they're rattling off, it sure sounds like they're deploying like you figured they would."

Flynn felt himself beginning to relax. Not much, though. Just a little. At least one element of this clusterfuck was going according to his initial plan. He'd known the Raven Syndicate's radio transmissions would be too highly encrypted for them to break. But he'd also been pretty sure that the regional police communications networks were far less sophisticated and vulnerable to interception. Being right about that meant they had a window into what some of the numerous Russian forces now arrayed against them were doing.

Hynes frowned. "So essentially the cops are out in force, and we're surrounded?"

"Which is why we're not planning to stick our heads in the noose just yet," Flynn said.

The broad-shouldered, former U.S. Army soldier snorted. "Gonna have to do that sometime, sir," he pointed out. "Because I sure as hell don't plan on taking up permanent residence in this crappy country."

Despite his own inner misgivings at how badly this mission had already gone astray, Flynn offered the other man a confident smile. "Ye of little faith, Cole. I have a cunning plan."

"Counting on it, sir," Hynes said simply.

Flynn nodded. He'd been recruited into Four in the aftermath of two separate covert operations that had exploded in the CIA's face a few years ago. Both times, he'd put his life on the line to salvage whatever was possible from Langley's largely self-inflicted disasters. Despite that, since he'd just been a lowly captain in U.S. Air Force intelligence, he'd been the one tapped as a scapegoat for the agency's errors. In the CIA's game of musical chairs, the loser was always the one without any political pull. Ultimately, however, he figured he'd actually come out ahead. Joining the Quartet Directorate had given him what he craved: the opportunity to act decisively against hostile forces without being second-guessed or hobbled by superiors who were more interested in protecting their own careers than in defending the United States.

The same went for Hynes and Vucovich. They were among the few survivors of the last Langley-orchestrated debacle. Fiercely loyal to Flynn himself, they'd somehow tracked him down and finagled their way into the Quartet Directorate. And while they were both a bit rougher around the edges than Four's usual recruits, they'd each proved their worth when it counted—and in extreme circumstances. He owed them a lot.

Muscling up the heavy door revealed a pitch-black interior. It smelled of dust, sweat, grease, old food, and, faintly, fresh paint. Moving quickly,

Flynn and his team wheeled their heavy Ural motorcycles in through the open door and then went back for the rest of their gear. As soon as everything was safely inside, they rolled the metal door back down.

Flynn was careful not to turn on the overhead light until the outer door was fully closed. Its single incandescent bulb flickered to life, buzzing softly as it cast harsh shadows across the single room.

Over half the available space was taken up by a single large vehicle entirely covered by a tarp. Sleeping bags, a camp stove, and a screened portable toilet and washbasin filled the rest of the limited square footage.

"Ah, home sweet home," Van Horn murmured. She shrugged. "But I'm still rating it one-star on Yelp."

"It's not exactly the Ritz-Carlton," Flynn conceded. He checked his watch, a Vostok Amphibian model—Russian-manufactured like all the rest of their gear. Midnight had come and gone hours ago. But late though it was, they still had work to do. He looked around the intent group of faces. "All right, people. Let's get to it. We'll grab some shut-eye once we're finished. Clear?"

Heads nodded.

Suiting his actions to his words, Flynn grabbed a duffel bag full of their weapons and other equipment and lugged it over to the tarp-covered vehicle. Behind him, the others began wiping down the Ural motorcycles and sidecars with bleach-covered cloths, painstakingly removing fingerprints, DNA, and any other identifying traces from the machines. They needed to leave nothing behind that could be tied to them.

SIX

THE NEXT DAY

Compared to the other rooms full of expensive furniture and priceless art, Pavel Voronin's private office on the dacha's second floor was a study in simplicity. It was occupied only by a plain wood desk, several monitors and other computer equipment, and a few functional chairs. The extravagance elsewhere was mainly for show, intended to impress high-ranking visitors with his wealth and sophistication. This was a room suited for serious work.

Moodily, Voronin pushed aside a tray holding his untouched meal. His mouth thinned. Being openly targeted for assassination worked as an appetite suppressant. He looked across his desk at Kiril Rodin. "So?"

"Annenkov's patrols have returned. There's no sign of any hostile forces remaining in the vicinity."

Voronin snorted. "Leaving us with no understanding of what just happened."

"For the moment," Rodin agreed. "But we've recovered valuable evidence—shell casings and fragments from both the drone and SAM missile that were used against us."

"And?"

"Early analysis suggests those who carried out the attack were using Russian-made weapons," Rodin said.

"How . . . interesting." Voronin's expression hardened. "So maybe we do have an enemy close to home."

Rodin shook his head. "I wouldn't jump to conclusions. We're not the only ones who understand how important it is that the equipment used in black ops can't be traced. If foreign agents *were* involved in this effort to assassinate you, they'd have been fools to use their own country's weapons. Besides, a Russian bullet is just as lethal as anything made by the Americans or the Israelis or others in the West."

Reluctantly, Voronin nodded. The other man had a good point. The international black market was awash in firearms, missiles, and explosives. Dangle enough hard currency in front of the right people—whether they were shady arms dealers or corrupt officials—and you could obtain practically anything without inconvenient questions being asked. Over the past several years, the Raven Syndicate had acquired its own substantial arsenal of foreign-made armaments through just such methods.

Rodin's smartphone pinged. He glanced down at the screen and scrolled through the new message he'd received. After a moment, he looked up again. "Annenkov just relayed the most recent reports from the local police units."

"To what effect?" Voronin snapped.

"Their checkpoints haven't turned up anything significant so far. They've made a few arrests but only of known criminals—small fry wanted mostly for petty offenses," Rodin said with a shrug. "Drugs. Some shoplifting. A drunken assault here or there. Nothing severe. And nothing that would tie any of them to last night's attack."

Voronin scowled. "Then what's your recommendation?"

"We should take this to a higher level," the other man replied. "It's time to bring the official security services into the mix. Without cooperation from the Ministries of Internal Affairs and Defense, we can't expand the search area as needed, let alone implement the more extreme measures that might be required to find, identify, and arrest or eliminate those responsible for hitting us."

Voronin's frown grew deeper.

"There is no question that rumors are already circulating in Moscow," Rodin pointed out. "We can't keep an attack of this magnitude under wraps forever."

"And I suppose you've already personally briefed Zhdanov on the incident?" Voronin commented dryly.

"Of course," Rodin acknowledged.

Voronin gritted his teeth. The gray-haired bastard had never bothered to hide where his ultimate loyalties lay. Why expect him to start pretending now?

Rodin spread his hands. "The president understands your concerns. But he has assured me they are unfounded. He's certain that no one official was involved in any of this."

With an effort, Voronin forced down the urge to swear aloud. The other man was manipulating him—and quite openly too. Now, if he continued to refuse to bring the FSB and military into the loop, he could be seen as doubting Zhdanov's sworn word. From there it would be a short and undoubtedly fatal step to being accused of treason, which gave him no real choice but to agree.

Elaborately, he shrugged. "All right. Make the arrangements. But I want an all-out effort from the security services in return, with nothing held back. And I want our own people in Moscow—all of them, operational specialists and analysts alike—deployed to backstop the different ministries. We need to know everything the FSB and the others find, *when* they find it. I want our own eyes on everything they do . . . or don't do. Is that understood?"

Rodin nodded. "*Quis custodiet ipsos custodes*? Who will watch the watchers?" he quoted. "Evidently, we will."

"Exactly. And put Kondakov in charge," Voronin ordered.

Again, Rodin nodded. Prior to his own appointment by President Zhdanov as the head of Special Operations, Vasily Kondakov, a former colonel in the GRU, had been the oligarch's top deputy in the Raven Syndicate. Neither man especially liked the other, but there was no doubt about Kondakov's competence—or his allegiance to Voronin.

NEAR THE A108 MOSCOW BIG RING ROAD
THAT SAME TIME

The checkpoint on the outskirts of Voskresensk was sited just short of a major intersection. Temporary barricades narrowed the road at this point to only one lane in each direction. Four police cars, patrol lights flashing, were parked off to the side. Two black-uniformed officers handled the job of methodically inspecting every vehicle headed north toward Moscow. Six more were armed with assault rifles and shotguns and alert for any sign of trouble.

Satisfied with what he'd seen, Police Junior Lieutenant Konstantin Tikhonov stepped back and gestured the old Volvo sedan he'd been examining through the checkpoint. "Go on. Pull ahead. You're cleared."

"Who's going to explain to my boss why I'm late for work?" demanded its lone occupant, a sour-faced woman, to no one in particular. Tikhonov ignored her. With a final, irritated sniff, the woman put her car in gear. It lurched forward in a thick cloud of acrid diesel exhaust and sped off along the road.

Tikhonov turned his head away to hack out a rasping cough.

"Nasty-smelling fumes, sir," his warrant officer said sympathetically. He waved a hand at the long line of cars and trucks crawling slowly toward their checkpoint. "All this backed-up traffic is spewing a lot of crap into the air."

The lieutenant shrugged. "It can't be helped. You heard the major. No terrorists will get through here on our watch." He straightened up and carefully readjusted his peaked officer's cap to the regulation angle. Then, imperiously, he signaled the next vehicle waiting in line to move forward.

It was another older model, this time a UAZ 3741 van. Popularly nicknamed "*Bukhanka*" or "Loaf" because its oblong shape made it look oddly like a wheeled loaf of bread, this particular Soviet-era make was badly dented and absolutely filthy. Dust and dirt streaked the windshield of its two-person cab. Logos stenciled across its cargo section's grimy dark green sides showed that it belonged to the local Oliva Paint and Varnish Factory.

Tikhonov's lips curled in disgust. "If that's a loaf of bread," he murmured to his subordinate, "it's a damned moldy one."

"It's a working vehicle, sir," the warrant officer pointed out.

The lieutenant frowned. "Shoddy equipment equals shoddy work. Keep that in mind, Vlasov."

"Yes, sir."

The panel van lurched to a stop at the checkpoint. At Tikhonov's signal, its middle-aged driver laboriously rolled down his grimy window. He and his assistant were as unkempt as their vehicle. Clad in paint-stained coveralls and sweat-stained T-shirts that bulged over rolls of belly fat, it was obvious that neither had shaved or even bathed for at least a day.

Tikhonov stepped closer to the cab. His nose wrinkling at the stale smell of fried onions, he snapped his fingers impatiently. "Identification!"

Stifling a yawn, the driver handed over his license. With evident difficulty, his equally overweight assistant dug his ID card out of a back pocket.

Tikhonov scrutinized them carefully. They appeared genuine. He handed the cards back. Then, frowning in sudden thought, he studied the van's cargo compartment. It was big enough to hide a multitude of contraband—or just possibly a few armed and dangerous terrorists attempting to escape the scene of their crimes. "What are you carrying back there?" he asked.

The driver stared back at him in bewilderment. "Why, paint, of course," he said finally. "Got a big order from some fancy office renovation project in Moscow." With a heavy sigh, he craned his head at the long line of vehicles backed up behind them. "We're gonna catch hell from the bosses for being so late on this delivery."

Tikhonov snorted, unmoved by the sob story. He'd already heard some variation of it a hundred times this morning. "Show me!" He put his hand threateningly on the 9mm pistol holstered at his hip, then he checked the light on his bodycam, to make sure it was working. Recording everything was standard procedure these days for any traffic stop, especially one that might go sour.

With a shrug, the driver shut off his ignition and tossed the keys to his assistant. "You heard him, Ivan. Open her up."

The other man clambered down out of his side of the cab. Fumbling to find the right key, he ambled around to the back. With a grunt, he unlocked the van's two back doors and then hauled them both wide open.

Tikhonov leaned forward to take a closer look. Rows of paint cans, many of them rusting and badly dented, filled the back of the van from floor to ceiling. He pursed his lips, feeling let down. So much for his hunch. "Some of those containers look very old," he commented acidly. "Are you pawning off junk on your customers?"

Unfazed, the assistant shrugged his rotund shoulders. "A paint can is a paint can," he pointed out. "And cans cost money. Besides, you can refill 'em as many times as you want as long as you do it with the same color of paint." He tapped one of the cans. "You want me to open this up and show you what's inside, too?"

A horn honked loudly from somewhere farther back in the line of stalled traffic.

Tikhonov sighed, acknowledging defeat. "Never mind." He flapped his hands, signaling the other man to close the van. "You can go." He turned away toward the next vehicle in line, dismissing the battered old paint company vehicle and its scruffy occupants from his mind.

———

Once they were several hundred yards past the police roadblock, the UAZ's driver, Shannon Cooke, breathed out in relief. "That sure as hell wasn't much fun." He shifted uncomfortably in his seat. "I hate wearing these damned prosthetics," he grumbled. "I sweat under them like a pig."

Slouched in the seat next to him, Nick Flynn nodded. "It is a shame to hide all our natural beauty under these disguises," he agreed, laughing. "I guess that's one of the downsides of being a wanted criminal."

"Criminal?" Cooke protested. "I am not a crook. A hunted, highly dangerous foreign spy, sure. But not a crook."

"You say 'tomato'; the Russians say 'tomahto,'" Flynn said with a grin. He twisted around to open a partition between the cab and the cargo area. "Everybody okay back there? Still nice and cozy?"

"Cozy? Seriously? By sardine standards, sure. By human standards, no," Van Horn retorted. "I'm recommending a new recruitment protocol to Br'er Fox." That was her pet nickname for their boss, Carleton Frederick Fox, the head of the Quartet Directorate's American station. "The next time we pull one of these stunts, we only bring circus-trained contortionists."

Flynn understood her complaint. Together with every piece of their equipment and all their weapons, Van Horn, Kossak, Hynes, and Vucovich were crammed into a small section of the panel van's cargo compartment—with barely enough room to do anything more than sit elbow-to-elbow in the darkness. The rest of the space was taken up by the false facade of paint cans carefully stacked up to conceal them from anything but a determined inspection. Their cramped hiding place might not be comfortable, but as a desperate measure to avoid detection, it was undeniably effective.

MOSCOW, RUSSIA
A FEW HOURS LATER

Located more than eleven miles south of the Kremlin, Moscow's Biryulyovo Zapadnoye district was a mishmash of middling tall apartment buildings dating back to the mid-twentieth century, light industry, auto and electrical repair workshops, retail stores, warehouses, and a large number of walled or fenced-in lots used to store goods or old cars and trucks. Amid Russia's current economic slump, many commercial buildings and storage areas were out of business—abandoned by owners and tenants who couldn't afford to pay their mortgages, rents, or taxes.

Driving carefully to avoid drawing any unwanted attention, Cooke turned off one of the district's main roads and onto a narrow, much-quieter side street. At this time of day, there were no pedestrians in sight. Children were in school. Their parents were working. And the homeless and chronically unemployed preferred to congregate in the area's tree-lined parks, where at least there was shade and the possibility of cadging enough rubles for a meal or a drink or a pack of cigarettes.

Halfway down the street, he pulled over to the curb and parked, idling the van's engine. They were just a few yards from a padlocked gate. The low-walled compound it secured was a maze of rusty metal storage sheds, weather-beaten crates and boxes, graffiti-covered shipping containers, and a slew of wrecked vehicles, most of which had long ago been stripped of any usable spare parts. The whole area reeked of decay and neglect.

Cooke checked his mirrors carefully. "Looks clear," he commented.

Flynn nodded. He slid open the panel to the cargo area. "We're at our next stop," he announced. "Ready to work your electronic magic, Wade?"

Moving cautiously to avoid stepping on anyone's fingers or toes, Vucovich scooched past the others in the rear of the van. He poked his head and shoulders out through the narrow opening, blinking a few times against the bright sunlight. Then he squinted through the grimy windshield toward the gate. They had a good line of sight from here and could easily observe the CCTV camera covering the entrance.

"I'm on it, sir," Vucovich confirmed. He brought out a tablet computer and powered it up. A few taps on its screen opened a list of the wireless networks operating in the vicinity. One was highlighted, thanks to some preliminary hacking he'd done when they'd first visited this area a few days before. This was the network connected to that particular closed-circuit surveillance camera. His eyes narrowed in concentration as he signed into the network and then navigated through several menus until he confirmed that he had control of the camera. From there, it was easy. Activating a subroutine he'd already planted made sure that its live feed would be replaced by a prerecorded loop shot earlier. Even if someone figured out later what he'd done, there still wouldn't be any video recording of their vehicle entering the lot. "All set," he reported with satisfaction.

"Nice work, Wade," Flynn said, and he meant it. The Russian capital city's vast surveillance system was part of what made operating covertly here incredibly difficult. Moscow had more than one hundred and fifty thousand CCTV cameras in use. Nastier still, the government had also installed facial recognition software to help track so-called "criminals and dissidents." Admittedly, the odds that anyone would ever check the footage from this one camera out of so many were relatively low, but Flynn wasn't in the mood to take any more risks just now—not after his carefully planned move against Voronin's country estate had somehow tripped the oligarch's own elaborate security systems and then promptly cratered.

Minutes later, Cooke pulled up outside a dilapidated shed in the far corner of the lot. No one could see them from the street; all of the buildings overlooking this section were boarded up.

Inside their new temporary safe house, Hynes stopped dead. "Oh, just swell. Another fricking dump," he said. He shook his head gloomily, surveying the stained concrete floor and stacks of dusty cardboard boxes lining the walls. "'Join the Quartet Directorate,' they said. 'See the world,' they said. 'Live the life of international intrigue and adventure,' they said." He scowled. "How come nobody said a damned thing about spending most of your nights and days in a bunch of flea-bitten rat-traps?"

Hiding a smile, Van Horn laid a comforting hand on his shoulder. "Actually, they did, Cole. It was on page fifty-two of your contract," she said kindly. "Right below the provisos on death, dismemberment, crippling injury, and the total lack of a profit-sharing plan."

"Well, crap," Hynes said, sounding rueful. "I knew I should have read the fine print more carefully."

SEVEN

Flanked by Rodin, Voronin watched closely while Russia's president, Piotr Zhdanov, inspected the burned-out wreckage of the Kazan Ansat gunship shot down over his estate during the attack. A light breeze rustled through fire-scorched trees, sending little ash swirls dancing across the broken fuselage. Twisted pieces of the helicopter's shattered composite rotor blades littered the forest floor.

"A near-run thing, Pavel," Zhdanov commented off-handedly. Almost idly, he prodded at a piece of charred debris with his foot before turning away. His hard brown eyes sharpened. "Who knows? If those mysterious intruders had gotten a little closer before being detected by your defenses, they might have succeeded in blowing your head off."

Voronin nodded tersely. He was all too aware of the danger he'd been in, and still was, since those who tried to kill him remained on the loose. He was equally aware that the president was careful not to run any risks on this visit to the Raven's Nest.

Rotors clattered somewhere overhead. Several long-nosed Ka-52 Alligator attack helicopters were on station, orbiting low over the surrounding terrain. Their mast-mounted Phazotron FH-01 millimeter wave radars probed the air and ground constantly, hunting for the slightest sign of any developing threat. The gunships aloft were matched on the ground by the wheeled armored fighting vehicles and troops of a full army motorized battalion. Zhdanov himself wore heavy plates of bullet-resistant armor over his lightweight jacket, shirt, and slacks. His glowering bodyguards ringed the crash site, weapons at the ready.

Voronin eyed the president carefully. He had aged significantly, even over the past several months. What had once been a fringe of thinning gray hair above Zhdanov's round face was almost gone. He had visibly lost weight, and the shadows under his eyes were even more profound and darker. His hands trembled slightly at rest, either from pent-up stress or perhaps some undisclosed neurological disorder.

The old man is dying, Voronin realized callously. Not immediately, to be sure. And certainly not quickly. He might linger for years, becoming ever sicker and weaker. But he was dying, nonetheless. Sooner or later, the precarious stability represented by the president's tight-fisted rule would end. And one way or another, Russia would awake one morning to find Piotr Zhdanov gone and a new master in the saddle.

All of which made it even more important for him to regain the fullness of his own power as soon as possible, the younger man thought coldly. The old man's death or permanent incapacitation would open the floodgates—unleashing all the pent-up political rivalries among the Kremlin's inner circle.

Inside the privacy of his own mind, Voronin sneered. That any of the shambling, geriatric dinosaurs around the president seriously believed they were fit for the office was a testimony to their own idiocy, or, just as likely, their own fast-encroaching senility. For Russia to have any hope of surviving as a great nation, let alone reclaiming her status as a superpower, she needed a leader of enormous intellect, energy, and utter ruthlessness. A leader willing to kill millions of people, or even more, if that proved necessary.

Voronin knew he was the only man among Russia's ruling elite who deserved real power. But it was equally evident that none of his would-be rivals would tamely hand the reins to him. He had to be ready to seize his chance the instant it arose. All of which made gaining the president's approval for VELES even more critical. After his previous two failures, only its resounding success could firmly reestablish him as Zhdanov's unchallenged right-hand man and his logical successor.

As if in answer to his thoughts, the president frowned and swung toward Voronin. "I wonder? Is it possible this sudden assault on you is somehow related to your new special project? The one you plan to brief me on today?"

At that, Rodin stepped forward. He lowered his voice. "This may be a conversation best reserved for a more secure area, Mr. President," he pointed out respectfully. "Besides their weapons, who knows what else our unwelcome guests may have carried with them?"

Thoughtfully, Zhdanov surveyed the dense woodland around them. "You worry that these intruders might have planted intelligence-gathering devices?" he asked.

"It's certainly possible," Rodin said. "We're checking, of course. But such a search will take time." He shrugged. "For now, I suggest it would be wiser to adjourn to the safety of the dacha. Our security personnel sweep the whole building every day for listening devices. We can speak freely there."

"Very well," Zhdanov agreed. He turned to Voronin and gestured. "Lead on, Pavel. Show me what you have in mind."

————

Once through the dacha's solid bronze doors and inside its high-ceilinged central hall, Zhdanov gratefully shed the bulky vest of ceramic armor plates his bodyguards had insisted he wear while outdoors. "There. Now I feel more like a man and less like a fucking tank on legs."

Voronin smiled politely, hiding his contempt for the older man's coarse turn of phrase. "Welcome to the Raven's Nest, Mr. President," he said simply, then snapped his fingers.

Servants immediately appeared to usher them all into a large living room deeper inside the building. They laid out a selection of drinks on a sideboard—vodka for Zhdanov, lemon-flavored hot tea for Voronin and Rodin—and then withdrew just as silently. The president jerked his chin toward the door, ordering his bodyguards out as well. Obeying, they filed out of the room and closed the doors behind them, leaving the three men alone.

Sipping his tea, Voronin led the others to a group of leather high-backed chairs arranged in a conversational arc facing a large-screen display. They sat down. Zhdanov tossed his vodka back with a single gulp, then he shook out a cigarette and lit it. He took one deep drag before looking over at the younger man. "So, Pavel, what is this new project of yours? What do you claim we can achieve?"

"Victory, sir," Voronin told him confidently. "For Russia. And for you." A tap on the screen of his smartphone brought the bigger screen to life. "A victory achieved through the intelligent application of advanced science."

Zhdanov listened carefully while the younger man outlined the nature of the new biological weapons developed on his orders—weapons equally matched for Russia's protection by disease-resistant seed stocks and targeted fungicides. Footage shot at the Kameshkovo Institute amplified and verified his claims.

To his credit, the president instantly grasped the implications. Using these genetically engineered bioweapons would enable Russia to trigger mass famine and chaos among its enemies, especially the United States—whose highly productive agricultural sector was the envy and the underpinning of the entire civilized world.

Nevertheless, as Rodin had already warned, Zhdanov was not a fool-hardy man. "The scientific work you've sponsored is remarkable," he admitted. But then he leaned forward, pinning Voronin with his hard-eyed gaze. "Whether or not it represents a practical weapon is another matter completely."

At his direction, the younger man scrolled back to the imagery of dead and dying crops shot inside the Institute's maximum-security green-houses. The president waved a hand at the pictures on the screen. "Our responsibility for triggering such a catastrophic food crisis would have

to be completely hidden," he insisted. "Desperation makes people willing to do many otherwise unthinkable things. And what will it profit
us to starve the Americans if they decide to drench us all in nuclear fire
in retaliation?" He turned back to Voronin. "You've already brought us
too close to the brink once, Pavel," he reminded the other man coolly.
"We may not be as lucky another time."

Voronin controlled his expression. The failure of his last grand
scheme had ended with the detonation of a tactical nuclear warhead
deep in the American heartland—something that could easily have triggered a catastrophic, all-out nuclear exchange between the two countries.
Only Moscow's abject apologies and its willingness to pay substantial
compensation for the fortunately limited human and property damage—
along with the cold-blooded sacrifice of several military officers Voronin
had suborned, falsely branding them as having been in bed with Middle
Eastern terrorist groups—had persuaded the feckless American political
establishment to overlook such a "regrettable incident" in the interests
of "world peace." But not even the current U.S. administration, rud-
derless though it was, could be expected to ignore a successful Russian
biological weapons attack on American agriculture.

"I agree wholeheartedly, sir," he assured Zhdanov. "Which is why
I've made sure we have a plan that will allow our agents to successfully
infect America's most vital and productive agricultural regions with our
weaponized disease spores—and do so *without* being detected."

Zhdanov leaned forward. "Explain this plan of yours to me," he
demanded.

Speaking confidently and using video imagery and maps for emphasis, Voronin laid out what he intended. It was a detailed, comprehensive,
and thoroughly persuasive summation of an inherently complex scheme.

When he finished, Zhdanov sat back, plainly impressed by what he'd
heard. For a long moment, he sat silent, obviously weighing options in
his mind. At last, he looked up. "So when can you be ready to initiate
your VELES operation?"

"In less than a year," Voronin assured him. "While the plan is complex and involves a large number of separate elements, we can move

forward with most of them simultaneously. This includes the production of sufficient stockpiles of our weaponized fungal spores as we also quietly replace significant portions of our own seed stocks with disease-resistant strains. And while that's in progress, we can be acquiring the special equipment needed to covertly deliver these new weapons inside the United States."

Zhdanov held up a hand. "Listen closely, Pavel," he said. "You may proceed with all preparations that can be completed inside *our* national territory, including stockpiling these new bioweapons and hardening our domestic agriculture industry against their effects. Should our enemies uncover what we're up to, we can pass those measures off as reasonable defensive precautions against a potential biological attack by other nations. Understand?"

Voronin nodded.

"You may even conduct tests of your bioweapon delivery systems within the safety of our borders," Zhdanov continued. "*But* you are strictly forbidden from conducting *any* covert operations related to VELES inside the United States or any other Western nation until I give you my explicit authorization." He shook his head. "Someone has you in their sights, Pavel. Maybe the CIA. Maybe Israel's Mossad. Or possibly Britain's MI6. Until we figure out exactly who is after you—and just how far they've penetrated your Raven Syndicate's security—I won't risk moving too far ahead with this plan of yours." His voice sharpened. "Are my orders in this regard clearly understood?"

Tightly, Voronin nodded. From the older man's tone, it was obvious that he had neither forgotten nor forgiven his earlier failures. Nor had he missed Voronin's determination to ignore directives if he judged the president had suddenly become unnecessarily cautious.

"Good," Zhdanov said. "Because the slightest deviation from my orders this time will force my hand. You are a useful man, Pavel, to me and to the Motherland, but I will not overlook further treasonous disobedience."

Again, Voronin nodded. He was acutely aware of cold-eyed Kiril Rodin, the president's handpicked executioner, at his side. Although he remained outwardly calm, inside he felt rage boiling up. For all of Zhdanov's bluster about reclaiming Russia's preeminent place on the world stage, he was again showing himself to be as timid and unimaginative as the rest of his advisers.

Against his wishes and all his inclinations, Voronin was once again forced to bend a knee to a lesser man like Piotr Zhdanov. One day though, he vowed silently, that would change. And when the moment arrived, Russia's current leader would learn—too late—who was indeed the master and who was the servant. An ancient adage ran comfortingly through his mind. "Treason doth never prosper; what's the reason? For if it prosper, none dare call it treason."

EIGHT

LENINGRADSKY RAILWAY STATION, MOSCOW

THAT SAME TIME

Mingling with the steady flow of other travelers arriving from the nearby Komsomolskaya Metro stop, Laura Van Horn strolled briskly through the main doors of the train station—one of the ten serving the Russian capital and the oldest. It dated back to the middle of the nineteenth century, a product of the Tsarist empire's first significant expansion of railroads. Seen from the outside, Leningradsky Station looked very much like a Renaissance-era Italian palazzo set down in the heart of Moscow, complete with a pale-yellow exterior and an ornate, green-domed, central clock tower. High, arched windows provided ample natural light to its ground floor in the spring and summer.

The station's interior, however, was considerably plainer and more modern. Yellow lines striped the concrete floor of its main hall. Brightly lit shops and restaurants occupied the sides, and escalators headed up toward more food and retail outlets on the upper level. Digital monitors flickered at several points, showing the scheduled trains, their destinations, departure and arrival times, and track assignments.

For this morning's expedition, Van Horn had dyed her naturally dark hair a sunny, eye-catching blonde. She towed a small, soft-sided, rolling

suitcase and wore an elegant, expensive business suit. A large shopping
bag from one of Moscow's most exclusive clothiers over one shoulder
and a stunning Swiss-made Longines watch on her wrist completed the
look she was going for—that of a sophisticated, high-powered female
executive on the go.

Concealed behind a pair of designer sunglasses, her eyes scanned her
surroundings. The rail station, usually bustling near the departure times
of express trains bound for Saint Petersburg, was even more congested
than usual. Long lines of passengers were backed up from the far doors
which opened onto Leningradsky Station's train platforms and tracks.
Uniformed police officers, supervised by stern-faced men in dark, un-
fashionable suits, were grouped near those exits.

Well, well, well, she thought. Something was very definitely up.

Unhurriedly, Van Horn made her way through the crowds to one
of the station's information kiosks. A balding, middle-aged clerk behind
the counter looked up appreciatively at her approach.

"*Ya mogu vam pomoch', Gospozha*?" he asked politely. "Can I help
you, miss?"

She flashed him a thousand-watt smile, noting how he unconsciously
straightened up and threw back his shoulders. It was almost Pavlovian,
she thought with inner amusement. *Careful there, Laura*, she told herself with an inward grin. With great power came great responsibility, so
maybe she owed it to the world to hold back a little.

Van Horn smiled brightly and said in perfect, colloquial Russian,
"Oh, I hope so." She nodded toward the mass of people near the platform doors. The crowds were growing by the minute as more and more
travelers flooded into the station. "I have some time before my train
leaves, but that looks pretty bad. Is there some major delay on the lines?"

The information agent shook his head. "No, miss. There's no problem with our rail service." He shrugged. "There's a heightened security
alert in place. The authorities are checking IDs and asking more questions than usual." He smiled back at her. "But you shouldn't have any
trouble. I've noticed that they're only selecting men for more extensive
screening. Not any of the ladies."

Van Horn thanked him warmly and continued deeper into the station. Instead of joining the line waiting to clear security, she headed for one of the coffee shops not far from where the police and dark-suited security officers were bottlenecking everything. As she walked past them, she didn't bother hiding her curiosity. It would be more suspicious if she ignored what was going on.

Eyeing the checkpoint confirmed what the information kiosk clerk had told her. Men were being pulled out of the line in ones and twos. Police officers carefully scrutinized their identification cards or passports while they were asked a few questions. Some were waved through after this quick inspection. Others were ushered over to plastic chairs at folding tables, where they were subjected to a more intrusive interrogation by plainclothes officers, all of whom were using laptop computers— obviously to confirm details of what they were being told whenever possible.

Van Horn's lips thinned slightly. Yep, she thought, recalling the old children's rhyme, "Come into my parlor, said the spider to the fly." Well, there were many spiders here, all spinning their webs to trap the unwary. Arriving at the coffee shop, she paused for a moment to make a little show of checking her watch and studying the nearest departures and arrivals board. Then, with a shrug, as if to indicate that she still had time to kill before her train left, she entered the shop and ordered a black coffee to go.

Carefully sipping at the scalding liquid, she exited the café and looked around again. She'd found out what she needed—now to make a discreet exit. Two trains—one a high-speed express, the other a slower, local train—were scheduled to arrive in the next several minutes. The timing would be tight but manageable. After ditching the remains of her coffee in a trash can, she turned on her heel and headed for the nearest ladies' room.

Once she was inside a stall in the restroom, Van Horn moved into action. First, she doffed her sunglasses and glittering Swiss watch and shrugged out of her business suit and heels. Rolls of padding extracted from her shopping bag added weight to her hips and stomach. Cheek pads fattened her face. Then she pulled on a shapeless, frowsy blouse and baggy pants, and a pair of the plain, sensible shoes that a middle-aged, ordinary working woman might wear. Carefully, she inserted a pair of brown-tinted contacts to conceal her blue eyes. Finally, she donned a brown wig streaked with gray over her hair. Her small rolling case and luxury shopping bag were tucked away inside a much larger folding bag from one of Saint Petersburg's cheap discount stores.

Her transformation complete, Van Horn exited the restroom and joined a steady stream of passengers now crowding into the rail station from the platforms. Her formerly long-legged stride was gone, replaced by the much slower, near-shuffle of a heavyset woman exhausted after a long, crowded train trip.

Altering her appearance so drastically was intended to avoid the awkwardness of anyone who'd noticed her earlier wondering why she'd entered the station and then turned around to leave without boarding a train. With the Russian security services apparently on high alert, she needed to do whatever she could to avoid raising suspicions.

Walking slowly, Van Horn went back outside and headed for the Metro. This time she didn't try to hide her frown. She had a lot to report to Flynn and the others. And none of it was good news.

IN MOSCOW'S BIRYULYOVO ZAPADNOYE DISTRICT
A SHORT TIME LATER

Inside the dilapidated metal shed they were using as a temporary safe house, Nick Flynn looked around the circle of worried faces. "So there it is," he said quietly. "Based on what Laura saw, the Saint Petersburg rail exit route is closed to us." He held up one of their carefully forged identity cards. "These are solid enough to stand up to a quick visual check. But the moment anyone runs one through an official database, we're fucked."

Heads nodded. The Quartet Directorate's document forgers were experts in their fields. They did top-notch work. But without access to the vast computer files Russia maintained on its citizens, there were hard limits to what they could achieve.

Cole Hynes frowned. "We've got other problems too, sir," he said. "The rest of you guys speak perfect Russian. Me and Wade can't. We've got enough vocabulary to answer some basic questions, sure. But if we got pulled aside by one of those cops for a real conversation?" He shook his head. "We'd screw it up." He snapped his fingers. "And that would be that."

Flynn nodded. Their Russian language deficits had been one of the strongest arguments against bringing the two former soldiers on this mission in the first place. But he'd decided that the team's likely need for their other specialized skills tipped the scales in their favor. His jaw tightened. Where did you draw the line between the natural cockiness required to undertake the daring, extremely hazardous missions Four handed out to its operatives . . . and sheer, stubborn bravado? Well, he thought bleakly, it was starting to look like he might be about to find out the hard way.

Tadeusz Kossak leaned forward to make a point of his own. "It is not just the Saint Petersburg exit closed, then," he said carefully. "It is all of them. Certainly, any rail route heading west is now too dangerous for us to use." He shrugged. "Why should the Russians focus their attention only on one train station? It would be illogical. There must be similar heightened security measures in place everywhere."

Flynn agreed with him. Manpower was not a problem for the Russian security and intelligence services. "Yeah, I'm pretty sure you're right, Tad. My bet is that, censorship or no censorship, a lot of bitching about the travel delays caused by these unexplained ID checks will leak out into Russian social media by sometime tonight. Certainly by tomorrow morning at the latest."

"So maybe we sit tight for now and wait out this security crackdown," Shannon Cooke suggested. "And then make our run for the border later."

Flynn shook his head. "I'd be on board with that if we had a more secure safe house," he said. "But this one is way too exposed. We can't hope to hide that we're camped out here much longer."

He saw their heads nod in agreement. Abandoned or not, the odds of somebody stumbling across them in this old storage lot were already uncomfortably high and rising all the time. It wouldn't matter much whether it was just kids looking for somewhere exciting and off-limits to play—or a few of the homeless hunting for a place to crash or for old junk they could sell. When locals started gossiping about strangers hiding out here, all hell was likely to break loose.

After a short silence, Van Horn frowned. "Okay, Nick. If we can't get out by train and we can't stay here, then I guess we go north."

"Figure so," he admitted.

"Br'er Fox isn't going to be real happy about this," she commented. "Using the north crossing was supposed to be our last resort. Things could get messy."

"Messier, I think you mean," Flynn said. One side of his mouth turned down. "What we sold as a precise, surgical incursion to take out Voronin hasn't exactly gone according to plan, remember?"

Cooke grinned. "Now, don't be too hard on us, Nick," he counseled earnestly. "Plenty of top-notch doctors fall back on big saws and other extreme measures to take care of tricky cases, don't they? Considering the opposition we ran into, I'd say we were in the ballpark for a certain, admittedly very loose, definition of 'surgical.'"

Hynes snorted. "Geez, remind me never to schedule any serious medical care in your neck of the woods."

"Kill or cure, Cole," Cooke said with a devilish glint in his eyes. His Virginia drawl thickened a bit. "Getting treated by a good, old-fashioned country doctor might make a man out of you. Or a woman, I guess, if his scalpel slips."

For a few seconds, Hynes just stared back at him. But then he started to laugh, followed by everyone else. Flynn let them go on for a while, grateful for Cooke's successful effort to break the growing tension. They'd all been on edge since Laura returned from Leningradksy Station with her bad news.

But as soon as they quieted, he started issuing rapid-fire instructions. Before heading north, they had preparations to make—and make quickly. With their next move decided, he had the sudden, uneasy sense that they were running out of time much faster than he'd hoped.

NINE

THAT EVENING

A midnight black Mercedes Sprinter van drove south through Moscow's busy, brightly lit nighttime streets. Its license plate bore the unique letters and codes, which would tell any Russian policeman that the vehicle was connected to the FSB, Russia's Federal Security Service—and therefore free to speed, run red lights, and break other traffic laws as necessary. That was a blind. The van actually belonged to the Raven Syndicate, which paid high fees—both officially and under the table—for its stock-pile of such plates and the special driving privileges they conferred. The practice was common among Russia's ruling political and economic elites, who saw no reason to inconvenience themselves by obeying laws and regulations intended for ordinary citizens.

Traffic noises from the crowded streets outside filtered into the back of the windowless van, where Pavel Voronin sat between Kiril Rodin and balding Vasily Kondakov. The Sprinter was equipped as a mobile command post, and their seats faced a bank of computer displays and secure communications gear. One of the monitors showed a convoy of several dark-colored vans trailing behind them. These vehicles were carrying a platoon-sized force of heavily armed Syndicate troops.

Voronin frowned. He was generally reluctant to operate so openly inside Moscow—preferring to reserve the use of his organization's veteran mercenary special operators for work beyond Russia's borders. Unfortunately, his continuing doubts about how far he could trust those running his country's military and security services left him no choice. Relying solely on his own people was the only way he could be sure that this move against those who'd tried to assassinate him wouldn't be betrayed.

Of course, that still left open the question of whether or not this was a wise use of their resources. When Kondakov urgently declared that he had immediate, actionable intelligence on their enemies, the haste required to organize an armed force and get it moving hadn't allowed any opportunity for a detailed briefing. Well, better late than never. Voronin turned toward the other man. "All right, Vasily. Convince me this isn't just a wild goose chase."

"It might be," Kondakov admitted. Behind his horn-rimmed spectacles, his eyes were watchful. "But it's our best lead yet."

Rodin snorted. "Our only lead, you mean."

"True," Kondakov retorted. "But if you're scared of wolves, don't go into the woods."

"Enough," Voronin snapped, holding up a hand to interrupt their argument before it went any farther. He was well aware there was no love lost between the two men. Rodin had usurped Kondakov's position as chief of Special Operations, relegating him to a lesser role in intelligence gathering and internal security. And if encroaching on what had been the former GRU colonel's sole turf wasn't bad enough, Rodin had also insisted on cutting him out of the loop for VELES. Kondakov knew that some new major operation was in the works, but nothing more.

Both men subsided.

He fixed his cold gaze on Kondakov again. "Go ahead. Walk me through your reasoning on this."

"It starts with CCTV footage obtained at the Leningradsky rail station," the other man explained. "Since we cannot fully trust the competence of the Ministries of the Internal Affairs and Defense—or their reliability, for that matter—I've assigned my best analysts to review recorded imagery from their security checkpoint operations at Moscow's important transportation hubs."

Voronin nodded.

Rodin's lip curled slightly. "A singularly tedious and unrewarding exercise, I would think."

"Not for those who pay attention to important details," Kondakov countered. "My people understand the importance of the work they're doing."

"Go on, Vasily," Voronin said mildly. "So your analysts found something?"

The other man nodded. "An incongruity. A small one at first glance. But one with great significance upon closer inspection." He leaned forward to the keyboard before him and entered a command. Surveillance camera footage shot at Leningradsky Station earlier that day appeared on one of the screens. A quick tap on a control zoomed in on one of the travelers shown entering the main hall—an attractive, well-dressed blonde.

Voronin felt one of his eyebrows go up. "A woman?" he asked in surprise. So far, they had been focused on searching for male suspects—the kind of tough-looking, physically-fit men capable of carrying out a commando-style raid on his estate.

"Observe," Kondakov said simply, letting the surveillance footage play.

They all watched silently as the woman stopped at an information kiosk, chatted briefly with its attendant, and then strolled casually down the station hall past the checkpoint and into a coffee shop. Minutes later, she emerged, threw away her disposable coffee cup, and entered the nearest women's restroom.

"Ah, a great mystery," Rodin said, not bothering to hide his scorn. "A woman drinks coffee and then has to take a piss."

Unfazed, Kondakov adjusted the playback speed. People now moved through the frame in skittering jerks as first minutes and then hours raced by.

Voronin was the first to figure it out. "She never comes out of that restroom," he realized.

"Correct," Kondakov agreed. "Or more accurately, she does emerge—but not in the same guise." He touched the controls again, rewinding the CCTV footage and slowing it down. Several minutes after the attractive blonde went through the door to the ladies' room, a very different woman—much older, dowdier, and plumper in appearance—came out and joined a flood of newly arrived passengers headed out of the station. "Her tradecraft was excellent," he commented matter-of-factly. "If one of my analysts weren't something of an obsessive compulsive, we would never have spotted the switch."

Fascinated, Voronin watched the woman shuffle out through the main doors and vanish. It was hard to believe she had any connection to the elegant blonde they'd first observed, let alone that she was the same person. He turned to Kondakov. "What then? Do you know where she went?"

"My team was able to recreate her later movements," the other man confirmed. "At least while she traveled through the Metro system."

Voronin nodded his understanding. With more than nine million riders a day, Moscow's Metro was the primary means of transportation for most capital residents. That made the system a focal point for police and security service surveillance. Between the thousands of CCTV cameras covering every entrance, exit, and station platform and the government's advanced facial recognition software, a known suspect couldn't easily evade detection. "And?"

"This woman shuttled between several different Metro lines in rapid succession, timing it precisely so that she transferred from arriving underground trains to others which were about to depart, usually with only seconds to spare."

Interested now, Rodin leaned forward. "That's classic practice to evade any human tail."

"She's definitely a professional intelligence operative," Kondakov agreed. "In my judgment, one of the highest caliber."

"Whose operative is she?" Voronin ground out through clenched teeth. "Which country, which organization, employs this spy or assassin?"

Kondakov shrugged. "That is still unclear. Even once we have her in our hands, I suspect it will require prolonged and rigorous interrogation to pry out the truth." He smiled thinly. "She should be an interesting challenge."

Voronin nodded, appreciating the other man's intentions. Among his many talents, the former GRU colonel was a skilled torturer. With an effort, he pulled his mind away from the anticipation of future pleasure and back to the business at hand. "And after she finished playing this game of Metro hopscotch? What then?"

"She took the Black Line south," Kondakov said, "and finally exited the system at the Anino Metro stop, near the Moscow Ring Road." He pulled up a new set of images. "Cameras outside the station caught her heading east on foot into the Biryulyovo Zapadnoye district."

"And from there?" Voronin demanded. "Where did she go?"

"We can't be sure," Kondakov said carefully. He took off his glasses and polished them with his handkerchief for a few seconds, plainly buying time to consider the best way to impart what he knew would be extremely unwelcome news. "Not precisely, at least," he said at last. He put his glasses back on and spread his hands. "The local CCTV network in this part of Moscow is comparatively sparse, with many of the cameras off-line for various reasons."

Voronin stared at the other man, his hands balled into fists. "Are you telling me that you lost her after all of that, Vasily? That she's completely disappeared on us?"

"Not completely," Kondakov replied. He opened a digital satellite map of Moscow on the screen. Zoomed in, it showed the Biryulyovo Zapodnye district in intricate detail—displaying every street, alley, building, and patch of open ground. "My people have scanned the footage from every surveillance camera covering the borders of this area. Our target doesn't appear. Not once. So we're reasonably confident that she hasn't doubled back on us again. Which means this district was her intended destination."

"Even if that's true and not just wishful thinking to save your ass," Rodin spoke up frostily, "the original point still stands. This *is* a waste of time and resources." He pointed to the map with disdain. "Close to a hundred thousand people must live in this district. Most of them are probably tenants occupying block after block of apartment buildings. We'd need hundreds of armed men to carry out a thorough search in any reasonable amount of time. As it is, we have fewer than forty troops with us."

Kondakov smiled back at his rival. "If we needed to go door-to-door through every apartment block, your premise would be correct. But we don't."

Voronin eyed him closely. "And why is that?"

In answer, Kondakov zoomed in the satellite map until the screen showed only a tiny part of the district—the segment closest to where CCTV cameras had last spotted their female suspect. Instead of rows of apartment buildings, this area was mostly given over to a few dozen tiny commercial enterprises—everything from automotive repair shops to electrical supply outlets to building materials warehouses and storage lots.

Before Rodin could object further, Kondakov used his mouse to highlight a few locations. "According to tax records, these particular buildings and lots are abandoned," he explained. "Which makes them ideal temporary hiding places for foreign agents—or others—who evaded the initial net cast around the Raven's Nest and are now desperately exploring ways to escape from Russia."

Voronin nodded appreciatively, seeing what the other man was driving at. "You think that's what this woman was doing for these would-be assassins? Scouting the train station to learn if tighter security measures were in place?"

"Just so."

"All roads and railways lead to and from Moscow, and a large urban area does offer many nooks and crannies in which to conceal oneself," Voronin mused aloud. He glanced back at Rodin. "So?" he asked. "What is your assessment now?"

The other man's eyes were hooded. Plainly, he was not happy about having walked so easily into the clever analytical trap Kondakov had set for him. But then he shrugged, obviously deciding he would gain nothing by further argument. "Assuming these guesses are accurate, we should have enough men on hand to handle the job," he said carefully. "Especially if we can take these people we're hunting by surprise."

Voronin straightened up. "All right. Let's get this done." He looked at Kondakov. Since the older man was in charge of the Raven Syndicate's internal security apparatus, this was now his operation to command personally. "Make sure you've blocked the exits from these different places you've identified, and then send the rest of your teams in hard and fast. Roust anyone there. Shoot if you must, but take prisoners for further interrogation if possible."

"And after we're done questioning these people?" Kondakov asked calmly. "What then?"

"Kill them," Voronin said. His eyes were icy. "No one comes after me and escapes alive."

BIRYULYOVO ZAPADNOYE
A SHORT TIME LATER

A squad of Raven Syndicate troops in night-gray camouflage and body armor crouched on the far side of a low wall. A two-man sniper team on the roof of a nearby building reported that the storage lot the wall surrounded was full of rusting, abandoned cars and trucks, old shipping containers, boxes, and crates, and a couple of weather-battered metal sheds.

As a young officer cadet, Igor Nemov had been earmarked for service with the Spetsnaz. After intense, often dangerous, training and several years of active duty for absurdly low pay, he'd been persuaded to transfer his hard-won skills to the Syndicate instead. Since the mercenary organization served Russia's national interests, he saw little significant moral difference between being asked to kill for the State or for Pavel Voronin. And if that were so, why not do the same job for substantially more money?

"Strike Three-One, this is Strike Three Overwatch. No movement in the target area. Everything still looks quiet," a voice whispered through Nemov's radio headset.

He clicked his mike to acknowledge the sitrep from his sniper team. Taking a shallow breath and then another, he waited uneasily while the seconds ticked slowly past. From the quick, pre-raid briefing they'd been given, the people they were hunting tonight were dangerous as hell,

highly trained professional killers. Taking them by surprise was essential if they were hiding out somewhere in this abandoned lot. Because
otherwise, Nemov and his men were in for an ugly fight.

"*Strike Group, this is Command,*" he heard Kondakov radio at last.
"*All units are in position. Wait one.*"

Nemov tensed, raising his clenched fist so the rest of his assault squad
could see it. The plan was to hit multiple possible hiding places simultaneously. Doing so inevitably reduced the number of troops available to
take out any site, which was risky. But it was either that or mass more
forces against one location at a time and risk hitting empty air—while
making enough noise to spook their intended targets and give them time
to bolt for some other safe haven. Kondakov had made it abundantly
clear that was *not* an acceptable outcome.

"*Execute,*" Kondakov said coolly. "*Now.*"

Nemov pumped his fist twice. "Go! Go! Go!" he hissed.

Instantly, two of his men yanked sharply on cables attached to coiled
barbed wire they'd cut earlier. The wire, strung along the top of the wall
years ago to deter thieves, fell aside with a soft, metallic *twang*.

With their way now clear, Nemov and his squad swarmed over the
low wall and dropped into the darkened lot, fanning out, weapons at
the ready. They drifted past abandoned vehicles, mounds of old crates,
and empty shipping containers—probing carefully for any signs of an
ambush or concealed sentries as they moved deeper into the area.

One of the two sheds in the far corner of the lot was plainly abandoned. Only empty blackness loomed behind its wide-open entrance.
The other had a door that was shut. Assault rifle up and aimed, Nemov
glided silently toward the shed. His troops moved with him. He was
sweating now. No light showed under the door, but what did that matter
if armed men were concealed inside, waiting to spring an ambush?

Rapid hand signals deployed his Raven Syndicate squad into a tactical stack alongside the door. From front to back, their heads nodded
as each man confirmed he was ready. Silently, Nemov counted down.
Three. Two. One.

His finger jabbed inward, unleashing his troops.

The man in the lead smashed a battering ram into the flimsy door. It broke open with an earsplitting crash. He rolled aside, clearing the way for the soldier behind him to lean in and lob a flash-bang grenade through the pitch-black opening.

WHAAMM.

The grenade went off with a shattering roar. A cascading shower of blinding pyrotechnics suddenly lit the night. The troops waiting behind the grenade thrower rushed in right on the heels of the blast—deploying to the right and left, ready to open fire at the slightest sign of movement.

The shed was unoccupied, empty of anyone, hostile or otherwise.

Nemov was the last man inside. He paused at the doorway to scan the empty room through experienced eyes. His pulse pounded in his ears. He felt jittery and knew that the sensation was a symptom of the adrenaline flooding his system in anticipation of a deadly, close-quarters battle slowly ebbing away.

"Shit," one of the Syndicate troopers growled. "This was a waste of time."

"I don't think so, Gennady," Nemov retorted. "Lights," he called out in warning. Then he flipped up his night vision goggles and flicked on a powerful flashlight. Its bright beam darted here and there across the interior of the shed, highlighting scuffed patches on the floor and other places where the old cardboard boxes lining the walls looked to have been disturbed.

At his gesture, some of the men dragged the boxes away, revealing sacks of recent food trash—mostly containers from surplus Russian Army field rations—and stacks of paint cans. Staring at them, one of his men tentatively suggested, "Homeless mooks?"

Nemov shook his head. "Ever met a homeless guy who was this neat and tidy? Or one who collects full cans of paint?"

"No, sir," the other man admitted.

"Me neither," Nemov said with a grimace. "Which probably means all this crap was left behind by the people we've been hunting." Dourly, he keyed his radio, preparing to report in. He was sure the news that their targets had already abandoned this safe house would not be well-received.

TEN

MERCURY CITY TOWER, MOSCOW

AN HOUR LATER

Under a dark, star-filled sky, the floodlit Mercury City Tower's bronze-tinted reflective glass glowed, transforming the 340-meter-high skyscraper into a soaring pillar of fire on Moscow's night skyline. Slanting, steplike recesses along one side gave the structure a tapered look. These unique architectural elements added to its apparent height and set it apart from its closest neighbors—the other ultramodern office and residential high-rises spiking skyward as part of the city's International Business Center. Eleven huge skyscrapers were packed into a small area, considerably less than a square kilometer, on the left bank of the Moskva River. Several more enormous buildings stood at different stages of construction—left unfinished amid the current economic downturn.

Forty-four stories up, Pavel Voronin prowled around his spacious private office. Ordinarily, its breathtaking views over the bright city lights of Moscow put him in a good mood. But not tonight. Tonight, he felt caged and restless. More suited by nature and temperament to be a predator among other, lesser men, he intensely disliked the realization that some group—as yet unidentified—had him in its sights.

Nor was this an empty threat. Their assault on the Raven's Nest could easily have succeeded in killing him.

He scowled. If nothing else, the debacle there had proved that his defenses were weaker than he had assumed. The wooded, thinly populated countryside around the Raven's Nest offered too many separate avenues of infiltration and attack.

That was why Voronin had decided to retreat here for the time being—to this towering, reinforced concrete-and-steel skyscraper. Three of the Mercury Center Tower's seventy-five floors housed the Raven Syndicate's corporate headquarters. Offices of other corporations, five-star restaurants, high-end retailers, and opulent apartments owned by some of Russia's richest and most powerful citizens filled the rest of the space. Consequently, the security systems protecting its easily guarded entrances and elevator banks were state-of-the-art. Now, bolstered by his armed personnel, they should be effectively air-tight.

He stopped pacing and stared out a window. Safe or not, his decision to take refuge in the Mercury City Tower still rubbed at his pride. It wasn't that he lacked for anything here. The living quarters adjacent to his office were comfortable, even lavish. And if anything, he was in closer touch with events and his most important subordinates.

No, Voronin understood, what gnawed at him was the knowledge that he had to take counsel of his fears for the first time in his adult life. Before the recent attempt to kill him, anyone with any sense had feared Pavel Voronin. But now, he thought sourly, it was as if his pursuers had abruptly turned his life upside down. He was the one who was afraid, and it was an unpleasant sensation.

His office door chimed suddenly. What now? Irritably, he turned away from the view outside and went back to his desk where he glanced at his computer monitor. The feed from a security camera showed Vasily Kondakov waiting just outside. A pair of Voronin's bodyguards had just finished patting him for concealed weapons.

Composing himself, Voronin sat down. He tapped an icon on his smartwatch, disengaging the door's security lock. Thick steel bolts retracted, and the door swung open, admitting his chief of internal security.

Voronin curtly gestured Kondakov to the chair in front of his desk. It took effort to control his mounting frustration. Showing signs of anxiety in front of his subordinates would be unwise. Men obeyed the strong and despised the weak. Assuming a feigned look of mild curiosity, he waited until the door locked again before nodding to the other man to begin. "So, Vasily, I assume this unscheduled visit means you've found something useful?"

"I believe so," Kondakov said carefully. "Ever since our raid on that enemy safe house came back empty-handed, my analysts have been working to develop new leads."

"And?"

"Reviewing reports and bodycam footage from the web of police checkpoints you ordered deployed immediately after the assault yielded results," Kondakov said. He synched his tablet with a large digital screen on the closest wall and opened a file. It showed surveillance footage from a checkpoint on the outskirts of Voskresensk, close to a junction with one of the main roads to Moscow.

Voronin watched silently as a battered early model UAZ panel van pulled up for inspection. Video from a young police lieutenant's bodycam showed him checking identification cards from two heavyset, disheveled men riding in the cab. Moments later, the view shifted around to the back when he insisted on inspecting their cargo.

Kondakov froze the image on a wall of paint cans, old and dented, that seemed to fill the van's cargo space from top to bottom.

"Paint?" Voronin asked, perplexed. "What's so significant there?"

In answer, the other man tapped at another file, opening a single digital photo. Shot inside the abandoned shed Raven Syndicate troops had raided only hours before, it showed a collection of rusting cans stacked along one wall. His finger indicated the image. "They are identical."

Voronin grimaced. "That van," he realized. "It was carrying the enemy agents we've been hunting."

Kondakov nodded. "Judging by the cargo capacity of the vehicle and the amount of food trash recovered from the shed, this is a small, very highly trained team. I estimate its strength as being in the range of no more than four to six individuals."

"So few?" Voronin growled. "How is that possible considering the losses they inflicted on our security forces?"

"Surprise, speed of action, and the use of superior fire power at every point of contact," the other man said bluntly. "These people are very good at what they do. Which makes them extremely dangerous."

Tight-lipped, Voronin sat back. "What else do we know?"

"We pulled the names and ID numbers of the van driver and his assistant off the police officer's body cam footage and ran them through a host of official databases," Kondakov said. "They don't match up with any known citizen or resident alien."

"Meaning their ID cards were forged."

Kondakov nodded.

Voronin frowned. "And the van? Its license plate, I mean. Was that a fake too?"

"No," the other man said. "The number is genuine. It was even registered to a UAZ panel van of a similar model year and make."

"But not the same one?"

"No. Available records show the vehicle associated with this plate number was junked several years ago." Kondakov spread his hands. "And once again, I'm forced to admire the tradecraft of our opponents. They constructed a solid defense against any cursory inspection or traffic stop. A police officer running the number of that plate through his computer wouldn't turn up anything suspicious."

"I don't want these bastards admired," Voronin snapped, unable to hide his irritation any longer. "I want them dead!"

Hurriedly, Kondakov bobbed his head in agreement. "A quick review of traffic camera footage from the area shows that van was last seen on roads that lead to the safe house we discovered. But that's where we've run into a dead end. There's no sign of the vehicle anywhere in the district now."

"Which means these enemy agents are on the move again," Voronin said, working hard to regain control over his temper.

Kondakov nodded.

"Knowing this, can you track them using the traffic camera network?"

Kondakov shrugged. "That would be . . . difficult," he admitted. "Attempting to do so would mean combing through every frame of footage shot in the Moscow region. At a minimum, I estimate that represents well over a hundred thousand hours' worth of video."

Voronin frowned. "The proverbial needle in the haystack, then?"

"Worse, I'm afraid," Kondakov told him. "Millions of vehicles traverse the local roads and highways daily. And of those, tens of thousands are UAZ vans of the same make and model year."

"I grow weary of being told what cannot be done, Vasily," Voronin warned. "Particularly since the people who tried to kill me may already be making a run for one of our borders."

Kondakov nodded again. "That is their most likely move," he agreed. "And it gives us a chance, if only a small one, of intercepting them." He replaced the images on the wall screen with a large digital map of Russia, centered on Moscow. A swipe across his synced tablet drew a large red line through the highways leading west and southwest toward the Baltic states, Poland, Belarus, and Ukraine. "I consider these the least likely escape routes. Our frontiers there are relatively heavily guarded and the target of significant surveillance. Any attempt to cross them illegally, whether by vehicle or on foot, would be unnecessarily risky."

"True," Voronin acknowledged.

Another sweep of Kondakov's fingers drew a similar line across the roads and highways leading south toward Georgia and Azerbaijan. "The same thing applies here. Tensions are high in this area and, consequently, so is our security."

Voronin pointed southeast at the routes connecting Russia with Kazakhstan. "And those?"

"Across the steppes?" Kondakov shook his head. "While it's possible, I judge that to be a low probability. The terrain there is so open that any covert attempt to cross the border might easily be spotted by ground or air patrols. Again, if it were me, I would assess the risks of making such a move to be too high."

"Then you believe these terrorists are headed north?"

Kondakov nodded. "I do. Our border with Finland runs for more than thirteen hundred kilometers, most of it through woods and uninhabited land. Plus, it's relatively lightly guarded at the moment. Except along the southernmost portion, most of our Cold War–era perimeter fences, tripwires, and other defenses have been dismantled."

Voronin considered that. The course of action suggested by the other man made sense from their mysterious enemy's perspective. "So you want me to ask for new police roadblocks on the highways heading north, into Russian Karelia and the Murmansk area?"

"Unfortunately, there's no time for that," Kondakov said, shaking his head. "It will take hours for any request to work its way down through the bureaucracy of the Ministry of Internal Affairs. And even more time to organize special units of trained police officers. By then, this possible trail will be far too cold."

Voronin frowned. "Then you want to use our own people for this effort?"

"We have two helicopters on standby," Kondakov reminded him. "With just enough range and payload capacity to deploy four-man security teams into positions for a possible intercept on the two most likely routes. And the farther outside Moscow we send them, the better the odds that one of the UAZ vans they stop and inspect will belong to our targets."

"Four-man teams?" Voronin queried sharply. "You keep praising the competence of these enemy agents. What makes you confident that a mere handful of your security troops can deal with them?"

"Surprise works both ways," Kondakov pointed out. "After all, no one, no matter how highly trained, can remain alert forever. And the more distance they put between themselves and Moscow, the more these people should let their guard down."

Voronin made his decision. "Very well. Organize it. Get your intercept teams moving as quickly as possible." He frowned. "But we need a backstop in case you've guessed wrong."

Kondakov nodded. "We should ask President Zhdanov to order a special heightened state of alert for all border districts adjoining hostile countries," he said slowly. "Our Border Service units should be on the lookout for any unauthorized vehicles, particularly UAZ-made vans, which attempt to enter their controlled zones."

Voronin considered the proposal. The FSB commanded Russia's 170,000 Border Guard troops. Taking into consideration the sheer length of the nation's frontiers, that seemed like a pathetically small number. On the other hand, its U.S. counterpart, Customs and Border Protection, had fewer than 22,000 armed agents. And Russia's government, at least, attempted to regulate all movement near its borders. He nodded to himself. If those who'd tried to kill him were really on the run, desperately trying to escape from Russia without being caught, it made sense to throw as many obstacles as he could into their path. He picked up the secure phone on his desk and punched in a two-digit number. Politically weakened though he was, he still had a direct line to the Kremlin.

It rang just once before being answered. "Executive Office of the President," said a quiet, businesslike voice on the other end.

"This is Pavel Voronin," he declared. "I need to speak to President Zhdanov personally. The matter is urgent and involves grave issues of state security."

ELEVEN

SOME HOURS LATER

Nick Flynn fought down a powerful urge to yawn. Stiffly, he forced himself to sit up straighter in the passenger seat of the ancient UAZ 3741 van. He knew he was so tired that, once he started yawning, he'd have a hard time stopping. After more than thirty-six hours on the run with only short periods of rest in cramped, uncomfortable safe houses, fatigue toxins were accumulating fast in his body.

He glanced at Tadeusz Kossak behind the wheel. The other man looked as drained as he felt. No surprise, he thought. Sleep had been a luxury for all of them ever since this mission kicked off—both precious and in extremely short supply.

Flynn narrowed his eyes against the headlight glare as a large tractor-trailer truck roared past on the opposite side of the highway, heading south toward Vologda. Moments later, a white SUV coming up behind them flashed its high beams in warning and then pulled around and quickly passed them, red taillights dwindling rapidly as it faded into the distance and darkness. Apart from them, the road was empty.

Off to the east, the sky was beginning to lighten, gradually turning a pale gray above the forest of pine, birch, and spruce trees that lined the highway. It would be dawn in less than an hour.

"I think we may be heading into trouble," Kossak said suddenly, peering intently through the van's windshield. He took his foot off the accelerator, allowing the UAZ to slow a little. His left hand drifted from the steering wheel down to the butt of the 9mm MP-443 Grach pistol stuffed between the edge of his seat and the door.

Flynn followed his gaze. There, about a mile up the road, he could see lights moving on the verge and what might be a lightweight orange barricade blocking the right-hand lane. He squinted, trying to make out more details in the poor light. "Some kind of an accident scene? Or maybe a sobriety checkpoint?"

The Pole shook his head. "There aren't any vehicles in sight," he said tightly. "And whoever is manning that barricade just waved the SUV that passed us right on by, even though it was clearly speeding."

Flynn felt cold. Kossak's night vision was phenomenal, one of the traits that made him such a superb long-distance marksman. If he couldn't see any police cars or trucks parked near that checkpoint, they simply were not there. Since the nearest town was miles away, the strong possibility was that the people ahead of them had been flown into position by helicopter. And ordinary Russian traffic cops didn't have access to helicopters.

Suddenly wide awake, thoughts raced through his mind in rapid succession. They'd switched the van's license plates and painted over the corporate logo on its sides, but the model and make made it comparatively easy to spot—assuming their enemies had some inkling of what type of vehicle they were using and where they might be headed. *Score that as a likely big fat "yes" on both counts*, Flynn realized, eyeing the shadowy figures moving into position near the orange barricade. Blowing through the checkpoint or making a sudden U-turn away from it weren't realistic options. The UAZ was mechanically reliable, but it wasn't exactly high-powered or nimble. As soon as the bad guys were sure that they had a valid target and radioed it in, it would be impossible for his team to shake any search and pursuit, especially since the road network in this part of Russia was sparse.

Which left only one real option, Flynn knew. One that was all too likely to get them killed. "If this really is aimed at us, we'll have to punch out from the inside," he murmured to Kossak. He reached down into the carrying case between his feet, extracted his compact PP-2000 sub-machine gun, and slid it into the narrow gap between his seat and the passenger side door. The Pole nodded. He loosened his Grach pistol in its holster, making sure he could draw it in a hurry if necessary.

Flynn craned his head back around toward the open panel into the UAZ's cargo area. "We're coming into a probable red zone," he warned loudly, using the Four slang for an enemy position. "If things turn hot, bail out fast and go hard."

"Got it," Laura Van Horn replied. "ETA?"

Flynn looked through the windshield again. They were now within a quarter mile of the checkpoint. A figure had stepped out onto the high-way and, using a hand-held flashlight, signaled for them to pull over. "Maybe thirty seconds," he said.

"Well, hell," Van Horn said conversationally. "Good thing none of us could sleep back here in this fricking sardine can." The sound of weapons being chambered accompanied her words.

Kossak braked to a gentle stop near the orange barricade. He rolled his window down as the flashlight-wielder approached. "What's up, of-ficer?" he asked politely, narrowing his eyes against the beam hitting him right in the face.

"None of your business," a harsh voice growled. "What are you people doing on the road so damn early?"

The Pole shrugged. "Got an emergency plumbing job at one of the hotels in Lipin Bor," he said casually, naming a lakeside town some miles ahead up the highway. "The manager there is shitting himself that his guests won't have hot water when they wake up."

"They don't have any plumbers of their own in Lipin Bor?" the man holding the flashlight snapped in disbelief.

Kossak shrugged his shoulders again. "The manager's my cousin," he said. "He likes to keep his business in the family."

Squinting himself against the glare, Flynn saw two more men edging around toward the back of the van and a third positioned off to the front.

They all wore night-gray camouflage uniforms, body armor, and carried assault rifles. *That tears it*, he realized coldly. These were definitely Raven Syndicate goons, not regular Russian traffic police. He turned toward Kossak and raised his voice a little so that Van Horn and the others in the back of the van could hear his warning that they were being flanked. "Hey, Yuri, I got another text. Now Piotr says the *two* toilets at the *rear* of the building are clogged, too. And he's starting to freak out about when we're going to get there."

"Great," Kossak sighed. He looked at the man pinning him in the flashlight beam. "Hey, is this going to take much longer, officer?"

"Not really," the other man said grimly. "Now get out of the van! Both of you!"

Well, so much for subtlety, Flynn thought. "You heard him, Yuri," he said, forcing a nervous edge into his voice. "We need to get *out*."

"Sure, sure," Kossak replied. "No problem, officer." He leaned over to grab the door handle with his right hand, seemingly unintentionally lowering his head toward the more solid cover of the dashboard, and simultaneously drawing the 9mm Grach with his left hand. His finger curled around the trigger and squeezed repeatedly, firing several quick semi-armor-piercing shots right through the driver's side door at the Syndicate trooper holding the flashlight on him.

Hit at least twice at point-blank range, the Russian stumbled backward.

Flynn exploded into action himself, grabbing his submachine gun and slamming the passenger's side door wide open as he threw himself out sideways. His right shoulder and hip slammed into the ground as he swung the muzzle of the MP-2000 toward the gunman positioned at the front of the van.

Flashes stabbed the night as that Russian fired a wild burst directly into the vehicle. Slammed by 7.62mm rounds, the UAZ's windshield shattered, and pieces of torn metal flew away from its broad, blunt nose.

WHAAMM. A flash-bang grenade went off somewhere behind the vehicle—tearing apart the darkness with dozens of strobing pulses of dazzling light. Weapons stuttered, accompanied by yells and agonized screams.

Flynn ignored the chaos unfolding all around him. His field of vision narrowed to the Raven Syndicate trooper he'd identified as his primary target. Everything seemed to be moving in slow motion as his nervous system and brain kicked into overdrive. From his position on the ground, he could see the other man's assault rifle swinging away from the bullet-riddled front of the UAZ to aim at him. But then his own submachine gun's front sights settled into position first, and he opened fire on full auto—burning through half a magazine in less than a second. The Russian jerked backward, hammered off his feet by multiple hits that ripped through his legs, chest, and head.

An eerie silence descended across the scene, broken only by high-pitched whining and pinging noises from the UAZ's wrecked engine. Through his gunfire- and explosion-numbed ears, Flynn heard Van Horn call, "We're clear back here! All hostiles are down and dead." He scanned the ground ahead of them. Nothing moved. Slowly, he raised up off his side. "Clear to the right front, too," Flynn reported. "Tad?"

"*Gówno*. Shit," Kossak answered through clenched teeth from somewhere on the other side of the van. "I've been hit."

They found the Pole lying half-in and half-out of the bullet-riddled van. Multiple splotches of blood were spreading across his back and both legs of his jeans. Bits of metal gleamed in the center of each small wound. While none of the 7.62mm rounds fired into the front of the van had struck him, they'd blown a hail of sharp-edged splinters across the cab and into Kossak.

While Hynes applied field dressings to the Pole's wounds and Cooke and Vucovich dragged the four dead Raven Syndicate troops out of sight into the nearby woods, Van Horn pulled Flynn aside for a quiet consultation. "None of those injuries are going to be fatal, but one thing's for sure, Tad's not going to be walking on his own—at least not very far—until all those splinters are dug out and his torn-up muscles have time to heal," she said.

Flynn nodded. "We'll have to carry him to the rendezvous point," he agreed. Fortunately, one of their gear bags included a foldable portable stretcher.

"Which brings us to our next big problem," Van Horn pointed out, jerking her head toward the shot-up UAZ van. "It doesn't look like any of us are going very far, and we're still what? Something like five hundred miles from where we need to be?"

"Thereabouts," Flynn said with a nod.

Van Horn folded her arms. "And you've got a solution for that?"

"I do," Flynn said with a sigh. "But I don't like it much." He indicated the lightweight orange barricade in front of their wrecked van. "I figure we make use of what the Syndicate has provided and run our own unofficial traffic stop on the next big vehicle, preferably a tractor-trailer truck, that comes along."

She whistled softly. "You know we'll have to bring the driver along with us? At least until we can safely drop him off somewhere he won't be found for a while."

"Yeah, which means we'll be adding kidnapping and carjacking to our list of felonies," Flynn admitted. "On the other hand, I don't imagine that'll make much real difference if the Russians grab us before we can break across the frontier."

Van Horn's eyes roved around the site of their recent battle. Then she smiled crookedly. "I guess not. Because between this shootout and the mess we made back at Voronin's estate, I figure we're already at the top of the Kremlin's Most Wanted List."

TWELVE

REPUBLIC OF KARELIA, RUSSIA
LATE EVENING

Nick Flynn moved warily through the ancient pine woods—on the lookout for dead tree branches and slippery, half-buried rocks among the ferns and thick green moss carpeting the forest floor's shallow ledges and hollows. Van Horn followed him, with Hynes and Vucovich carrying Kossak on their portable stretcher, and Cooke bringing up the rear. They were all being cautious, both to avoid making excessive noise and to reduce the chances of someone twisting an ankle. Heavily burdened as they were by one wounded teammate, they couldn't risk any further injuries.

They'd ditched the tractor-trailer truck they'd hijacked several hours before, abandoning it on a deserted side road, along with its bound and gagged driver. If necessary, Flynn figured an anonymous phone call to the Russian authorities once they were safely in Finland would ensure that the poor guy was retrieved.

Coming to a place where the forest gradually sloped away to the west, Flynn paused for a moment to check his bearings. Squinting, he peered through the trees, ignoring the whirling swarms of mosquitos and biting flies whining through the sweltering gloom. Off across a stretch of lower ground just ahead, he spotted the red-tinged glint of fading sunlight on water. They were getting close to the eastern shores of Lake Kamennoye. He glanced down at his watch. Although it was almost ten at night, the sun was just now sliding below the horizon. Long black shadows stretched eastward.

Laura Van Horn moved up beside him. She nodded toward the faint glimpse of water. "That it?" she asked, pitching her voice low so that it couldn't be heard more than a few feet away.

"Should be," Flynn said. The hint of a smile twitched at the side of his mouth. "Unless I got us turned around somehow and this is one of the other sixty-some-odd thousand lakes in Russian Karelia."

"Not funny, Nick," Van Horn growled quietly. She thumped his ribs with her elbow. "Might not be safe to piss me off just now. I'm hot and sweaty, and not in a good way."

"Affirmative on that," he acknowledged. Then, before she could elbow him again, he led the way down the gentle slope. Following him, the team pushed across the level ground, skirting trees and boulders and denser patches of underbrush. Closer to the lake, the woods were even thicker and more tangled.

After a few minutes, Flynn reached the edge of a rutted dirt road. According to the maps he'd studied, it ran parallel to the lake shore for several miles. He felt the tension tightening his shoulder blades ease up a little. Reaching this landmark meant they were getting close to their planned rendezvous point.

But then, just as he was about to cross the narrow road, he picked up the unmistakable sound of a vehicle moving somewhere not that far off. It was getting closer fast.

A Russian patrol, Flynn realized. Reacting fast, he dropped into the nearest cover—a clump of ferns growing around a fallen log. Van Horn went prone near a tree. So did Cooke. Vucovich and Hynes carefully lowered Kossak's stretcher and went to ground behind a group of moss-covered boulders.

The engine noise grew even louder.

Flynn lay still with his eyes narrowed to slits, observing the road through a slight gap in the ferns. Suddenly, a UAZ-469 utility jeep appeared from the north, driving into sight around a shallow curve. It carried a pair of armed Border Guard soldiers in forest-pattern camouflage and soft-billed caps. Accompanied by the grinding sound of shifting gears and the crackling hiss of a radio, the small four-wheeled vehicle bumped along the rutted dirt road, heading south. The heads of both the driver and his passenger were on constant swivel—meticulously scanning the forest around them in all directions.

Suddenly worried that the gleam of his eyes might give him away in the fading light, Flynn carefully lowered his head. He held his breath as the jeep rolled on only yards away from his hiding place, waiting for the startled yell that would confirm he'd been spotted. His hand edged toward the stock of the PP-2000 submachine gun slung over his shoulder.

The shout never came.

Instead, the jeep just kept going until it disappeared from view around another bend in the road a hundred yards farther south.

Flynn breathed out slowly. Russia's territorial forces were a lot more active than he'd anticipated. This was the second patrol they'd had to avoid since starting this trek through the rugged Karelian countryside.

He frowned. Technically, the area they were traversing was part of a nature preserve. That made it strictly off-limits to everyone, except accredited scientists and carefully guided eco-tourists. Yeah, well, he thought, it was becoming painfully evident that the Border Guards hadn't gotten the memo. Or, more likely, they didn't give a damn about endangered local animals and plant life. Not when Moscow must be demanding immediate action to tighten security along its frontiers with the West.

Flynn sighed. Tempting as it was to lie hidden among these ferns for a while longer, that wasn't an option. With Russians on high alert, he and his team needed to keep moving. He got back to his feet and stood listening for a moment, just in case the local Border Guards commander had decided to play it cute by sending out a second jeep to act as a rearguard for that last patrol.

But except for the irritating, persistent whine of mosquitos, there was only silence. Nothing else stirred in the gathering shadows.

Reassured, Flynn darted across the rutted dirt track and immediately dropped back into cover on the far side. As soon as he signaled that it was clear, Van Horn and the others followed him over the road.

Once they were reunited, they moved on toward the shore—pushing through the trees and bracken. The sun was now well below the horizon, and the light around them was softening, fading into the gray melancholy of twilight.

Suddenly, from somewhere not far ahead, they heard a low whistle.

Flynn, Van Horne, and Cooke immediately halted and took a knee with their weapons up and ready. Vucovich and Hynes sank to the ground, still holding the stretcher between them. Kossak, pale from pain and blood loss, pulled his pistol.

Unhurriedly, moving slowly to avoid spooking them, a camouflaged shape stood up from the undergrowth only a few yards away. To his intense relief, Flynn recognized the narrow, sharp-nosed face, keen blue eyes, and graying brown hair of Rytis Daukša. The Lithuanian was a veteran of his small nation's most secret and elite anti-terrorist unit, *Aitvaras*. After joining the Quartet Directorate, he'd been recruited into a European action team like the one Flynn had formed for Four's American station—commanded by Tony McGill, a former sergeant in the UK's SAS. McGill, Daukša, and several others had fought beside them the previous year during a daring commando raid deep into communist Cuba.

Flynn and the others lowered their weapons.

Silently, the Lithuanian beckoned them to follow him through the last stretch of forest and down to the water's edge. Lake Kamennoye stretched to the west, toward Finland. Without a trace of wind, the lake's waters were still, reflecting the image of every tree and boulder encircling it as if in a mirror.

Daukša jerked a thumb back toward the dirt road they'd crossed, now invisible among the trees and lengthening shadows. "Something has the orcs stirred up. That Border Guard patrol you just evaded makes three in just the past few hours," he commented quietly. "Your doing, I presume?"

"Could be," Flynn admitted. "We might have pissed off a few people."

The Lithuanian grinned at him. "One of them being our not-so-good friend Voronin, I understand—" He broke off as the sound of clattering rotors abruptly shattered the silence of the forest.

They all squatted down and froze in place in the shadows.

Suddenly, a dark-and-light-green-painted Mi-8 troop transport helicopter roared low across the lake about a mile away. In its wake, the downwash from its spinning blades churned the water into a froth of rippling white foam. Red and green and white navigation lights blinking, the helicopter flew on to the north—and eventually vanished into the rapidly growing darkness. The noise of its engines and rotors faded away.

Daukša hummed softly. "This man Voronin has a very long reach."

"So it seems," Flynn agreed. "Which is why we're in a bit of a hurry here, Rytis."

With a somber nod, the Lithuanian turned, brought two fingers to his mouth, and whistled softly again.

As if by magic, another member of Four's Europe-based action team suddenly appeared less than ten yards away down the shoreline—flipping aside the camouflage netting that had hidden him from view until that moment. Einar Haugen had served with Norway's Special Operations Commandos before signing on with the Quartet Directorate. Tall, square-jawed, and blond-haired, he resembled the Vikings of legend, but Flynn knew the big man had hidden depths, including a quirky, dark sense of humor that left even Cole Hynes in awe.

Flynn glanced wryly at Daukša. "Got anything else up your sleeve?"

The other man shrugged. "Not me. But Einar does."

They joined the Norwegian at the water's edge. Immediately, Flynn found his eyes pulled to four dark green inflatable rafts. Drawn up on shore, they had been concealed beneath Haugen's camouflage netting.

"These are packrafts," the blond-haired man explained in fluent, but accented English. "Compact and comparatively light, they are used by backpack enthusiasts who want to combine water travel, even white-water rafting, with hiking trips into the wilderness." He knelt by one of the rafts and patted its resilient, polyurethane-coated nylon fabric side. "These are a marvel of design. Uninflated, each raft weighs less than fourteen of your American pounds. Plus, they can be packed down to a twenty by ten inch roll."

Flynn was impressed. Inflated, each of the rafts looked to be about six feet long and almost four feet wide. "What's their carrying capacity?"

"Two adults and up to several hundred pounds of equipment," Haugen replied. "Plus, I have made some special modifications of my own." He moved around the raft and waved a hand at a small assembly fixed to its stern, complete with a miniature three-bladed propeller. "See?"

Flynn stared. "You've equipped these rafts with motors?"

"*Ja*," the Norwegian said with a proud look. "Very efficient, light-weight electric marine motors. They have enough battery power to carry us across this lake. Ten miles or so." His smile grew broader seeing the American's amazed reaction. "Much easier and quieter than trying to paddle so far, eh?"

"Pretty slick, Einar," Flynn acknowledged. "Pretty doggone slick."

THIRTEEN

LAKE KAMENNOYE

A SHORT TIME LATER

As soon as the last traces of light faded from the western sky, they hauled their rafts off the rock-strewn shore and scrambled aboard. It took only moments to lower the outboard motors into the water and engage the propellers. Accompanied by a low, barely audible, whine, the inflatables veered out into the lake and forged ahead at nearly five miles per hour. Daukša and Haugen were in the lead boat, followed by Flynn and Van Horn. Vucovich shepherded the bandaged Tad Kossak in the third small craft, and finally, Cooke and Hynes brought up the rear. As a precaution, they stayed fairly close to shore, no more than fifty yards out. That way, if they ran into trouble, they'd at least have a shot at darting swiftly back into hiding.

As the miles and minutes steadily unrolled, the voyage took on an eerie, almost otherworldly feel. In the darkness, each inflatable raft carved its own narrow, arrow-shaped furrow through a vast black field of tiny, brilliant lights—the stars sprinkled across the heavens above reflected in the lake's calm, untroubled surface. And in this deceptively peaceful setting, with nothing to do but follow the dimly seen shape of the boat ahead, Flynn found it all too easy to let his mind drift.

Over the past several days, he'd had to be laser-focused, first on

trying to carry out the team's assigned mission to kill Voronin, and afterward, when everything went wrong, on the urgent task of getting
everyone safely out of Russia. Doing so had required every ounce of
his tactical skill, courage, ingenuity, and determination. Now, though,
he had just enough breathing space to look ahead and consider what
might come next.

Flynn's jaw tightened. He was sure they'd managed to throw a serious
scare into Voronin, but that wasn't what they'd needed to accomplish.
Frightened or not, everything they knew about the Russian oligarch
suggested he wouldn't abandon his efforts to destroy the United States
and make his own country the world's preeminent power.

This left the Quartet Directorate only two real choices: Either give
up any thought of going after Voronin directly or commit to a second
attempt to eliminate him—a mission made inherently more complex,
more dangerous, and far less likely to succeed by their first failure. Shaken
though he was by the strength of Voronin's defenses, Flynn already knew
which course of action he'd be arguing for. What he didn't know yet
was how he could look his teammates in their eyes and convince them
he wasn't proposing a modern-day kamikaze mission.

Two staccato mike clicks through his headset brought him sharply
back to the present. That was one of the emergency signals Daukša had
briefed them on before setting out across the lake. In response, Flynn's
hand flashed to the tiny outboard fixed to their raft's stern. A quick
button press cut battery power to the motor. The raft slowed immediately, gradually losing momentum until it barely drifted across the water.

Quickly, he looked around. Three darkened oblong shapes bobbed
silently nearby. The others had cut their own engines too.

Crouched low in the front half of their raft, Van Horn pointed
ahead. He leaned to her left to get a better line of sight on whatever had
spooked Daukša and Haugen. He saw the answer right away.

They were close to a place where a large island sat astride this arm of
Lake Kamennoye, narrowing it so that only two channels—each scarcely
fifty yards wide—linked to the broader expanse of water beyond. Taking
advantage of this natural choke point, the Russians had built a one-lane,

north–south road across the lake here, spanning both channels with the aid of a couple of small steel beam bridges supported on concrete piers.

The Lithuanian had been leading them toward the northernmost passage, planning to glide smoothly under the span before motoring back onto the broader lake. At night, in this restricted nature preserve, and under normal circumstances, they should have been able to slip through without any trouble.

Which made it too damned bad that the circumstances were anything *but* normal, Flynn thought, seeing the shape of a UAZ jeep parked on the bridge only about a hundred yards away. A reddish glow from lit cigarettes revealed two Russian Border Guards leaning on the railing while they stared across the darkened lake. One said something indistinct. The other laughed.

Instinctively, Flynn crouched even lower in the little raft. Even at this relatively short distance, their inflatables should be virtually invisible, just black shapes riding silently on equally black water. But would their luck hold? His mouth quirked upward. Relying on luck was an amateur's move, like figuring you could roll into Vegas with a couple of thousand bucks in your pocket and plan on coming out a millionaire. Sure, it could happen, but you certainly couldn't count on it.

From the set of Van Horn's shoulders, he suspected her thoughts were running in the same direction. When she pulled out her 9mm Grach pistol and started threading a suppressor onto its muzzle, he was sure of it. He leaned forward and touched her arm.

She glanced back with a raised eyebrow. Her ordinarily generous mouth was tight-lipped.

Flynn shook his head slightly, indicating the weapon in her hand. She was a crack shot, as he had good reason to know. A hundred yards, though, was an extreme range for a pistol. Hitting anything at that distance would be tricky, especially with her first shot. It would be worth trying if the Russians spotted them first—but not before. For now, their best hope was to wait this out.

Reluctantly, Van Horn nodded. She finished fitting the suppressor to her pistol but refrained from taking any other immediate action.

Several minutes slid by, each a seeming eternity.

Finally, one of the Russians flicked his cigarette out over the railing. It vanished into the water with a soft *hiss*. He straightened up and snapped an order to the other man. Obeying, the soldier dropped his own cigarette onto the bridge and ground it beneath his boot heel. Then he walked around the jeep and climbed into the passenger seat. The first Border Guard took one last look out across the water, shrugged, and slid back behind the wheel. Moments later, the jeep's engine coughed to life, and it drove off.

In the lead raft, Daukša keyed his mike once. That was the signal to proceed. Swiftly, Flynn and the rest restarted their outboard motors. Battery-driven propellers whirred quietly into motion, and the little convoy of small boats moved on again toward the low, overhanging bridge—heading west into the channel, and, ultimately, out onto the wider lake.

Two hours later, the four rafts nosed up along a narrow gravel beach on the far shore. Everyone except Kossak scrambled over the sides, into ankle-deep shallows, and hauled the inflatable boats onto the beach. Vucovich and Hynes loaded the wounded Pole back aboard his stretcher.

Quietly, Daukša and Haugen moved down the line of rafts. They showed everyone how to deflate and stow their inflatables in rucksacks with practiced ease. They did the same for the outboard motors, which broke down into separate, easily carried components.

Thirty minutes after landing, Flynn and the others were ready to move on. The shortcut across Lake Kamennoye had saved them from what would otherwise have been an arduous and time-consuming trek through miles of rugged wilderness—in constant danger of being intercepted by roving Border Guard patrols. Trying that while carrying a stretcher-bound wounded man might have proved impossible. As it was, they were now less than two miles from Russia's border with Finland.

With the Lithuanian and Norwegian on point, the group headed off through the forest at a rapid clip. The skies behind them would begin to brighten in less than two hours. Given the tight timing, they needed to press on as quickly as possible without crashing through the woods like wild elephants on a rampage.

But then, around two hundred yards from the frontier—which along this stretch of the border was nothing more than a wide clearing cut through the forest, with occasional wooden posts to indicate which side of the line you were on—their luck ran out. They had just reached the edge of a small glade, the last open space before the border itself, when Daukša suddenly flashed the hand signal for "contact front."

Like the rest, Flynn went prone. Bushes and tree trunks provided some cover and concealment. Controlling his breathing, he listened carefully. Voices murmured ahead of them, accompanied by boots crunching through brush. Moments later, a Russian patrol emerged on the far side of the clearing.

There were six Border Guard soldiers. Five had assault rifles slung over their shoulders. But the sixth trooper held the most dangerous weapon of all on a leash—a German Shepherd tracking dog. *Shit, shit, shit*, Flynn thought bleakly. Thanks to their advanced camouflage, the humans might miss them, but that damned dog would be right on top of them the second it caught their scent . . . which would be any moment now.

He sighed inwardly and readied his submachine gun. Minimizing collateral damage had been one of the primary conditions imposed on this mission by the Quartet Directorate's various heads of station. Their directives were clear. Voronin himself and his Raven Syndicate mercenaries were fair game. But shooting up ordinary Russian conscripts and regular police officers was something they'd wanted to avoid if possible. Four might consider itself at war with the enemies of the West, but it was not usually a war waged without limits.

Carefully, Flynn cradled the compact PP-2000, settling its stock against his shoulder while his left hand moved to the foregrip. His right forefinger slid just outside the trigger guard. He frowned. He didn't want to kill these Russians, but it sure looked like he and his team wouldn't have much choice. And no matter how this ultimately played out, an ambush that ended up with dead Russian border troops was bound to cause one hell of a ruckus. Those higher up in Four might understand the necessity, but no one was going to thank him for possibly triggering a small-scale shooting war along the Russo-Finnish border.

A boot nudged his leg.

Flynn glanced over and saw Haugen shake his head minutely. The big, blond Norwegian had a small radio transmitter in his hand. He smoothly pulled out its extendible antenna with a tight, satisfied grin. Then he thumbed on the power switch and pressed a button along its side.

Ear-splitting bursts of what sounded like automatic weapons fire erupted somewhere off in the woods to the north. Flashes tore the night sky in strobing pulses. Periodic loud, grenade-like *bangs* echoed through the trees.

Over at the far edge of the clearing, the Russians dove for cover. Frightened voices called back and forth as the soldiers fumbled frantically to ready their weapons while staying prone. The German Shepherd, meanwhile, was straining at its leash—desperately eager to chase down the strange noises it was hearing.

"What the hell is going on, Sergeant?" Flynn heard one of them yell to their leader.

"Fuck if I know, Yvgeny," the other man growled. Like most Russian noncommissioned officers, he was little more than a conscript himself—albeit one with a slightly higher level of education. "But stay down unless you want your head blown off."

Slowly, the staccato rattle of gunfire and sharp, cracking grenade blasts faded away, leaving only a heavy, stunned silence in their wake.

Abruptly, the sergeant's radio crackled to life. "*Line Patrol Delta, this is Base. We've just received reports of small-arms fire somewhere in your operating area. What's your status? Are you engaged with hostiles?*"

"Negative, Base," the fresh-faced sergeant replied. "The action, whatever it was, was somewhere to our north. But the shooting's died away now."

"*Copy that. Listen closely. You are directed to immediately investigate the source and find out what is going on. Exercise great caution. Be advised that the foreign terrorists we've been looking for could be responsible.*"

Keeping his finger carefully off the transmit button, the Russian noncom hawked and spat to the side. "No shit," he muttered, sounding disgusted and out of sorts. Then he keyed his mike. "Understood, Base." Gloomily, he levered himself upright and swung around to stare at the rest of his men who were still lying down—nervously aiming their rifles toward the northern edge of the small forest glade. "You heard the major," he snapped. "On your feet, *parni*! Spread out and stay sharp."

With loud grumbling, murmured curses, and an evident lack of enthusiasm, the Border Guard troops climbed back to their feet. Then, chivvied along by their equally reluctant leader, they slowly fanned out and moved north. Only the dog showed any eagerness for action.

Once the Russians vanished among the trees, Flynn turned to Haugen. He felt a huge grin spread across his face. "That was a damned effective distraction, Einar."

The former Norwegian commando shrugged nonchalantly. "Rytis and I rigged up a few dozen firecrackers and some pyrotechnics before coming to meet you," he admitted. "It seemed a useful precaution."

From out in front, Daukša whistled softly. "This is our chance," he hissed, getting back up. "Let's go!" Then he turned and trotted west toward the border.

Flynn and the rest followed him. With the nearest enemy patrol distracted and chasing phantoms, they reached the frontier without any further trouble.

Once inside Finland, they pressed on through the woods to where two passenger vans were parked beside a narrow, paved road. Alerted by an earlier coded message Flynn had sent after the attempted highway ambush, a Quartet Directorate-affiliated EMT was waiting there for them. After a quick examination, he started working on Kossak's injuries, extracting metal splinters and fragments and sewing up the jagged wounds they left behind. The Pole bore his treatment in stoic, tight-lipped silence.

While the others wearily loaded their equipment aboard the waiting vehicles, Daukša pulled Flynn aside. "We need to get on the road, Nick," he said firmly. "And move swiftly."

"To avoid unnecessary hassles with the locals?" Flynn guessed.

The Lithuanian nodded. "Four has friends inside the Finnish Border Guard, and they agreed to turn a blind eye to tonight's border crossing operation. But their patience isn't endless."

Flynn smiled. "Especially since things got a little . . . noisy?"

"Possibly so," the other man admitted with a grin. "Moscow will complain bitterly. Naturally, to no avail. But it would still be best for our Finnish friends if they could swear convincingly that they didn't encounter anyone crossing into their national territory without permission."

"'You didn't see me. And I was never here,'" Flynn said, quoting the traditional black ops mantra.

Daukša nodded again. "Sometimes the old ways are best," he agreed.

Made aware of the need to keep up the pace—at least for a bit longer—it took only a few more minutes for the Quartet Directorate team to finish loading their gear and pile aboard the two vans, with Kossak stretched out and finally able to sleep with the aid of a morphine patch. Daukša took the wheel of one and Haugen the other. They pulled away, driving south toward Helsinki.

With a deep sigh of fatigue, Flynn settled into one of the rear seats of the second passenger van. Van Horn slid in beside him and gave him a quick, hard kiss. "I missed doing that," she said with a mischievous grin.

"So did I," he admitted.

"Well, buckle up, cowboy," she promised huskily. "Now that we're safe and sound, I plan on making up for lost time."

Flynn closed his eyes. "Yes, ma'am."

Van Horn looked more closely at him. "I'm sensing a 'but, Laura,' there, Nick," she said quietly. "Care to share it with me?"

He shrugged. "It's not that complicated," he told her tiredly. "I just can't shake a feeling that this was just the start of the shit hitting the fan. A lot of folks were sour on this mission from the get-go, so the after-action debriefings will likely be pretty brutal."

"Ah, the brass," Van Horn said in understanding. "Our esteemed lords and masters and the rest of the 'I told you so' crowd."

Flynn nodded. Some of Four's different national and regional stations had been reluctant to approve the American attempt to kill Pavel Voronin. They'd viewed the proposed assassination attempt as excessively dangerous and far too likely to endanger the shield of secrecy so vital to the Quartet Directorate's continued survival and success. His team's failure would probably give even more ammunition to the nay-sayers who wanted to stick to a defensive, reactive policy in the face of the ongoing threat from Voronin's Raven Syndicate.

Van Horn looked him squarely in the face. "So we get more push-back from the same people who wanted to turtle up in the first place?" she observed. "You going to let that stop us from trying again?"

Wearily, Flynn smiled. "Oh, hell no. At least not if I can figure out a new plan. One that won't get us all killed for no purpose."

She leaned in for another, even longer kiss. "Now there's the Nick Flynn I know and love," she said in satisfaction when she came back up for air. "Ornery and stubborn . . . and right."

FOURTEEN

MERCURY CITY TOWER, MOSCOW

THE NEXT DAY

Pavel Voronin glowered across his desk at Vasily Kondakov. "You're certain that these enemy agents have escaped?" he ground out.

The other man nodded. "The truck they stole after eliminating our ambush team was found by Border Guard troops, along with its kidnapped driver, only about a kilometer outside the security zone. Between the driver's story of what happened to him and these reports of a patrol lured away from the frontier by what turned out to be command-detonated pyrotechnics, there's no doubt."

"And what do the Finns say about this incident?"

"They deny any involvement," Kondakov said. "To use their exact words, I quote: 'An isolated episode of apparent hooliganism on Russia's sovereign territory is an issue for the Russian government to resolve. It is of no concern to Finland.' Unquote."

"The Finns are laughing at us. Right in our faces," Voronin said bitterly.

Kiril Rodin had been staring out the floor-to-ceiling windows that formed one wall of Voronin's office while Kondakov delivered his briefing. Now he turned around. "Of course, they are," he said. "Without hard evidence proving those we were hunting crossed into Finland, Helsinki has what it most wants and needs: plausible deniability." He shrugged his shoulders. "No doubt our foreign ministry will issue a pro forma protest, but the matter will die there."

Voronin shared the older man's cynicism. During the Cold War, the Finns had been ostensibly neutral in the prolonged conflict between the West and the Soviet Union, and thus vulnerable, at least to some extent, to saber-rattling by Moscow. But now that Finland was officially a member of the NATO alliance, the calculus had changed. Leaning too hard on Helsinki these days carried a risk of escalation that no one in the Kremlin wanted or believed Russia could afford.

Indeed, Voronin understood the equation better than anyone. Russia's strategic position had been worsening for decades. Its situation had now deteriorated to the point where any conventional military clash with its rivals, feckless though the Europeans and Americans were, could only end in humiliating defeat. Of course, he thought icily, that was precisely why the Raven Syndicate covert operations he'd organized over the past several years relied so heavily on unconventional weapons, especially on weapons of mass destruction. The only realistic paths to victory when the weak confronted the strong were stealth, secrecy, and a cold-eyed readiness to inflict mass casualties in a deniable surprise attack. Voronin's mouth twitched slightly. After all, why challenge an enemy to honorable open combat when it was safer and surer to stab him in the back and cut his throat for good measure?

With an effort, he pushed those more significant considerations aside for the moment. None of his schemes to wreak havoc on Russia's chief rival, the United States, would bear fruit if his enemies succeeded in killing him. Keeping that fact in mind, Voronin grasped, only reinforced the paramount importance of ensuring his personal safety. He turned his attention back to Kondakov. "All right, these bastards have successfully slipped out of another noose—killing more of our men in the process," he snapped. "What does that tell you?"

"That the operatives who attempted to kill you are definitely foreign agents working for a hostile power," Kondakov replied. "They were not under orders from anyone in our military or the security services."

Voronin nodded. That was likely enough. The Finns would have had no reason to ignore the criminal activities of rogue FSB, GRU, or Spetsnaz members. No, whoever these would-be assassins were, they were not Russians—or at least not Russians paid by any of his political enemies here at home. He looked over at Rodin with a raised eyebrow. "And you share this view?"

"I do," the gray-haired man said bluntly. "I will go further. I believe that the Americans employ these enemy agents, either the CIA itself or one of their other covert operations-capable intelligence organizations."

Voronin frowned. "The Americans? Haven't they always been too afraid of our possible retaliation to risk direct, lethal action on our soil?"

"Historically, yes," Rodin said. He arched a brow. "But the circumstances have changed, thanks largely to your own actions. By now, the Americans must have tied you to the various planned attacks against them. Considering how close they've come to total disaster, with millions under threat of death, it should be no great surprise that, to use their own idiom, the gloves have come off." He folded his arms. "And while their first attempt on your life fell short, it did come tantalizingly close to achieving success."

"You think these enemy agents will try to kill me again?" Voronin kept control over his voice with a tremendous effort.

"If it were my assigned task, I certainly would," Rodin said. "Now that the Americans seem to have shed their traditional squeamishness about 'wet work,' at least where you're concerned, we can expect more attempts on your life, always, of course, at times and places of the enemy's own choosing."

Voronin clenched his jaw, restraining a blistering stream of profanity that would otherwise have come tumbling out. He did not want to reveal how much he'd been shaken by the other man's coldly professional assessment. But whether he liked it or not, Rodin's reasoning was unassailable. If the CIA had connected him to the nuclear explosion in their homeland—and suspected that it was only a tiny taste of an even larger and far more destructive plan—the Americans had every reason to want him dead.

He forced himself to consider the situation with as much objectivity as he could muster. It was not easy. He was more used to being the hunter, not the hunted. The feeling—no, he thought grimly—the certainty that he was marked for death was not one he could push off to the side and compartmentalize. It had begun to consume his waking thoughts and even to invade his dreams.

Enough, Voronin told himself fiercely. Since he was under attack, he must first look to his defenses—and then seek some means of turning the tables on those who wanted to kill him.

At least one thing was evident in all this mess. He could not plan on returning to the Raven's Nest. Not any time soon, at least. His country estate was too vulnerable, too exposed. Despite the overconfident promises made by the Syndicate's security specialists, its defenses, the product of months of work and billions of rubles, had almost been penetrated by a single small commando team. Another assault by a larger group, or by one employing more sophisticated and powerful weapons like armed aircraft or missiles, might succeed.

Voronin determined to formalize the earlier decision to shift his residence to the Mercury City Tower. As a practical matter, the building represented the most defensible point available. Using it as his headquarters was the safest option. Access to this level, dozens of floors above the ground, was limited to a handful of closely guarded elevators—controllable only by carefully screened individuals with the appropriate security clearances and high-tech biometric IDs. Better yet, the whole building effectively lay at the very heart of the Russian state, only a few kilometers from the Kremlin itself. Anyone coming after him would first have to penetrate a cordon of the tens of thousands of police, state security officers, and soldiers deployed to safeguard the capital.

Rodin nodded on hearing his reasoning. "Sensible," he agreed. A slight smile creased his lean face. "Although no defense is ever truly impregnable. We would all do well to remember that."

Voronin jerked his head toward the door. "Consider me warned," he snapped. "Now get out."

Still smiling, Rodin sketched a half-mocking salute and left.

Kondakov watched him go through narrowed eyes. When the outer door latched behind him, he turned back to Voronin. "That man is a troublesome son of a bitch," he warned. "You'll need to finish him one day. Before he finishes you."

"A fact ever in the forefront of my mind," Voronin agreed, with a sour grunt. "For now, though, his master, Zhdanov, still has me on too tight a leash. I can't move against Rodin without moving against the president at the same time. And that will not happen."

The other man nodded. He'd heard the implied but unspoken "at least not yet" lurking behind Voronin's carefully chosen words. Behind the lenses of his glasses, his eyes were hooded. "Son of a bitch or not, though, Rodin is not entirely wrong. Staying purely on defense is a bad idea."

"I agree," Voronin told him. "Which is why I have another assignment for you, Vasily. An important one. Certainly more important, anyway, than chasing around after my bodyguards as a glorified chief of internal security."

"Ah," Kondakov said, with an air of deep satisfaction. The last months of playing second fiddle to Kiril Rodin had been difficult for him, especially since he'd grasped early on he was being kept in the dark about the next major Raven Syndicate operation aimed at the United States. He leaned forward. "So then, what are your orders?"

Voronin steepled his hands. "I want you to assemble a special hunter-killer team," he said bluntly. "It should include our best covert operators and most skilled assassins."

"Men who are also fluent English speakers?" Kondakov guessed.

Voronin showed his teeth. "Exactly so." He tapped his desk. "Once you've organized this team, I want them ready to move overseas immediately. They will be under your personal command. You have the necessary experience."

Kondakov nodded. Before switching his allegiance to Voronin and the Raven Syndicate, he had headed Unit 29155, the GRU's special assassination squad. Under his leadership, its highly trained killers had operated secretly around the globe, eliminating defectors, political dissidents, and even foreigners deemed threats to Russia's national security.

"The instant we obtain actionable intelligence on anyone involved in this attempt to kill me, I want them liquidated," Voronin went on coldly. "It doesn't matter if they're working for the CIA, Israel's Mossad, MI6, or someone else. And I don't give a damn if there's collateral damage when your team kills one of these people—whether it's their wives, children, parents, friends, neighbors, or even their damned pets. This is not a moment to show weakness. I'm willing to stack up corpses like cordwood if necessary." He scowled. "Despite what Rodin may believe, I'm convinced that the American intelligence services and their political masters are still weak and squeamish. Maybe, if we shed enough blood, they'll abandon this absurd quest for revenge."

FIFTEEN

AVALON HOUSE, WINTER PARK, FLORIDA

SEVERAL DAYS LATER

Nick Flynn turned off a quiet residential street and continued up a long, curving private drive fringed by tall palm trees. Through more trees ahead, dazzling morning sunlight reflected brightly off the still waters of a small, almost circular lake. He parked his rental car in front of a grand, two-story mansion overlooking the water and got out.

Built in the 1920s as the Florida winter retreat for a wealthy New York financier and his family, Avalon House wouldn't have looked out of place in classical Spain. Its century-old red clay roof tiles, muted yellow stucco walls, tall, arched windows, and wrought-iron entry gate conveyed a sense of both serene, enduring elegance and the confident self-assurance of old money.

If anything, this impression was strengthened by the weathered bronze plaques fixed beside the heavy oak front door. Their old-fashioned lettering indicated the mansion was now leased to three relatively obscure, but obviously long-established and seemingly respectable organizations—Sykes-Fairbairn Strategic Investments, the Concannon Language Institute, and the Sobieski Charitable Foundation.

It was a classic case of looks being completely deceiving, Flynn thought with amusement as he approached the entrance. Sykes-Fairbairn

Investments and the others were actually about as respectable as a honky-tonk bar operating out of the basement of a Baptist church. They were front groups for the Quartet Directorate, some of the many it had created to cloak its clandestine activities over the years.

Avalon House was the headquarters for Four's American station, a gift by one of its founding members. He'd been an heir of the same wealthy banking family who originally owned the mansion. As a young man during the Second World War, he'd served in the Office of Strategic Services, the OSS—the precursor to the CIA—and seen the dangers looming over the postwar world.

Among its other advantages, the mansion was a long way from Washington, D.C. To some, Flynn supposed, it would seem strange for a worldwide private intelligence outfit to site one of its major operational centers in an area more commonly associated with theme parks, beaches, and vacation resorts. But that was exactly the point. The Quartet Directorate kept its existence secret by staying off everyone's radar. Avoiding the Beltway's toxic maelstrom of rival federal intelligence agencies, keen-eyed foreign spies, busybody journalists, and ego-inflated politicians and government bureaucrats made that easier.

He pushed the buzzer and looked up at the camera above the big door. A second later, its built-in biometric sensors confirmed his identity. With a soft click, the door swung open. It revealed a brown-tiled foyer commanded by a large reception desk. Entries on the left and right led deeper into the building. At the foyer's far end, a wide, curving staircase swept up to the second floor.

Laura Van Horn turned from where she'd been chatting with the Korean-American woman behind the reception desk. Elaborately, she checked her watch. "Well, look who finally showed up. What did you do, Nick? Blow up the traffic on I-4 or something? Gwen and I were discussing whether or not she should send out a search and rescue team."

Flynn raised an eyebrow. "Search and rescue? That seems like over-kill," he said with wounded dignity. "I'm barely five minutes late. And that's because my red-eye flight from Heathrow was delayed. We only landed in Orlando an hour ago." After leaving Finland, Van Horn and the rest of the team had flown on ahead. He'd stopped over in London for an extra day to brief his European counterparts on exactly where and how the operation against Pavel Voronin had gone off the rails. He shook his head. "Besides, how much trouble do you two honestly think I could get into in five minutes?"

A tiny smile danced around the edges of the other woman's prim mouth. To anyone who didn't know her well, Gwen Park would have seemed completely unthreatening—just an ordinary, though very fashionably dressed, receptionist or secretary. But like so much else involving the Quartet Directorate, her outward appearance was a facade. She was both a skilled marksman and an expert in hand-to-hand combat. And before she took over as the head of Avalon House's security detail, she'd spent several years in the field, masterminding undercover counterterrorist and intelligence operations deep in Southeast Asia's deadly Golden Triangle.

"Do you really want me to answer that, Mr. Flynn?" Park asked with mock severity. She indicated the computer on her desk. "I have an alphabetized spreadsheet here. It starts with 'A,' for arson."

"We didn't burn down any public or private buildings," Flynn protested. "At least, not during this most recent mission."

Park nodded. "As Laura has assured me." Her smile widened. "That's almost a first for you, Nick."

"I do my best," he said virtuously. Then he grinned. "Besides, in my defense, I'm usually left unsupervised."

"So I gather," Park said, sharing an amused look with Van Horn. "But since you're aware that Four counts on its people taking independent action when necessary, that may not be as persuasive an argument as you'd think."

Flynn spread his hands in surrender. "Using logic and reason against me, Gwen? Really? No fair." He nodded up the stairs. "I suppose they're ready for us?"

She nodded. "Mr. Fox and the others are waiting for you both in the study."

Flynn sighed. This was not going to be a pleasant meeting. He turned to Van Horn. "When you poked your head in there earlier, did you spot any firing squads, blindfolds, or last cigarettes in evidence?"

"None that I noticed," she reassured him.

Flynn took a deep breath and held out his hand to Van Horn. "Okay then, shall we, ma'am?" he asked gravely, yielding to his full, native Texas twang for once. "Go up there and ride out the storm together, I mean?"

"Ah, polite and old-fashioned as ever," she commented.

"It must be my childhood training," he drawled. "I just can't seem to shake it."

Smiling, Van Horn took her hand in his and led him up the sweeping staircase.

———

Most of Avalon House's upper floor was used as temporary quarters for Quartet Directorate agents who needed rest and recuperation between stressful field assignments. The upstairs study, however, was reserved for important meetings and planning sessions. Originally the inner sanctum of the financier who'd owned the mansion, it was full of old and comfortable, although somewhat worn, furniture. Four's heads of station tended to allocate their budgets to operations, not fancy accoutrements.

When Flynn opened the door to the study, he immediately noticed the rest of his team grouped at a table. Tadeusz Kossak, still recovering from his shrapnel wounds, had a pair of crutches propped up beside him. Carleton Frederick Fox, the head of Four's American station, sat across from the younger men. A projector screen tied into Avalon House's secure computer network was set up to one side, where everyone could see it.

He resisted the impulse to burst out laughing. Tough and experienced covert operators that they were, Cooke, Hynes, and the others were all trying to play it very cool. But somehow the overall vibe was one of a bunch of nervous schoolboys summoned to the principal's office for a scolding.

He couldn't fault them. There was no getting away from the fact that they had promised the Quartet Directorate a definitive result— Pavel Voronin's death—and then ended up only escaping from Russia by the narrowest of margins, leaving Voronin still alive behind them.

Fox, a thin, middle-aged man with graying hair, nodded pleasantly toward the two open chairs. "Nick. Laura." His pale eyes shone behind a thick pair of wire-rimmed glasses. Except for the powerful intellect and craftiness his gaze revealed in unguarded moments like this, Fox could easily have been mistaken for the boring money manager or mid-level government bureaucrat he so often pretended to be.

Flynn dropped into one of the indicated seats. Van Horn took the other. Silently, he braced himself for the sharp-tongued, after-action review and critique he knew he deserved. In hindsight, it was painfully clear that his original mission concept had been far too reliant on luck. Failing to give Murphy's Law—"whatever can go wrong, will"—its due was a cardinal sin for any special ops planner. Worse yet, their intelligence on the defenses and alarm systems protecting Voronin's Raven's Nest had proved to be woefully inadequate—yet another shortcoming that had nearly ended up getting all of them killed or captured. His shoulders tightened. Fox might be justified in removing him from command of the action team. Or even busting him back to junior agent-in-training status, assigned to count paper clips and pencils in some middle-of-nowhere back office.

Instead, the older man surprised him. "First, let me say how glad I am to see you all alive and well," he began, peering at them over his glasses. "In light of the opposition you faced—both from the Raven Syndicate and Russia's legitimate military and internal security forces—escaping virtually unscathed was no small feat."

"Unscathed, maybe, but not exactly covered in glory," Flynn felt compelled to point out with a lopsided smile.

Fox shrugged. "As I've mentioned before, Nick, glory isn't something we in Four care much about."

"Maybe not," Flynn admitted. "But accomplishing the mission *does* matter. And that's where we came up short."

"Short as in 'did not pass Go. Did not collect two hundred dollars.' *Did* almost get our sorry asses shot to shit," Cole Hynes clarified helpfully.

Flynn stifled a chuckle at the carefully neutral expression he saw on Fox's face. He knew the older man was unsure how to take the former army enlisted soldier. Like Wade Vucovich, Hynes was not a product of the Quartet Directorate's usual screening processes—which tended to gravitate toward recruits with more formal education and a higher social status. If Flynn had to guess, he'd bet that was probably a holdover from the organization's early days. Most of its original American founders had come out of the World War II–era Office of Strategic Services, which had recruited so heavily from Ivy League universities, Wall Street, and even Hollywood that many regular military men had quipped its acronym, OSS, really stood for "Oh So Social."

"Pretty much," he agreed. Flynn turned back to Fox with an apologetic look. "Which is why I imagine the 'I told you so's' are flooding in from all over?"

"Perhaps not as much as you might expect," the older man said. "Remember, Voronin's determination to target the United States with weapons of mass destruction first tipped the balance in favor of direct action against his Raven Syndicate. And some new developments have made it clear that he has every intention of pursuing these dangerous ambitions. Given that, I'm reasonably confident my colleagues at the other Four stations can be persuaded to authorize another attempt to preempt his continuing efforts by killing him."

"New developments?" Flynn asked. "Like what?"

Fox said nothing for a moment. Watching him closely, Van Horn suddenly leaned forward, her eyes alight. "Spit it out, Br'er Fox," she said. "You're looking awfully content considering the circumstances. Which means you've been raiding the henhouse again. Heck, I can practically see the feathers poking out the sides of your mouth." She sat back again and folded her arms. "What is it you know that we don't?"

"One of the other Quartet Directorate stations has a mid-level intelligence asset in the Moscow area," Fox said carefully. "An asset who is occasionally privy to knowledge of Voronin's movements—at least in and around the Russian capital."

Flynn stared at him. "Why are we just hearing about this intel source now?" he asked finally.

"Because the very existence of this asset has been a closely held secret," the older man explained. "One confined, in fact, to a handful of Four's most senior people, and even then only on a strict, need-to-know basis."

"And I suppose we didn't need to know," Flynn realized.

Fox nodded. "Correct. Given the perceived odds against your team succeeding in killing Voronin without being captured or killed, the Four station in control judged that revealing the existence of this asset to you was too great a risk." He shrugged. "For what it's worth, I concurred in their decision."

Van Horn snorted, half in amusement, half in irritation. "Nice vote of confidence, Br'er Fox."

"Unfortunately, there's usually a gap between probable outcomes and desirable ones, Laura," Fox told her. "I do my best to keep that fact firmly in mind."

"So what's changed now?" Flynn asked.

"First, this intelligence asset has been able to identify a location Voronin has apparently made repeated visits to over the past several months—including the same day you carried out your attempted reconnaissance of his estate," Fox told him. He picked up a small wireless remote and activated the projector screen. It lit up, revealing a high-resolution overhead view of a large complex of modern buildings. Many of them, those in the very center, appeared to be roofed with glass. The entire compound was surrounded by barbed wire fences and dense forest. "This picture was obtained during a recent pass by a commercial imaging satellite," Fox explained. He nodded at the screen. "It shows a facility known as the Special Research Institute for Plant Genetics."

"Which does what, exactly?" Flynn pressed.

Fox shrugged. "Therein lies the rub. To the best of our knowledge, this so-called Institute is entirely unconnected to the ordinary world of scientific research. The scientists employed there have never published papers or test results in any known scientific or technical journals. In fact, it seems impossible even to learn precisely who works at this Institute, let alone what exactly they're working on."

"That level of secrecy suggests we're looking at a bioweapons lab of some kind," Flynn realized.

Fox nodded. "The analysts we've consulted agree."

"Run by the Russian government?"

The older man shook his head. "It seems not. What little we can dig up suggests that the Institute is a private facility."

Flynn grimaced. "Funded by Voronin and the Raven Syndicate," he guessed.

"Quite probably," Fox agreed. His expression grew somber. "Given the name, it at least seems likely that the facility's research efforts revolve around creating new biological weapons aimed at plants, rather than at people directly."

"At food crops, you mean," Flynn said.

The older man nodded again. "American agriculture is the linchpin, not only of this county, but of the whole world's food supply. If some new and untreatable plant diseases were unleashed against us, the damage inflicted on our crops could easily trigger devastating famines, both here and around the world."

Looking alarmed, Wade Vucovich leaned forward. Flynn remembered that he'd grown up on a farm before joining the military. "Can we pass the word to our own government about this?" he asked, almost hesitantly. "Maybe get them to put pressure on the Russians to back off before Voronin pulls the trigger on whatever he's got planned?"

Fox sighed. "Unfortunately not. All we have to go on is this one set of sadly uninformative satellite photos and a considerable amount of conjecture. Generating serious action by Washington would take a great deal more hard evidence than we are ever likely to be able to produce—at least in time to matter."

Flynn knew the older man was right. After all, the need to act directly and swiftly against threats—circumventing bureaucratic inertia—had been a driving force behind the creation of the Quartet Directorate in the first place. "Which makes it even more important than ever that we nail that son of a bitch Voronin ASAP," he realized. Then he grimaced. "But to be honest, Br'er Fox, as of right now, I can't see a hope in hell of ever being able to covertly penetrate the sensors and defenses around the Raven's Nest. Not and get close enough to take an effective shot at Voronin."

"That brings me to the second piece of critical intelligence pro-vided by Four's asset," Fox said quietly. "Voronin is no longer using his country estate. It seems your attack frightened him sufficiently to shift his residence."

"To where?"

In answer, the older man tapped the remote control, replacing the satellite image of Voronin's suspected bioweapons lab with a photo of a huge, bronze-colored skyscraper. Along with several others of similar size, the 1,100-foot-tall ultramodern structure loomed over Moscow. "According to our information, he's moved here. To the Mercury City Tower in the city's International Business Center."

"Which is where the Raven Syndicate has its main corporate of-fices," Flynn remembered.

"The organization occupies three full floors," Fox confirmed. "Start-ing on the forty-third floor, about two-thirds of the way up."

Flynn stared at the image of the massive skyscraper. Every aspect of his mission planning process had just been upended in the blink of an eye. As difficult as it would have been to get to Voronin when the oli-garch was sheltering behind the defenses of his country estate, would going after him inside a vast honeycomb of steel and concrete be any easier? "How solid is this intelligence?" he asked Fox.

"Very solid," the older man assured him. "According to our source, Voronin has moved his personal chef and several prized pieces of his art collection to the Mercury Center Tower over the past few days."

Van Horn nodded. "That fits." She frowned. "Our boy Pavel is all about the finer things in life. Well, those, plus mass murder."

Flynn understood what she meant. The Quartet Directorate's pro-file of the Russian showed him to be highly educated and able to move easily among the globe's wealthy, cultured elites. Initially groomed by Russia's Foreign Intelligence Service, the SVR, to be a deep-cover spy in the West, he'd been educated at the Philips Exeter Academy, one of America's oldest and most prestigious prep schools. He was then sent as an undergraduate to Oxford. After that, he returned to the US where he earned an MBA from Harvard Business School. What his polished background didn't reveal was that Voronin was also a ruthless psychopath, one perfectly willing to cause the deaths of tens of millions to advance his interests and those of his native country.

"This International Business Center place is pretty much in the heart of Moscow, right?" he asked Fox. "Close to the river?"

The other man nodded. He opened a satellite view of the Russian capital's downtown area. Then he scrolled a cursor to highlight the tight cluster of skyscrapers that made up its newly developed financial core. A red dot blinked on the exact location of the Mercury City Tower.

Flynn studied the map in silence, and then he shook his head in disbelief. "So Voronin's parked himself forty-plus stories off the ground . . . right in the center of this uber high-end business district? A district that's chockful of Russia's richest and most powerful corporate leaders and politicians, all of whom have their own security personnel and bodyguards? One that's also just a block away from Moscow's brand-new city hall? And which, to top it all off, is less than three miles from Russia's Ministry of Defense and the Kremlin itself?"

Cooke whistled softly under his breath. "Not exactly an easy target."

"Not hardly," Flynn agreed. He turned back to Fox. "How much intel do we have on this building's layout and security systems?"

"Virtually none at the moment," the older man said with regret. "Essentially just what's publicly available on the internet. Which, I'm afraid, boils down to a few articles on its design and construction, a handful of sample luxury apartment floor plans, and a few glossy PR photos touting some of the tower's public spaces. Worse yet, we have absolutely no useful information concerning the three floors owned by the Raven Syndicate."

"Swell." Flynn took a short, sharp breath and let it out. "Effectively, then, we just got knocked back to square one on this op. Hell, maybe even farther back than that because, as of right now, this whole situation we're up against looks like a disaster just waiting to unfold."

"The task has certainly become even more complicated and dangerous," Fox acknowledged. "You know that no one will think the worse of you or your team if you want to reevaluate the feasibility of this mission, Nick—"

Flynn held up a hand to stop the older man right there. "I didn't say we were quitting, Br'er Fox," he said. "I just don't plan on going off half-cocked this time." He glanced around the table at Van Horn, Cooke, and the others. "As of this moment, intelligence gathering is our top priority." They nodded.

"That's going to take boots on the ground," Van Horn pointed out. "Inside Moscow."

Flynn sighed. "Not exactly a place I really had on my bucket list for a repeat visit so soon, but you're right."

Fox cleared his throat. "Unfortunately, infiltrating back into Russia could prove somewhat more difficult than in the recent past," he warned. He toggled the remote, throwing another set of photographs up onto the screen. Taken from a CCTV camera feed, these pictures were grainier and lacked the sharp definition of the other images they'd been studying. They showed Laura Van Horn in the two disguises—as an immaculately attired blonde in sunglasses and as a dowdy, heavyset middle-aged woman—that she'd used to scout the Leningradsky rail station.

Flynn was quiet for a moment. "Where did you get these?" he asked finally.

"From my counterparts in central Europe and the Baltic states," Fox replied. "They confirm these photos were sent to all Russian border crossings several days ago—only two days after you aborted your attempt to reconnoiter the Raven's Nest. Instructions were attached to consider this person," he nodded at the images of Van Horn, "as an armed and highly dangerous member of a known terrorist group. Moscow labeled her arrest and interrogation 'maksimal'no vozmozhnogo prioriteta,' 'of the highest possible priority.'"

Staring at the screen, Flynn felt the hairs on the back of his neck go up. Somehow, the Russians had fingered Laura as a target within hours of her visit to the train station. "Christ, those bastards were practically breathing right down our necks."

Van Horn took a deep breath and touched him gently on the arm. "Good thing you kept us moving fast, then." The rest of the team nodded somberly.

"I've had our best photo interpreters analyze these images," Fox continued. He looked across the table at Van Horn. "They concur it's unlikely that the Russians will be able to positively identify you."

"Glad to hear it," she quipped. "Because I kind of like my face the way it is now. Plastic surgery would be a bore."

"But—" Fox continued.

"Send me in then," Cooke interrupted. "I'm pretty damned sure nobody in Moscow has *my* picture." He smiled tightly. "Because if they did, I'd already be dead."

That drew murmurs of agreement from the rest of the team. Cooke was a veteran of the U.S. Army's ultra-secret Task Force Orange. Over the years, he'd operated clandestinely in different hostile countries—collecting vital local intelligence for U.S. Special Forces operations.

"Do you have something in mind, Shannon?" Flynn asked.

The Virginian's fingers drummed lightly on the tabletop. "Right now, the Russian border security goons are undoubtedly twitchy as all hell," he noted. "But I figure that's bound to ease up in a week or two."

Flynn knew he was probably right about that. The longer military and security forces were kept on high alert, the more fatigued, less efficient, and less observant they generally grew. It was just human nature, and there was no real way around the problem—short of handing their duties over to robots and artificial intelligences, a course that carried its own set of distinct complications.

"If you give me time to work up a solid new cover, I'll slip in and see what I can dig up on the scene," Cooke proposed.

Reluctantly, Flynn signaled his assent. Sending the other man into Russia for a close reconnaissance of the Mercury City Tower was better than sitting on their asses doing nothing. But short of Cooke somehow scoring a personal tour of the Raven Syndicate's corporate headquarters, including an in-depth briefing on its security systems—which seemed about as likely as Voronin deciding to give up everything to become a Trappist monk—they were still going to fall well short of having enough hard intel to craft a solid, survivable plan. And that was a problem.

SIXTEEN

HIGH-ALTITUDE FLIGHT TEST CENTER,
WEST OF VOLGOGRAD, RUSSIA

SOME WEEKS LATER

Under the early morning summer sun, fields of ripening wheat spread from horizon to horizon before ultimately disappearing into the heat haze. Small clusters of buildings and barns dotted the landscape. Each was a farming village where life had not changed much in decades. Unpaved roads spoked outward from every little settlement, meandering lazily around low hills, along the rims of erosion-carved ravines, and across dry, tree-lined creek beds.

A single surfaced road ran straight through this isolated rural area. It came to an end at a large fenced-in military complex. A guard shack manned by soldiers barred entry to unauthorized visitors. Long low cement-block buildings—subdivided into offices, barracks, workshops, and storerooms—lined one side of the facility. The rest of the compound was open ground, a vast field of short-cropped wild grass turning brown in the scorching summer heat.

Several green, canvas-sided military trucks and a red-painted fire engine were parked near the center of the compound. They formed a rough circle around a huge, undulating sphere of clear polyethylene film. Less than a thousandth of an inch thick, this sphere was slowly expanding, swelling as it inflated. A flexible hose connected it to one of the trucks. Pumps whirred, feeding hydrogen to the massive balloon through this hose.

Within thirty minutes, although it was still only a fraction of its ultimate size, the balloon had achieved enough buoyancy to bob skyward. Composite fiber cables tightened, tethering it to the ground as it grew even bigger. Flight control equipment, communications gear, ballast, and the other components of its one-ton payload were mounted on a frame attached to the base of the still-expanding envelope.

A Russian air force captain stared upward at the inflated balloon as it tugged harder against the tethers holding it captive. His eyes narrowed, judging the proper moment. Finally satisfied, he spoke into a hand-held radio. "Cease fueling and detach," he ordered.

Immediately, the truck-mounted pump shut off. Seconds later, now empty of hydrogen, the long flexible hose disconnected from the half-inflated balloon and dropped to the ground.

"Go for launch," the captain reported. He took one final look around his ground crew. One by one the technicians gave him a thumbs-up signal. "Launch!" he commanded. His crewmen obeyed instantly and yanked hard on their release controls. With simultaneous sharp pops, the tethers still attached to the balloon broke loose and fell away.

Freed now, the rippling teardrop-shaped envelope soared higher, hauling its payload off the ground. It gained altitude with astonishing speed, and as the balloon climbed into thinner and thinner air, the hydrogen gas inside expanded enormously. By the time it reached the stratosphere's lower edge, the envelope blossomed into a huge, elongated sphere more than seventy meters in diameter. Within minutes, it was just a tiny bright dot silhouetted against the immense blue dome of the sky—discernible only because of the sunlight twinkling off its translucent film surface.

Flanked by a gaggle of uniformed air force officers and ringed by his bodyguards, Pavel Voronin stood watching the launch with intense interest. Now he glanced toward the highest-ranking officer, a colonel named Fyodor Kardashev. "Most impressive, Colonel." His head turned skyward again, following the glowing speck as it drifted eastward on the prevailing wind. "What is the maximum altitude planned for this flight?"

"Thirty thousand meters," Kardashev replied. "Close to one hundred thousand feet as the Americans measure it."

"And you can actually steer this machine, even without engines or propellers?"

The colonel nodded. "To a remarkable extent, our atmosphere shares many similarities with the earth's oceans," he said. "Depending on the altitude, currents of air flow at varying speeds and in different directions. So, just as a sailing ship can change course by trimming its sails, we can command the balloon to gain or lose altitude—shifting between separate air currents to control its course and speed over the ground."

Voronin shaded his eyes. The balloon, so massive when seen up close, was now almost invisible. "What is the vehicle's flight duration? How long can it stay aloft?"

"This design? Up to twelve days, given reasonable weather," Kardashev said.

Voronin nodded. Although he'd been briefed earlier on the capabilities of Russia's military high-altitude balloons, seeing a launch for himself went a long way to confirming the practicality of his plans. It had been worth coping with the burdensome restrictions imposed by his security team for safety's sake, including hastily rerouted flights and sudden vehicle changes that had added hours to this trip outside Moscow.

"Very well, Colonel," he said. "As I said, I'm extremely impressed by your operations here. I'm convinced that your unit's equipment and special expertise are precisely what my project needs."

Kardashev clasped his hands behind his back. "Your interest gratifies me, Mr. Voronin," he said, choosing his words with evident care. "However, let me be blunt. I cannot place my design teams or training staff at your disposal without an explicit order from the General Staff, one confirmed in writing by President Zhdanov himself. I hope you understand this."

Voronin smiled pleasantly, concealing his irritation. Word about the unfortunate fate of other Russian military men caught up in the Raven Syndicate's covert operations had obviously leaked out. To mask Russia's involvement in the most recent of these, several of those officers had been falsely accused of treason and then summarily executed. Kardashev had no intention of risking the same fate. Given the circumstances, he supposed that he couldn't fault the colonel for being cautious. But he still despised the idea of having to go running, hat in hand, to the Kremlin at every significant stage of VELES. He'd grown used to those involved in his plans obeying his orders without hesitation. Learning that was no longer the case was a humiliating reminder of his diminished status.

"Of course, I understand, Colonel," Voronin lied. He needed Kardashev's specialized equipment and expertise. If he had to crawl for now to get them, so be it. "I'll contact the president immediately. You'll have the authorization you need within a matter of days at most."

SEVENTEEN

MOSCOW

LATER THAT DAY

A decaying, five-story brick apartment building overlooked an entrance to the International Business Center, the one closest to the bronze-colored edifice of the Mercury City Tower. The contrast between the older building's rusting iron balconies and flaking, discolored walls and the gleaming office and residential tower just across the street could not have been starker. The low-rise apartment building was an eyesore—an ugly throwback to when this section of the city had been a bleak, cheerless factory district. That was before Moscow's newly enriched corruptocrats and ambitious politicians swept in with their grand schemes for urban renewal. The factories were gone three decades later, bulldozed and dynamited into oblivion. And in their place had come skyscrapers filled with banks, investment firms, gourmet restaurants, and luxury flats.

But somehow, through an odd twist of fate, this rundown block of apartments had survived the mania for redevelopment. Generations of lowly assembly-line workers, their wives, and children had spent their lives inside its ugly walls, often with two or three families crammed cheek-by-jowl into a single small set of rooms. Now, however, more than half the apartments were vacant, judged unsafe even under Russia's notoriously lax health standards.

There were plans on file to tear the building down. But they were on hold, a victim both of Russia's slowing economy and bureaucratic inertia. In the meantime, a handful of primarily elderly tenants moved like ghosts through narrow, dingy hallways lit dimly, if at all, by flickering, low-wattage bulbs. Broken risers and missing banisters marked stairwells that smelled powerfully of mold and old garbage.

Four flights up, Shannon Cooke perched on an overturned crate in the darkness of an abandoned apartment. To deter squatters and vandals, sheets of plywood shuttered its windows. He'd drilled a small hole in the board covering the nearest opening, a hole just large enough to slot in the lens of a miniature video camera. Wirelessly connected to his tablet computer, it filmed the main barrier-guarded entrance to the Mercury City Tower's underground parking garage. Right now, it showed the normal flow of late afternoon Moscow traffic. Cars, small trucks, buses, and yellow taxi cabs streamed slowly east and west along the broad avenue outside.

With a soft grunt, he stretched his stiff arms and legs. He'd been keeping track of comings and goings from the skyscraper—at least those visible from this concealed vantage point—for several days, sleeping only in short snatches when he could no longer stay awake.

Keeping one eye on the screen, he unwrapped a protein bar and took a bite. *Ah, all the texture of the finest cardboard*, he thought, chewing steadily, *but without any of its natural wood pulp flavor*. Crunching down one or two of the concentrated energy bars in an emergency was fine. Living off them for days wasn't much fun. Even Russian army rations—with their packs of gooey processed cheese, stale crackers, overly sweet apple jam, and lumpy, ready-to-heat beef and barley porridge—would be a feast in comparison. Unfortunately, he couldn't risk anyone catching the smell of cooked food wafting out of what was supposed to be an empty apartment. The elderly Russian pensioners clinging to their own shabby, rent-controlled flats were a nosy bunch.

Cooke felt a wry smile cross his face. He'd signed on to snoop around

Voronin's corporate headquarters of his own free will. And in doing so, he'd broken the first important military commandment: Never volunteer. So, while bitching to himself about the consequences might have made him feel a little better, it didn't do a thing to change the overall situation. Boredom, discomfort, and exhaustion were the three guaranteed constants of any solo surveillance operation. Years of covert work around the world, almost always in Third World hellholes, had taught him that the hard way.

Well, at least this particular operation was nearing its conclusion. Or so he hoped. But several variables had to shake out in just the right order for that to happen. First, the assessment by Four's still-unidentified intelligence asset that Voronin was basically holed up inside the Mercury City Tower had to prove accurate. Second, Flynn and Van Horn had to be right in tying the ownership of a private aircraft, a Bombardier Global 7500 executive jet based at Moscow's Vnukovo Airport, to the Russian oligarch. And finally, the flight tracking data Fox had been emailing him all day needed to actually mean something. Currently, it showed the jet in question heading to Moscow on a return flight from Volgograd.

Cooke knew there was a chance he was committing a classic blunder. Leaping to a desired conclusion using assumptions loosely pinned together by wishful thinking was a common error in the intelligence business. But he'd spent enough days and nights cautiously poking around the Mercury City Tower to realize continuing to play it safe wasn't going to yield any useful information. Sometimes you just had to roll the dice and hope you got lucky.

His smartphone buzzed softly. He answered it. "Yes?"

"Mr. Zimin," a familiar voice said, "this is the pharmacy. Your prescription for blood pressure medication is ready for pickup. A three months' supply."

"Can you deliver it instead?" Cooke asked. "I can't leave the office just yet."

"Certainly," the other man said. "But we would, of course, need to add an 18 percent surcharge to cover our fuel and labor costs."

"I see," Cooke said, hesitating briefly as though he were doing the mental math needed to figure out how much more he'd be paying for delivery. "That's a bit steep," he said at last. "I'll swing by when I can and pick the pills up myself."

The caller thanked him for his business and hung up.

Cooke considered what he'd been told. Tony McGill—the head of the Quartet Directorate's European action team—was acting as his backup on this surveillance op. Masquerading as a Russian businessman in Moscow for a meeting with clients, the Englishman had checked into Vnukovo's Doubletree by Hilton earlier in the day. The hotel, located directly across the street from the airport, offered good views of the flight line from its upper-floor rooms. And now, using Four's special word code, McGill had confirmed that the executive jet they were tracking had just landed at Vnukovo, where a convoy of six vehicles was meeting it.

Cooke's pulse quickened. While he supposed there was a slim chance McGill had actually spotted a different Russian VIP, maybe some other corporate chieftain with similarly expensive tastes in personal aircraft, the safe bet now was that this was Voronin. And that he would soon be returning to his lair.

Less than an hour later, Cooke was sure.

His concealed peephole camera picked up a group of tough-looking men in dark suits as they left the Mercury City Tower. Moving briskly, they joined a trio of uniformed police officers on duty at the parking garage entrance. Two of the newcomers flashed ID cards and then snapped orders. With indifferent shrugs, the cops moved aside, leaving what he was sure were Raven Syndicate security personnel in sole command of the entry barrier.

Cooke's mouth tightened. It was clear who was running the show over there. His fingers scrolled across his tablet, zooming the camera in to take a closer look at those men in dark suits. Discreet bulges under their jackets marked concealed weapons. Several carried attaché cases far more likely to hold compact submachine guns than corporate paperwork. That was a lot of firepower on tap. Way too much for the anticipated arrival of any regular building resident or visitor—no matter how wealthy or high-powered they might be compared to most Muscovites.

He zoomed the camera back out. Moments later, it picked up a line of six black limousines turning onto the avenue from the direction of the Third Ring Road. That was the most direct route for anyone coming from Vnukovo International. "Gotcha, Pavel, you rat bastard," he murmured.

Swiftly, Cooke slipped the tablet into his pocket and grabbed a bike helmet and backpack from beside the overturned crate he'd been sitting on. Then he clipped a walkie-talkie to his bright orange reflective vest and inserted a pair of earbuds. It was time to put on a show.

Cautiously, he cracked the door he'd jimmied open days before and stole a look outside. His eyes flicked left and right. This floor's dimly lit hallway was clear. None of his unwitting neighbors were in sight.

Aware that the clock was running, Cooke slipped through the door and descended the stairs to the ground floor. There, a battered service door let him out into a narrow alley. His bicycle was chained up at the far end, well out of sight of the street. He unlocked the bike and, moving faster now, wheeled it back down the alley. He came out onto the street in time to see the last of the black limos turning in through the entrance to the Mercury City Tower's underground garage. Moments later, its red tail lights disappeared down a ramp.

After settling the neon red plastic bike helmet firmly on his head, he swung a leg over his bicycle and started off—weaving in and out between slow-moving cars and trucks as he cut across the avenue and angled toward the huge skyscraper. Horns blared behind him in irritation, but he only shrugged his shoulders and kept pedaling. It was all part of the act. Bike messengers were the same the world over—always in a hurry, heedless of their own safety or that of others, and relying on quick reflexes to get out of any jam.

One of the Raven Syndicate security men saw him coming and curtly flagged him to a halt on the pavement. "You there!" he growled, striding closer. "Where the fuck do you think you're going?"

"Easy there, comrade," Cooke said soothingly. He let go of the bike's handlebars and took out his earbuds, letting the other man hear the heavy metal blasting out of them. "It's no big deal. I'm just making a delivery. That's all."

Impatiently, the security man snapped his fingers. "Show me!"

"Hey, no problem," Cooke said, sliding the backpack off his shoulder. He unzipped it and pulled out a thick manila envelope. He indicated the recipient's address, which was an apartment on one of the upper floors of the Mercury City Tower. "See?"

Scowling, the guard took the envelope from him and examined it through narrowed eyes. Slowly, he turned it end over end, poking at the seals and flaps as if to make sure they hadn't been tampered with.

While he waited patiently for the man to finish checking out the package, Cooke risked a casual glance around. He wasn't the only one who'd been pulled aside. The other Raven Syndicate security men were stopping every pedestrian or vehicle trying to enter the immediate area. *Paranoids R Us*, he thought coldly. Voronin's people weren't taking any chances, especially while their master was out in the open—at least to the extent that a heavily guarded gated parking garage could be considered as "the open."

Apparently satisfied, the guard thrust the envelope at him. "All right, you can go." He stepped back and waved toward the skyscraper's elaborate front entrance. Tall metal structures—part modern sculpture, part light fixture, and part shelter from rain or snow—lined the walkway. Tubular steel columns supported overhanging glass panels. They were clearly intended to convey the impression of oak trees in autumn, down to the scattering of red and gold leaf symbols imprinted on each transparent panel. "Report to the security desk in the main lobby. They'll handle everything from there."

"Thanks, comrade," Cooke said with a polite nod. Reinserting his earbuds and humming along with his music under his breath, he walked his bicycle over to where several bronze-tinted sliding glass doors opened into the lobby. He chained up the bike and went inside.

His first impression of the Mercury City Tower's lobby was one of immense space. The ceiling rose at least fifty feet above a vast white marble floor. Its recessed translucent panels glowed with light. Yards-long digital screens lined the walls, showing the latest news and advertising the virtues of the building's commercial tenants—an array of luxury retail stores, wealthy business enterprises, and highly rated and very exclusive restaurants.

Cooke's second impression was that he'd just set foot inside an armed camp. At the far end of the enormous open space, rows of key card–operated turnstiles blocked access to huge elevator banks. Beyond the turnstiles, airport-style metal detectors and X-ray screening machines provided an added layer of security against smuggled weapons or explosives. Armed guards were visible everywhere he looked. Those seated at the security desk wore jackets emblazoned with the Mercury City Tower's corporate logo. Others in dark suits, with the hard-eyed look of veteran soldiers, were posted to observe the key card-controlled entrances and the elevators. *Those must be more of Voronin's men*, he determined.

Still humming softly to himself, he walked nonchalantly across the cavernous space to the long desk manned by the skyscraper's own rent-a-cops. One of the guards looked up from the computer screen he'd been watching. "Yes?"

Cooke pulled out his earbuds. "Got a delivery for someplace on the forty-sixth floor," he said, unzipping his backpack and retrieving the thick manilla envelope. "What's my best way there, comrade?"

The security man snorted. "There isn't one . . . *comrade*." He snapped his fingers. "Hand that over. Our internal mail service will take it from here."

Regretfully, Cooke shook his head. "No can do," he said. He flipped the envelope around to show the other man the form attached to the front. In bold red lettering, it stated, CONFIDENTIAL FINANCIAL MATERIAL. SIGNATURE REQUIRED FOR DELIVERY.

With a frown, the security guard swiveled toward his closest colleague. "What's procedure here, Yuri?"

The other man shrugged. "Call the addressee. If they want the envelope, give this clown a visitor's pass and send him on up."

Nodding, the first guard swung back and peered closely at the name and address on the envelope. Then he entered the information into his computer, highlighted the appropriate number, and had it dialed by the system's internal communications network. "Mr. Povetkin? This is the front desk. A signature-only package for you has just arrived. Should we send the messenger up?" He listened to the answer coming through his headset and then nodded rapidly. "Yes, sir. No problem. Yes, sir. Thank you." When he disconnected, he looked over at Cooke with a sour expression. "Okay. You can go on up." He reached into a drawer behind the desk and tossed him a bright yellow key card plainly marked TEMPO-RARY. "Use that to pass through the turnstiles. But don't forget to drop it off here on your way out. Clear?"

Cooke nodded. "Clear as a sunny day." He smiled. "Anything else I should know?"

"Yeah," the guard told him. "You go in. You take the elevator to the right floor. You deliver your package. You come back down. That's it. Don't go wandering around. That card tracks your movements, so if you deviate in the slightest, we'll know—and we'll arrest your sorry ass for criminal trespass. And then we'll probably beat the shit out of you for making our jobs harder. Got it?"

Cooke whistled. "That's hardcore, comrade. Got it." He leaned over the desk with a friendly grin and lowered his voice a notch. "Hey, what's with all the high-tech security? Got a super-famous sports star living here? Or some big-name film actress or maybe a pop singer?"

The guard leaned closer himself. "You really want to know the truth?" he asked quietly.

"Sure."

"It's none of your damn business. Now shut up and deliver your package."

Acting abashed, Cooke bobbed his head. "Shutting up," he muttered. *Crap, this place is wired up tighter than Fort Knox*, he thought. The yellow visitor key card got him through the turnstiles. But passing through the combination of x-ray and metal detector screening beyond them took several more painful and humiliating minutes. The Raven Syndicate troops assigned to the checkpoint did everything but subject him to a cavity search, and he had the clear impression they would gladly have tossed him out on his ear given even the slightest excuse. He noted that people who swiped red keycards to pass through the turnstiles were automatically waved past the additional weapons screening.

Cooke was feeling very thoughtful indeed by the time he finally approached the banks of elevators that opened into the lobby area. According to the limited information available on the internet, at least twenty passenger and nine separate freight elevators served the huge skyscraper. By his quick count, roughly half were accessible from this side of the building. But he immediately noticed that three of the elevators—two passenger and one freight—were indicated as RESTRICTED ACCESS ONLY. They could only be summoned using the special red key cards.

Careful *not* to show too much interest in those elevators, he moved instead to take one of the regular lifts open to visitors and ordinary residents. When the car doors pinged shut, he saw that the call buttons for floors 43-45 had been removed and replaced by a blank metal panel. No surprise, he thought. Those were the floors occupied by the Raven Syndicate. He studiously controlled his expression. Voronin and company were obviously not fond of uninvited guests.

Skipping over the empty space, Cooke tapped the button for the forty-sixth floor and rode up. Thirty seconds later, the high-speed elevator glided smoothly to a stop. With a soft chime, the doors opened into a wide corridor. He stepped out, immediately aware of the atmosphere of carefully crafted elegance created by the original artwork lining its wood-paneled walls. Like most of the Mercury Center Tower's upper levels, this floor was allocated to large luxury apartments.

He turned down the hall and ambled casually along, making a show of checking door numbers to find the correct address. All the while, however, he was using his peripheral vision to scope out his surroundings, including the location of the nearest emergency staircase. He paid special attention to the discreet placement of surveillance cameras. From what he could tell, the building's security team could observe every public space inside the Mercury City Tower at the push of a button.

Cooke reached the apartment he'd been looking for and rapped on the door.

A moment later, a dour-faced man attired in a long-sleeved white shirt, gray tie, pale blue vest, and dark slacks pulled it open. "Yes?"

"Mr. Povetkin?" Cooke asked, holding up the manilla envelope. Povetkin was a wealthy Russian private equity banker.

"No," the other man said. "I'm his personal assistant." He held out his hand. "I'll take that for him."

Cooke fumbled in his pocket for a pen. "I need a signature," he pointed out mildly. He waited while the assistant scrawled a signature across the form, detached it from the envelope, and handed it back. "Thanks, comrade," he said cheerfully, slipping the piece of paper into his pocket. Then he held out a hand, palm up. "Hey, any chance of a—"

The assistant shut the apartment door in his face.

"Tip?" Cooke finished. He shrugged his shoulders. "Guess not." He turned away, hiding a smile as he imagined the likely reaction of Povetkin when the banker read through the document he'd just delivered. It was an unsolicited invitation to participate in a project funded by Sykes-Fairbairn Strategic Investments, one of the Quartet Directorate's long-established front companies. Based on the cost structure, fees, and anticipated profits it disclosed, any rational businessman would shred the investment offer and dump it in the trash without a second thought. Then again, its sole purpose had been to provide him with a seemingly legitimate excuse to visit this heavily guarded building—so at least that part of his plan had worked like a charm.

Unfortunately, that was about the only positive result from today's reconnaissance exercise Cooke could see. The multiple overlapping layers of security he'd observed had given him a lot to think about . . . none of it good. Try as he might to be optimistic, it seemed clear that attempting to nail Voronin inside the Mercury Center Tower would end up being, in the memorable phrase coined by some ancient philosopher, "nasty, brutish, and short."

EIGHTEEN

TEMPEST FLIGHT, HIGH OVER RUSSIA

SEVERAL DAYS LATER

Lieutenant Colonel Valery Novik strained forward slightly against his seat harness. His bulky, bright orange full-pressure suit made movement inside the M-55 Geophysica's cramped cockpit difficult. He squinted through the canopy. Instrument panels and recently added displays left him only a narrow field of view. But what he could see around him was spectacular.

His twin-tailed, twin-engine aircraft was flying above eighteen thousand meters. At this altitude, the far horizon was nearly five hundred kilometers off, and he could plainly discern the earth's spherical nature. The ground curved away sharply to either side of his direction of flight. Ahead, the sky was a rich azure blue. Overhead, the atmosphere thinned—fading to paler and paler shades of that same hue until it vanished entirely amid the inky blackness of outer space.

With an effort, Novik pulled his gaze back down to his flight instruments. Except for cosmonauts, few pilots ever got the chance to brush so close to the upper limits of the sky. Russia had only five M-55 high-altitude jets still operational. The large, swept-wing aircraft were the rough equivalent of America's U-2 spy planes. While they were not combat planes, the M-55's predecessors were first developed during the 1950s to intercept unmanned American reconnaissance balloons flying over the Soviet Union. Later versions were dedicated mostly to military reconnaissance missions and to scientific research flights.

The pilot strongly suspected that today's highly classified flight was a hybrid of those typical missions—a test of cutting-edge science with significant military applications. But that was only a guess. The precise details of his plane's current top-secret payload were well above his security clearance.

Novik's eyes roved over the aircraft's complicated array of dials, gauges, switches, and multifunction displays—constantly checking and then rechecking his readouts in a highly disciplined pattern. The M-55 was a complex aircraft flying in a completely unforgiving environment. This high up, the margin between safety and catastrophe was thin, almost as thin as the atmosphere outside his cockpit. And on today's flight, the slightest technical glitch or fault could make the difference between a successful mission and an embarrassing failure.

A red diamond icon blinked on his navigation display, along with two sets of numbers—one for distance, the other for time—that were each spinning toward zero. "*Burya—Kontrolyu buri*," he radioed. "Tempest Flight to Tempest Control. I am thirty seconds out from the pre-plotted drop zone." His eyes darted to other control displays, picking out readings from key instruments. "Wind direction and speed are within predicted ranges. External air temperature is minus fifty-five degrees, Celsius."

"*Control to Flight*," the mission controller replied. "*Copy that. You are cleared to proceed.*"

"Affirmative, Control," Novik acknowledged. He tweaked his stick to the left, banking slightly to bring the drop zone icon squarely into the center of his navigation display. Satisfied, he reversed the bank, bringing the M-55's wings back level. Then he throttled down a notch, reducing the thrust generated by his two Soloviev D-30 turbofan engines. The aircraft slowed, shedding airspeed until it was right on the edge of stalling out. At this altitude, the amount of lift provided by the wings was greatly reduced.

Gritting his teeth, Novik held the aircraft steady, ready to throttle back up the second he felt the tell-tale shimmy in his control stick that would signal the M-55 was starting to depart from controlled flight. While he'd been briefed that today's test flight was vital to Russia's national security, he saw no point in unnecessarily risking both the plane and its highly classified payload.

The icon blinked from red to green. Now! He toggled a button on his stick.

In response, two streamlined pods mounted near the outer edge of each wing flared open. Tens of millions of tiny particles—none larger than ten microns, about the size of a droplet of mist—sprayed into the thin, subzero air. Tumbling in the wind and turbulence, the particles fanned out, forming an invisible cloud that trailed far behind Novik's speeding aircraft and then slowly began drifting down toward the ground far below.

TEMPEST CONTROL,
NEAR NIZHNY NOVGOROD, RUSSIA
THAT SAME TIME

Kiril Rodin had an excellent view of the proceedings from the back of the large, six-wheeled MPPU command and staff vehicle. He, Voronin, and Dr. Georgii Neminsky, the scientific chief for VELES, had flown here earlier in the day specifically to observe the results of this experiment. Apart from the three seats allocated to them, several workstations fitted out with advanced computers and communications gear took up the rest of the mammoth vehicle's interior. Uniformed technical officers manned these consoles, each assigned to monitor or perform a different aspect of the test.

Lieutenant Colonel Novik's cool, precise voice came clearly over the audio speakers. "*Control, Tempest Flight. Drop complete. Special materials containers read as empty. I am returning to base.*"

"Copy that, Flight," one of the officers replied, watching the monitors before him. One large display showed imagery transmitted by a long-range tracking camera. It captured the M-55 Geophysica, its twin-tailed shape blurred by sheer distance and speed. The rest of his screens mirrored telemetry from instruments aboard the aircraft. "We confirm that your payload containers show as empty."

In the seat next to him, another air force officer sat with a finger poised eagerly over a control on his console. His sleeve bore the emblem of the Radio-Technical Troops, a gold shield and radar dish superimposed over a silver aircraft fuselage. One of his monitors showed a truck-mounted antenna parked several hundred meters away. The antenna was slewed skyward. He glanced back at Neminsky. "Standing by to radiate."

The research scientist nodded. "Carry on, Captain."

The officer turned to his station. His finger stabbed down. "Pulsing now." His eyes darted to a second screen, this one a large radar display. A single blip near the center represented the M-55 aircraft. Immediately, a large blotch formed behind the plane. "Good hits," he reported. He looked back at Neminsky with a triumphant smile. "It worked, Doctor! We can track the cloud."

Rodin saw the scientist nod in approval, an action imitated by Voronin. He raised an eyebrow. "What exactly are we seeing?" he asked quietly.

Neminsky turned his head. "The test particles Lieutenant Colonel Novik just dumped into the atmosphere are radioactive," he explained. Seeing the look of disbelief on Rodin's face, he smiled. "Not dangerously so," he emphasized. "In fact, the amount of radiation emitted by these particles is essentially harmless—akin, in fact, to the levels produced by a common brand of ceramic dishes and cooking utensils manufactured by an American company up to the early 1970s. Millions and millions of people ate off and cooked with these dishes for decades without any noticeable ill effects."

Rodin stared at him for a long moment. "You're joking," he managed at last.

The scientist shook his head. "I do not joke, Mr. Rodin." He shrugged. "This so-called Fiestaware brand used uranium oxides to add vibrant colors to its glazes. The amounts were significant enough that the American government actually seized the company's original stockpiles of uranium as part of its project to develop atomic weapons during the Great Patriotic War."

"And because these small particles are radioactive, you can track them?" Rodin said slowly.

Neminsky nodded. "Precisely."

"How?" Rodin wondered. "I thought radiation could only be detected at relatively close range, using Geiger counters and dosimeters and the like?"

"This is an experimental technique," the scientist said. "A number of researchers worldwide have claimed it was possible to track radioactive particles using millimeter wavelength pulses from a ninety-five gigahertz W-band radar." He nodded toward the glowing cloud still visible on the radar screen. "As you can clearly see, they were right."

Rodin glanced at Voronin who had a wry look on his face. "Do I want to know how this all works?" he asked.

Voronin shrugged. "Do you have a physics degree?"

Rodin shook his head.

"Then, no," the younger man told him with unconcealed amusement. "All that matters to us is that Neminsky and his team can now track the diffusion of very small particles through the atmosphere. And then compare these real-world results to their computer-generated models for the dispersal patterns of other similarly sized materials."

"Like your weaponized fungal spores," Rodin realized, lowering his voice so that no one else could hear him.

"Correct." Voronin shrugged. "Without this data, we would be operating largely in the dark—forced to rely on software-produced guesstimates to plan our attacks inside the United States. With it, we can refine and adjust those plans in real time, considering the observed effects of wind and weather. There will be no unpleasant surprises or accidents." He smiled coldly. "As I promised President Zhdanov, our disease spores will hit their intended targets with near-absolute precision."

NINETEEN

THAT SAME TIME

A tiled veranda ran along one side of the Spanish-style mansion, looking out over the small lake bordering its carefully maintained lawns and flower gardens. Beneath the veranda's wood-beamed roof, ceiling fans whirred slowly, providing a cooling breeze. Battered rattan chairs and settees provided seating.

Nick Flynn sat slouched in a chair half-turned toward the pleasant view. Though his eyes were fixed on the sparkling, sunlit waters at the edge of the grounds, his mind was thousands of miles away. He was listening closely with Laura Van Horn and Fox while Shannon Cooke briefed them on his recently completed recon mission to Moscow. Dressed casually in shorts and khakis against Florida's summer heat and humidity, they had convened around a small round glass table.

Cooke, a bit ragged around the edges after several long days and nights under enormous stress, had returned late the night before. He looked better this morning, thanks to a few hours of sleep in a decent bed, a long shower, and a couple of meals that weren't prepared in plastic wrappers. Resilience was a key trait for any covert operator, and Cooke bounced back faster than most.

"Anyhow, slipping back across the border this time was easier than I figured it would be," the soft-spoken Virginian finished. "Those Russian border control guys are still focused more on people trying to infiltrate in—not so much on anyone trying to get out."

Fox finished jotting down some notes he'd been taking and then looked up. "Which brings us to the crux of the matter," he said to Cooke. "Based on what you learned in Moscow, do you believe an attack on the Raven Syndicate's corporate headquarters is feasible?"

"You want the short-hand version?" Fox nodded. "Feasible? Hell, no. Not in a million years," Cooke said bluntly.

Flynn sat up straighter and opened his eyes. He turned to face the other man. "Don't be afraid to get technical with us, Shannon," he said with a grimace. "What's the long version?"

"The long version? Sure. Here goes: It cannot be done. Period. End of story." Cooke shrugged. "I can't see any way to hit Voronin inside the Mercury City Tower—not with what we know now. We're still woefully short on the intel necessary to craft a plan that might work. Worse, I keep drawing a blank on any realistic approach to gather the information that we need."

Frowning, he ticked off some of what they were missing. Critically, they lacked access codes for the skyscraper's restricted elevators, which were the only ones that ran to the three floors housing the Raven Syndicate. Nor did they have schematics and other key technical specifications for the alarm systems used to secure the building's entrances and exits. And, aside from a rough guess at overall numbers based solely on his quick in-and-out visit, they were totally ignorant as to the extent of the local security forces.

"We don't even know where the tower's security control room is located. Or how well it's guarded," Cooke pointed out. "And that's a critical node."

Flynn nodded. Somewhere inside the mammoth skyscraper— whether on one of its seventy-five floors above the ground or the five subterranean levels was still a complete mystery—there had to be a control center, a place where security personnel were posted to monitor all the surveillance camera feeds and alarm systems. Saying that it was a critical node was almost an understatement. Because unless they could blind, bamboozle, or somehow otherwise neutralize those security systems, any attempt by armed attackers to reach Voronin's headquarters was doomed from the start.

"I get your point," he said to Cooke. "Whoever's in charge there could lock down every elevator at the slightest sign of trouble."

"Uh-huh. And that would leave the stairs as the only way up—or down, for that matter."

Flynn grimaced. "Trying to climb forty-plus fights of emergency stairs, against an alerted enemy?" He shook his head. "Count me out, brother. I'm allergic to mountaineering, especially when someone's likely to be shooting at me."

"Mountaineering? We're only talking about a few hundred feet, Nick," Van Horn said dryly. "You understand that's not exactly Mount Everest, right?"

Flynn grinned back at her. "I'm a Texas boy, Laura. Anything higher than a hundred feet qualifies as a mountain." He turned back to Cooke. "What else are we missing?"

"Up-to-date plans and schematics for the floors controlled by the Raven Syndicate," he replied. "When Voronin took the place over from his mentor, that guy he ratted out—"

"Dmitri Grishin," Flynn said. Grishin had been one of Russia's richest and most powerful oligarchs. Voronin had been his corporate troubleshooter and up to his neck in the older man's various illegal schemes and plots. But when one of those plans went off the rails, Voronin had betrayed his employer to Zhdanov—saving his own life and gaining control over the billions of dollars he'd then used to organize the Raven Syndicate.

Cooke nodded. "Yeah, him. Apparently Voronin spent a ton of money renovating those three floors once Grishin was out of the way." He shrugged his shoulders. "While in Moscow, I spent a couple of days making arms-length approaches to the contractors who handled the work. I'd hoped to get at least a quick look at their blueprints for the job."

"No joy?" Flynn guessed.

"None," Cooke admitted. "Voronin made sure all the paperwork came back to him as soon as the work was finished."

Flynn felt his jaw tighten. Even if his assault team could, by some miracle, make it up those forty-plus stories without triggering alarms and alerting Moscow's police and counterterrorist reaction forces, they'd be going in completely blind—without the slightest idea of the exact layout or any extra defenses the Raven Syndicate had put in place. Much as he hated to admit it, Cooke was right. Without considerably more information than they had now, attacking Voronin inside the Mercury Center Tower would only result in a blood-soaked fiasco. He said as much out loud.

"Then we go after Voronin when he's outside the building," Van Horn interjected. Her gaze was steely. "Sure, hitting a moving target isn't easy in some ways, but we can take out a car or limo—armored or not. Plus, the job's guaranteed to be much more doable than trying to pry him out of that stainless-steel rat trap he's forted up in."

Cooke stared at her. "You saw the surveillance video I shot from my stakeout position, right?" He tapped the tablet computer he'd just used to replay those scenes for them. "The one time I managed to spot Voronin on the move, he could have been in any one of six identical black limousines. Target discrimination would have been a serious challenge."

"Like I said, not easy," Van Horn replied with a shrug. "So we just RPG the shit out of the vehicles at the front and back to bottleneck the rest . . . and then blow the hell out of everything in between." Her smile was cool, more professional than amused. "That's basic ambush tactics, not rocket science."

Flynn shook his head in regret. "Tempting as it is, I don't think we could pull off a successful ambush. At a minimum, we'd require advance intelligence on Voronin's movements." He turned to Fox. "Can Four's special asset in Moscow provide us with that level of detail?"

"I'm afraid not," the older man said. "My understanding is that our source there operates well outside Voronin's orbit."

Van Horn frowned. "I don't see the issue. We set up in advance and wait for him to come into our sights."

"Setting up is the problem," Flynn pointed out. "I've studied the street maps of that area. There are multiple exits and entrances from the International Business Center. Voronin could use any of them, not just the one Shannon had his eyes on. There's no way we could guarantee having a strike team assembled close enough to take the shot."

Cooke nodded slowly. "That's not even considering the difficulty we'd have moving our people and their weapons and other gear into position without raising red flags for the local cops. Between the high-rollers who do business in those brand-new skyscrapers and the political bigwigs at Moscow's city hall, the police keep a close eye on comings and goings in that neighborhood."

"You managed it," Van Horn reminded him.

Cooke shook his head. "I was just one guy. Plus, I was totally unarmed. Infiltrating with an armed group would be an order of magnitude harder."

She sighed theatrically. "I hate you all and your inconvenient facts too. They're always getting in the way of my excellent plans to kill people and blow things up."

Fox smiled. "Even if it were not for the purely tactical issues involved, Laura, I wouldn't green-light any plan to ambush Voronin on Moscow's city streets." He borrowed Cooke's tablet and opened the surveillance video showing Voronin's convoy of limousines headed through traffic to the entrance of the Mercury City Tower. Then he froze it on a single frame where all six vehicles were visible. Using a stylus, he circled the other cars and trucks on the road around them, as well as the pedestrians lining nearby sidewalks. "You see the issue?"

Tight-lipped, Van Horn nodded. "Yeah. Stray rounds and explosive fragments travel."

"Exactly." Fox shook his head. "There's no chance you could ambush and destroy a convoy of that size in a crowded urban environment without killing and injuring dozens, perhaps hundreds, of innocent civilians—both on the streets and in the neighboring buildings."

She winced. "I take your point, Br'er Fox." Her mouth twisted slightly. "Sometimes it sucks to be the good guys."

"It does make our jobs more difficult," he agreed with a sympathetic nod. "On the other hand, I sleep better at night knowing that we're at least nominally on the side of the angels."

Privately, Flynn doubted that Voronin, psychopath that he was, ever lost any sleep over his own plans, which generally seemed to involve orchestrating the deaths of millions. But he understood Fox's broader point. Over its long history since the beginning of the Cold War, the Quartet Directorate had often proved itself quite ruthless in defense of the West. Nevertheless, there were ethical and moral lines Four would not cavalierly cross. Government intelligence services like the CIA or MI6 might occasionally carry out morally suspect and sometimes criminal actions under the cloak of "the needs of the state." But a private group like the Quartet Directorate had no such excuse.

"So if we can't hit Voronin at home in the Mercury City Tower . . . and we can't hit him on the move, what's left?" Cooke asked with a frown. "Praying that the son of a bitch gets hit by a meteor?"

One side of Flynn's mouth quirked upward. "Divine intervention would be nice," he agreed. "But I imagine God would be best pleased if we handle this ourselves. We'll keep banging away at this problem for as long as it takes to find a solution—one where the final score is: Quartet Directorate—One, Pavel Voronin—Burning in hell."

"Crap," Cooke groaned. He glanced at his watch. "I haven't pulled an all-nighter since—" His lips moved in silent calculation.

"College?" Flynn guessed.

Cooke grinned. "Nope. Got you. It was the day before yesterday, actually. My lone wolf scouting gig, remember?" He shrugged. "But I'm still jet-lagged as all get out. My brain isn't quite sure whether it's morning or sometime at night."

"Relax," Flynn told him. "I was speaking generally, not literally. I'm sure we could all use a break to rest and recharge." He checked his watch, then stood up and pulled Van Horn's chair out for her, gallantly offering her a hand. "Besides, Laura and I have a much-delayed date with some long-promised solitude, sunshine, and sand. We'll come back to this with fresh eyes in a couple of days."

She smiled as she took his hand and rose gracefully. "Ever the gentleman," she murmured.

Cooke laughed. "And smart, too, because I suspect you'd probably kill him if he bailed out on your plans for some R&R."

Van Horn shook her head. "You wrong me, Shannon," she said. "I would never *kill* Nick just for leaving me high and dry to fend for myself." Her eyes gleamed in sudden amusement. "But I do admit that I might be tempted to hurt him some."

TWENTY

THE NEXT DAY

Nick Flynn lay face down on a beach blanket. He could feel the warm sun soaking into his back and arms and legs. Muscles that had been knotted like triple-tied shoelaces for what seemed like months were starting to ease up as he finally allowed himself to relax. And right now, his only assigned task was to do absolutely nothing, only exist in this perfect moment—free of all worries and thoughts of the future.

Voronin. The Russian oligarch's name stirred in his subconscious, as noxious as the unexpected smell of rot and decay among flowers. Resolutely, he pushed it back down.

Instead, Flynn inhaled deeply. A soft breeze carried the salt tang of the nearby ocean to his nostrils. The peaceful silence surrounding him was broken only by the gentle murmur of waves hissing up on shore and the distant squawks of gulls circling over a nearby fishing jetty. Cocoa Beach was fifteen miles south of the Kennedy Space Center, but no launches were scheduled over the next several days. So the beach was free of the noisy, enthusiastic crowds that often flocked to watch rockets thundering into orbit.

Abruptly, a husky voice broke in on his thoughts. "You know, compadre, if I didn't like you so much, I'd really have to hate you right now."

Smiling, Flynn turned his head sideways to look at Laura Van Horn. Stunning in a skimpy cobalt bikini, she was sitting cross-legged in the shade of a large beach umbrella. Beyond her, the sands of Cocoa Beach were a dazzling white that merged with the greenish-blue waters of the Atlantic Ocean. "Hate me for anything in particular?" he asked lazily. "Or is this a more generalized, hypothetical loathing?"

In reply, she lowered her sunglasses so that he could see her bright blue eyes. He could read her answering smile in them. "It's the annoying way you can just lie out there under the sun for hours, without even a dab of protection . . . and never get sunburned. You only get browner and browner until you've got the perfect tan." She shook her head in disgust. "Nobody with an Irish surname like Flynn should be able to try that without frying lobster-red."

Flynn's smile widened into a lazy, complacent grin. "Well, I guess I can credit the maternal Tejano side of my family for that," he said. "It's not my fault I inherited good genes."

Van Horn snorted. "I hate genetics," she said darkly. "And while you're out there baking without pain or suffering, *I* have to slather on this stuff," she held up a bottle of SPF 50 sunscreen, "every thirty minutes on the dot, or I'll wind up looking like a stewed tomato."

"Yeah, maybe so, but you'd still be an incredibly sexy stewed tomato," Flynn corrected her.

Before she could kick sand at him, he rolled over and nodded at the bottle in her hands. "How about, as penance for my undeserved good fortune, I help you apply that stuff?"

Van Horn raised an eyebrow. "You seriously suppose offering to rub sunscreen all over my body qualifies as *penance*?" she asked, pretending to be scandalized. She pulled the bottle back a bit out of his reach.

Flynn laughed. "Hey, I'm a covert operator, not a theologian."

Just then, a burst of noise—loud, excited whoops and scattered clapping—erupted nearby. They turned to look for the source. The sounds were coming from the fishermen who packed the nearby jetty. One of

them had just landed a substantial catch, a fish that must be more than
three feet long, at least judging from the size of the tall, bearded man
who was proudly showing it off to his buddies. Dull blue on top, its
silvery belly scales shone in the sunlight.

Flynn whistled in admiration. "That kingfish has to be a forty-
pounder. Maybe more." He shook his head. "I'd heard they were mi-
grating close to the coast right now, but that's still one heck of a catch
off a jetty. I wonder what that guy is using for bait? Man, whatever it
is—" He stopped abruptly in mid-sentence, suddenly transfixed by a
slew of ideas sleeting through his brain.

Van Horn was still gazing at the kingfish as it was held aloft. "What
kind of bait for a monster like that? Not a clue, Nick." She grinned to
herself. "My preferred approach to fishing is just to drop a grenade in the
water and back the hell up. Maybe that's not exactly sporting . . . but it
does get results oh-so-much faster than you backwoods yokels dangling
worms in the water and hoping for some poor dumb fish to come swimming by." Hearing no response to her gibe, she turned back to look at him.

Flynn was just sitting there on the sand, staring off into thin air
with an intense look of concentration. Donning a frown, she waved a
hand in front of his face. "Hey, you! Non-flyboy! Over here! Remember me? The sexy, bikini-clad woman you were so hot-to-trot to slather
with sunscreen just a little while ago?"

Flynn came back to the present with a visible start. He reddened
slightly. "Sorry, Laura. I didn't mean to zone out on you."

"Don't sweat it," Van Horn told him kindly. Her eyes narrowed. "I've
seen that 'million miles away' expression before. So either you're suffering sudden-onset sunstroke or that clever head for tactics just kicked
out a solution to our problem. Namely, how do we successfully merge
a high-powered bullet with that scumbag Pavel Voronin's skull? Without ending up dead or in a Russian prison, I mean."

"Well, maybe not a complete solution," he said cautiously. "But I
do see at least the glimmer of an approach that might work."

She nodded. "And is this zigzag, streak of lightning in the brain
brilliant idea of yours something that'll go bad in the next day or two?"

"Not really," Flynn acknowledged. "What I've got in mind definitely isn't something we can pull off on the fly. It's going to take a lot of preparation and planning and a bunch of moving parts have to come together first." His mouth tightened. "But you should know that, if we end up putting my half-assed concept into action, we're both going to be in serious danger."

Van Horn smiled at him and raised her hand. "Ooh, ooh, let me guess, Mr. Flynn: We're talking about walking-a-tightrope-over-a-lava-pit-without-a-net levels of danger, right? Do I win a prize? Am I close?"

"Pretty close," he admitted.

"So basically a standard Quartet Directorate mission," Van Horn pointed out matter-of-factly. She handed him the sunscreen and scooted around to offer him her back. "Which is why you need to stop thinking right now. Let your subconscious do its thing in peace. And in the meantime, get busy massaging this lotion all over me. Not missing one single spot, nook, or cranny, mind you." She shot him an arch look over one slender, attractive shoulder. "Because, and trust me on this, Nick, once we're off this beach, you are *not* going to want my range of motion impeded by some lousy sunburn."

Flynn eyed her with interest. "Oh?"

She nodded. "You do know I kicked and screamed and all but held my breath to bulldoze Br'er Fox into cutting us lose even for this crappily short two-day leave?"

"I do," he agreed in a solemn manner. "Gwen Park was worried that she'd have to deal with a hostage situation unless he gave in."

Van Horn smiled again. "It was a near-run thing." She shrugged her shoulders. "Anyway, that's why the two of us are going to make use of every single hour we've been given. *Full* use. Is that clear?"

Flynn grinned back at her and flexed his fingers. "Why yes, ma'am. You can count on me. I'll get to working on that sunscreen right now."

TWENTY-ONE

MOSCOW

A COUPLE OF WEEKS LATER

At the chime from his office door, Pavel Voronin looked up from the report he'd been studying. Messengered over from the Kameshkovo Institute under close guard, it was a summary of Neminsky's most recent research. Stripped of all the usual technical mumbo-jumbo, it made for pleasant reading. The real-world data obtained from additional high-altitude test flights using the M-55 Geophysica aircraft continued to track closely with results from the scientist's computer models. Neminsky's initial estimate that they could sow enough weaponized disease spores in a single growing season to infect three-quarters of America's most productive agricultural regions—killing more than 95 percent of the affected crops—was beginning to look too conservative. Given careful planning, VELES could easily prove even more destructive than they'd first imagined.

He checked the screen on his desk. It was Vasily Kondakov, and, for once, the chief of internal security appeared uncharacteristically excited. Was there finally some news about the assassins who'd tried to kill him? Weeks had passed without Kondakov's people developing actionable intelligence that would enable his Raven Syndicate hunter-killer team to identify and target them. He scowled. Scrutiny of all known CIA,

MI6, and Mossad covert operatives hadn't turned up a single plausible suspect, certainly none that matched the female spy they'd spotted scouting the Leningradsky train station. It was almost as though his enemies had found some mysterious way to vanish off the earth's surface. But tempting as it was to assume they'd given up and gone into hiding, he knew that would be foolish. No, he thought coldly, those assassins were still out there, planning, plotting, and scheming against his life.

Irritably, Voronin closed Neminsky's report and slid it into his desk drawer. President Zhdanov's strictures remained in effect. Detailed knowledge of VELES was still limited to a handful of people inside the Raven Syndicate and the Russian government, and Kondakov remained outside that small circle.

Kondakov hurried in as soon as the secure door buzzed open and pulled out his tablet computer. "I've just been sent an urgent message from our mining operation in northern Sudan," he said. "You'll want to see it."

"Why?" Voronin asked. "Is some kind of trouble brewing there?"

The other man nodded. "Yes, there is, but it also represents an opportunity for us. If we act quickly and decisively."

The Sudan? Voronin frowned. This was not a development he'd expected. Besides its primary covert work for the Russian government, the Raven Syndicate operated worldwide—selling its military and intelligence expertise, services, and equipment to allied regimes and rebel groups across the globe. Among them was the corrupt military dictatorship of Sudan, which had now splintered into rival armed factions. Unable to pay for the Syndicate's services in hard currency, the faction currently controlling Khartoum had instead assigned him the rights to a gold mine near Al-Ibediyya, a small city on the Nile River roughly 350 kilometers north of the Sudanese capital.

At this mine, native workers, laboring almost as slaves under horrific conditions, blasted rocks out of the desert and shipped them to a nearby processing plant guarded by Voronin's security personnel and allied Sudanese paramilitary fighters. Once at this processing plant, the gold was extracted by leaching it out using cyanide and mercury. Afterward, these toxic substances were simply dumped into holding ponds without any concern for the local population's health. The operation was hugely profitable, pouring nearly a billion rubles a month, the equivalent of ten million American dollars, into the Raven Syndicate's corporate coffers. The prospect of potential trouble there was not welcome.

"Show me," Voronin snapped.

Deftly, Kondakov linked his tablet computer to the nearest wall screen. "As a precaution, we maintain a network of paid informants among the laborers, to keep an eye out for potential agitators or saboteurs," he said as a prelude. "Their reports allow us to 'disappear' potential troublemakers without much fuss."

Voronin nodded his understanding. His subordinate was describing a time-tested tactic, a favorite of the Soviet-era KGB and its modern successors. East Germany's secret police force, the Ministry for State Security, or Stasi, had gone even further in controlling dissent. By the time the Berlin Wall came tumbling down, it was estimated that the Stasi had recruited almost one out of every six East Germans to spy on friends, family, and coworkers. "Go on."

"Yesterday, one of these informants observed a clandestine meeting between two Westerners and some of the most disaffected miners— men we've been suspicious of for a long time," Kondakov continued. "Our man was able to covertly video some of this secret meeting using his cell phone."

"And now we have it?"

Kondakov nodded. "Recognizing its importance, our informant passed on the recording to his Syndicate controller at the processing plant, who, in turn, immediately forwarded it here to Moscow." His finger double-tapped an icon on his tablet, opening the video file they'd been sent.

Voronin gazed at his wall screen as the recording began to play. His eyes narrowed. The video was grainy, with poor lighting and even worse sound. From what he could tell, it seemed to have been shot in the back room of some tiny restaurant or coffee shop. But despite its technical imperfections, what the covert recording showed was clear enough. Two obvious Westerners—an attractive blonde woman and a fit-looking man—were speaking to a group of nervous-looking, rail-thin Sudanese workers through an interpreter.

"My analysts have double-checked the translations provided by our counter-intelligence officer stationed at the Al-Ibediyya processing plant," Kondakov said coolly. "They confirm that these Westerners are offering hard cash for inside information on our operations in the area . . . and for details concerning the strength and deployment of our local security forces."

Voronin felt his jaw tighten. "I see what you mean by potential trouble for us," he ground out.

Kondakov nodded. "This is definitely part of a clandestine reconnaissance effort aimed at our mining operation. But if you look closely at one of those Westerners, you'll see why I'm convinced this development also represents a golden opportunity for us." His tone subtly emphasized the word *golden*.

Perplexed, Voronin peered even harder at the poor-quality cell phone video. A moment later, his eyes widened in surprise. He stabbed his finger at the screen. "That woman! The blonde," he growled. "That's the same bitch you spotted at the Leningradsky Station. The one involved in the attack on me."

"According to our facial recognition software, the match is absolute," Kondakov agreed. He tapped at his tablet, freezing the video on another frame. It was centered on the fit-looking man seated next to the woman. "And if this woman's sudden appearance near our key facilities in Sudan were not significant enough, we've also encountered this other male foreign intelligence agent before. To our cost."

"Where exactly?" Voronin demanded.

Kondakov's fingers flew across his tablet, bringing up a series of still photos and sending them to the larger screen. "These pictures were taken by one of our operatives outside the Israeli embassy in Vienna more than two years ago," he explained.

Voronin leaned forward. The photos showed what was definitely the same man captured in the cell phone recording from Al-Ibediyya. He'd been caught on camera as he climbed out of a parked car and strode confidently toward the embassy entrance. The Russian scowled. Now he remembered this episode. In hindsight, it had signaled the eventual catastrophic failure of an earlier major Raven Syndicate operation aimed at the United States—an operation he'd codenamed MIDNIGHT. At the time, he and Kondakov had assumed the man in the photos was only a relatively low-level officer in the Mossad or perhaps in the Sayaret Matkal, a special forces unit controlled by Israel's military intelligence service. Later analysis of the limited evidence suggested that might not be the case . . . but none of Kondakov's people had succeeded in identifying the man. He'd shown up in Austria, begun unraveling MIDNIGHT, and then disappeared completely off the Syndicate's radar.

Until now.

Voronin glared at the screen for a moment longer before shifting his angry gaze back to Kondakov. "So now these two spies—both of whom have already done great damage to us—suddenly show up working side by side in Sudan and poking around our mining operations there? Why? What game are they playing?"

"It could be that, now that the enemy organization these agents serve has failed in its direct attack against you in Russia, it might be planning to strike softer, less heavily guarded Raven Syndicate targets," Kondakov suggested carefully. "Going after our Al-Ibediyya mining operation would fall into that category. Wrecking it would certainly deprive us of significant revenues."

"Not to mention notching another black mark against me in Zhdanov's eyes," Voronin muttered.

Kondakov nodded. A substantial fraction of the profits the Syndicate earned from its overseas enterprises made its way—however indirectly— into secret accounts controlled by the Russian president. Zhdanov would not be pleased to see his private income slashed because Voronin had failed to defend his operations from enemy attack. It would only add to Zhdanov's growing doubts about the younger man.

Unable to hide his frustration any longer, Voronin slammed a fist down on his desk, jolting the other man's tablet computer. "Who the hell are these people?" he snarled. Aware of his sudden lapse of control, he tried to regain his composure, lowering his voice before continuing. "And who are they working for?"

"Unfortunately, we still don't have any definitive information," Kondakov admitted. He waved a hand at the currently frozen video on the screen. "Both used perfect, unaccented English when communicating with their Sudanese interpreter."

"Which means nothing." Voronin shook his head. "I speak perfect English. So do you, for that matter."

Kondakov knew Voronin was right. A fifth of the world's population spoke English as a first or second language. The proportion was even higher among educated Europeans and Israelis. Certainly there was nothing special about the speech patterns they'd observed the two enemy agents using—at least nothing that could be used to narrow down their probable origins. "There is one way to resolve the issue," he pointed out.

"Which is?"

"Direct interrogation using . . . enhanced measures," Kondakov said. "I guarantee that will answer many of the questions which have troubled us."

Voronin smiled his understanding. The former GRU colonel had a justifiable confidence in his ability to elicit information using a mixture of physical pain and psychological pressure. "Then do you anticipate being able to lay your hands on these enemy spies?"

"Our people in Al-Ibediyya have them under surveillance now," Kondakov confirmed. "Their reconnaissance of our mining facilities is not yet complete. Better yet, there's no sign of anyone else providing security for them. And with your authorization, I can have my hunter-killer team on the ground there in less than twenty-four hours. We'll snap these agents up before they can run. Once we have them in our hands, squeezing the information we need out of them should prove easy enough."

"Do it," Voronin ordered. His pale eyes were expressionless, as frozen as a polar icecap. "But be sure they both suffer great pain before you finish them off. Make an example of them, Vasily."

TWENTY-TWO

PORT SUDAN INTERNATIONAL AIRPORT,
NEAR THE RED SEA, SUDAN

THE NEXT DAY

A sleek executive jet banked sharply over the sparkling, blue-green waters of the Red Sea and crossed the arid brown Sudanese coast, staying in a tight turn to line up on its final approach to Runway 34. Now heading almost due north, the Bombardier Global 7500 rolled back out of its bank and leveled off. Hydraulics whined and thumped as its underwing landing gear and nosewheel swung down and locked in position. Flaps whirred open, providing more lift as the aircraft shed airspeed and altitude. Off its port wing, the jagged, tumbled mass of the Red Sea Hills rose above a narrow coastal plain.

The jet touched down with a slight jolt and a puff of gray-black smoke from its tires. Braking smoothly as its big turbofan engines wound down, the Bombardier rolled down Port Sudan's long asphalt runway—rumbling past earthen revetments holding several Chinese-built Hongdu K-8 and Guizhou JL-9 two-seat jet trainers and light attack aircraft. The Sudanese Air Force flight school, although barely operational since the outbreak of factional fighting, was headquartered here.

Slowing further, the executive jet rolled by the main terminal building and tower. Several other passenger and cargo aircraft sat out on the apron. Since Khartoum International Airport was closed because of intermittent shelling by rival factions, Port Sudan was now the primary entry point for commercial air traffic and international relief supplies.

Past the terminal, the aircraft turned off the far end of the runway and onto a wide taxiway connected to a separate hard pad and hangar complex away from the airport's public areas. The Bombardier pulled up and parked beside an Mi-8 utility helicopter in Sudanese Air Force camouflage. Heat waves shimmered across the tarmac. The temperature was well over 100° Fahrenheit.

The jet's forward cabin door opened as soon as the engine whine faded into silence. Led by Vasily Kondakov, five men with weapons and gear bags slung over their shoulders trotted down the airstairs and headed directly to the waiting helicopter. Its engines were already spooling up. The six Russians climbed aboard, and the moment they were inside, the Mi-8 lifted off. It swung through an arc and then clattered off to the west—gaining altitude to clear the rugged peaks of the nearby hills. Al-Ibediyya was roughly ninety minutes flying time away.

Back at the airport, a tall, blond-haired man wearing a white polo shirt with the logo of the UN World Food Programme, the agency coordinating most food aid to the impoverished people of Sudan, lowered his binoculars with a satisfied smile. "And there they go."

"Are you sure, Einar?" his shorter, narrow-faced companion asked.

The big man nodded. The tail number of the Bombardier executive jet confirmed that it was the aircraft owned by Voronin through one of the Raven Syndicate's shell companies.

With a terse nod of his own, Rytis Daukša finished entering a short text on his compact, palm-sized satellite phone and hit the send button. It beeped softly, relaying his message through a commercial communications satellite high overhead. "Then we're set," he commented, sliding the phone back into his pocket. Their task here was done. Other events were now in motion.

ON THE OUTSKIRTS OF AL-IBEDIYYA, SUDAN
A SHORT TIME LATER

With Laura Van Horn behind him, Nick Flynn stepped out of the dim, relatively cool interior of the mudbrick house they'd been renting and into the intense heat of high summer. He donned his sunglasses and scanned the immediate area, checking again for the slightest hint of anything that seemed out of place. Their weather-beaten, white, older-model Toyota Land Cruiser was parked a few yards away in the wholly inadequate shade that a withered scrub acacia tree provided. Little swirls of dust danced across the dirt courtyard. Nothing else was moving.

Reassured, they headed to the Land Cruiser.

Flynn climbed behind the wheel, while Van Horn slid in on the passenger side. They wedged canvas-sided satchels under the center console between them. Both satchels had their flaps open, allowing quick access to the contents inside. With that done, Flynn refolded the sunshade that had narrowly kept the Toyota's interior from turning into an oven set on high. As it was, they were already starting to sweat.

He slid the sunshade behind his seat and glanced her way. "Okay, it's showtime. You ready?"

With her face a mask of concentration, Van Horn nodded. "You know me, Nick. I'm always ready."

"We are talking about the same thing, right?" Flynn said with a grin.

"Get your mind out of the gutter, mister," she said with a tight, answering smile. "Fun later. Work now."

"Roger that," he agreed.

After they finished putting on their safety belts, Flynn started up the Land Cruiser and put it in gear. He drove slowly through the gap in the courtyard's low mud wall. Deliberately, since being sneaky was not the point of this exercise, he signaled for a left turn and pulled out onto a hard-packed dirt road running north. It stretched ahead between other walled mudbrick houses and occasional clumps of scrub trees and brush. There was no traffic. With the sun high overhead, most people in this small city in northern Sudan were holed up indoors, waiting to emerge later in the evening when things cooled off.

Flynn glanced up at his rear-view mirror a hundred yards farther on. An equally battered dark blue SUV, a Nissan Patrol, had just turned onto the street behind them. Van Horn had her own eyes fixed on her passenger side mirror. "You see it?" she murmured.

He nodded. "Yep." He forced himself to avoid gripping the steering wheel tighter. His heart rate bumped up a notch. "Ivan One and Ivan Two. And they're right on time." Gently, he pressed down on the gas pedal, and the Toyota picked up speed. He checked his mirror again, watching the vehicle behind them. For a moment, they pulled away from the Nissan. But then its driver reacted and steadily narrowed the gap, closing the distance until he was only a couple of car lengths behind them.

"Like we figured, these guys aren't backing off," Flynn commented, feeling his pulse ratchet higher. Planned or not, this next move was going to be tricky. "The hook is in. Hold tight." Beside him, Van Horn nodded. She braced herself against the dashboard with her left hand. Her right gripped the handle above her door.

Flynn risked another quick look at his mirror. The Nissan was on their tail, hanging back no more than ten or fifteen yards. He breathed in and then out again in a disciplined rhythm, working to control his heart rate. *One. Two. Three.* Through the windshield, he saw a house ahead with a lone palm tree rising over its flat roof. He nodded tightly. He'd picked that out as a landmark on an earlier recon drive up this road.

Abruptly, he floored it. The Land Cruiser leaped ahead, racing up the street in a haze of tire-whipped dust. Mudbrick buildings and walls flashed by on either side, starting to blur as he kept accelerating.

Not far ahead, he spotted an opening between the buildings on their right. There it was! Gritting his teeth, Flynn cranked the wheel hard over, careening into a tight, high-speed turn that swung them onto a much narrower dirt road. It ran east toward the edge of town. A cloud of reddish dust billowed behind the Toyota.

Fifty yards down the little street, he jammed on the brakes. All four tires spun wildly as the Toyota skidded to a stop. Sand and pebbles spattered in all directions.

Slammed forward against his shoulder belt by the sudden deceleration, Flynn reacted fast. Fractions of a second counted now. When the Land Cruiser stopped moving, he slammed the gearshift into "park" and hit the release on his safety harness. It clicked open. Then he leaned over to the center console and yanked a PP-2000 submachine gun out of his open satchel. In the passenger seat next to him, Van Horn was doing the same thing. Without hesitating, they popped their doors open and stepped down onto the road, turning back to face the way they'd come with their weapons up and ready.

The red-tinged cloud of dust and sand kicked up by their tires still hung lazily in the air, obscuring the narrow entrance to this street. Flynn tucked the stock of the submachine gun against his shoulder, waiting. Any second now, he thought coolly, hearing the roar of an engine rapidly growing louder.

And then the blue Nissan burst out of the enveloping haze. Its brakes shrieked as it came to a sudden, fishtailing halt to avoid crashing into the back of their Land Cruiser.

Flynn and Van Horn opened fire before the Patrol's driver could try reversing out of danger. Their submachine guns stuttered, punching 9mm rounds into the other vehicle. More than a dozen shots from each weapon smashed through its dark-tinted windshield. Starred and cracked across its entire surface, the safety glass pane slowly collapsed inward. Their guns fell silent.

Breathing hard, Flynn took his finger off the trigger. With Van Horn covering him, he advanced on the bullet-riddled SUV. Reaching it, he yanked the driver's door open and stepped aside, quickly readying his submachine gun again.

"We're clear," Van Horn reported quietly.

Flynn peered in. Blood spattered the interior of the Nissan. The two men inside sagged back against its torn and tattered seats, only held upright by their seat belts. Their upturned, slack-jawed faces stared unblinking at the shattered windshield. Both Russians were clearly dead, shredded by multiple hits at point-blank range.

He swallowed hard against the sight of so much carnage and backed away. Just as he and Laura had planned, neither Raven Syndicate agent had a chance to pull a weapon. There was no room for fighting fair in this brutal secret war.

Van Horn was pale too, but she had a determined look. "Better them than us, compadre," she observed.

Flynn nodded. Those Russians had made their choice when they signed on with Voronin. He dropped out the half-spent magazine from his PP-2000, tucked it away, and reloaded. She did the same. This fight was just getting started.

In the sudden deathly stillness, they climbed back into their Land Cruiser. So far, no one had even dared to look out of the neighboring houses to see what all the gunfire meant. That was no great surprise, Flynn knew. Sudan had been embroiled in vicious civil strife for decades. Hundreds of thousands of people had been killed. Millions were refugees, either somewhere inside the country or forced to flee beyond its borders. Civilians had learned the hard way to keep their heads down and avoid entanglement with armed fighters—whether they were members of the rival Sudanese factions or foreigners.

Safely back inside their vehicle, Flynn and Van Horn donned tactical radio headsets. The time for subtlety and disguise was over. "Trawler Lead, this is Bait Two," she murmured into her mike. "Tango stalkers are down. Repeat, stalkers are down."

"*Copy that, Bait,*" Flynn heard Cooke reply. "*We're in position. Standing by. ETA now roughly forty-five minutes. Lead out.*"

"And there's our next cue," Flynn said. He put the Toyota in gear and pulled away from the ambush site. It took only a couple of minutes to reach the edge of Al-Ibediyya. There, they came to another dirt road rutted by the passage of heavy trucks. They turned onto it and drove northeast—headed out into the Nubian Desert, a barren, waterless wilderness that stretched for more than a hundred miles, all the way out to the rugged, equally bleak heights of the Red Sea Hills.

OVER THE NUBIAN DESERT
A SHORT TIME LATER

Vasily Kondakov leaned over from his bench seat to peer forward into
the cockpit of the Mi-8 helicopter. Past the helmeted heads of its three-
man Sudanese Air Force crew, he could see the desert unrolling before
them as they flew west—clattering low over its harsh, empty expanse.
With the sun almost directly overhead, there were no shadows to add
depth to the ground they were flying above. In places, dried up wadis
snaked through a landscape of reddish sand dunes. In others, slabs of
jet-black volcanic rock extruded through the lifeless surface, like spear
points thrust out of a dying man's back.

Kondakov's mouth thinned in irritation. Settled human life in northern Sudan was confined to a narrow band—one only a few kilometers
wide—centered on the Nile River as it twisted and writhed its way north
to Egypt and the distant Mediterranean Sea. And since only a single
paved road connected this region to the narrow coastal plains along the
Red Sea, helicopters and light aircraft were the most efficient and fast-
est modes of transportation. Knowing this, however, did not make him
any more comfortable at being forced to entrust his safety to the Mi-8's
helicopter's "local" flight crew.

Like many Russians, he harbored an unreasonable racial preju-
dice against most Africans—regarding them as unreliable at best, and
near-illiterate savages at worst. Learning that there was no airfield near
Al-Ibediyya suitable for the large Bombardier executive jet had come as
a severe blow, because it left his Raven Syndicate hunter-killer team dependent on their Sudanese allies for this final leg of the journey. Given
the circumstances, they would be lucky to arrive without further trouble at the gold processing plant.

Kondakov's dour musings were interrupted by the voice of the
Mi-8's copilot addressing him through his headset. Like the others, he
was tied into the helicopter's intercom system. "There is a radio trans-
mission for you, Mr. Kondakov," the Sudanese Air Force officer said
in heavily accented English, the only language they had in common.

"It is from your company's processing plant. I am patching this call through to you now."

The Russian sat upright in surprise. They were only thirty minutes out from Al-Ibediyya. What could possibly be so urgent that it could not wait until he was on the ground? "Go ahead. This is Kondakov," he snapped into his mike.

"*This is Duskhin,*" a voice tinged by static replied. "*We have a problem, sir.*"

Kondakov frowned. Oleg Duskhin was the Raven Syndicate officer assigned to command the security forces at the processing plant. According to his file, he was judged to be of only average competence. But the same assessment also showed that Duskhin was completely trustworthy, which was probably how he'd ended up in this African backwater where vast sums in gold could present an unfortunate temptation for abler but greedier men. "What is this problem?"

Duskhin hesitated for several long seconds. "*We've lost contact with the surveillance team tasked to keep track of those Western spies,*" he admitted finally. "*Given the situation, I would welcome further instructions.*"

Kondakov bit down on an oath. He was willing to bet that Duskhin's people had somehow screwed up and allowed the enemy agents to spot them. He realized that wasn't much of a surprise if he were being fair. The skill sets required to enforce a regime of terror among poverty-stricken Sudanese miners were not equal to the challenge of discreetly monitoring highly trained Western intelligence operatives. He sat quietly for a moment, weighing different options.

Perhaps unnerved by the continuing radio silence, Duskhin tentatively said, "*Perhaps I could deploy some of my other security troops to search for these people and try to discover what's happened to my surveillance team? We're only a few minutes' drive outside the town. That way, I might have more information for you by the time your helicopter lands?*"

"Absolutely not," Kondakov said. The idea of even more amateurs muddying the already roiled waters was not welcome at all. "Your guards will only get in our way," he said flatly. "My specialists and I will be on the ground shortly, and we'll take things from there. All I want from you are two fast vehicles, both fully fueled and in top mechanical condition. Is that clearly understood?"

Dushkin sounded relieved. "*Yes, sir. I'll organize that at once. We'll be ready for you the moment your helicopter lands.*"

Brusquely, Kondakov signed off. Then, with an exasperated sigh, he turned to the man next to him, the senior member of his hunter-killer team. Bullnecked Stepan Makeyev was a veteran of the GRU's shadowy Unit 29155—the death squad commanded by Kondakov for many years. Makeyev held an unsurpassed record for his number of liquidations of dissidents, traitors, and dangerous foreigners. Speaking rapidly, Kondakov outlined their current tactical problem.

When he was finished, Makeyev pursed his thick lips. "By the time we land, these spies will have a considerable head start on us," he pointed out. "Hunting them down may prove difficult."

"That's where you're wrong, Stepan," he said confidently. Running through the situation with the other man had given him time to think more carefully and recover his poise. "There's only one real direction they can run. And that's along the Nile road to Egypt. With this helicopter to scout ahead for us, it will be easy enough to find them." He shrugged his shoulders. "Now that Duskhin's idiots have tipped our hand, the only real difficulty may lie in taking at least one of these agents alive, which is our top priority." Smiling thinly, he fondly patted the hard-sided case in the other seat beside him. It contained some of his favorite instruments of torture. "I've been looking forward to practicing a few of my old skills."

Makeyev nodded. There was no real human expression on his broad face. "And what if the people we're hunting bolt off the Nile route and head out into the desert instead?"

"So much the better for us," Kondakov said with a careless shrug. He waved a hand at the lifeless vista outside the Mi-8's cockpit. "There's nothing out there. No gasoline. No water. Nothing. They would only drive into a blind alley without any way out."

TWENTY-THREE

OUTSIDE THE AL-IBEDIYYA GOLD PROCESSING PLANT

A SHORT TIME LATER

Five hundred yards outside the Raven Syndicate–owned compound, Tadeusz Kossak lay motionless in a shallow trough he'd laboriously scraped out of the sun-hardened soil the night before. His legs and lower back ached dully, a lingering reminder of the shrapnel wounds he'd suffered in Russia weeks earlier. While those injuries were healed now, at least enough to pass the scrutiny of a doctor who provided discreet, off-the-books medical services to Four's agents, he could still feel every one of them. But those pains were minor compared to his real enemy now, which was the heat.

His desert camouflage ghillie suit—one he'd handcrafted for himself using strips of lightweight, fire-resistant synthetic fabrics in tans, sand-yellows, light browns, and rock grays—broke up his silhouette and allowed him to blend perfectly with the arid landscape around him. Unfortunately, what the suit could not do was keep him cool under the blazing summer sun. In fact, it made the situation worse, since the ghillie suit's complex layers of cloth, netting, and bits of dried native brush trapped the substantial amount of heat generated by his own body even at rest. When combined with the already high daytime temperatures, it was almost unbearable.

Kossak shrugged inwardly, striving to ignore the sweat pouring off his face and body. No one in Poland's elite special forces or later in the Quartet Directorate had ever promised that his work as a scout and sniper would be easy or painless. Endurance and sheer grit in the face of intense physical discomfort were necessary traits for this work. As important in some ways, he knew, as the skill required to accurately hit targets at impossibly long ranges. Without his ability to sneak unde-tected to within the line of sight of an enemy, and lie hidden for hours or sometimes even days, his talent for precision shooting was nothing more than a carnival trick, or perhaps a way to rack up medals and awards in shooting competitions. He winced. He could not imagine being condemned to such a dull, meaningless existence.

He licked his blistered lips and then took a tiny sip of water from the CamelBak hydration pack he wore under his camouflage suit. It was scorching hot. Cautiously, he swished the water around the inside of his mouth, waiting for it to cool a little before swallowing.

Then, through his headset, the Pole heard Shannon Cooke's voice. "*Lead to all Trawlers,*" the other man radioed. "*Stand by. I have the Bait team's vehicle in sight. They're a couple of miles out, tooling up the southern track, poking along all nice and sedate—like an old married couple out for a Sunday drive after church.*"

Kossak smiled slightly. Long experience with Cooke had shown that the calmer and more "country" the Virginian sounded, the more keyed up he really was. The need to wait silently—in searing heat and mounting uncertainty—for the first elements of this intricate plan to come together must have been hard on him, too. "*Copy that, Lead,*" he heard Cole Hynes reply. "*Their timing is good. That Tango whirlybird is coming in from the east right now. I make it about five miles away, and I figure it'll be touching down in just a couple of minutes, tops.*"

The Pole nodded to himself in satisfaction. It was time for him to go to work. The heat-induced torment he'd been enduring inside the confines of his sweltering camouflage suit instantly subsided, pushed far to the back of his mind by the prospect of action. With slow, practiced movements, he pulled his long-barreled Lobaev DXL-5 heavy rifle into position. Like him, the weapon was swathed in strips of camouflage cloth to break up its distinctive silhouette. He sighted through the scope he'd attached, a Vortex Optics Razor HD Gen II, and panned slowly across the razor wire–fenced Russian compound—noting signs of movement.

Two large SUVs—one black and the other gray—had driven out of the processing plant's motor pool. They were now parked next to a large paved area that served as a helicopter landing pad in an isolated corner of the complex. Several hundred yards away, the plant's industrial and administrative buildings shimmered in the heat haze. Two Raven Syndicate security men cradling assault rifles nervously stood guard near the vehicles, looking miserable in their bulky body armor. A man he judged to be their boss had just climbed out of one of the air-conditioned SUVs. Clad in jeans and a short-sleeved linen shirt, he was dressed far more comfortably than his subordinates. But he also appeared ill at ease, obsessively checking his watch while he shouted at someone over his smartphone. One side of Kossak's mouth quirked up. Obviously, these men did not see the imminent arrival of a Syndicate bigwig as a blessing.

The Mi-8 appeared on the horizon. Rotor blades whirling, it swept low across the desert, rapidly taking on shape and definition as it approached. The big helicopter flared out when it reached the pad and slowly settled onto its tricycle landing gear. The shrill howl from its twin turboshaft engines diminished somewhat but did not fade away entirely. The Sudanese flight crew seemed ready to lift off again, just as soon as they had delivered their passengers.

Through his scope, Kossak saw the two Raven Syndicate guards double-time across the asphalt in response to a shouted order from their superior. They bent low under the Mi-8's still-turning rotors and yanked open one of its side doors. Half a dozen other men dropped out of the helicopter's aft cabin and immediately headed toward the waiting SUVs. Downwash from the spinning rotors whipped at their clothing.

Here we go, the Pole thought calmly. He zeroed in on the new arrivals, shifting his aim from face to face while mentally comparing them against the Quartet Directorate intelligence files he'd studied so thoroughly in preparation for this operation. He stopped at the sight of the tall, balding man wearing wire-rim spectacles who brought up the rear of the little group. That was Vasily Kondakov. There wasn't a shadow of a doubt in his mind. There was no mistaking that cruel, self-satisfied demeanor. This man, once a high-ranking officer in Russia's GRU, exuded power, which was appropriate for someone now believed to be Voronin's top deputy.

"Trawler Lead," Kossak radioed quietly, taking great pains to speak with absolute precision. "I have identified the primary target. Standing by for your order."

Meticulously, he adjusted his aim.

"*Understood,*" Cooke replied. "*Bait and all Trawlers. Confirm your readiness.*"

Kossak listened as a flurry of responses, all cool and thoroughly professional, but each conveying an unmistakable edge of eagerness, flooded through his headset. His finger settled into position against the trigger of his long sniper rifle.

"*All right, boys and girl. Light 'em up!*" Cooke ordered.

The Pole squeezed the trigger in the brief moment between one breath and the next. CRAACK. A 12.7mm round streaked downrange, slashing across the intervening desert at four thousand feet per second, three and a half times the speed of sound.

ON THE LANDING PAD
THAT SAME TIME

Kondakov mopped at his brow with a handkerchief while following the hunter-killer team out from under the helicopter's still-turning blades. He'd started sweating profusely the moment he stepped into the heat waves shimmering off the landing pad's asphalt surface. He frowned. It had been years since he'd been in the field himself. He was far more used to pulling other men's strings from the comfort of a climate-controlled office.

Still dabbing at his forehead, he straightened up at the edge of the pad and glanced back at the grounded Mi-8. As soon as his team was inside the SUVs waiting for them and ready to move out in pursuit, he would order the helicopter into the air again. Once aloft, it could scour the highway north along the Nile for any sign of those two Western agents as they undoubtedly scrambled to escape.

Kondakov nodded in satisfaction. His plan to box the enemy agents in from the air while closing around them on the ground wasn't complicated. Then again, he decided, it didn't need to be. No matter how skilled or desperate these operatives were, he and his men already held the winning hand in this little game. It was just a matter of time—

And then his eyes widened in horrified astonishment as the Mi-8's cockpit canopy shattered—blown inward by a massive, high-powered bullet. Hit squarely in the chest, one of the Sudanese pilots disintegrated in a spray of bright red blood and bone fragments, pulped by the enormous impact of a round capable of piercing steel. Half a second later, a second shot killed the other pilot.

For a moment longer, Kondakov stood frozen in disbelief, staring at the helicopter's smashed cockpit. But then, with a low growl, Stepan Makeyev knocked him flat. He smacked into the tarmac with a startled yelp and lost his grip on the small case containing his specialized torture devices. It spun out of his hands, landing a couple of meters away.

"Keep your damn fool head down, Colonel," the big man snarled from beside him on the ground, reverting to Kondakov's old GRU rank in the heat of the moment. Around them, the other Raven Syndicate hunter-killer team members had thrown themselves prone, too. They were already frantically clawing at their slung weapons and equipment bags.

Only meters away, a third heavy rifle round slammed into the front end of a parked SUV. Splinters spalled away from its smashed engine block. The next SUV rocked on its wheels, punctured by a fourth armor-piercing bullet that struck its fuel tank. The sickly-sweet smell of leaking gasoline permeated the air.

Pressed flat against the blisteringly hot tarmac, Kondakov craned his head to the side, desperately scanning the desert beyond the perimeter to pick out the enemy sniper who was methodically picking off targets. A sudden flash of movement off to his right drew his eyes. Only a few hundred meters away, a white Toyota Land Cruiser sped straight toward the coiled razor wire fence guarding the gold processing plant. A thick plume of dust trailed behind it.

Oleg Dushkin's two security men had spotted the oncoming vehicle at the same time. They dropped to one knee, sighting down the barrels of their 7.62mm KORD assault rifles. "Hostiles!" one shouted. "Engaging!" And then his head exploded, blown open by another 12.7mm round.

Spattered by blood and pulverized bone from his now-dead comrade, the second guard panicked. Screaming in terror, he scrambled to his feet and bolted for the nearest cover, one of their now-disabled vehicles. But before he'd taken more than a few steps, he was spun around by the crushing impact of yet another bullet. Killed instantly, the guard flopped to the ground.

"Well, shit, Colonel," Makeyev said conversationally to Kondakov. He slammed a thirty-round magazine into his weapon, a 9mm SR-2 Veresk submachine gun. "These fucking spies are hunting *us*, not the other way around." He unfolded the submachine gun's stock with practiced ease and set it firmly against his right shoulder. "This is starting to get ugly."

A loud, crackling hiss erupted out in the desert to their right, only about fifty meters beyond the perimeter fence. Makeyev stared in shock at a small rocket as it curved high into the air, uncoiling a length of flexible gray tube behind it. The little rocket sputtered through a shallow arc and fell inside the razor wire. Behind it, the gray tube thudded down over a stretch of the fence itself. "Incoming! Take cover!" he roared, burying his face against the tarmac.

WHAAAMMM.

At least a dozen grenades went off with shattering force in a split-second—tearing that section of the razor wire fence apart with thousands of sharp-edged fragments. A huge pall of dust and smoke obscured the area for several seconds.

Blearily, staggered by the enormous blast, Kondakov slowly lifted his head. He was just in time to catch sight of the Land Cruiser as it raced into the gap and then burst out of the smoke. Its tires shrieked, flinging dirt and rocks aside as the vehicle swung sharply and headed straight for them. It was still picking up speed.

"*Mater' Bozh'ya*. Mother of God," Kondakov stammered, transfixed by the terrifying sight of the Toyota seemingly determined to crush him beneath its wheels. Across the tarmac, the survivors of his hunter-killer team were moaning—dazed and deafened by the powerful explosion that had just ripped apart the perimeter fence. The processing plant's chief of security, Oleg Duskhin, lay crumpled off to the side like a tattered rag doll. Only Makeyev seemed capable of coherent thought or action. Grimly, the big man spat out a mouthful of blood and swung around, aiming his weapon toward the oncoming vehicle.

Seeing someone else prepared to fight back, Kondakov felt a brief surge of hope. Awkwardly, he fumbled for his pistol, a weapon he'd entirely forgotten until now. Swearing under his breath, he yanked his 9mm Udav out of its shoulder holster . . . and then saw a quadcopter drone blur past just overhead. Two small cylindrical objects tumbled toward the ground in its wake.

His mouth fell open in horror. "No—"

Both M84 stun grenades detonated with ear-splitting *bangs* and blinding flashes—flashes far brighter than the noonday sun.

TWENTY-FOUR

THE TOYOTA LAND CRUISER

THAT SAME TIME

Nick Flynn stomped hard on the brakes, slamming the Toyota to a screeching stop only a few yards from where stun grenades dropped by the drone had just gone off. Through its dust-smeared windshield, he could see bodies scattered across the tarmac. Some were dead. Others, those caught in the radius of the two blasts, were thrashing and rolling in pain. They'd been shocked and temporarily blinded and deafened.

Those Russians were fish in a barrel, he realized with ice-cold clarity. But equally, he knew, this tactical advantage wouldn't last much longer. Grabbing his PP-2000 submachine gun, he leaped out of the Land Cruiser. Out the corner of his eye, he glimpsed Van Horn doing the same thing on her side of the big white vehicle.

With his weapon up and set for controlled, semi-automatic fire, Flynn stepped to the side to gain a clear view of his chosen targets. His front sights settled on one of the Russians, a big, burly man who'd recovered enough to fumble desperately for his compact submachine gun, an SR-2 Veresk. Too late, pal, he thought. He squeezed the trigger twice. Hit by both 9mm rounds, the big man slumped forward and lay still, facedown on the asphalt in a spreading pool of blood.

Van Horn's PP-2000 stuttered, knocking down another of their enemies at point-blank range. Her target screamed and then fell silent.

Still on the move, Flynn swiveled toward the next Russian he could see trying to get up and fight back. He fired two more times. Hit in the stomach and chest, the Syndicate assassin dropped back to his knees and then folded onto his side, dying fast as he bled out. Off to his right, Van Horn shot another man crawling toward the cover offered by a black SUV.

That made four down of the five men they needed to kill, he thought coolly. So where was the fifth? Suddenly, he caught a flicker of motion at the very edge of his peripheral vision. More intelligent than his comrades, the last survivor among the Raven Syndicate hit squad had been lying doggo, playing dead behind another corpse. Now he reared up with the muzzle of his short-barreled submachine gun swinging toward Flynn.

Holy shit. Flynn spun toward this new threat—already aware that he was too late. His stomach muscles tensed, anticipating the impact of a hail of 9mm bullets that would rip him open.

Whaaackk. The Russian flew backward in a splash of red, hit straight in the center of mass by a 12.7mm armor-piercing round. He was dead before his mangled body thumped onto the tarmac.

"*Tango down,*" Flynn heard Kossak radio calmly.

Slowly, he let his breath out. "*Dzięki, Tadeuszu.* Thanks, Tadeusz," he said in Polish.

"*No sweat, Nick,*" the other man replied from his camouflaged hide five hundred yards outside the perimeter fence. "*I confirm all targeted hostiles are down.*"

"Got a live one here!" Van Horn called from close by. "And it's the big fish we were after."

Flynn moved to her side. There, curled up close to the first man he'd shot, was Vasily Kondakov. The senior Raven Syndicate executive was still dazed. He was pawing over and over at the tarmac, futilely trying to get a firm grip on a 9mm pistol he must have dropped when the stun grenades went off practically right in his face. His wire-rim spectacles hung askew, with both lenses cracked. Behind them, his eyes appeared unfocused.

Coolly, Van Horn kicked the pistol out of his reach. It went skittering back toward the Toyota. Then she brought her PP-2000 to bear, aiming straight at Kondakov's head. "Ready when you are, cowboy," she told Flynn. "Let's do this fast. Because I'm pretty sure this neighborhood is going to turn unhealthy real soon."

While she kept the Russian covered, he knelt and roughly bound the other man's hands and ankles using plastic flex cuffs, immobilizing him. They then dragged their prisoner over to the Toyota, unceremoniously stuffed him into the narrow gap between its front and rear seats, and slammed the rear doors shut. Flynn slid behind the wheel, while Van Horn went back to retrieve the small case Kondakov had been carrying when he climbed out of the Mi-8 helicopter.

When she got into the SUV beside him, Flynn nodded at the case. "Collecting souvenirs?"

She shrugged. "Figured it would be worth seeing what our boy Vasily back there thought was important enough to bring all the way from Moscow." She patted the case. "I have a hunch it'll make interesting viewing."

"Most likely so," Flynn agreed. He put the Toyota in gear and gave it some gas—cranking the steering wheel hard over to make a tight U-turn back toward the gap Hynes had blown for them in the wire perimeter fence. The moment they were through, he radioed Cooke. "Trawler Lead, we're clear. Our catch is on ice. So go ahead and pop the scene."

––––––––

Just beyond the fence, Cooke eagerly flipped back the sheet of desert camouflage cloth he'd used to conceal his shallow foxhole from prying Raven Syndicate eyes. He levered himself up to a kneeling position, ignoring the protests from muscles and joints that had been inactive for far too long. It had taken him half the night to crawl into this hidden position without being spotted—and then he'd been forced to lie curled up and cramped for hours more, unable to do so much as twitch a single muscle without the risk of blowing his cover. Finally, it was time for his payoff, he thought cheerfully. The chance to blow up stuff made up for a lot of inconvenience.

Cooke settled a yard-long, olive-drab fiberglass cylinder onto his shoulder. He squinted through the attached diopter sight, carefully aiming at the knocked-out black SUV closest to the cluster of bodies strewn across the tarmac. Not quite satisfied, he adjusted the angle of the tube slightly, elevating it to be sure his shot would clear the razor wire fence ahead of him. In this case, missing low and hitting that fence would be fatal, not just embarrassing.

His sight picture settled on target and held steady. "Shot out!" he warned over the radio and immediately triggered the weapon, which was a Russian-made MRO 72.5mm disposable rocket launcher.

WHUMMPH.

A small rocket flew out of the front end of the tube and streaked downrange. It carried a six-pound thermobaric warhead. Just above the black SUV, a small bursting charge went off inside the device—rupturing its casing and spraying atomized fuel in all directions. Milliseconds later, the warhead's main explosive charge detonated and instantly ignited this still-spreading fuel cloud.

WHAAAAMMM. With a searing orange flash, the SUV and everything for yards around vanished, first crushed by the blast's powerful shockwave and then consumed by the ensuing fireball.

Cooke nodded in satisfaction when he saw the mound of blazing wreckage he had just created. Now it would be impossible for the Raven Syndicate to positively identify any of those who'd been killed here . . . and, most importantly, to realize that Vasily Kondakov was *not* among the dead.

He dropped the spent rocket launcher back into his foxhole and clambered out. Then he turned and sprinted toward Flynn's Land Cruiser, which had just pulled up not far away. From other points outside the Raven Syndicate compound, he could see Hynes, Vucovich, and Kossak also loping toward the waiting vehicle. Now that they had what they'd come here for, it was high time they bugged out.

ATBARA AIRPORT, SUDAN
SOME TIME LATER

Atbara was another river city like Al-Ibediyya, a scattering of mudbrick
houses, minaret-topped mosques, and other buildings lining the lifegiv-
ing Nile's east bank. It sat roughly forty-five miles south of the Raven
Syndicate's gold processing plant.

Outside the city, Flynn surveyed the small structures clustered to one
side of a single, mile-long dirt runway with a skeptical look. He and Van
Horn stood shoulder-to-shoulder a few yards from their parked SUV.
Its engine was still idling to provide air conditioning for the rest of the
team and their prisoner. The only other vehicles in sight were a pair of
derelict pickup trucks placidly rusting beside a tin-roofed building. This
seemed to serve as a combination terminal, baggage handling facility,
and ticketing office on the very rare occasions when a plane landed here.
Right now, the building was deserted. "Airport's kind of a highfalutin
term for this place," he commented.

"It is definitely on the rustic side," Van Horn agreed. Orchestrating
this part of the operation had been her job. "Which is just what we want
now," she pointed out. "No fussy officials asking inconvenient questions
and demanding paperwork we don't have, right? And no nosy tourists
taking awkward, not-so-easily-explained pictures. No witnesses at all,
unless you count them," she jerked a thumb toward a couple of stray
dogs taking refuge in the minimal shade provided by the nearby building.

Flynn laughed. "I imagine they'd sell us out for food scraps, but I
doubt Voronin has any canine translators on staff."

"See? That's why this place is perfect."

He nodded. Just then his palm-sized satellite phone pinged. He
glanced at the text scrolling across its inch-wide screen: *Pegasus inbound on final.* Shading his eyes, he peered to the southwest. Sunlight
glinted off wings as a single-engine turboprop, a Pilatus PC-12, banked
toward the runway. Even at this distance, it was distinctive, with a sleek
needle nose, wide, low wings, and a high, cantilever T-tail. Pressurized
for high-altitude flight, fast, and long-ranged, the Swiss-made aircraft

could also operate easily and safely from rough, unpaved landing strips like this one. That made it ideal for their purposes, and it also helped explain why the Pilatus's military variant, the U-28A Draco, was a particular favorite of the U.S. Air Force's Special Operations Command.

"Ah, right on time," Van Horn said with a satisfied smile. "I do love it so when a brilliant plan comes together."

Flynn nodded more cautiously. He was keenly aware that they were now approaching what was likely to be the most difficult, disagreeable, and, at the same time, the most vital phase of this mission. Nothing else they'd accomplished here would matter if they couldn't pull off what he had in mind.

They watched in companionable silence as the PC-12 came in, descending swiftly toward the end of the runway. Despite the rough surface, it touched down with barely a jolt and taxied over to where they stood waiting. Dust and sand churned up by the aircraft's five-bladed propeller drifted away on the light wind.

The Pilatus rolled to a stop only a short distance away. Its prop kept turning and with a low whine, the plane's forward clamshell-style door swung down.

On cue, the Toyota Land Cruiser's ignition switched off. Cooke and the rest of the team climbed out with their captive and headed toward the waiting aircraft. Flynn and Van Horn moved to join them. As a precaution, they hustled Kondakov along at the center of the group—using their bodies to shield him from scrutiny. The Russian was blindfolded, with his hands cuffed behind him. His mouth was taped shut.

Once aboard the PC-12, Kossak led the Raven Syndicate officer to the back of the passenger cabin. Without saying a word, the Pole roughly forced the other man into a seat and strapped him in. All the window shades were pulled down, leaving the interior dimly lit.

Equally quietly, Cooke and the others took their seats and buckled in. The cabin was surprisingly large for a single-engine aircraft. It had room for them all, with a couple of empty seats left over. The unnatural-seeming hush was a direct result of Flynn's earlier instructions to keep conversation to a bare minimum. Kondakov, though still plainly shocked by this sudden reversal of fortune, was not a fool. It would be better all around to avoid giving him any clues as to where they were now headed or what might happen to him once they arrived.

Up at the front of the aircraft, Flynn pulled the door back up and closed it. The high-pitched, howling whine of the PC-12's twelve-hundred horsepower Pratt & Whitney engine fell away sharply, muffled by the plane's excellent soundproofing. He turned and poked his head into the cockpit.

Van Horn had just finished strapping herself into the copilot's seat. The pilot was a former colleague of hers from Alaska's Air National Guard, Jack "Ripper" Ingalls. Like Flynn himself, she'd recruited Ingalls into the Quartet Directorate in the aftermath of a failed hunt for a hijacked Russian stealth bomber prototype. Four always sought out people with specialized skills and an ingrained willingness to take risks in a good cause.

"Take her up when you're ready, Rip," Flynn said quietly.

Ingalls nodded. He released the brakes and increased his throttle setting a notch. The PC-12 started moving again, bumping northeast along the dirt runway's rutted surface.

When it reached the far end, Ingalls swung the aircraft through a tight half-circle, lining up on the center of the brown strip that now stretched ahead to the southwest. He reapplied the brakes, and they rocked to a stop. His eyes ran over his gauges and displays one more time. On his right, Van Horn did the same.

Satisfied by what he saw, Ingalls ran his throttle forward, increasing power to the PC-12's engine. The noise level inside the cockpit increased markedly.

"Still looking good, Rip," Van Horn reported. Her eyes were fixed on the engine readouts. "Pressure and temperature look good. No faults. No anomalies."

Ingalls nodded. "Rolling now," he said. He released the brakes again and began his takeoff roll. The Pilatus almost leaped ahead, speeding down the dirt runway. When it reached an indicated speed of eighty-two knots, he pulled back slightly on his yoke. Like the thoroughbred it was, the aircraft smoothly lifted off and climbed into the sky—gaining altitude and air speed with astonishing swiftness for a prop-driven plane. Its landing gear whirred closed within seconds of leaving the ground.

At ten thousand feet, Ingalls banked gently around to the northwest, settling on a course that would take them most of the way to their next destination. Flynn went back to the main cabin. Cooke and the others had unbuckled their seat belts and were either stowing their weapons and equipment or silently changing into fashionable civilian clothes. He joined them. Where they were headed now, the last thing they could afford was to appear as they were in reality—a group of heavily armed, highly trained special operators who'd just carried out a successful surprise attack against a superior enemy force. For the next phase of this mission, discretion was, by far, the better part of valor.

TWENTY-FIVE

DAKHLA OASIS AIRPORT, EGYPT

SOME HOURS LATER

At the feel of a hand gently laid on his shoulder, Nick Flynn woke from a light doze in his seat. With nothing to do on the flight north from Atbara except worry about what came next, he'd allowed himself to drift off. He opened his eyes to find Laura Van Horn leaning over him. She nodded toward the open cockpit. "We've started our descent into Dakhla," she murmured softly into his ear.

He unbuckled and went forward with her. While she slid back into the copilot's seat, he squatted down to get a better view through the cockpit window. The arid wastes of Egypt's vast Western Desert extended in every direction—a brown, waterless expanse littered with gray and black boulders and stretches of wind-blasted gravel. The single visible exception lay directly ahead, where a fifty-mile-wide swath of groves of palm trees and green, irrigated fields surrounded towns of mudbrick and quarried brown stone.

This was the Dakhla Oasis, deep in the desert—more than two hundred miles west of the Nile River valley. It was the largest and most populated of the seven oases scattered across this otherwise hostile environment. It had been inhabited for thousands of years despite its isolation, or perhaps because of it. Dakhla's archaeological treasures ranged from prehistoric rock carvings to ruins and clay tablets from Egypt's Old King-dom to a Roman fort and temple that dated back to the time of Nero, as well as fortifications and a minaret erected early in the Islamic conquest.

A little south of the settled area, Flynn could see the long, mottled, gray and brown line of what had once been an eight-thousand-foot-long paved runway. Since there were no longer any scheduled commercial flights to Dakhla's airport, it had been allowed to fall into disrepair. Nearly half the landing strip's surface was cracked and pitted or half-buried by drifting sand. What was left was kept open for the smaller aircraft used to fly in archaeological teams, parties of wealthy adventure tourists, or the occasional central government administrator from Cairo.

Ingalls glanced back over his shoulder. "We'll be on the ground in about ten minutes."

"Did you get any probing questions from the airport operations folks?" Flynn asked.

"Nope," Van Horn assured him. "This airport's practically a ghost town, except when it's tourist season or some wannabe Indiana Jones–types show up looking for the Holy Grail or the Lost Ark. Right now, there's just one guy in charge, and his whole work force adds up to a couple of aircraft and fuel handlers, plus maybe a night watchman to guard the gate." She shrugged. "From what I can tell, the airport manager, a Mr. Nabil Bashir, is bored out of his skull most of the time. So he's really looking forward to welcoming our Mr. Hopper and his party to the oasis and arranging ground transportation and lodging for them at the finest local hotel."

"Lucky Mr. Hopper," Flynn said with a wry grin. He went back to his seat and buckled back in.

During their planned stay on the ground here, Shannon Cooke would become Mr. Francis Hopper, a wealthy American entrepreneur with a passion for Egyptology. According to the flight manifest they'd prepared for the local Egyptian authorities, he was accompanied by his personal pilot, Ingalls, an executive aide, Kossak, and two bodyguards, Vucovich and Hynes. No mention was made of Flynn, Van Horn, or their prisoner. As far as the official paperwork went, they simply didn't exist.

Ingalls was as good as his word. The PC-12 touched down right on time and taxied north along the weathered runway. Looking out the aircraft's left side, the slowly setting sun produced a glare off yellow-brown dunes of quartz-rich sand. Off to its right, the Pilatus rolled past huge circular fields of wheat grown using center-pivot irrigation. While they were still rolling, Van Horn climbed out of the copilot's seat and came back to join Flynn. When they arrived, it wouldn't do for anyone to spot a second pilot, especially a woman, in the cockpit.

Near the far end of the runway, Ingalls swung the plane through a tight right turn and slowly taxied across a concrete apron toward the airport's small, whitewashed terminal and tower building. Three Egyptians stood waiting to greet them at the designated parking stand. One, a thin, young-looking man in a light cotton suit, was undoubtedly the local manager, Nabil Bashir. The other two were older and wore reflective vests that identified them as ground crew. One carried a bright yellow cable to connect the PC-12 with the nearest AGPU or Aircraft Ground Power Unit. The AGPU would provide electrical power for the Pilatus's systems while it was on the ground.

Once the Pilatus came to a full stop, Flynn slid his window shade up a few inches and peered out. He was pleased to note that the only aircraft currently on the ground at Dakhla was a twin-engine Embraer Legacy 500 business jet in the nondescript colors of a Europe-based charter airline. If all went well, he thought, mentally crossing his fingers, the presence of that plane should let him tie up one of the loose ends of this particular mission, at least temporarily. He pulled the shade back down.

Ingalls shut down his engine and switched off the cabin lights. Late afternoon sunlight through the cockpit windows now provided the only illumination inside. Cooke and the others were already gathering near the forward door. The pilot scooted past them to lean over to Flynn. "We're hooked up to ground power, so I can leave the fans running," he said very quietly, pitching his voice low enough to avoid being heard by anyone but Flynn and Van Horn. "But you guys won't have any air conditioning. It's going to get pretty hot in here before the sun sets."

"How hot exactly?" Flynn asked.

"You ever see *The Bridge on the River Kwai*?" Ingalls said. "Remember the iron box the Japanese shoved the British POWs in for torture? About that hot, I'd guess."

Flynn nodded somberly. He jerked his chin at Kondakov, who was still blindfolded, gagged, and tied up in the back of the plane. "In this case," he told the other man, "that might be more of a feature than a bug."

"Except you'll be riding it out with him," Ingalls pointed out.

Flynn grinned. "I didn't say this was a perfect plan. It's just the only one we happen to have."

"Better you than me, brother," Ingalls said, patting him on the shoulder. Then the pilot went forward to open the aircraft door. A gust of hot air blew in off the sunbaked concrete apron outside. Cooke, adopting the persona of Francis X. Hopper, multimillionaire and archaeology enthusiast, swaggered down the steps to meet the local Egyptian welcoming party, accompanied by his entourage. Ingalls shut the curtains to the cockpit and followed them all out. Moments later, the PC-12's cabin door swung back shut, plunging the cabin into darkness.

Suddenly, Flynn heard the faint rustle of clothing from the next seat over. He leaned across the narrow aisle to bring his mouth close to Van Horn's ear. "What exactly are you doing?" he murmured, in Russian. By now, Kondakov's hearing had probably recovered somewhat from the stun grenade blasts that had initially deafened him.

"Getting as comfortable as I can while we wait," she answered patiently in the same language. Even in the dark, he could sense the playful smile she shot him. "Mister X back there is blindfolded, remember? So I don't see the point in sweating my ass off any more than I have to. But don't get any big ideas about close contact. Like I said, this is about cooling off, not heating up."

She had a point, Flynn realized. As Ingalls had warned, the PC-12's interior cabin temperature was already climbing. And here they were, stuck in the dark, waiting out the remaining hours until this little airport closed. Stripping down would, at least, minimize some of the discomfort.

TWENTY-SIX

ABOARD THE PILATUS PC-12

LATER THAT NIGHT

Fully clothed again, Flynn checked his Vostok watch. Its luminous hands showed that it was past ten at night. Unequipped to handle night flights, Dakhla's airport shut down as soon as the sun set. He raised the window shade to look outside. Except for a few tiny lights on the Embraer business jet parked across the apron, the entire airport was dark. He pulled the shade back down and leaned over to tap Van Horn's shoulder. It was time to go to work.

With a nod, she left her seat and went forward to the cockpit to turn on a few of the PC-12's cabin lights. In their dim glow, Flynn got busy—setting the scene as they'd planned. First, he retrieved a portable, high-wattage gooseneck lamp and plugged it into an outlet on the seat facing Kondakov. Understandably miserable, the Russian sat slumped against his seat belt, drenched in sweat.

Van Horn came back to join him, lugging the other prop they'd chosen for this high-stakes drama. It was the case Kondakov had brought with him from Moscow. She set it down where it would be visible and walked around behind the prisoner.

At her nod, Flynn aimed the lamp hood right into the other man's face and flicked it on—suddenly bathing Kondakov in a harsh, unwavering white glare. Van Horn leaned forward and tore away the Russian's blindfold and gag. Then before he could react, she stepped around him and dropped casually into one of the two facing seats. Flynn took the other.

Casually, her foot slid Kondakov's case forward into the light. It was open now, revealing a gruesome array of torture instruments—electric drills, saws, needles, and pliers among them.

Blinking painfully against the dazzling glare after so many hours in darkness, the Russian swallowed painfully. His mouth was quite evidently as dry as dust, probably both from fear and dehydration. His eyes widened slightly when he noticed the two people seated across from him. Seen only in silhouette behind the bright lamp beam, they were little more than vague, unrecognizable shapes. "Who are you?" he stammered in English. "What do you want from me? If it's a ransom, I promise my employer will pay handsomely for my safe return."

At that, Van Horn uncoiled and leaned forward into the light, allowing Kondakov to see her more clearly. "Oh, Vasily," she chided him in flawless, conversational Russian. "You know very well who we are. Or at least you already know our faces, if not our names. Or our affiliations. But you must also know that we are not interested in money. Not a single ruble, dollar, or euro."

"Then what do you want?" he said, reverting to his own native tongue with a look of despair.

Now it was Flynn's turn. "Information, of course," he said easily, also in perfect Russian. "Why else would we have gone to so much trouble to keep you alive in the midst of so much death?" He noticed Kondakov's gaze drift, almost unwillingly, toward the open case of torture devices.

The blood drained from the Russian's face. "And if I refuse to answer your questions?" he forced out.

Van Horn smiled. "Are you afraid we might try to pry what we need out of you, using your own instruments?" Her foot tapped the case again, almost fondly. "Delightfully ironic though it might be, I can promise you that we are much too civilized for such a barbaric course of action."

Kondakov breathed out in obvious relief.

Now it was time to push. *And push hard*, Flynn thought. Half the secret of a successful interrogation was to keep your subject off-balance until he broke—whipsawed back and forth between abject fear and desperate hope, however implausible. "My colleague is right," he said. "We won't torture you ourselves." But then he shrugged. "If you won't cooperate, we'll simply hand you over to others who are less squeamish than we are, and who possess fewer scruples."

"What others?" the Russian asked. He was almost whispering.

Van Horn's smile widened. "Come now, Vasily," she coaxed. Her foot prodded the case of torture instruments one more time. "You've built a career on torture and murder and the death of innocents. Surely your imagination can summon up any number of those who would be very glad to have the chance to extract their revenge from you—one torn fingernail, broken bone, or gouged-out eye at a time?"

Kondakov's face paled even more.

Seeing that, Flynn exulted inwardly. The psychological profilers working for the Quartet Directorate had been on target. Like many sadists and killers, the Russian was something of a physical coward himself. He took pleasure in inflicting on others what he most feared himself. Flynn turned to Van Horn. "Maybe we should hand him over to the survivors of one of the Syrian resistance groups?" he suggested casually.

"A good choice," she agreed. "They can be quite . . . inventive." Her eyes hardened. "And who can say how far they might go if given a chance to even the score with the Butcher of Latakia?"

Flynn noticed how Kondakov almost unconsciously squirmed backward against his seat in barely suppressed horror. No surprise there, he thought grimly. While still a high-ranking officer in the GRU, the Russian had carried out many gruesome covert operations for the Assad regime allied with Moscow. Among other atrocities, he had personally supervised the torture and execution of dozens of political dissidents and rebels—even going so far as to order the deaths of innocent women and children in front of their accused husbands and fathers. The prospect of ending up helpless in the grip of those whose families and clans he had helped destroy had to be terrifying beyond any rational ability to calculate.

Kondakov's mouth opened and closed soundlessly for several long seconds, just as though he were a hooked fish gasping its life out at the bottom of a boat. He was, Flynn thought dispassionately, almost literally frightened out of his wits. "And if I give you the information you're looking for?" he managed to finally stammer. "What then? You promise to kill me cleanly?"

Flynn tensed. *Ah, shit*, he thought. This was the moment he'd been dreading. Vile though Kondakov was, and vital as it was to obtain the information they so desperately needed, he couldn't help feeling this was a filthy process—one that could stain his soul. And convincing though her own cynical, ruthless act was, he knew Laura Van Horn shared his doubts and worries. He decided to fall back on the truth—though admittedly not the *whole* truth. It was the only way he knew to sound absolutely convincing. "Kill you? Not at all," he said honestly. "If you answer our questions, and answer them truthfully, we'll cut you loose. Completely unharmed. You have my word on that."

The Russian stared back at him. "You'll free me?" he repeated in clear disbelief. "But how can you? How can you be sure that I will not tell my employer exactly what it is that you're looking for?"

Van Horn interceded, not bothering to hide her amusement. "Seriously, Vasily?" she said. "You would go running back to Pavel Voronin after you fucked up so badly and let yourself get captured?" She shook her head in disgust. "Are you really that stupid? Or that suicidal?" She shrugged. "From what we know of your employer, he'd pat you on the back . . . and then feed you feet-first into a furnace."

Flynn saw Kondakov blanch at that reference to an unimaginably brutal method of execution sometimes favored by the old Soviet KGB. She had struck a shrewd blow. Nevertheless, he had the distinct impression that the other man still hoped that he could talk his way out of trouble with Voronin—if only he could somehow make it back to Moscow in one piece. On the other hand, he could also sense that Kondakov's resistance to answering their questions was weakening.

The issue, Flynn recognized, hung in the balance. Abruptly, acting on instinct as much as on reason, he decided that it was time to gamble.

It was time to push Kondakov to the breaking point and see what happened. He donned a cruel smile. "It's your call," he said coolly, as if he didn't give a damn what the other man decided. "Keep silent and die screaming under the knives of Syrian rebels. Or give us what we're interested in and walk away without a scratch." Pointedly, he checked his watch. "And, pleasant though this conversation has been, we're not screwing around anymore. You've got just thirty seconds to choose which way this all goes down."

Kondakov's eyes darted back and forth between them, a reflection, Flynn was sure, of the man's inner turmoil as he desperately cast about for some other alternative. If anything, he looked even paler than before—with skin that was more corpse-gray than a living man's.

"Fifteen seconds," Van Horn said flatly. "The clock is ticking, Vasily."

Flynn saw the Russian break. His body slumped like a snowman melting under a blowtorch. "I will answer your questions," he sighed.

"Smart choice," Van Horn told him. She shot a meaningful glance at Flynn. *Don't trust this son of a bitch*, it said. *At least not very far.*

He nodded. Neither of them had any real illusions about Kondakov. To save his life for the moment, the Russian would give them what they wanted. But there was no doubt that he still harbored thoughts of buying his way back into Voronin's good graces later—using any information he obtained as collateral. No matter how coyly you played it, Flynn understood, any interrogation ended up being a two-way street. The questions you asked inevitably revealed almost as much about your own interests or intentions as the answers you received told you about those of the enemy you were cross-examining.

Despite this, Flynn opted to kick things off by zeroing in on some of the key information they needed. At this point, trying to hide their objectives would only be wasted effort. "All right, Vasily," he said pleasantly. "Let's start with how the security measures for your Raven Syndicate offices at the Mercury City Tower are organized—"

As question followed question, he saw Kondakov begin to realize what they must be planning. The other man's eyes widened subtly. But by this time, Flynn had gained enough insight into the way the

Russian's mind worked that he could sense whenever Kondakov tried to lead them astray. He could credit that perception to his U.S. Air Force intelligence training and a natural gift for reading people. "Tells" were just as common in interrogation as around a poker table.

When at last they were finished, it was almost dawn. Completely exhausted, Kondakov sat slumped in his seat. Flynn knew that neither he nor Van Horn looked much better. He glanced at her. She nodded silently, entering a brief text message on her satellite phone. They'd learned as much as they were going to from their prisoner, and now it was time they got moving.

Flynn stood up and brusquely replaced Kondakov's blindfold. Then, before the surprised Russian could react, he unbuckled the seat belt and dragged him upright. "What is this?" The other man was taken aback and unable to hide the undercurrent of fear in his voice. "Where are you taking me now?"

"Away," Flynn replied shortly. Still holding the Russian tightly by his pinioned arms, he waited while Van Horn opened the forward cabin door. Faint smells of aviation fuel and diesel exhaust wafted in through the opening, along with the pale gray light of very early morning. "We're not fools, Vasily," he continued. "We're not dropping you off anywhere close to us."

Temporarily mollified, and obviously aware that he was helpless with no real choice but to obey for the time being, Kondakov reluctantly allowed them to guide him down the stairs and onto the tarmac. Keeping quiet, they marched him across to the other parked aircraft, the Embraer Legacy 500 executive jet.

Alerted by Van Horn's text message, a stocky, gray-haired man stood waiting patiently for them at the foot of the Embraer's airstairs. Flynn recognized him immediately. For many years, Mikolaj Soliński had been the chief of Poland's foreign intelligence service, the *Agencja Wywiadu*. Now he headed the Quartet Directorate's central Europe station. Two tough-looking younger men flanked him.

At a terse nod from Soliński, Flynn pulled out his pocketknife and sliced through Kondakov's flex cuffs, freeing the other man's bound wrists. Then he shoved the Russian in the small of his back, sending him staggering across the tarmac. Immediately, the two men waiting with Soliński stepped forward and firmly took Kondakov by the arms.

"We have the prisoner," one of them told Flynn formally. He flashed a card that identified him as an agent of Poland's internal security agency, the ABW. "They are waiting for this man in Warsaw. My superiors have many questions about several mysterious deaths for which he may have been responsible."

Shocked, Kondakov swung his blindfolded head toward where Flynn stood watching. "What are you doing?" he demanded weakly. "You promised me my freedom!"

Flynn shook his head. "We promised to cut you loose without a scratch," he reminded the Russian. "And that's exactly what we've done."

He stepped back as the younger Poles hauled a still-protesting Kondakov up the stairs and into the waiting aircraft. He glanced at Soliński. "How long can your people hold that bastard incommunicado?"

The gray-haired man shrugged. "Six weeks, perhaps. Certainly no more than eight. After that, it will be necessary to begin formal judicial proceedings if we want to hold him longer, which means informing the Russian authorities that he is alive and in our custody."

Flynn nodded his understanding. He shook hands with Soliński and then turned back to the PC-12 Pilatus. Walking beside him, Van Horn shook her head. "Six weeks? That sure doesn't give us much time for planning and prep work."

"Nope," he agreed, already working through what they'd learned from Kondakov. "I guess that means we're just going to have to buckle down and stop taking it so easy."

She snorted. "Easy? Hell, Nick. *Nothing* about the past few days was easy."

Flynn shot her a wry, sidelong smile. "Compared to what's coming our way next? Yeah, I think it actually was."

TWENTY-SEVEN

THE NEXT DAY

Pavel Voronin and Kiril Rodin silently followed one of Zhdanov's aides into the president's private office. Heavy drapes covered every window, blocking any view of the courtyard below. A ceiling fan over the president's ornate desk barely stirred the haze of gray cigarette smoke.

Zhdanov looked up from the pile of reports he'd been reading. His expression was not welcoming. Sourly, he waved at the pair of gilt chairs in front of his desk. "Sit down," he growled. "Both of you."

They obeyed. Casually, Voronin unbuttoned his suit coat and crossed one leg over the other, determined to appear completely unfazed by this abrupt summons to the Kremlin. Behind this pose of studied calm, however, he was on full alert. He was well aware that his life might hang in the balance here, potentially forfeit if he misread the situation to the slightest degree. It was apparent that Zhdanov was in a dangerous mood—one that sometimes moved him to acts of violence. As he aged and his health declined, Russia's authoritarian leader was becoming increasingly arbitrary. In recent months and years, a number of once-trusted subordinates and longtime political allies had learned the hard way what it meant to displease him. A few were dead. The rest were locked away in harsh conditions and under close guard.

With a grunt of disgust, Zhdanov finished the report he'd been perusing. After tossing it back on the pile in front of him, he picked up a cigarette that had been sitting smoldering in his overflowing ashtray. He took a deep drag, filling his lungs with smoke, and then irritably ground it out. Considering the older man's well-known craving for nicotine, Voronin half-expected him to immediately light up another. Instead, the president simply leaned back in his chair with his hands laced over his stomach. And then, for a long, increasingly uncomfortable moment, he said nothing, merely observing Voronin and Rodin from under heavy-lidded eyes.

Voronin held his silence. Given Zhdanov's obvious vexation, he would gain nothing from opening this conversation. He had the sensation of walking a tightrope, with a ravenous tiger pacing hungrily below him. Beside him, Rodin kept his own mouth shut, perhaps having made the same internal calculation.

At length, the president sighed and shook his head. "Tell me, Pavel," he said conversationally, "would you have said that your man Vasily Kondakov and his handpicked team were competent? That they were a group of top-notch professionals?"

"Yes," Voronin said simply. Shading the truth of what he had believed would gain him nothing. "In all cases, their training, years of field experience, and collective record of success against Russia's enemies would have suggested nothing less."

"I see." Zhdanov let that hang in the air for a moment. Abruptly, he rocked forward in his seat and banged a fist on his desk. "Then how do you explain what happened yesterday in Sudan?" he snarled. "Maybe you can tell me how a group of supposedly experienced professionals walked straight into an ambush and got themselves butchered!"

Voronin kept a tight grip on his own expression. Privately, he shared the older man's surprise and fury at how easily and quickly Kondakov and his team had been eliminated. But again, he knew he would gain nothing by revealing his feelings to Zhdanov. The former GRU colonel had been his most trusted subordinate. Criticizing the other man now would only make him look weak. He shrugged. "The first reports from the scene are not clear," he said carefully.

Zhdanov snorted. "Since there were no survivors from this attack, that's hardly surprising," he snapped. He shook his head. "Listen closely to me now, Pavel. You've sold your Raven Syndicate's intelligence and military services to me and your other clients around the globe based on your people's supposedly unparalleled expertise in their respective fields. More disasters like this will put your reputation at risk, perhaps even obliterate it, and if that happens, you will be of no further use to me. Do you understand?"

Voronin nodded tightly. Crude though it was, the other man's threat was quite clear. Unmarked graves across Russia were full of those for whom Zhdanov had no further use.

"Now, give me the truth," Zhdanov continued. "Is the Sudan processing plant still operational after this catastrophe?"

There was the real crux of the president's concern, Voronin suddenly understood. The death of Vasily Kondakov or any of the others with him, no matter how swift or humiliating those deaths might have been, was of little real importance to Zhdanov—except possibly as a rhetorical club with which to beat him about the neck and shoulders. It seemed that the continued flow of rubles from the sale of Sudanese gold mattered most to the president. Nearly half the profits from Al-Ibediyya went to the Russian government, and a substantial portion of that money ended up in Zhdanov's secret bank accounts. Considering that he already exercised total power over all government spending, subject only to nominal oversight from his rubberstamp Duma and Federation Council, Voronin couldn't see why the president cared so much about those hidden funds. Perhaps, he thought cynically, it was mainly as a means of keeping score. Some of Zhdanov's predecessors had looted trillions of rubles from the treasury during their tenures in office. It was possible, he supposed, that the old man across the desk viewed his ability to out-steal all of them as one more measure of his own success.

"The gold plant is undamaged," Voronin assured the president. "Its processing operations continue without interruption." He shrugged. "I've already dispatched additional security personnel to replace those lost in the attack, so we should have no trouble with the labor force."

Zhdanov frowned. "And what about those Western agents? The ones you sent Kondakov and his team to capture? Are they in a position to cause us further trouble?"

For the first time in this meeting, Kiril Rodin spoke up. "We're confident they've already left the scene," he said quietly. "Everything we know strongly suggests they were acting as bait for the ambush force that killed Kondakov and the others. In our judgment, the gold processing plant was never their real objective. This was an operation deliberately designed to lure a senior Raven Syndicate executive into range and eliminate him."

"As part of this vendetta by someone against Pavel here and his organization?" Zhdanov suggested.

Rodin nodded. "Yes, sir." He shrugged. "And it worked to perfection. Kondakov walked right into their trap, like a lamb led meekly to the slaughter."

Voronin worked even harder to control his demeanor. By extension, Rodin's withering assessment of how easily Kondakov had been tricked applied equally to him. Both of them had seen only what they wanted and leaped immediately to the flawed conclusions their enemy had intended all along. Being reminded of his mistakes was galling, and from the studied innocence of the other man's expression, he could tell Rodin had enjoyed his chance to do just that. The day would come, he vowed darkly, when Zhdanov's pet spy and assassin would bitterly regret his continuing insolence.

Zhdanov leaned back in his chair, clearly thinking about what he'd been told. His hands busied themselves shaking another cigarette out of the crumpled pack on his desk and lighting it. He puffed reflectively for a moment, and then sat forward again. "These continuing efforts against you and the Raven Syndicate trouble me, Pavel," he said, stabbing his cigarette at the younger man for emphasis. "Is it possible that they are somehow related to your new operational project, to this VELES? Has someone breached your secrecy? Is stopping you from proceeding with your intended bioweapons attack what motivates them?" His eyes were cold. "Because I tell you plainly that I will not countenance any further work on this scheme of yours—no matter how promising it may be—if there is even the slightest chance that the Americans have learned what you plan on doing to them." He shook his head. "Remember, I'm interested in sabotaging the United States from within, *not* in sparking an open military confrontation we cannot hope to win!"

"Our security for VELES remains completely intact," Voronin promised. "In any case, it's clear that Kondakov was the intended target of this most recent ambush—not me. More importantly, he had absolutely no involvement in, or even knowledge of, anything connected to VELES, so there was never any real risk that our plans might be compromised."

Zhdanov looked at Rodin. "Is that true?"

The other man nodded. "At my insistence, Kondakov was kept completely out of the loop," he agreed. "Even if he'd somehow been captured alive, he wouldn't have been in a position to tell, or sell, any vital secrets." He shrugged again. "And since he and everyone with him died on the scene, we have even less to worry about."

Zhdanov was pleased by that. He turned back to Voronin with a sardonic look. "You should be grateful that Rodin insisted on such precautions," he said pointedly. "To be honest, Pavel, I suspect many of your earlier failures can be traced to carelessness on your part where security was concerned. Too many people knew too much about your various plans, which is why information about them seems to have always reached the wrong ears." He smiled thinly. "The old adage is always apt: Three men can keep a secret. So long as two of them are dead."

"Something I will remember, Mr. President," Voronin said steadily. It occurred to him that there were three of them in this room right now. Considering his long-range intentions for both Zhdanov and Rodin, perhaps that was an omen.

Zhdanov nodded. "And on that same subject, who will be replacing Kondakov as your internal security chief? You'll need someone better suited to the task than he proved to be."

"I've selected Anton Saitov," Voronin answered. "He was Konda-kov's senior subordinate."

"A logical choice, perhaps," Zhdanov commented. "But is that your only reason?" He turned to Rodin. "What do you think?"

The other man shrugged. "I vetted Saitov myself. He's a veteran of the FSB with extensive experience in counterterrorism and secu-rity work. In my view, he's tough, well-trained, and more than ruthless enough to do the job."

That was an understatement, Voronin thought. Among other tasks, Saitov had worked undercover for the FSB, infiltrating the far-right, ul-tranationalist Russian Imperial Movement. During his time undercover, he'd carried out covert assassinations of the group's more troublesome and independent-minded leaders—clearing the way for others who were more willing to obey the Kremlin's secret orders. Enticing him to join the Raven Syndicate had been a sensible move. And while Saitov might lack Vasily Kondakov's outward polish and advanced education, his skills and more recent hands-on operational experience probably made him a better fit for their internal security needs. Although he was reluctant to admit as much, Voronin also suspected Saitov was cunning enough that he would have spotted the trap laid for Kondakov before it was sprung.

Where it counted, Kondakov's death changed nothing. VELES would proceed unimpeded. If anything, Voronin thought, the fact that his enemies seemed to have shifted their efforts to attack what they per-ceived as the Syndicate's weak points rather than coming after him again directly was a vindication of his decision to move to the Mercury City Tower. So long as he remained secure in his fortified headquarters, he should be safe from any realistic threat.

TWENTY-EIGHT

SEVERAL DAYS LATER

Fox's office was small and simply furnished, with just a desk, a couple of comfortable chairs for visitors, and an inexpensive-looking desktop computer. Its best feature was a large picture window that looked onto one of the mansion's lush tropical gardens full of vibrant blooms in brilliant colors. At the moment, however, the view out the window showed a solid wall of clouds boiling ever closer. Lightning flashed in the distance, crackling across the darkening sky. Seconds later, a low rumble of thunder rattled the windowpanes. A gust of wind stirred the plants outside.

One of Florida's typical summer afternoon thunderstorms was on the way, Nick Flynn knew—watching more distant bolts slash out of the heavens toward earth. It was like clockwork. What had been a bright blue sky dotted here and there by a few puffy white clouds would vanish, swallowed up by towering gray and black masses of storm clouds. Torrents of wind-driven rain would lash down, hammering the ground with astonishing force. Within moments, lawns, sidewalks, and parking lots would all be an inch or more deep in running water, leaving tourists caught unprepared by the sudden deluge, soaked to the skin and splashing frantically toward the nearest shelter. Twenty minutes later, the skies would clear, leaving little evidence of the downpour except for a few rapidly evaporating puddles . . . and the fattened profits of the area's theme parks and souvenir shops that made a killing selling rain ponchos and umbrellas at ridiculously inflated prices.

"Earth to Flynn," Laura Van Horn murmured, nudging him gently in the ribs. "Ixnay on the storm-chasing and wool-gathering." She nodded toward Fox, who had just reached the last page of their report on the Al-Ibediyya ambush and their subsequent interrogation of Vasily Kondakov.

The older man looked up. "So Kondakov claims not to know any details about the Raven Syndicate's larger plans?"

"Beyond the bare fact that Voronin is definitely preparing another major operation of some kind aimed at the U.S.?" Flynn said. He shook his head. "Nope. He says he was being kept totally in the dark."

"Do you believe him?"

Flynn nodded. "Yeah, I do. He was pretty bitter about the whole situation. Being demoted and then pushed onto the sidelines clearly pissed him off."

"Kondakov blamed that on the new guy Zhdanov put in place," Van Horn clarified. "As part of some big shakeup ordered after we blew Voronin's last operation to hell in Cuba."

Fox tapped the report. "This man Kiril Rodin?"

"That's him," Van Horn said. "Apparently, he's supposed to act as Zhdanov's eyes and ears inside the Raven Syndicate."

"And to ride herd on Voronin himself." Flynn cleared his throat. "Kondakov described Rodin as an assassin as well as an informer. The rumor is that he's worked for both the SVR and the GRU in the past. Supposedly, he's also there to put a bullet in Voronin if Zhdanov decides that's necessary . . . or maybe just politically advantageous."

Fox nodded. "Based on your coded emails from Egypt, I asked some of my contacts in several different intelligence agencies, both here and elsewhere around the world, to run Rodin through their hostile agent databases." Like other Quartet Directorate heads of station, the older man maintained discreet, arm's-length relationships with people in the official intelligence and military services. None of them were privy to Four's real secrets or even to the complete picture of its aims and capabilities, but they did know enough to be of some help in carefully limited circumstances.

"Anything useful turn up?" Flynn asked.

"Nothing concrete," Fox replied. "Just a very rough physical description and unconfirmed reports that someone with that name has been employed—for wholly unspecified reasons—by a number of Russian intelligence organizations over at least the past twenty to thirty years."

Flynn stared at him in surprise. "The guy's been a spook for maybe three decades, and that's all that bounced back?" He frowned. "Heck, that's practically blank slate territory."

"Indeed, it is," Fox agreed. "And in this case, I suspect the very absence of information is a vital form of information itself."

Van Horn looked amused. "That sounds incredibly wise, extremely Zen, and also totally obscure, Br'er Fox. Care to share the plain English version?"

"It means that Kiril Rodin will likely prove to be a dangerous and highly capable opponent."

Flynn saw what the older man was driving at. There were only two real explanations for how someone like Rodin had managed to stay so far off everyone's radar, despite a lifetime spent in the shadowy world of spies and covert action. One was by being a complete non-entity, a sort of glorified file clerk, who was content to push papers from one desk to another and then go home, proud of another workday consumed by insignificant, bureaucratic busywork. But that clearly wasn't Rodin's story. Why would Zhdanov trust a backroom SVR or GRU hack to impose his will on someone as intelligent, ambitious, and murderous as Pavel Voronin? And that made Kondakov's conviction that Kiril Rodin was an assassin even more troubling. If so, the mysterious Russian must have been killing people on orders from Moscow for decades—and doing so without ever leaving a trail.

Van Horn tilted her chin at Fox. "Out of curiosity, if we ran the same kind of database search on you, would we get similar results?" she asked.

"Quite possibly," the older man admitted with a crooked half-smile. "Depending on the name you used in your search, of course."

Flynn held his countenance steady. He'd always respected Fox's superb leadership, powers of analysis, and gritty resolve to do everything he could to help his agents complete, and if possible, survive their hazardous missions. Now, for the first time, he realized there was an even more profound, more complex edge to Fox. In retrospect, it only made sense. After all, before becoming Four's head of the American station, Fox must have been a field operative, someone just as willing to put his own life on the line to complete missions as those he now commanded.

"Interesting," Van Horn said, obviously filing the information away for further consideration. She came back to the task at hand. "Well, if this guy Rodin is such a bad-ass, maybe we should figure out how to motivate him to knock Pavel off for us. Dead's dead, after all, no matter who pulls the trigger."

The older man nodded. "That would certainly be an elegant solution, especially since Voronin seems to be on thin ice with Zhdanov." He shrugged. "Sponsoring another botched operation would likely be the final straw."

"And that's where we start going in circles, Br'er Fox," Flynn pointed out. He shook his head. "Maybe Zhdanov would do the job for us if we could somehow sabotage Voronin's next covert operation, but we can't take the risk of waiting until he's ready to unleash whatever new biological weapons his pet scientists are cooking up. Instead, we have to get inside this son of a bitch's OODA loop and take him out. Doing that is our best chance to disrupt whatever he and his damn Raven Syndicate have in the works."

He saw Fox and Van Horn nod their understanding. Breaking into an enemy's OODA (observe-orient-decide-and-act) loop was a key principle of strategic and operational planning. Initially formulated by a brilliant U.S. Air Force officer, Colonel John Boyd, it was simple in concept, but enormously difficult in execution. Essentially, the technique offered a weaker, but more agile and faster-acting, combatant a means of defeating a stronger, but slower and more ponderous, hostile force. And like many human endeavors, its roots could be traced back to the Bible. Bigger, stronger, and better-armored Goliath had swaggered forth to battle expecting to chop David into pieces with his iron sword . . . right up to the second the shepherd boy had brained him with a simple stone hurled from his sling. Once you had an opponent reacting to your moves, instead of carrying out his own carefully laid plans, you were halfway home.

"Which leads me to the obvious question," Fox said finally. "Can you and your team accomplish the mission?"

Flynn looked the older man straight in the eyes. "It won't be easy. It sure as hell won't be safe. But, yes, I'm confident that we can."

Van Horn nodded her agreement.

"And your assessment is based on what you learned from Kondakov?" Fox pressed.

"Correct." Flynn laid another set of papers on the desk, plus the red access key card they'd obtained from their Russian prisoner. The documents included rough sketches of several of the Mercury City Tower's above-ground and subterranean floors. Others showed strength estimates for the Raven Syndicate and building security forces and details about their usual deployment patterns and armament. He waited patiently while the other man examined the material.

After several minutes, Fox lifted his head with a questioning look. "On quick inspection, I don't see any obvious weak points in Voronin's security arrangements," he said carefully.

"That's because there aren't any," Van Horn told him. "Trust me on this, Br'er Fox. Nick and I spent days studying the tactical situation from every angle we could think of—digging through what we've been told to find even the smallest gap we could exploit. Trouble is, we both came up with zero, zip, *nada*. Shannon Cooke wasn't wrong when he said this place is locked down tighter than Fort Knox."

Fox frowned. He picked up Kondakov's red key card. "And this?"

"A dead end, I'm afraid," Flynn said. "We were pretty sure the Raven Syndicate would cancel his building access as soon as they thought he was dead. Nevertheless, I'd hoped we could use that card as a template to forge our own versions. It would have been a nifty way to dodge their weapons screening and gain access to those restricted elevators." He shrugged. "I ran my idea by some of our technical people. Once they analyzed the way those key cards are programmed, they shot me down fast."

"Why?"

Flynn nodded at the plastic card in Fox's hand. "Because whenever a card is scanned, the individual biometric data coded inside it is automatically double-checked against a special database maintained by Mercury City Tower security."

"So using a key card containing information that's not already in their system—"

"Would only trigger every damn alarm in the whole building," Flynn acknowledged.

Fox winced. "And I suppose a similar problem would affect any forged visitor key cards?"

"Yep." Flynn confirmed. "They may not contain biometric info, but they're still clearly individually coded in some fashion."

"Plus, those temporary cards don't have restricted elevator access, and you can only pick them up at the lobby security desk," Van Horn pointed out. "And even if we had some way to slip weapons by the metal detectors and screening machines at the entrances, not even rent-a-cops would be dumb enough to hand out visitor passes to a whole bunch of strangers. No matter how politely we asked."

Fox frowned at them over the top of his glasses. He indicated the papers on his desk. "Then, if there aren't any gaps or other vulnerabilities in Voronin's security for you and your team to exploit, I don't see how you can hope to succeed," he said. "While I'm willing to accept the risk of casualties in any operation, I am not prepared to countenance a suicide mission."

"And I don't plan to go on one," Flynn countered. "There's an old quote that dates back to the famous Carthaginian general Hannibal, when his officers protested that his idea of crossing the Alps to invade Italy was nuts. He told them, 'I will find a way, or make one.'" He offered the older man a tiny cockeyed smile. "There's our plan in a nutshell.

Since we can't *find* any serious hole in Voronin's existing security arrangements, we're going to *make* a hole of our own."

Fox eyed him narrowly for a long silent moment. "I assume you do know that I'm going to need a bit more detail than simply the recitation of a pithy military aphorism, Nick?" he remarked at last, with just the faintest hint of amusement in his voice. "No matter how apt it may be."

"I kind of figured you might," Flynn admitted. He leaned forward. "Okay, here's how Laura and I see this going down—"

Over the next half hour, he laid out the gist of the plan they'd concocted to penetrate the security systems at the Mercury Center Tower and move a strike team into position to kill Pavel Voronin—along with as many of his Raven Syndicate's senior executives as possible. Fox listened intently, occasionally nodding in either agreement or understanding.

When Flynn finished, Fox sat back in his chair, his eyes half-closed while working through what he'd just heard. His fingers drummed softly on his desk as a rhythmic accompaniment to his deep, focused thought. At length, he sighed and looked back across the desk at Flynn and Van Horn. "You won't have much of a margin for error or accident," he observed.

"Practically none," Flynn conceded. "This either works out the way we intend, or it all goes down in flames right from the start." He knew that was an inherent weakness of their plan, and it worried him. Tacticians preached the need for alternate avenues of approach and contingency plans to cope with the friction—a fancy term for "shit going wrong," as one of his instructors had laconically observed—inherent in any clash between armed enemies. It was good advice. Unfortunately, in this case, there were no other avenues of approach to the problem. Voronin's defenses were so tight, they'd only get one chance to breach them. "But we have to take this shot now or walk away. Because, as soon as the Russians learn that Vasily Kondakov is still alive, all bets are off."

Fox nodded. "Very well. You have my approval to go ahead." One of his eyebrows ticked upward. "Which raises the question of how you intend to infiltrate your team and all of the special equipment you need back into Russia."

"That's Task One," Flynn acknowledged. "And it will be a grade-A bitch, especially because of the time pressure we're up against. Not to mention all of the extra border security measures the Russians have added since our last, noisier-than-we-wanted visit. We sure as heck can't plan on slipping the whole team across the frontier in one go."

"That would be . . . unwise," Fox said. "So you're going to break into smaller groups?"

Flynn nodded. They would send only two agents across the border at any one place. As an added security measure, the full details of their plan—its final rendezvous points, precise methods of attack and evasion, the cover identities for others in the group, and the like—would be communicated only to individuals as necessary. In effect, his action team would operate on a strict need-to-know basis until almost the last moment. He wasn't pleased about that proviso. Until now, he'd kept Cooke, Kossak, and the others in the loop on every operation. But the risks this time were just too high. If the Russians captured any of his people crossing the frontier, they needed to be kept from learning exactly how Flynn intended to penetrate Voronin's defenses.

"A sensible precaution," Fox said. His eyes sharpened. "Of course, you and Laura will be the unavoidable exceptions to this rule . . . since the plan is entirely your creation. Both of you, by definition, know too much." Flynn and Van Horn nodded. "Which makes it all the more unfortunate that you are, in fact, the Quartet Directorate agents most at risk in this madcap enterprise," Fox continued. "As the inevitable downside of your acting as bait to lure Kondakov to Sudan, I imagine your photographs are now plastered across every Russian border checkpoint, international airport, and seaport from the Baltic all the way east to the Pacific coast."

"Likely so," Flynn agreed. He glanced at Van Horn.

She smiled. "That's exactly why Nick and I have worked out our own special way in," she told the older man. "What's the best way to avoid getting picked up at checkpoints or airports or ports, do you suppose?"

"Bypassing them entirely," Fox said straightaway.

Van Horn nodded. "Yep." She shrugged. "Now that makes what we're planning a little complicated. We'll need to buy some new equipment, for a start. Plus, we'll have to charter a ship."

The older man suddenly bent his head and pinched his nose in poorly concealed dismay. "And all of this is going to cost a lot of money?" he guessed with a long-suffering sigh. Over the past couple of years, critical covert operations conducted by Flynn and Van Horn had cost several million dollars—primarily to procure cutting-edge aircraft and other pieces of equipment that had proved essential. Thanks to wise investments made decades ago by its wealthier founding members, Four had deep pockets . . . but its resources were not unlimited. Fox could only hope that his two best field operatives would somehow keep that firmly in mind.

Flynn grinned. "Ah, Br'er Fox, you know us all too well," he admitted, only slightly abashed.

TWENTY-NINE

MERCURY CITY TOWER, MOSCOW

A COUPLE OF WEEKS LATER

A long motorcade turned into the main entrance of the skyscraper's underground parking garage. The security guards and uniformed police officers on duty there immediately stiffened to attention. Slowly, the cavalcade of flag-decked black limousines and unmarked vans drove past and down the ramp. Their tires squealed on the garage's concrete surface, echoing shrilly throughout its cavernous, multi-level interior.

Five levels below the surface, the long column of vehicles rolled to a stop. Doors banged loudly up and down its length as armed soldiers and members of the president's security detail fanned out to form a shield against would-be assassins and curious onlookers alike.

Once his bodyguards were in place, President Piotr Zhdanov emerged from his personal car, an armored Aurus Senate L700 limousine. Buttoning his suit coat, he stood for a moment, allowing his eyes to adjust to the bright artificial glare of the overhead LED lights. Then he swiveled his head to an aide. "Well?" he demanded. "Where is he?" The aide murmured an answer in his ear, accompanied by a respectful nod toward a small nearby elevator.

Zhdanov swung in that direction and spotted Pavel Voronin standing there, closely hemmed in by several members of the president's advance security detail. He hid a smile at the carefully neutral expression the younger man had adopted. No doubt Voronin would have preferred the protection of his own Raven Syndicate bodyguards, but that would not happen. Not for this mysterious meeting, at least, whatever it truly portended. The only armed men allowed in the president's immediate presence were those known to be utterly loyal to him.

He jerked his head, signaling Voronin to approach. The guards parted slightly, stepping aside just far enough to make room for the other man to obey.

"Welcome to the Mercury City Tower, Mr. President," Voronin said politely. He indicated the elevator behind him. "This is my executive lift. We can take it up to my offices whenever you're ready."

Before answering, Zhdanov's eyes sought out the senior officer of his advance detail. The hard-faced man nodded slightly, confirming that his men had checked everything for possible threats and they were completely safe. Satisfied, the president turned back to Voronin. "Very good, Pavel. Let's get this done, shall we? I don't want people to ask too many questions about what I'm doing here."

"Nor do I, sir," he assured him. "But I think you'll find this visit today well worth your time."

Zhdanov nodded curtly. "I'm counting on it." He followed Voronin to the elevator and waited while the other man swiped a card through a security reader. A light on the machine glowed green, and gleaming metal doors slid open. Two unsmiling security men squeezed into the elevator with them. There was no conversation during the short, fast ride up forty-four floors.

Kiril Rodin was the only person waiting for them when the doors opened again. He nodded his head in polite greeting. "If you'll follow me, Mr. President, everything is ready for you." At Zhdanov's silent acknowledgment, he turned and led them along a corridor.

The president noted the empty offices on each side. "Where is everyone?" he asked.

Rodin looked back over his shoulder. "As a security precaution, we've temporarily ordered everyone off this entire floor," he explained. "Only Syndicate personnel cleared at the very highest level are exempt."

"Excellent," Zhdanov approved. "The fewer eyes to see and mouths to blab, the better."

They entered a large conference room not far from Voronin's private office. Zhdanov took the comfortable leather chair indicated by Rodin. A snap of his fingers sent his bodyguards back outside to guard the door. Alone with the other two men, the president swung around to face them. "All right," he snapped. "I'm here. Now tell me why. That vague line of bullshit you sold my top aides, 'vital matters of state security, etc.' had better bear some resemblance to the truth."

"I apologize for the imprecision and ambiguity," Voronin said calmly. "But the need for absolute secrecy you've rightly insisted on made it impossible for me to be any clearer."

"So this does involve VELES," Zhdanov said with satisfaction.

Voronin nodded. "Our planning has now reached the point where I believe a full operational briefing is in order." He half-turned and pitched his voice to the audiovisual control room at the back. "Lights!"

Immediately, the conference room darkened and a wall-sized display screen lit up. Most of it was dedicated to a digitized topographical map of North America. Voronin picked up a remote control and touched a small button on its side. Substantial portions of the map now glowed a soft red—mostly confined to a vast swath of the United States between the Rocky Mountains on the west and the Adirondacks on the east. "The American heartland, the core of its agricultural production," Zhdanov commented.

Voronin nodded. "And our primary target." He touched another button. Smaller sections of the display lit up, showing videos of enormous high-altitude balloons lifting off and soaring into the stratosphere.

Zhdanov frowned. "What are those supposed to be?"

"The most efficient means of delivering our lethal payloads," Voronin replied. Another button push made a sprinkling of balloon-shaped icons appear at different points on the map of the United States. As each icon appeared, it moved—purposefully propelled along the illustrated air currents. Behind each indicated balloon, vast stretches of the target area turned a sickly green color, a visual representation of the effects of the weaponized fungal spores it was sowing, spreading death from the skies.

Zhdanov scowled. "Balloons?" He shook his head. "What are you playing at, Pavel? This isn't some kind of children's game! American F-22 or F-35 fighters can knock your slow-moving gasbags out of the sky with a single missile each."

Voronin smiled. "Perhaps. But the Americans can't hit what they won't even be looking for."

"Explain that," Zhdanov snapped.

"We will use their Pentagon's earlier mistakes against them," Voronin said. "The Americans were humiliated when a Chinese balloon-lofted spy platform slipped through their air surveillance network and rode the winds at will over their homeland. After that incident, they adjusted the filters on those radars to better detect slow-moving objects like high-altitude balloons."

Zhdanov's scowl deepened. "Yes, I remember. As I said, the Americans will see your gasbags as they launch and shoot them down with ease!"

"No, Mr. President," Voronin said with absolute confidence. "They will not." Seeing the older man's face reddening with mingled rage and confusion, he went on more quickly. "The Americans won't do so, because that first humiliation with China's spy balloon led to others which were even more embarrassing. Not long afterward, the U.S. Air Force downed several other unidentified high-altitude objects—using Sidewinder missiles that cost half a million dollars. But it turned out that the balloons they'd destroyed so expensively were probably nothing more than stray private or commercial balloons, either ones that had been used for advertising purposes or that may have been carrying weather sensing and other scientific instruments." Voronin smiled again. "These episodes generated so much political and social media ridicule that now no one in NORAD or the Pentagon, or especially in the White House, has any appetite for, or interest in, tracking slow-moving objects over the United States itself."

"Like the story of the boy who cried wolf," Zhdanov murmured.

Voronin nodded. "Exactly. NORAD's air surveillance radars track unidentified objects crossing *into* North America's controlled airspace. Anything flying *over* the interior is monitored loosely, if at all, by the civilian air traffic authorities." He shrugged. "We will use this willful blindness against them. In fact, by the time the moment arrives to launch VELES, the Americans will not only avoid interfering with our operations, they will be actively encouraging them."

"Encouraging your balloon flights? Why on earth would they do such a foolish thing?" Zhdanov asked, surprised.

Voronin's slight smile grew more openly predatory. "The first step will come when you authorize me to begin covert operations inside the United States. With your permission, I intend to set up a new front organization there—one the Americans will believe to be a non-profit climate change research group."

The president's face betrayed his continuing confusion.

"The current U.S. administration is wholly committed to fighting climate change, and it actively encourages and even supports environmental organizations it sees as political allies in this struggle," Voronin explained. "Based on past experience with earlier covert operations on U.S. soil, I'm confident this means no one in the American intelligence or national security apparatus will be interested in looking too closely at a group the White House views as friendly to its interests."

Zhdanov's face cleared. "Essentially, you'll be hiding in plain sight, preparing to strike with the Americans none the wiser."

"Precisely," Voronin said with undisguised satisfaction. "In the months before we activate VELES, my operatives, posing as researchers, will conduct multiple high-altitude balloon flights. We'll use components—polyethylene balloon envelopes, flight control equipment and software, and scientific instruments—sourced entirely from American or other Western suppliers."

"So that nothing you're doing will lead back to Russia," the president quickly grasped.

Voronin nodded. "During these test flights over the continental U.S., we'll collect data on changing weather patterns, stratospheric air currents and temperatures, and dozens of other variables. The Americans will understand this effort as a normal study of climate change. What they'll miss is that the same meteorological data will greatly assist our mission planners in refining their targeting parameters."

"Clever. Very clever, Pavel," Zhdanov approved.

Voronin smiled and lowered his head, willing to let the older man believe he valued his praise. "We reap one other benefit from these routine high-altitude flights," he continued. "Watching our research balloons lift off over and over should also lull the American air traffic control observers into complacency, so that they won't see anything wrong or dangerous when our real plant disease-spreading flights take to the skies."

Zhdanov's gaze drifted back to the large digital map of the United States, which now showed whole regions glowing the pestilent green of contamination. Flickering numbers along the top of the screen showed computer-generated estimates of crops destroyed and deaths from spreading famine and the collapse of civil order. Six months out from the projected start of Voronin's operation, as diseased crops across the American heartland rotted in the fields, the predicted deaths were already in the millions and climbing fast. A thought occurred to him. He looked at Voronin. "What about famine relief efforts by America's allies? Could emergency food shipments from overseas mitigate the damage your weapons will inflict?"

Voronin shook his head. "The United States is currently the world's largest agricultural exporter. With its crops destroyed, no other combination of countries will be in any realistic position to make up the shortfall. And even if its allies were willing to ration food to their own citizens to send aid to America, the logistic challenges involved would be insurmountable. The world's most recent severe famines have affected fewer than ten million people. We will be triggering starvation among more than three hundred million."

Impressed, Zhdanov turned to Rodin. "What do you think of this? In your judgment, is it safe for us to proceed with this next phase of VELES?"

"I have to admit that the plan is excellent," he said. "And nothing in these first secret operations inside the United States carries any serious risk of exposure. The moment of truth will only come when we begin shipping stockpiles of Dr. Neminsky's weaponized spores to our field operatives."

Zhdanov nodded and made his decision. "Very well," he told Voronin. "You may begin. Set VELES fully in motion."

THIRTY

WAKKANAI HARBOR, HOKKAIDŌ PREFECTURE, JAPAN

THAT SAME TIME

Wakkanai, a small city on the northeastern tip of Hokkaidō, the northernmost and second largest of the four Japanese home islands, lay less than thirty miles from the nearest piece of Russian territory, Sakhalin Island. In Nick Flynn's view, that made it an ideal jumping-off point for their attempt to slip secretly into Russia's Far Eastern region. From the foot of the gangplank of the *Nikkō Maru*, he looked out across the harbor.

Bright lights gleamed in places, illuminating the dark water lapping gently at piers and an assortment of vessels tied up alongside wharves. Most were small seagoing fishing boats no more than sixty to eighty feet long—much too small to serve their purpose. The *Nikkō Maru* was a different story. She was the type of fishing vessel known as a seiner, one that caught fish using enormous conical nets trailed off her stern, and at nearly a hundred and sixty feet in length, she was large for her class.

"We're all set," Laura Van Horn said from behind. Flynn turned. Accompanied by a slender, middle-aged Japanese man, she was walking down the gangplank with a satisfied smile on her face. She jerked a thumb at the ship behind her. "Our cargo's secure."

Flynn followed her gesture and saw a tarped shape about the size of a Ford F-150 pickup truck lashed down to the *Nikkō Maru*'s foredeck, close to the powerful winches ordinarily used to lower and raise the ship's fishing nets. The sailors who'd helped hoist it aboard from a flatbed truck parked close by on the wharf were already dispersing to other duties.

"I've spoken to Captain Nakaya," the Japanese man, whose name was Hideki Takada, reported. "He confirms that the most recent weather forecasts look favorable. He's ready to set out whenever you are."

Flynn nodded gratefully. Takada was the head of the Quartet Directorate's Japan station. Contacted by Fox for help, he'd thrown himself wholeheartedly into coordinating this part of their operation, including arranging the charter of the *Nikkō Maru* from its corporate owners, who had assisted Four in the past. He'd also been instrumental in recruiting the crew for this voyage. Some were Quartet Directorate part-timers, agents who could be activated out of ordinary civilian life when their special skills were required for particular missions. Others, like Captain Nakaya, were retired veterans of the Maritime Self-Defense Force, Japan's navy. Before joining Four, Takada had been a high-ranking officer in the Defense Intelligence Headquarters, Japan's equivalent of the Pentagon's Defense Intelligence Agency, the DIA. He'd pulled strings left in place from his years of government service to find the reliable and thoroughly discreet men and women Flynn and Van Horn would need to attempt this high-risk endeavor.

"Thank you, sir," Flynn said. "We really appreciate everything you've done for us."

"It's Hideki. Not, sir," Takada reminded him gently. It was a point he'd made at their first meeting the day before. Four had no rigid hierarchy, preferring to operate as a group of equals wherever possible. Responsibilities, including command authority, were assigned based on talent, experience, and specialized skills, not strict seniority.

Flynn nodded. That was one of the things that had attracted him to the Quartet Directorate in the first place. During his service with the U.S. Air Force, he'd never played the game of kissing the asses of superior officers just because they outranked him . . . which was probably one of the reasons he'd found himself in such hot water when the

CIA came looking for a convenient scapegoat for its own screwups. He grinned. Nick Flynn, Principled Rebel, sure sounded better than Nick Flynn, Too Stubborn For His Own Good.

"Besides, no thanks are necessary," Takada continued. "My people and I fully understand the importance of your operation. Voronin and his Raven Syndicate are a menace to us all. The sooner you finish them, the safer we will be." He glanced back at the ship with more than a hint of longing. "You know, I almost wish I could go with you." His teeth flashed in a quick smile. "It should be quite entertaining."

Flynn believed him. Four's Japan Station chief was quiet and thoroughly professional on the surface. Still, he and Van Horn had already figured out that the other man had hidden depths, including an almost piratical dash and an equally avid inclination to take whatever chances were required to complete a mission. In fact, over dinner and drinks the night before, Takada had proudly traced his ancestry back to Japan's ancient seafaring clans, the *kaizoku*, who were either pirates or traders as circumstances dictated. With that in mind, it was no surprise that he'd ultimately chosen the more freewheeling Quartet Directorate over the duller bureaucratic confines of Japan's Defense Intelligence Headquarters. "Entertaining might not be the word I'd have chosen," he said carefully.

"Thrilling? Exhilarating?" Van Horn suggested with obvious amusement. "Am I getting warmer?"

"Not exactly," Flynn said. "Much as we'd like to have you along," he said to the other man, "whatever you can do to run interference for us here could make all the difference. If things don't go as planned at the airport tomorrow, all the luck and skill in the world won't help us."

Takada nodded more seriously. "You can count on me," he assured them. "I will make sure everything gets off the ground there without a hitch."

"Then we'd best get aboard," Flynn said with an inquiring glance at Van Horn.

She nodded. "Yep. Our gear's all stowed. And we've got a tight schedule to keep. Places to boldly go. Bad guys to shoot. New infinitives to split."

"Please do not rub it in," Takada said. "Remember, we also serve who stand and wait to distract excessively curious government officials."

Laughing, they both thanked him again, this time offering him a slight bow. Since they were colleagues in Four, it was appropriate to use the brief dip of head and shoulders that represented the "bow between equals." Takada returned the gesture, but then insisted on shaking their hands warmly. It was a custom he'd picked up over years of working closely with Westerners.

With a final goodbye wave, Flynn and Van Horn turned and strode up the gangplank. They made their way aft to the *Nikkō Maru*'s raised pilothouse.

Captain Koichi Nakaya, short and powerfully built with a shock of close-cropped white hair and a trim beard, turned to them. "You are ready to depart?"

Flynn nodded. "We are, captain."

"Very well," Nakaya said gravely. He picked up a walkie-talkie and rattled off a quick series of orders in Japanese. The ship's diesel-electric engine came to life with a deep, throaty rumble, turning over at low RPMs. Pale gray exhaust eddied away from the single short funnel behind the pilothouse. Satisfied by what he saw on his repeater gauges, the captain issued more orders.

Through the windows, Flynn saw sailors moving toward the fore and aft mooring lines holding them to the wharf. Others gathered near the anchor winch. He heard Nakaya snap a final series of crisp commands into his walkie-talkie. The other man's years of experience as a naval officer were apparent both in his confidence and in the disciplined, professional way his sailors sprang immediately into action. There was none of the easygoing behavior he'd noticed aboard the other fishing vessels homeported at Wakkanai.

Moments later, with her anchor raised and lines coiled aboard, the *Nikkō Maru* edged away from the wharf, turned slowly, and headed out of the harbor—steaming northeast across Sōya Bay at fifteen knots. Flynn and Van Horn stayed in the pilothouse, watching everything with interest. It took about an hour for the ship to clear the headland of Cape

Sōya and turn east into the La Pérouse Strait between Hokkaidō and Russian-owned Sakhalin Island.

It was then that Nakaya handed the wheel over to his junior deck officer and stepped back. He turned to the two Americans. "We have now left the territorial waters of Japan. Welcome to the open ocean."

Flynn glanced out the pilothouse windows in surprise. They were still well within sight of the coast. The lights of fishing villages and country homes twinkled against the dark silhouettes of low, forested hills. At this point, the strait was less than twenty-seven miles wide. From the heights of Cape Sōya on a clear day, it was possible to see Russian territory. "Come again?" he asked. "I'm no sailor, but this looks a little bit crowded to count as open ocean."

"It is more a matter of legality than of actuality," Nakaya explained. "We Japanese only claim ownership out to three nautical miles here. This enables American warships and submarines carrying nuclear-armed missiles and bombs to transit the passage without violating our long-standing prohibition on such weapons." He smiled wryly. "And so, you see, we remain true to our deeply felt convictions . . . without being idiotic about it."

"Smart thinking," Flynn agreed.

Nakaya shrugged. "The practice preserves a comfortable illusion, which is good enough for most of my countrymen." He nodded toward the door. "You should both get some food and rest now. We stay on this course for another seven hours. That will take us east into the Sea of Okhotsk, well out onto the open ocean in truth, rather than just legal fiction."

"What happens then?" Flynn asked.

"We turn north and reduce our speed to ten knots," Nakaya replied. "If all goes well, that should bring us to the waypoint you've selected at the correct time. We will be roughly ninety nautical miles off the Russian coast shortly after sunset tomorrow."

"And then shit gets real," Van Horn commented.

The captain nodded gravely. "Yes, Ms. Van Horn," he agreed. "That is true indeed."

TEMPORARY CHECKPOINT,
ON THE RUSSO-BELARUSIAN BORDER
A SHORT TIME LATER

Tadeusz Kossak, smartly dressed in an expensive, hand-tailored business suit and stylish designer sunglasses, paced irritably back and forth beside a luxury Mercedes S-class sedan with Belarussian license plates. Wade Vucovich, dressed far more simply in the off-the-rack blazer, button-down shirt, slacks, and plain black tie appropriate for a driver who might also double as a bodyguard, stood a little apart with his arms folded patiently. To all appearances, he was listening while his "employer" fumed about the "ridiculous" holdup they were currently experiencing. In reality, Kossak's expressive behavior was intended largely to divert attention from his companion, whose Russian language skills weren't up to prolonged questioning.

Still muttering curses, the Pole glanced around at their surroundings. It was already late in the afternoon, with the sun settling toward the west. Closer at hand, orange cones were strung across the M1 Motorway toward Smolensk and Moscow—diverting all eastbound traffic from Belarus to this abruptly reopened border crossing station. Every vehicle, without any exceptions, was thoroughly searched before being passed through. Besides the Border Guard officers and enlisted personnel manning this post, he noted the presence of at least a platoon-strength unit of regular soldiers together with their wheeled fighting vehicles. He frowned. The Russians weren't screwing around. They were ready to apply overwhelming force at the slightest sign of trouble.

Impatiently, Kossak swung back to the Mercedes. He uttered a new litany of nearly silent profanity as he watched one Border Guard methodically paw through the sedan's open trunk. At the same time, another poked and prodded around its front and rear seats and then dug into the glovebox. When at last they finished and flashed thumbs-up signals to the officer supervising their search, he muttered, "Finally, by God!"

He turned immediately to the officer with his hand held out for their forged Belarussian passports. "So much for our so-called customs union," he growled. On paper, citizens of the Eurasian Customs Union—those of Russia, Belarus, Kazakhstan, Armenia, and Kyrgyzstan—were supposed to be exempt from customs inspections and most border controls when traveling from one member state to another.

The Russian shrugged. "I regret the delay," he said, perfunctorily and with obvious insincerity as he returned their passports. "But this is a necessary precaution. We've received serious warnings about possible terrorist incidents."

Kossak sniffed in disbelief. "Oh? Involving what? Wives, girlfriends, and grandmothers?" He waved a contemptuous hand toward a separate section of the checkpoint where all couples, women traveling alone, and even family groups were being subjected to far more intense screening and interrogation.

The Border Guard officer only shrugged again. "Moscow makes the rules, Mr. Manaev," he said. "We simply enforce them."

Minutes later, once the two Quartet Directorate agents were safely inside the Mercedes and speeding onward toward Moscow, still 270 miles away, Vucovich let out his breath in a huge, relieved sigh. "Jesus, Tad," he said, glancing back over his shoulder at the Pole. "I'm really glad we weren't carrying any contraband or weapons this time around. Those guys weren't screwing around."

Kossak nodded. "True enough, Wade." His mouth tightened. "Ordinarily, I would be very happy that our earlier activities have spooked these Russian bastards. But now I admit that the timing is unfortunate."

Vucovich turned back to the road. "Yeah, unfortunate is right. Which kind of makes me wonder how exactly we're supposed to nail that MF'er Voronin without any guns or explosives and such."

"A fair question," Kossak admitted. "But how does that old English poem go? 'Ours is not to reason why—'"

"'Ours is but to do or die,'" Vucovich finished the quote for him. "I had a teacher in high school who made us read it. And that one line stuck in my head." His mouth turned down. "Because it sounded really stupid to me. General Patton had it right. You win by making the other poor dumb son of a bitch die for his country."

Kossak nodded in approval. "Not quite as noble, perhaps. But infinitely preferable." He shrugged his shoulders. "In this case, we hope that our own courageous leader knows what he is doing."

"Captain Flynn will come through for us," Vucovich said stoutly. "He always does."

"Of that I have no doubt, Wade," Kossak agreed.

THIRTY-ONE

MASHTAKOVO CHECKPOINT,
ON RUSSIA'S BORDER WITH KAZAKHSTAN

THAT SAME TIME

With a Kazakh-produced Camel Blue cigarette dangling nonchalantly from his mouth, Shannon Cooke cranked the steering wheel of his KamAZ big rig hard over. "Here we go," he muttered to Cole Hynes, who was seated next to him in the cab. Both men had stripped down to sleeveless undershirts in the summer heat. Neither had shaved for several days.

The heavy truck swung slowly off the two-lane highway and onto a side road that ran through the Russian Border Guard and customs station. Its white concrete buildings were the only man-made structures in sight. Elsewhere, the treeless Central Asian steppes spread to the far horizons, flat and almost entirely featureless.

The setting sun hung very low in the west, and Cooke had to squint against its red-tinged glare as he followed the signs directing them to a high bay vehicle inspection shed. A bored-looking Border Guard holding a clipboard waved their truck inside and then signaled them to stop.

The Russian waited until Cooke stubbed his cigarette out in the dashboard ashtray. Then he nodded at the long, five-axle dump trailer they were towing. "What's your load?" he asked.

"Slag and ash," Cooke said with an indifferent shrug. "Making a haul to a cement plant outside Ryazan."

At this, the Border Guard looked even more bored than before. Slag and ash, among the byproducts of smelting iron and steel, were a common Kazakh export to Russia. When blended as an aggregate into ordinary cement, the powdery, granular materials created a more durable and longer-lasting form of Portland Cement, which was useful for all types of construction projects. For a moment, it was obvious that the Russian was tempted to overlook the rest of the inspection process and just wave them on through. But a quick glance over his shoulder showed that an eagle-eyed NCO was observing him.

The guard sighed and jotted down the truck's license number on his clipboard. "Wait here," he told Cooke. "I have to do a visual inspection." He trudged back down to the dump trailer. Then, grumbling under his breath, he scrambled up onto one of the trailer's large tires. He clung to the side of the trailer with one hand, and then raised up on his boots just high enough to lift the tarp tied down across its cargo bed. Peering underneath, he saw only a layer of dark gray ash mixed with brownish chunks of iron ore slag. A breeze stirred up some of the ash, and the Russian sneezed violently. He shook his head, dropped the tarp back into place, and jumped down to the ground. Swiping at his nose, he came back to the cab and scribbled across the rest of the form on his clipboard. Finished, he flipped it over. "Show them your papers, guys," he said with a jerk of his head toward the adjacent passport control office, already turning away to move down the line toward the next waiting big rig.

Cooke and Hynes climbed down out of the truck cab and sauntered over to the office. Its scuffed linoleum floors, banged-up counters, scratched plexiglass partitions, and faded official posters were a testimony to the sameness of cheaply built government buildings worldwide. The Mashtakovo passport office had a function. No one in authority wanted to spend any more on its utilitarian form than was necessary.

The two Quartet Directorate agents joined the end of a line of others waiting to show their documents. One by one, those ahead of them were called up to one of the counter windows manned by Border Guard officers. When it was finally their turn, they handed over their Kazakh passports as demanded. The names on their forged identity documents were Russian. Out of nineteen million people in the Central Asian republic, four million were ethnic Russians.

The Border Guard officer behind the window inspected their passport pictures and their faces closely for a few moments—comparing them against other images on his computer screen. Cooke was sure those were grainy surveillance photos of Flynn and Van Horn.

Apparently satisfied, the Russian stamped their passports and tossed them back. "You carrying any drugs," he asked blandly.

Without much expression, Cooke shook his head, as did Hynes.

"Vodka?"

This time Cooke grinned. "A few bottles," he admitted. "For personal medicinal use."

The Border Guard officer snorted. "Just stay off the sauce while you're on the road," he warned as he waved them on their way. "The police aren't going easy on drunks after accidents these days."

Cooke sketched a salute as he turned toward the door with Hynes on his heels. On their way out, both men noted that non-ethnic Russians and all female travelers were being questioned much more closely. They exchanged glances. Flynn and Van Horn would have been in trouble if they'd attempted a crossing here. There were limits to how long any disguise could hold up under prolonged inspection.

As soon as they climbed back into their truck and shut the doors, Hynes slumped back against the seat. "Okay, that wasn't a whole lot of fun. But it went easier than I thought it would," he said, relieved.

As he put the big KamAZ into gear and pulled out of the inspection shed, Cooke shot the younger man a sidelong grin. "Now, Cole," he said kindly. "I'm just guessing here, but I'm betting you won't be talking about how *easy* things are once I hand you a shovel and tell you to dig all of our crap out of the back of this rig."

"No, sir," Hynes agreed with a short, barking laugh. "I don't believe I will be. That's definitely going to be one hell of a messy, back-breaking job." The cases containing all the special equipment, weapons, clothing, and other gear their action team would need in Moscow were buried in the dump trailer they were towing—concealed about four feet down under its layers of compacted slag and ash.

ABOARD THE *NIKKŌ MARU*, IN THE SEA OF OKHOTSK
THE NEXT NIGHT

The sun had set, leaving the fishing vessel in almost total darkness. On its foredeck, the glow from deck lamps fell across its power winches and the tarped, pickup truck–sized shape lashed there. The only other sources of illumination visible, besides a pale quarter-moon high in the west, were the ship's red and green marine navigation beacons and a small, bright white light fixed to the masthead.

Nick Flynn came down the short ladder from the pilothouse and moved forward across the deck to join Laura Van Horn at the port railing. In the diffuse radiance from the nearest lamp, he could see that her hair was now dyed auburn. His own dark hair was a much lighter shade of brown. Both alterations were part of the preliminaries required for their new disguises. She was gazing out across the surface of the sea. It was calm, ruffled only by a few shallow waves rising and falling on their way east toward the distant shores of Kamchatka. "The weather looks good," he reported. "Captain Nakaya says both the wind conditions and sea state are close to ideal for our purposes."

"Now there's a welcome change," Van Horn said, turning to him with a quiet laugh. "I thought we might have to try launching in a gale for tradition's sake."

Flynn nodded, remembering how they'd first met. Her crippled C-130J had made an emergency landing in the middle of a blizzard at his last U.S. Air Force duty station, an isolated radar post in northern Alaska, right on the edge of the frozen Beaufort Sea. Next had come their first critical Quartet Directorate mission together, where his assault team had been forced to make a daring, high-altitude jump into the trailing edge of a fierce North Atlantic storm. "For small favors, I am devoutly grateful," he replied. "I've had enough snow and ice and howling winds to last a whole lifetime."

"Me, too," she agreed as her gaze returned to the ocean. "You know the Russians use this area, the Sea of Okhotsk, as a bastion for their missile submarines, right?" she said thoughtfully. "Could be a real short ride for us if one of them pokes its periscope up for a look-see at just the wrong time."

Flynn eyed her closely. "That's not exactly a pleasant hypothetical. You feeling all right?"

Van Horn shrugged. "Just a little antsy is all. Must be pre-mission jitters. I'll be all right on the actual night."

"Um, Laura?" he said carefully. "This *is* the night."

She smiled up at him. "See? I feel better already."

Flynn put his arm around her. "Anyway," he continued. "As it happens, I did run the numbers on the possibility of encountering one of those Russian missile subs."

"Really?"

Seeing the amused look Van Horn gave him, he shrugged defensively. "Hey, I like to be thorough when planning an operation. Sue me." He gestured out across the darkened ocean. "Anyhow, the Sea of Okhotsk contains around six hundred thousand square miles of open water. And the Russians currently have a total of four SSBNs operational with their Pacific Fleet . . . of which, maybe one is on patrol at any given moment. So considering how little of the ocean can be seen from a raised periscope—"

She shook her head in wonder. "You seriously pulled together all these numbers? Honestly?"

Flynn grinned. "It was a twenty-hour flight from Orlando to the airport at Sapporo. And you know I never sleep well on planes. I got bored." He moved on. "The upshot is that the odds work out to about two hundred thousand to one in our favor."

"That good, huh?"

"For submarines, anyway. Just don't push me for the odds on any other aspect of this mission," he said.

"Wouldn't dream of it," Van Horn assured him.

Flynn nodded. "Good decision." He looked her in the eyes. "So? You ready to do this?"

"Roger that," she answered, and gave him a short, sharp hug. "Let's move."

While Flynn headed back to the pilothouse to alert Nakaya and his crew, Van Horn took out her satellite phone and connected it to a constellation orbiting high overhead. She scrolled through a menu of the message presets she'd loaded before setting out on this sea voyage and chose one at the top: PLAY BALL. The phone beeped softly, indicating her text had been transmitted. Less than a minute later, a reply arrived: GAME ON.

Committed now, she moved toward the tarped shape on the *Nikkō Maru*'s foredeck. Moments later, a group of Japanese sailors arrived. Under her supervision, they stripped away the tarp—revealing the shape of a SeaMax M-22 FW amphibious light sport aircraft with its wings folded back for easier transportation.

Unhurriedly, Van Horn moved around the aircraft, conducting a detailed inspection to make sure that nothing had been damaged while the SeaMax was in transit—first in the hold of a cargo aircraft bound from the United States to Wakkanai's regional airport and then during this short trip aboard ship. When its wings were folded, the aircraft was remarkably compact, but even when they were fully deployed, it would still be a very small, lightweight flying machine. Powered by a one-hundred horsepower, four-cylinder Rotax 912ULS engine mounted in a pusher configuration above a strut-braced high wing, the M-22 was only a little over six feet high and barely longer than a minivan. Its fuselage was no wider than an adult human's outstretched arms. Fully fueled, the little seaplane's maximum takeoff weight was just a bit over 1,300 pounds.

Flynn came back onto the foredeck, carrying their gear. He stopped, watching while Nakaya's crewmen slowly unfolded the tiny M-22's wings and horizontal tail stabilizers and locked them into position. Turning to Van Horn with a look of mock dismay, he said, "Whoa, whoa. Hold up here a sec. Where's the rest of this thing? Did we leave pieces behind on the wharf at Wakkanai by accident?"

She wagged her finger in reproof. "No bitching allowed, Nick. I showed you the full specs on this bird, remember? And you signed off." She patted the sleek fuselage. "Don't pay any attention to the bad man, baby. He's just a mean, old gravel cruncher," she murmured, using the U.S. Air Force slang for an officer who wasn't a trained pilot. She turned back to him. "Now, repeat after me: 'The SeaMax is one sweet, flying machine. And this is going to be fun.'"

Flynn felt an eyebrow go up. "Fun?"

Van Horn shrugged her shoulders. "I say 'fun.' Or maybe 'thrilling' is a better word. But you'd probably define what we're about to try as 'gut-wrenchingly hazardous.' Anyway, it's all just a question of perspective." She smiled crookedly. "Have a little faith, cowboy. This is a magnificent, mother-loving aircraft, and it's going to be okay."

Knowing when he was beaten, Flynn matched her expression. "Yes, ma'am. Whatever you say."

She shook her head. "You can't fool me. I know you're only being so agreeable because your life is going to be completely in my hands for the next several hours."

"Probably so," he agreed. "And very attractive hands they are too," he confided.

Her eyes gleamed. "Flattery, Nick? Well, it'll probably get you somewhere." She patted the amphibious plane again. "Which, in this case, should be deep into Russian territory long before the sun comes up."

THIRTY-TWO

WAKKANAI AIRPORT,
HOKKAIDŌ PREFECTURE, JAPAN

THAT SAME TIME

Hideki Takada, head of Four's Japan Station, stepped out onto the outer walkway around the top of Wakkanai Airport's glass-enclosed control tower. He leaned against the metal railing and looked out across the field. Bright lights illuminated the 7,200-foot-long runway below, creating a striking contrast with the shadowy waters of Sōya Bay on the other side. To the west, distant white, orange, green, and red lights twinkled along the shore, showing where the outskirts of Wakkanai met the coast road. Beyond that, wooded hills, tinted faintly silver by the light of the quarter-moon still high in the sky, rose to form a natural amphitheater around the small city, pinning it against the sea. Ordinarily, Takada, who had something of a poetic soul like many Japanese, would have savored this nocturnal joining of natural beauty with man's designs. This evening, though, he had more pressing matters at hand.

He raised his binoculars and focused on a portable trailer in a grass field between the runway and the control tower. A pair of small satellite communications dishes topped it. The trailer had been flown in aboard the same cargo aircraft that had delivered the SeaMax M-22 light

amphibious plane now aboard the *Nikkō Maru*. It had been accompanied by yet another small flying machine—one currently positioned a
mile away at the far end of the runway.

Any minute now, Takada thought, tensing slightly. Laura Van Horn's
coded text from the fishing vessel far out at sea had been the trigger for
the next critical moves here. Given the problematic constraints imposed
by flight times and fuel, everything at the airport had to proceed exactly
as planned. There was no significant room for error or delay. Suddenly,
a woman's voice came through his radio headset. "*Wakkanai Tower, this
is Hermes Nine-Zero-Zero, request departure from runway zero-eight per
approved flight plan.*"

"*Hermes Nine-Zero-Zero, Wakkanai Tower,*" he heard the controller
stationed in the tower behind him reply just as coolly. "*Winds light at
zero-nine-zero, cleared for takeoff, runway zero-eight. Have a good flight.*"

"*Thank you, Wakkanai, rolling now.*"

Takada smiled in relief. In person, former U.S. Air Force staff sergeant Sara McCulloch was a petite redhead with a wicked sense of
humor. But when she was seated at a remote piloting station and controlling one of her beloved unmanned aerial vehicles, or UAVs, she was
a consummate professional, utterly calm and absolutely focused. No one
listening to her would have suspected tonight's exercise was anything
but the routine demonstration flight it had been billed as.

He swung his binoculars to the right and followed the drone Mc-
Cullough was now controlling as it accelerated down the runway. To
an untutored eye, the small aircraft would have looked something like a
pregnant praying mantis—an impression created by its bulbous domed
nose; the streamlined cargo container slung under its long, thin fuselage; a pair of broad, narrow wings; an aft-mounted pusher propeller;
and finally, three down-angled tail fins.

Takada's mouth tightened. The positioning of those tail fins was
unfortunate, the one glaring hole in the clever cover story he'd put together to explain away this flight. The Quartet Directorate's heads of
station assumed many different roles to conceal their real activities.
In his case, he chaired a consulting firm rumored to have close ties to

major defense contractors in Japan and abroad. Acting in that capacity, he'd sold Wakkanai's airport director and staff on the idea that he was currently assisting an Israeli aviation company that was interested in entering the Japanese market.

Supposedly, this evening's discreet flight was intended to exhibit the capabilities of a Hermes 900 drone equipped for maritime surveillance—a mission of great importance to an island nation like Japan so dependent on overseas trade. That was made more believable because other countries, ranging from Iceland to those of the European Union and the Philippines, were already flying Hermes 900s for the same purpose. Unfortunately, a real Hermes 900 UAV would have had two *up-angled* tail fins, rather than three down-angled ones. The drone speeding down the runway, though otherwise almost indistinguishable from the Israeli design, was actually an American-made General Atomics MQ-1 Predator. Four had managed to secretly acquire this remotely piloted aircraft several years before when the U.S. Customs and Border Patrol retired its Predator surveillance fleet. And Takeda's primary concern right down to this moment was making sure that no one with an annoying eye for detail spotted the anomaly and started asking difficult questions.

With a muffled whine from its pusher propeller, the Predator lifted off and climbed into the night sky. It banked sharply right and flew out across Sōya Bay. Within minutes, the UAV was invisible in the darkness.

Takada breathed out. He'd done his part. This phase of the mission was safely underway. Whether or not it succeeded or ended in utter disaster now rested on the slender shoulders of Sara McCulloch, and equally on those of Laura Van Horn.

IN THE SEA OF OKHOTSK
A SHORT TIME LATER

Nick Flynn felt the SeaMax M-22 lurch and sway slightly from side to side as it was slowly hoisted off the *Nikkō Maru*'s deck by one of the powerful winches ordinarily used to deploy and stream the ship's heavy fishing nets. When they were high enough for the seaplane's floats to clear the starboard side railing, the direction of travel changed. Now the winch spun, swinging them away from the ship, out over the open sea. The rocking intensified. He was tempted to close his eyes, but suddenly sensed that would be a really bad idea. Motion sickness wasn't usually a problem for him. Still, this sensation of sitting in the open cockpit of a very small aircraft as it dangled from a cable and swung up and side-ways—all while still connected to a vessel that was also gently rolling and pitching in light seas—was unsettling.

The winch motor slowed and then stopped. They were far enough out from the *Nikkō Maru*'s starboard side to avoid any risk of slamming into the hull. He glanced to his left where Laura Van Horn had her head craned out over the side of the cockpit, checking the sea below.

"Looks good to me, Captain," she reported into her headset mike. "You can have your guys lower away when they're ready."

"*Affirmative, Ms. Van Horn*," Nakaya radioed back. "*Stand by.*" He snapped a command in Japanese to the winch crew.

Instantly, the machine's motor whirred again, this time lowering the attached amphibious plane so gently that it touched the surface of the water without more than a tiny splash as it slapped into an oncom-ing wave. The aircraft settled deeper in the water. Its nose rose and fell slowly. Back on the ship, the winch operator ran his motor for a few seconds more, paying out some slack in the cable.

Moving gingerly in the cockpit's tight confines, Van Horn swiveled to face aft and climbed up on her seat to reach back along the fuselage. Working quickly, she detached the clamps holding them to the cable. It reeled back in and vanished overhead. Freed now, the SM-22 bobbed up and down on the waves. The *Nikkō Maru* gradually drew ahead of them.

She wriggled around, dropped back into her seat, and donned her safety harness. Then she glanced at Flynn. "Okay, now that I'm reason-ably confident we're not about to sink, let's get this baby sealed up." Obeying, he reached up and pulled the aircraft's large bubble canopy closed and then latched it.

While he strapped himself in, Van Horn's hands danced across her instrument panel, readying the seaplane for flight. Displays and gauges lit up as they powered on. She tapped a button in the center of the panel. One small light turned red. "Our transponder is off," she confirmed.

Flynn nodded. On this covert attempt to penetrate hostile airspace, one of the last things they wanted was a simpleminded radio transponder primed to blurt out their location and identity at the slightest brush of a radar beam. Of course, flying without a functioning transponder was technically illegal for any civilian aircraft operating in controlled airspace. But considering how many other rules and regulations they were about to break, the overall effect was probably comparable to adding a charge of jaywalking to grand larceny and arson.

"Ready for your owl eyes?" he asked, rummaging behind his seat to grab their night vision goggles.

Van Horn took the pair he presented with a low, husky laugh. "Well, I could try this stunt by guess and by Braille—" she offered.

"No," Flynn said firmly. "Crashing is strictly contraindicated." He settled his goggles over his radio headset and switched them on. His surroundings brightened immediately, turning nearly as clear as day, thanks to the image intensifiers that multiplied whatever ambient light there was. But one effect of that was the lack of any distinct color. Everything in sight—the waves rolling across the sea, the *Nikkō Maru*, and the confines of their cockpit—appeared only in monochrome shades of black, white, and gray.

Van Horn donned her own night vision gear, then rechecked her displays. Satisfied by what she saw, she reached up to the overhead panel in the center of the bubble canopy and punched the ignition switch. Their four-cylinder Rotax 912ULS engine coughed to life. The aircraft's three-bladed pusher propeller began turning on the high wing above and behind them. Her eyes flicked right and left, scanning her readouts one final time. "Oil pressure and engine temperature both look good," she said aloud. With a glance at Flynn, she added, "We're ready to roll."

"Roll?" he countered.

"Okay, bounce might be more accurate," she admitted. Her right hand settled on the center stick, while her left hand gripped the throttle lever located just below the canopy. "Hang tight, compadre. Here we go." Suiting her actions to her words, Van Horn pushed her throttle forward a notch. The engine responded smoothly. She fed in more power. Seawater splashed across the nose as the M-22 motored across the surface—bouncing a little and skipping across the top of the low waves as it picked up speed. A plume of white foam and propeller-whipped spray lengthened behind its streamlined hull.

After a takeoff run of around five hundred feet, the light seaplane reached a speed of forty knots and, with a minor jolt, broke free of the water and climbed into the air. Van Horn toggled her stick, leveling out just two hundred feet above the ocean. She caught up with the *Nikkō Maru* and banked into a slow orbit around the ship, noting how she needed to apply rudder, as well as use her stick. The little seaplane shuddered and yawed slightly as it hit small pockets of turbulence. She nodded to herself. This aircraft required constant control inputs because of its high, wing-mounted engine, wing struts, and floats. It wasn't a smooth flier. Instead, it danced through the air, and its pilot needed to be ready to join the dance.

Confident that she had the feel of the aircraft, she broke out of her slow circle and headed west for the distant, unseen coast of Sakhalin Island, throttling up until they were hitting nearly one hundred knots. Behind them, the *Nikkō Maru* altered her own course and increased speed, steaming south back toward Japan.

They were now on their own.

THIRTY-THREE

LOW OVER SAKHALIN ISLAND, RUSSIA

SOME TIME LATER

The SeaMax wove along a narrow, winding ravine, rolling first to the right, then to the left, and then back again along its trace. Steep, forested slopes climbed high above the low-flying aircraft, just as they had from almost the first moment it crossed the island's east coast. Sakhalin was nearly six hundred nautical miles long from south to north, but only twelve miles wide at its narrowest point, and it was largely a mass of mountains, ridges, and hills. Spring-fed shallow streams cut these ranges of higher ground into innumerable gullies and gulches. Here and there, wider valleys had been carved by bigger rivers that generally flowed north or south along the island's spine before they turned to find outlets to the sea.

Flynn gripped the edges of his seat as Van Horn banked sharply from side to side to avoid smashing into the wooded heights hemming them in. Under her night vision goggles, her face was a mask of total concentration. The center stick in her right hand was in constant motion as she went from one tight, rolling turn to the next. Her feet continuously worked the SeaMax's pedals, applying left or right rudder as needed. One second, he'd see near-vertical, tree-studded slopes flashing past just outside the bubble canopy, seemingly close enough to reach out and touch.

Moments later, he'd be staring nearly straight down into the churning waters of the stream they were currently following as it tumbled and snaked its way west toward lower ground.

It was like riding the world's most exciting roller-coaster, Flynn decided with an inward gulp—except for the fact that they weren't on rails, and roller-coaster cars didn't go spinning off end over end to smash into rocks and trees with a fatal burst of fuel-fed flame if the ride operator made the slightest error. The fact that they were making this wild, death-defying, low-altitude flight for good reasons didn't make it any less gut-wrenching.

It all came down to their need to avoid detection. The seaward approaches to Russia's Far East were shielded by overlapping layers of air surveillance and air defense radars—radars that were, in turn, tied to regiments of fighter aircraft and surface-to-air missile batteries. Penetrating those defenses was possible for advanced stealth aircraft like America's B-2 Spirit bombers and its F-22 Raptor and F-35 Lightning II fighters. Doing the same thing in a civilian light sport aircraft, whose straight, strut-braced wing and cruciform tail configuration rendered it about as stealthy as a zebra trying to hide in the middle of a litter of Dalmatian puppies, was a much more challenging task.

What Van Horn was doing now involved fundamentals of basic physics. The radio waves emitted by ground-based air surveillance and tracking radars could not penetrate solid masses of stone and earth. To avoid being spotted, you either had to fly very low—while also keeping far enough away from any active radar to stay below its horizon—or you needed to fly a carefully planned course that maximized the masking effect of rugged terrain. She was employing both tactics on this critical flight.

Trying to navigate through Sakhalin's maze of mountains, razor-edged ridges, and twisting watercourses would have been challenging enough in an advanced military aircraft equipped with sophisticated computer navigation systems and terrain-following radar linked to a heads-up display. Making the same journey in a light sport plane without any navigation aids beyond a GPS-linked digital map was an order of magnitude more difficult. Only her tremendous skill as a pilot and her uncanny ability to anticipate danger and react quickly gave them any chance to survive . . . let alone succeed.

Flynn glanced in Van Horn's direction. Sweat streaked her face. Her firm jaw was set. But the fingertips of her right hand appeared relaxed on the stick. That was a mark of her experience, he realized. A rookie pilot trying a stunt like this would probably end up clutching his stick with a rictus grip—and likely over-control the aircraft into a crash.

He felt the M-22 roll back to wings level. Ahead through the canopy, he could see that the ravine they were following narrowed sharply as it cut through a belt of rock that was harder and denser than the limestone, sandstone, and other, softer soils that formed most of Sakhalin Island. The stream that had cut this gorge over millions of years dropped from ledge to ledge in a cascade of small waterfalls and rapids. Spray, gray in his night vision gear, splashed high across rock faces. He swallowed hard. All his confidence suddenly vanished. They weren't going to fit through that gap. Or rather, he suspected, they would, but only until the ravine jinked unexpectedly in a different direction. What happened next would be bad, as in "Star Wars X-Wing fighter caroming off the walls of the Death Star trench and exploding in a ball of fire" levels of bad.

"Uh, Laura . . ." Flynn said faintly.

Ignoring him, she held her course for several seconds, but then pulled back sharply on the stick and went to full power. The little seaplane responded immediately, clawing up through the air to clear the rocky escarpment barring their path. Even with the one hundred horsepower Rotax engine doing its best, their airspeed bled off fast. Before the SeaMax could stall out, she dropped the nose, practically shaved the tops of the fir trees lining the crest, and then descended almost straight down the gentler slope on the other side of the ridge, picking up speed on the way.

Flynn breathed out in relief. They were through the central range of mountains and coming out onto a narrow coastal plain. Tiny specks of light far off to his right pinpointed a small fishing village on Sakhalin's west coast. Through the canopy, he could make out a large body of water stretching as far as his assisted eyes could see to the north and south. They were approaching the Tartar Strait, which separated the long island from Russia's mainland.

Freed for now from the need to focus so intently on avoiding terrain obstacles, Van Horn glanced across the small cockpit. "Is there a problem, Nick?" she asked innocently. "Because I think maybe you were about to say something back there? Just before we *didn't* hit that cliff? Which is kind of weird, actually, because I'm pretty sure you know this isn't my first nap-of-the-earth rodeo."

He reddened slightly, suddenly relieved that their night vision gear only revealed shades of light and dark. "*Mea culpa*," he murmured contritely. "*Mea maxima culpa.*"

"*Te absolvo*," she responded with a quick grin.

"Now you know Latin, too?"

Van Horn laughed. "Saw it in a movie once." As soon as they crossed the coast, she altered course to the northwest and steadied out at around a hundred feet above the waves. They flew on into darkness.

Flynn kept busy now scanning the horizon ahead of them. The SeaMax wasn't equipped with radar or radar warning receivers, so they were reduced to the Mark I Human Eyeball to detect possible threats. Short of a miracle, that wouldn't do them much good if they encountered Russian aircraft on patrol, but one of his rules—taught long ago by his mother, who was as fierce as she was loving—was that bitching about what you didn't have was a complete waste of time and energy. You did your best with what you had, and if you sat idly by on your ass and whined instead, well, that was entirely on you.

He sat upright in his seat, suddenly spotting faint lights out on the horizon to their north. "Contact, contact, contact," he snapped to Van Horn. "Lights low at our three o'clock, some ways off. I can't make out if the lights are stationary or moving slowly. Not aircraft, I'd guess, but those could be Russian helicopters."

She leaned past him to take a look for herself. "That's a ship," she said with confidence. "A big one." She pushed the stick forward. The little seaplane dove, nosing toward the ocean's surface until it practically skimmed the waves. The lights vanished over the edge of their suddenly narrowed horizon.

"A ship?"

Van Horn nodded. "Probably the Vanino-Kholmsk train ferry."

Flynn considered that. Half a million people lived on Sakhalin Island, and everything they couldn't produce on their own had to come by sea. The ferries shuttled dozens of rail cars full of goods between the mainland and the island. Unfortunately, the ships didn't follow any fixed schedule, departing on their half-day to day-long voyages whenever the weather and the availability of cargo dictated. Given their unpredictability, encountering one of the ferries at sea was a definite prospect, but there were other, less appealing possibilities. "Is there some reason you don't think that was a Russian Navy destroyer or corvette transiting the strait on its way to or from Vladivostok?" he asked quietly.

She snorted. "You kidding? We were maybe only fifteen miles out when I dove for the deck. At that range, a warship's air search radars would have been lighting up our ass in seconds." Her eyes roved the horizon. "And we'd be eating missiles right about . . . now."

Nothing happened. They continued flying without incident, juddering slightly in the gentle winds pushing waves eastward across the strait.

"So your reasoning is: We're not dead; therefore, it wasn't an enemy warship?" Flynn asked after a moment longer.

Van Horn nodded. "Pretty much."

"Hmmph," Flynn said, chewing on her logic. Then he shrugged. "Okay, that works for me."

They arrowed onward, still practically hugging the waves. After several minutes, Van Horn leaned forward, eyeing the GPS-linked map open on the cockpit's right-hand multifunction display. A tiny white cross marked "RP" was in sight, not far ahead of their indicated position. "We're a couple of minutes out from the rendezvous point. Now we find out how good our planning really is."

Flynn nodded. Left unsaid, but fully understood by both of them, was that this was essentially a make-or-break moment. This mid-air rendezvous was critical. Sure, if it didn't come off for some reason, they could still press on with their infiltration attempt, but their overall odds of success would drop to near zero—and their timing for the planned attack on Voronin would be blown to hell.

Van Horn throttled back, slowing the seaplane to around eighty knots. Then she reached out and tapped an icon on her left-hand multifunction display. It turned green. The IR beacon fixed to their tail was activated. With that done, she flipped a switch to turn on a very low-powered tactical radio. "Seabird to Kingfisher," she called. "Do you copy?"

They both heard only the faint hiss of static through their headsets for a long moment.

"Seabird to Kingfisher," Van Horn said again. "Do you copy?"

This time there was a response. "*Kingfisher to Seabird. I read you five by five,*" they heard Sara McCulloch reply from her remote piloting station at Wakkanai Airport, more than two hundred nautical miles south of their present position. "*I'm at your four o'clock, estimate three miles out. I have your beacon in sight and am turning to slot in close behind you.*" Her transmissions were being routed to the Predator UAV by satellite link and then relayed on to them by an equally short-range radio.

Instinctively, Flynn craned around to hunt for the approaching drone. At three miles, it was little more than a tiny bright dot in his night vision goggles. He watched the Predator move around behind them. Small windows at the rear of the M-22's cockpit offered forty-five degrees of aft visibility. But within moments, the distant dot of the UAV vanished, obscured by the seaplane's solid wing mount. With a slight shrug, he turned back. Now it was up to the two aviators.

Carefully and precisely, calling out their airspeeds and courses at every step, Van Horn and McCulloch jockeyed their respective aircraft into a tight trail formation—with the Predator ending up roughly a hundred yards behind the SeaMax's tail. "*Kingfisher is in position, Seabird,*" McCullough said finally. "*Hanging on your six.*"

"Copy that," Van Horn replied. "Making my initial turn." She banked slightly to the right, bringing the seaplane's nose around to the north.

"*Following you around,*" the drone pilot confirmed.

Van Horn rolled back out of her gentle turn, and now the two small aircraft flew north, farther up the Tartar Strait, for the next preplanned navigation point. From there, another course change would take them almost due west, aiming straight for the Russian mainland.

THIRTY-FOUR

SEVERAL HOURS LATER

Close to a hundred and thirty nautical miles from where they'd crossed the Russian coast, Van Horn banked the small seaplane into a gentle left turn, curving off the generally northwest course they'd been following for the past couple of hours. Flynn felt a tight smile crease his face and just as quickly disappear. "Generally northwest" was an inadequate way to describe what had, in reality, been another twisting, winding, hop-scotching flight over and between ridges and hills, down into valleys, and just above the treetops of dense, moonlit forests. Along the way, he'd only caught occasional glimpses of the lights of small villages or isolated cabins. Russia's Far East was, by and large, very thinly populated.

They were approaching the mile-wide Amur River. Most of the region's people and industries clustered along its banks. So far, they'd successfully evaded Russia's air surveillance and air defense radars. But the Amur Valley was the place where they were most in danger of being spotted visually. Any truck driver or river barge captain observing two unidentified aircraft, one of them an unmanned drone, winging low across the water here—especially this late at night—would almost certainly report his sighting to the authorities. And that could trigger a dangerous cascade of responses by Russia's air defense network, ranging up to scrambling a Beriev A-50 AWACS airborne radar plane and its accompanying fighters. Being hunted from the sky would be fatal. Terrain masking and low-altitude flight were ineffective tactics against airborne radars capable of sorting out moving targets from the rest of the ground clutter.

Van Horn took them low behind a range of wooded hills that ran roughly parallel to the Amur at this point. She contacted the Predator. "You still with me, Kingfisher?"

"*On you like glue, Seabird,*" McCulloch assured her. There was nonetheless a note of strain in the other pilot's voice. Even with the IR beacon attached to the SeaMax M-22's tail as a guide, the task of remotely flying her Predator so low through this rough, hilly country was daunting. Her flight control inputs to the UAV were relayed through a satellite link, so there was always a short delay—usually much less than a second—before the Predator responded to her commands. That kind of delay didn't sound like much, but it meant the drone would fly more than a hundred feet between the time she commanded a maneuver and the time it finally responded. A lag like that wasn't critical when flying straight and level at high altitude. But jinking through tight terrain, it meant McCulloch needed to constantly think ahead of her next sudden turn or change of altitude— anticipating, instead of simply reacting. Doing that was possible for a sufficiently trained and skilled pilot, but it was also inherently exhausting.

Van Horn pulled back gently on her stick, slightly pitching the plane's nose up to begin her slow climb. Flynn looked out the right side of the bubble canopy. They'd been zooming near the base of the hills they were using as cover against visual and radar detection. "And . . . here we go," she murmured, raising M-22's nose again, only a couple of degrees. They ascended another fifty feet, climbing just high enough to pop above the top of the hill.

Immediately, the whole panorama of the Amur River Valley opened out before Flynn's eyes. He scanned the ground swiftly but methodically—first looking for signs of movement on the nearby roads and the closest stretch of the river, and then systematically widening his search sector by sector, all the way to the far edges of his vision. "We're clear," he reported after a moment. "I don't see any moving vehicles on the highway or the local roads. And there's no river traffic anywhere in sight."

Van Horn nodded. It was exactly as they'd hoped. It was already well past midnight, local time, and they were far enough away from the larger riverside cities and towns to significantly reduce the odds of encountering any insomniac long-haulers or barge crews. But low odds weren't the same thing as a guarantee, so scouting first before committing had been the right move. "We're good, Kingfisher," she relayed to McCulloch, hunched over her terminal and flight controls hundreds of miles away. "Executing my turn . . . *now.*"

She rolled the SeaMax into a tight turn back to the northwest, leveled out, and dropped its nose to plunge down the other side of the hill, practically shaving the tops of the trees carpeting its far slope. When the ground flattened out, she took them right down onto the deck and flew straight toward the wide black ribbon of the Amur.

As always, flying so close to the ground intensified the impression of speed for Flynn. He knew they were only traveling at around eighty knots—not that much faster than you could drive a car on some Texas backcountry roads—but this low, it still felt more like they were hitting Mach Three. In what seemed like the blink of an eye, their little seaplane flashed across a two-lane highway and zoomed out over the water.

He tensed. They were completely exposed out here on this broad, flat river, with higher ground rising on each side of the valley. All it would take was for one Russian to be looking out onto the Amur at the wrong time from the wrong place, and they'd be completely hosed. Suddenly he knew how a cockroach skittering across a kitchen floor must feel when the light suddenly snapped on.

Forty seconds later, they reached the other side of the river and came back over the land. Even steeper and higher ridges and forested heights rose ahead of them. Van Horn banked slightly north, aiming for a narrow gap in this jagged chain of hills. Flynn felt his stomach clench in anticipation of yet another breakneck roller-coaster ride. Which was worse, he wondered? A wild run through rough country? Or that horrible feeling of total vulnerability he'd just experienced?

If he was being honest, he'd have to admit that neither of those was his real problem. On a daring raid into Cuba the year before, his Quartet Directorate team had flown some highly experimental, turbo-jet-powered hoverbikes. During the mission, he'd discovered that he enjoyed high-speed, low-altitude flying—at least if he was at the controls. But those hoverbikes didn't have anywhere close to the range and payload needed for tonight's mission, and he couldn't fly the SeaMax safely to their planned destination.

His problem, Flynn knew, was not being in charge of his own fate. And that sucked. Both emotionally and intellectually, he was more than willing to trust Laura Van Horn with his life. She was the best pilot and had the steadiest nerves of anyone he'd ever met. Unfortunately, knowing that didn't help much in combating his conflicting emotions. At his core, he craved responsibility and control and hated dependence. He always wanted to hold the reins. And for better or worse, Flynn realized, this aspect of his personality wasn't ever likely to change. Then again, he recognized, neither was the reality that he couldn't fly this aircraft. And Van Horn could. It was a zero-sum equation with only one correct answer.

So, for the time being, he'd have to toughen up, endure the ride, and do his best not to jostle her elbow. Flynn tightened his grip on the edge of his seat. And just in time, because she suddenly moved the stick hard over and worked her feet on the rudder pedals—rolling them into another sharp turn to follow the natural trace of the valley. As if Van Horn could read his racing thoughts, he noticed one side of her mouth curl into a tiny half-smile. "Hang tight, Nick," she said kindly. "Another ninety minutes or so should see us through the worst of this."

"I'm fine. It's all good," he replied, a bit too enthusiastically.

Her smile widened. "You know, you're a really bad liar sometimes."

There was no right response to that assertion, so he opted for a dignified silence . . . which lasted only until she abruptly threw the M-22 into another tight bank to avoid a sharp-edged spur of rock that suddenly loomed up around the next bend. "Oh, shit," he said tightly as the world seemed to spin around their canopy.

Van Horn's grin grew even wider, which hardly seemed either possible or fair. But, in the end, he had to admit that she was as good as her word. About an hour and a half later and roughly a hundred nautical miles beyond the Amur, they broke past the high country and flew out across a wide plain. Small streams curlicued in intricate, ever-winding patterns through grassland and small groves of scrub trees and brush.

A large, roughly kidney-shaped, lake appeared ahead of them. A quick glance at the GPS-linked map on their right multifunction display confirmed it was Lake Chukchagir, deep in the heart of Russia's Oldjikan State Nature Preserve. "Kingfisher, I have our landing zone in sight," Van Horn radioed.

"*Copy that, Seabird,*" McCulloch replied. "*What's your fuel state?*"

Van Horn checked a small indicator on her left-hand display. "We'll be flying on fumes in about fifteen minutes." She glanced at Flynn. "Good thing we'll be landing in ten, right?"

He nodded. Although the SeaMax M-22 was rated for a range of around five hundred and fifty nautical miles without reserves, terrain-following flight burned significantly more gas. When planning this mission, they'd known they would be pushing right up against the edge of the plane's fuel capacity, with almost no margin left over for errors in navigation and absolutely none for any attempt to abort and return to the *Nikkō Maru.*

Van Horn banked into a gentle right turn, bringing them around low over the lake. She made a pass, closely studying the surface through her night vision goggles. Flynn did the same on his side of the cockpit. "Looks doable," she commented. "No rocks. No obvious shallows or sand bars."

"Same here," he reported.

She circled back the way they'd come and lined up again on the lake, flying parallel to its wooded southern shore. She nosed over slightly, lowered the aircraft's wing flaps to generate more lift, and simultaneously reduced her throttle setting. Behind them, the Predator broke away and began slowly orbiting over the lake at two hundred feet.

Shedding airspeed, the M-22 seaplane glided down out of the sky. A few feet off the water, Van Horn pulled the stick back a scooch to bring its nose mostly level. Then she cut her throttle a little more. They settled smoothly onto the surface with only a minor jolt. Small plumes of foam and spray splashed out from under the aircraft's streamlined hull and wing floats, dwindling as its speed through the water fell off. Decisively, she pulled her throttle all the way back and cut the engine. The propeller slowed and stopped turning, leaving them coasting across the lake, gradually losing way. A retractable water rudder allowed her to steer until the aircraft finally drifted to a complete stop—and ended up rocking gently about fifty yards offshore.

Flynn raised the bubble canopy. They sat together silently—watching and listening intently for even the slightest indication that their landing had drawn any unwanted attention. But nothing stirred in the darkness beyond the water's edge. The only sound nearby by was the droning noise of the Predator's turboprop engine as it circled low overhead.

"Shall we?" Flynn said at last, gesturing toward the shore.

Van Horn nodded. She used their low-powered radio one last time. "Kingfisher, this is Seabird. We're ready to go ashore. The winds here are extremely light, with only occasional gusts from the north-northeast at less than three knots. You can make your drop whenever you're ready."

"*Roger that, Seabird,*" McCulloch responded. Overhead, the Predator under her command broke out of its slow orbit and climbed away to the north until it reached an altitude of five hundred feet. Then it circled around to fly back toward the lake's southern shore. "*Dropping now.*"

The cargo container slung under the UAV's long, thin fuselage broke free and plummeted toward the ground. Its parachute snapped open a second later, billowing wide to slow the container's plunge dramatically. Sliding downwind, it thudded into soft ground about a hundred yards from the water's edge. The parachute's canopy fluttered briefly in the ground breeze and then collapsed.

"Good drop, Kingfisher," Van Horn said. "Thanks for your help. And good luck on the way out."

"*You too, Seabird,*" McCulloch answered. "*Safe travels. Kingfisher out.*" Her mission accomplished, she turned the Predator drone to the southeast and flew away, shedding altitude as she went. Assisted by a computer-generated map created during their inbound flight, McCulloch was confident she could safely retrace their low-altitude, radar-evading route. And her UAV should have just enough fuel remaining to make it back out over the Tartar Strait before self-destructing.

As soon as the drone disappeared from view, Flynn and Van Horn got busy. It took them a couple of minutes to drag a compact raft out of the cockpit's narrow cargo space behind their seats and inflate it using a CO_2 cartridge. Then Flynn held the raft steady while Van Horn climbed aboard with their two small travel cases. She repaid the favor, using one of the wing struts to hold them in place, while he swung himself over the side of the cockpit.

Before they left, Flynn leaned back in and carefully activated the timers on a pair of small charges fixed to the SeaMax's cockpit floor. Their lights blinked green. Not wasting any more time, he dropped lightly back into the little raft and pushed away from the floating seaplane.

With a mischievous grin, Van Horn handed him a pair of collapsible plastic oars belonging to the inflatable. "You were a Boy Scout, right? You must know how to use these things."

"And you don't?"

She shrugged, still smiling. "Knowing how is not the same thing as doing. Besides, I see this as a fair division of labor. I got us *here*," she indicated the lake. "So you get us *there*," she said, pointing toward the shoreline.

"Fair enough," Flynn agreed with a quiet laugh. He took the oars and swiftly rowed them ashore where they grounded on a gravel and sand beach. Not far inland, reeds and tall grasses swayed in the light breeze. They scrambled into the shallows and then pulled the raft up and out of the water.

Out on the lake, a sudden, muffled *THUMMP-THUMMP* signaled the detonation of their scuttling charges. With the bottom of its hull blown wide open, the SeaMax M-22 settled rapidly and sank out of sight in a white bubbling froth of foam. Flynn and Van Horn watched it go. Although Lake Chukchagir was only twenty feet deep at that point, its waters were murky, and the bottom was both muddy and choked with weeds. Their now-wrecked aircraft should lie safely hidden in its shallow depths for several years and maybe even longer.

When the lake's surface grew still again, Van Horn sighed. "Scratch one more perfectly good airplane. I hope I don't end up making a habit of this."

"I think it only counts as a loss if you wreck it while flying," Flynn said consolingly.

"What was that then?"

"Necessary expenditure of mission items in a previously approved manner," he said with a straight face.

Van Horn stared at him. "Did you just make that up on your own?"

Flynn shook his head. "I had a couple of buddies in ROTC who wound up in logistics. They taught me some of the lingo."

"Be careful, Nick," she warned. "That's some serious dark side of the Force shit right there. And once you go too far down that path, you can never return to the light side."

"Which is—" he prompted.

Van Horn shrugged. "Flying, shooting missiles, blowing things up, killing bad guys. You know, the good stuff."

"Point taken," Flynn said. He motioned toward the nearby clump of reeds and tall grasses where the Predator's parachuted container had come down. "Speaking of which, we should get moving. We've got a train to catch, remember?"

She nodded. Together, carrying the small inflatable raft, they sloshed across the soft, almost swampy ground.

The cargo container was about eight feet long, four feet wide, and four feet high. It was canted slightly, with one end partially dug into the mud. It took them only a short time to reel in the parachute and bundle it up into a compact mass of fabric. Scraping away the mud took only a bit longer.

Flynn knelt and undid the straps holding the container shut. Van Horn helped him push it open. Under a layer of mesh netting, more straps secured a Russian-made Tula TMZ 5.951 off-road motorcycle in place. He nodded approvingly. Long out of production, Tula bikes were favorites among Russian hunters and outdoor enthusiasts—primarily due to their ruggedness and reliability. It was precisely the kind of machine they needed to traverse this wilderness area, and best of all, it wouldn't attract any unwelcome attention.

Working as a team, he and Van Horn unstrapped the motorcycle and then muscled the heavy machine up and out onto the ground. The now-deflated raft, oars, and bundled-up parachute took its place. More work camouflaged the airdropped cargo container itself with cut grasses and reeds. When they were done, Flynn eyed their handiwork critically. Sinking the case in the lake would have been better, but it was too heavy to drag all the way out into deep enough water, especially across muddy ground. Plus, hauling it through the reeds would undoubtedly have left traces that would be visible from the air. So, while this wasn't a perfect job of concealment, it was their best option right now. After all, this was a nature preserve, off-limits to almost everybody, except a few Russian biologists and a handful of forest rangers. The odds of anyone stumbling across the container anytime soon should be somewhere between slim and none. He glanced around at the empty, silent landscape surrounding them and shrugged. As it was, he'd put his money on none.

Quickly now, they washed off in the lake and changed their clothes. Then Flynn strapped their bags to the motorcycle's rear, swung his leg over, and hit the ignition. Its single cylinder, 12.5 horsepower engine coughed to life. Van Horn hopped on behind him.

Slowly, using his night vision gear to help find a path through the dark woods lining the lake, Flynn drove south, picking his way around trees and thickets of brush with care. According to the maps and satellite photos they'd studied, they were about two miles from an old logging track that would eventually lead into the region's sparse road network.

KOMSOMOLSK-ON-AMUR RAILWAY STATION
THE NEXT NIGHT

Carrying their small bags, Flynn and Van Horn strolled arm-in-arm through the open doors of the bright pink-and-white stucco railway station and onto the platform. A long passenger train of silver and red cars stood there, obviously ready to depart.

Flynn was now dressed in the Russian Army's everyday uniform for an officer—olive-green slacks, a tight-fitting zippered jacket in the same color, and a peaked cap. His documents, meticulously crafted by the Quartet Directorate's best forgers, identified him as a Major Alexei Lokhanov, currently serving in a signals regiment assigned to the Far Eastern Military District. He also carried papers authorizing him to take a month's leave on a honeymoon. Van Horn, dressed comfortably for travel in jeans, a white blouse, and a lightweight jacket, now called herself Tatiana Lokhanova, his wife. She had papers to prove it, of course. Not that anyone had spent much time studying them. This deep inside Russian territory and so far east of Moscow, most identity checks were cursory.

And that, Flynn thought with satisfaction, was precisely why they'd just made such a difficult long-range penetration flight. For all its perils, complications, and significant expense, it had been their safest way into Russia.

Conversing fondly in informal Russian, they boarded the waiting train and went along a narrow corridor to the sleeping compartment reserved in their name more than a week earlier. Once they were safely inside and out of earshot of the car's dour female attendant, Flynn tossed his major's cap onto one of the two fold-down beds and turned to Van Horn. "So," he said with a teasing grin. "We've got a nine-hour ride to Khabarovsk, where we catch the westbound Trans-Siberian Express, right?"

She nodded. "And after that, we've got another six days on the rails before we reach the Moscow areas. What's your point?"

"It's just this," Flynn continued, still smiling down at her. "What do you suppose we can possibly do to keep ourselves busy for all that time?"

Van Horn slipped her arms around his waist and stepped closer. "Well, Major Lokhanov," she said, looking up into his face with a sly smile of her own. "It just so happens that I've got quite a few ideas I plan to share with you."

With a slight lurch, the train started rolling.

THIRTY-FIVE

VLADIMIR, EAST OF MOSCOW

A WEEK LATER

Located approximately one hundred and twenty miles east of Moscow, Vladimir had once been one of medieval Russia's most important and powerful cities. The glories of its ancient past survived in a number of beautiful, gleaming white, gold-domed Russian Orthodox cathedrals, some of them close to a thousand years old. Sadly, none of the architectural brilliance that had produced such marvels of design was reflected in the city's main railway station, which was an ugly, boxy structure built out of pale gray concrete slabs and glass in all the worst traditions of Soviet-era construction. The best that could be said about it was that it was functional.

Wearing ordinary civilian clothes now, Nick Flynn and Laura Van Horn stepped down off the train and onto the main platform. Holding hands, they walked into the station itself, then headed straight for the nearest exit, acting very much like a newly married couple with eyes only for each other—paying no apparent attention to the other travelers milling around ticket windows or food kiosks. Once outside the station, however, they spotted a solidly built man in a dark suit and a chauffeur's cap waiting on the pavement. He held up a hand-written sign that read "LOKHANOV." It was Tadeusz Kossak.

Flynn tamped down on any sign that he'd recognized the Pole. Instead, he walked over with a quizzical look. "I'm Lokhanov," he said. "Alexei Lokhanov." He nodded at Van Horn. "And this is my wife. Are you here for us?"

Kossak nodded impassively. "Yes, Mr. Lokhanov," he said, indicating the dark blue S-model Mercedes sedan parked at the curb behind him. "Some of your friends arranged this ride as a honeymoon gift."

For friends, read Br'er Fox, Flynn realized, since no one else on his team had been briefed on their cover story before making their own way into Russia. He turned to Van Horn. "Look, Tatiana," he said. "We don't need to take a taxi after all, thanks to Mischa and the rest of the guys. See, they're not total losers after all."

She smiled. "Well, Alexei, they're still drunken louts. But at least they're generous, drunken louts."

"Half a win is better than no win at all," Flynn said with a wink at Kossak.

Stoically, exactly like a hired car driver who had no intention of getting involved in the affairs of his passengers, the Pole politely held the Mercedes's rear door open for them. As soon as they were inside, he slid behind the steering wheel and smoothly pulled out onto the station access road. Coming to a parking barrier, he slid his ticket into the machine, paid what he owed, and then turned the Mercedes left onto the next street over.

Once they were safely in traffic, Flynn leaned forward. "Any problems I should know about, Tad?" Although the Trans-Siberian Express train they'd been riding for the past six days had Wi-Fi, he'd calculated that using it to contact Fox back in the U.S. or any others on his team for anything short of an actual emergency would have been much too risky. Given the limited number of emails and texts emanating from any train, the FSB and other Russian intelligence services would have a relatively easy time spotting anything remotely suspicious. You couldn't hide in a crowd if there wasn't one.

Kossak shook his head. "Nothing significant," he said. "Wade and I arrived almost a week ago. And Cooke and Hynes got in a couple of days later, with all our equipment."

Flynn nodded. That was good news. He'd been confident that burying their gear under a load of slag would get it past any border security checks, but it was nice to have his confidence confirmed. It also meant that Cooke and Hynes had successfully ditched their big rig and dump trailer at Ryazan as planned and acquired another vehicle. "Any developments since then?"

"None," the other man told him. "We've just been waiting for the two of you to show up." He studied the pair of them in his rear-view mirror. One eyebrow went up. "So?" he asked casually. "How was your long train trip together?"

"Nicely boring and very restful," Flynn lied smoothly, ignoring a sharp elbow jab from Van Horn. "We managed to catch up on a lot of sleep."

Kossak's mouth twitched as he plainly fought the temptation to laugh out loud at such an obvious load of nonsense. Instead, he simply smiled. "*Ah*," he said gravely. "Restful. Of course. I understand completely." He returned his attention to navigating Vladimir's busy streets. When they came to an intersection with the Volga Highway, the M7, he turned west toward Moscow itself.

They were still some distance from the capital's outskirts when Kossak turned off the highway and onto a narrower country road leading northwest. Within minutes, they were traveling through a rural landscape marked by villages, groves of birch and pine, and farms broken into family-sized plots. Most of those small fields, orchards, and gardens probably belonged to Muscovites who wanted to get away on weekends and holidays for fresh air and home-grown fruits and vegetables. Some miles farther on, the Mercedes stopped at the entrance to an unpaved road that led off into a patch of woodland. The way ahead was closed off by a chain-link gate.

Kossak flashed his lights four times.

Responding to the signal, Cole Hynes stepped out from the shadow of the trees. He wore a cloth cap and a leather jacket and had a submachine gun slung over one shoulder. With a quick nod, he opened the gate for them and stood waiting until the Mercedes pulled all the way through before latching it shut again. As they drove up the dirt road, Flynn glanced back and saw Hynes vanish again into the woods. He hadn't just been waiting for them to arrive. He was clearly on sentry duty.

A few hundred yards up the road, the sedan came out of the surrounding forest into a clearing. A wood-framed house painted a light blue sat at one end, while a creek-fed pond lay at the other. Although it was more isolated than most, Flynn judged this to be a typical Russian dacha, the type of small country home Moscow's more prosperous inhabitants preferred for occasional getaways. A black Mercedes-Benz Sprinter van was parked near the house on a patch of gravel. Kossak pulled up alongside the van and switched off his ignition. Then, acting as their chauffeur to the last, he opened the rear door for them.

As soon as Flynn and Van Horn got out of the car, Cooke and Vucovich appeared in the doorway of the house. "Hey, amigos!" Cooke chirped. "*Mi casa es su casa*. Welcome to Cooke Manor East."

Flynn laughed. Like many of the Quartet Directorate's original founders, Cooke came from a wealthy family. They owned quite a lot of land in southwestern Virginia's rugged backcountry. His neighbors there, and Cooke himself, for that matter, referred to the large, elegant family home built by his grandfather as The Manor. He waved a hand at the dacha and pond. "*¿Tu casa*, Shannon? Your house? What're you doing? Buying up Russian real estate now?"

"Well, more like borrowing it, I guess," Cooke admitted. "The actual owner's a local *Mafiya* bigwig."

"And this organized crime boss doesn't mind us squatting on his property for a spell?" Flynn asked carefully.

Cooke grinned. "Oh, I figure he probably would . . . if he knew about it. But as it happens, the poor son of a bitch is currently doing a long stretch of hard time in a Russian prison."

"And this crook's old neighbors aren't at all curious about new folks turning up out of nowhere?" Van Horn asked with a skeptical note in her voice.

Cooke shrugged. "The nearest neighbors are about a quarter mile that way," he said, pointing deeper into the woods. "Plus, we get the strong impression they're used to looking the other way when it comes to things happening around this place."

Flynn thought back to the sight of Hynes on guard at the gate to the property. In that cloth cap and leather jacket, he'd looked very much like one of the stereotypical *patsani*, the Russian slang term for a criminal gang's foot soldiers. "And is it just possible, say, that the locals may have gotten the mistaken impression that we might be *Mafiya* too?" he asked with deliberate casualness.

"Could be," Cooke said, donning an innocent expression that wouldn't have fooled anyone. "Folks do seem a little skittish for some reason. We sure haven't had anyone come around hoping to bum a cup of sugar lately."

Van Horn snorted. "Uh-huh. Well, I suppose we'd better plan on being long gone before any of the real *Mafiya* boss's underlings get wind of underworld rivals horning in on his weekend vacation place."

"The exact timing of that kind of depends on you and Nick," Cooke pointed out. "So far, the rest of us have been operating in the dark."

Flynn and Van Horn ducked their heads, acknowledging the justice of the other man's implicit complaint. It was one thing to understand the importance of safeguarding vital information. Finding yourself on the outside of that need-to-know loop was quite another.

They followed the other three men into the house. It was comfortably, if not luxuriously, furnished—with a couple of small bedrooms, one indoor bathroom, what appeared to have been a study or office for the *Mafiya* owner, a living room with a sofa and entertainment center, and an eat-in kitchen. Van Horn looked around in approval. "Nice," she murmured. "Or at least a heck of a lot better than the dumps we hid out in the last time we were here."

"Crime does seem to have paid our host reasonably well," Cooke agreed. "Up to the moment that the cops nailed him anyway."

While she took their bags into one of the bedrooms, generously vacated by Cooke, Flynn sat down at the kitchen table and sent a short email to Fox in Four's word code, reporting their safe arrival. Moments later, he received a simple acknowledgment from the older man and a couple of sentences that appeared to be ordinary family gossip. When Van Horn returned, Flynn silently showed them to her. She nodded in understanding. Translated, Fox's postscript read: Support group in position and standing by. Signal when ready to proceed.

That night, over a simple dinner of frozen, prepackaged meals bought at a local grocery store, Hynes asked the question on their minds. "Okay, sir, what's our next move?"

"Getting tired of being on vacation?" Flynn countered with a slight smile.

Hynes snorted. "I don't mind the part where nobody's shooting at us," he said. "But Wade and I are in sleeping bags in the living room. And he snores. A lot. It's like trying to sleep next to a diesel generator."

"I snore?" Vucovich said in genuine surprise.

Flynn hid a grin. At the isolated Alaskan radar post where he'd first commanded the two men, fellow soldiers had groused that Vucovich's snoring should be classed as a prohibited nonlethal weapon under international law. Apparently, no one had ever told him.

"You both snore," Kossak said bluntly. "So loudly that I can hear the two of you through the walls of my room. And it is not a pleasant duet."

Smiling openly now, Flynn held up his hand. "Okay, I get it. Y'all are on the edge of going stir-crazy. So listen up. I've got one more important piece of prep work scheduled for tomorrow morning." He turned to Kossak. "And for that, I'll need you to act as my chauffeur one last time, Tad."

The Pole shrugged. "That will not be a problem."

"Good." Flynn looked around the table. "Once that's finished, we should be all set to pull the trigger on the main operation. Laura and I will brief you on the full plan tomorrow evening," he promised.

He could see the others perk up at the prospect of imminent action. No matter how safe they seemed to be at the moment, no one could forget they were deep inside hostile territory. Every passing hour and day only increased the chances of something going wrong. Time was not their ally.

"Does this plan of yours have a code name?" Cooke asked.

Flynn nodded. "We opted for a classic," he said. "It's called NEMESIS."

"Short and sweet and on point," Cooke agreed. "I like it."

THIRTY-SIX

OFFICE OF PROCYON SERVICES UNLIMITED,
THE ARBAT DISTRICT, CENTRAL MOSCOW

THE NEXT MORNING

Flynn made a show of reading through the entire charter agreement, comprised of several pages of intricate fine print. Clauses and numbered subclauses of dry legalese were nested like the smaller and smaller figurines that were part of a traditional Russian Matryoshka doll. When at last he reached the last page, he looked across the desk at Daniil Zemtsov, Procyon's managing director. "Everything seems to be in order," he said.

Zemtsov nodded. "The instructions you relayed from your principal during our correspondence were quite . . . detailed," he said carefully.

Flynn shrugged. "He *is* a man who knows his own mind."

"Naturally," Zemtsov hastened to agree. He inclined his head toward the walls of his office, which were full of photographs of other famous people who'd used his company over the last couple of decades. They ranged from rising politicians to successful entrepreneurs and entertainment industry superstars. "All of our clients are people of great wealth and power. We are quite used to accommodating their usual needs for—" The businessman stopped abruptly as Flynn held up a hand in warning.

"Do not make the mistake of assuming that my employer is typical in any way, Mr. Zemtsov," Flynn said quietly. "You are an intelligent, well-connected man. I assume you've heard any number of rumors about our various endeavors."

Uneasy now, Zemtsov moistened his suddenly dry lips. "Some," he admitted cautiously, obviously not sure how much it would be safe to reveal. Many of the stories he'd heard revolved around episodes of extreme violence and mysterious, unexplained, and unprosecuted deaths. Others indicated that his prospective client was closely connected to the Kremlin, especially President Zhdanov. If even a quarter of those rumors were accurate, the corporate chieftains and celebrities he usually dealt with resembled this new customer as closely as guppies did a great white shark.

"Then you should understand how important it is to satisfy him in this matter—important to your company's reputation . . . and to you, personally," Flynn warned. "My employer demands extreme efficiency. And complete discretion. He does not accept excuses for failures or inadequacies." He smiled coldly. "Nor do I, for that matter."

Zemtsov swallowed hard. The man sitting across the desk from him was said by those in the know to be nearly as dangerous as his master. "Everything will be ready at Bykovo, as promised," he hastened to say. "Complete with the required crew."

Flynn nodded.

"We'll also file all the necessary official paperwork under our corporate name," Zemstov continued. "There will be no need to refer to your principal or your organization in any documentation filed with the authorities. Everything will stay in-house here."

Flynn allowed a little more warmth to slide into his voice. "Very good." He took out an expensive fountain pen and swiftly initialed and signed the charter agreement at each indicated place. With that done, he retrieved a bank draft from the inner pocket of his perfectly tailored suit and slid it across the desk. "I believe this will cover our transaction," he said.

Zemtsov stared down at the draft. It was for more than nine million rubles, roughly one hundred thousand American dollars, and it was drawn on one of the world's most exclusive financial institutions, Geneva's Banque Privée Edmond de Rothschild. His eyes widened greedily.

The amount was 20 percent over what Procyon usually charged for such a charter.

Flynn stood up to go. "You have my private mobile number," he said. "Contact me at once if there are any problems."

"There won't be," Zemtsov assured him hurriedly. He climbed to his own feet and ingratiatingly offered his hand. "And thank you! It's been a great pleasure and privilege handling this matter for you, Mr. Kondakov."

THE DACHA, OUTSIDE MOSCOW
THAT EVENING

Under the light of a shaded lamp, Flynn looked around a circle of intent, determined faces. He opted to be blunt. These people were all professionals. They were also trusted comrades and friends—and in Laura Van Horn's case, much more. They deserved the truth exactly as he saw it, not the kind of smoothly packaged, optimistic BS some staff weenies used to boost the morale of frontline troops assigned to hazardous duty.

"I'm not going to sugarcoat this," he began. "There is no margin for error on this mission. If anything major goes wrong, we're probably all dead."

Heads nodded. They'd all read Cooke's report on the security setup at the Mercury City Tower, and the details of what Flynn and Van Horn had learned about Voronin's own defenses while interrogating Vasily Kondakov.

"Here's the deal," Flynn continued. "Even if everything goes according to plan, NEMESIS will still be risky as hell for all of us. We'll have to be at the top of our game—ready to go in hard and fast." He met their eyes. "And when things go south, as they surely will, each of us must be ready to act without hesitation. To do whatever it takes to accomplish this mission. There's no use in trying to play it safe. We won't get another crack at Voronin. Not in time to matter. So this is all-or-nothing."

Hynes raised a hand. "Uh, sir?"

Flynn nodded. "Go ahead, Cole. You've got a question?"

"Not exactly," Hynes said. "More of a comment. See, as pre-game pep talks go, I thought you might want to know that yours kind of sucks. Big-time. No disrespect intended, of course."

That triggered grins and half-stifled snorts of laughter from around the table.

"He's right, you know," Van Horn said gently to Flynn. She patted his hand. "Maybe in the future when we do something batshit crazy like this, you should think about leading with the positive. Say something like, 'Hey, we might not die. If we get incredibly lucky, that is.' Something along those lines."

Flynn couldn't hide his own answering grin. "*Et tu*, Laura?" he asked in a hurt tone. Then he turned to Hynes. "Thanks for the constructive criticism, Cole. I'll do my best to keep it in mind for the next time. Assuming, of course, that there will be a next time."

"Always glad to help out, sir," the other man told him.

With the tension broken slightly, Flynn turned to the details of their plan. "Okay, what's the best way to clear a defended building?" he asked.

To his surprise, Wade Vucovich spoke up first. Tall and almost gangly, he was usually the quietest one in the group. "From the top down, sir," he said. "At least that's what they taught us Joes in urban combat training."

Flynn nodded. "Bingo. And the training and doctrine are right in this case. So that's exactly how we're going to work NEMESIS."

Cooke eyed him quizzically. "Please tell me that you're *not* planning for us to helicopter to the top of that damn skyscraper and then rappel down about four hundred fricking feet to where Voronin and his goons have their offices?" His soft Virginia drawl lengthened. "I've got a lot of hidden talents, but playing Spiderman ain't one of them."

"I thought about it," Flynn admitted and then shrugged. "But even I am not *that* loco."

"Could have fooled me," Van Horn murmured.

He flashed her a quick half-smile and then moved on. "No mountaineering is required. Instead, we're taking exactly the opposite approach." Ignoring, for the moment, the puzzled looks this statement prompted, he shifted his gaze back to Cooke. "And, as it happens, you've got the starring role, Shannon."

The other man folded his arms and leaned back with a sardonic look. "Oh, joy. Should I be flattered? Or just scared shitless?"

"Both, probably," Flynn replied. He glanced around the table with a serious expression. "Now, listen up, folks, because here's how this is going to work—" When he finished explaining the tactics they would employ and the timing involved, he sat back. "Any questions? Any comments?"

There was a long moment of silence while the other team members digested what they'd just been told. Finally, Hynes whistled softly and shook his head. He stared across the table at Flynn with an almost admiring look. "Hell, sir. You weren't kidding about how dicey this plan is, were you?"

"Nope. I meant every single word," Flynn said softly. He studied the other man. "So, Cole? Are you in? Or out?" Ordinarily, at this stage of a mission, he wouldn't have even dreamed of offering anyone a chance to bail out. But now that they were all face to face with the cold, hard reality of what they were being asked to try, he found he couldn't do anything else but give them the option. He thought wryly that, if he'd had a sword, he could have drawn a line in the dirt outside and dared them to step across it, like Colonel William Barrett Travis did at the Alamo.

Hynes shrugged. "Oh, I'm in, sir. Win or lose, this will be one heck of a ride." One by one, Shannon Cooke, Tadeusz Kossak, and Wade Vucovich nodded solemnly in agreement.

Flynn breathed out, feeling both heartened and uneasy in the same moment. They were fully committed now. NEMESIS would kick off early the next morning—and there was no going back once it did.

THIRTY-SEVEN

KHAMOVNIKI DISTRICT, ACROSS THE MOSKVA RIVER
FROM GORKY PARK, MOSCOW

THE NEXT MORNING

Several late-model cars, a mix of Ladas, Hyundais, and Kias, were neatly
parked around a tree-lined courtyard. Five- and six-story-high brick and
concrete-block apartment buildings rose on all sides, except for a single
entrance to the nearest street. Shannon Cooke stood quietly in the cover
of the trees. According to what they'd been told, the man he was waiting for was a creature of habit, at least on his home turf. He came fully
on alert as a burly, shaven-headed man strolled out of the closest apartment building, smoking a cigarette.

Cooke took in the tattoos visible on the man's thick neck. That
was Anton Saitov, the Raven Syndicate's new internal security chief, no
doubt about it. The hard-eyed man matched the description Kondakov had provided. Those tattoos were souvenirs of his undercover "wet
work" inside the neo-Nazi Russian Imperial Movement.

Saitov took a deep drag on his cigarette and then tossed it aside.
Blowing out a lungful of pale blue smoke, he moved toward his vehicle, a steel-gray Lada Granta, reaching into his pocket for his car keys.

Cooke stepped out from under the trees. "Anton Sergeevich Saitov," he called out formally, holding up what would appear from a distance to be a police warrant card. "A moment, please. We have a few questions for you."

Saitov spun toward him fast. His eyes narrowed. The Russian seemed to hesitate for a moment, but then his attention focused even more intently on the card in Cooke's hand. With snakelike swiftness, his hand darted inside his jacket pocket and came out holding a 9mm SR-1 Vektor pistol—a type favored by members of the FSB and GRU for close-in fighting. One of their nicknames for the weapon was *Gyurza*, Viper.

"*Khuy tebe*! Fuck you!" Saitov snarled. "You're no cop." His pistol was already moving into line with Cooke's chest when there was the sudden *cough-pop* sound of a suppressed weapon firing. A round red hole appeared in the center of the Russian's forehead, accompanied by a sudden splatter of blood, brain matter, and shattered skull fragments out the back of his head. Killed instantly, he went down without a sound.

"Well, crap," Cooke murmured, as he bent over to pull the Vektor from Saitov's dead hand. "That could have gone better."

"Not likely," Nick Flynn said matter-of-factly, from off to the side, still standing under the trees. He detached the magazine of his Lebedev PL-15 pistol and thumbed in another round to replace the one he'd just fired. Then he reinserted the magazine and unscrewed the still-warm suppressor attached to its barrel. "Kondakov warned us this guy Saitov was a paranoid SOB. He was never going to fall for the phony cop routine."

Cooke shrugged. "Yeah, I guess not." He shook his head in disbelief. "The bastard sure was fast, though. I thought he had me."

"Which is why I'm just as glad he's not going to be around for the rest of this little escapade," Flynn agreed, sliding his pistol away out of sight as he joined Cooke by the body. Working quickly and efficiently, the two Quartet Directorate agents searched Saitov's corpse—retrieving both his red restricted access Mercury City Tower key card and his Raven Syndicate photo ID card. With that done, they lugged the dead man over to a dumpster in one corner of the courtyard and heaved him inside out of sight. That way, given reasonable luck, it would be a while before anyone found the body.

Unhurriedly, Flynn and Cooke left the courtyard and went their separate ways. They each had different roles to play in the next phases of this complex, precisely timed plan.

MERCURY CITY TOWER
A SHORT TIME LATER

After paying his fare plus a generous tip in cash, Cooke climbed out of the taxi that had brought him to the skyscraper's front entrance. Carrying a large briefcase, he strode through the bronze-tinted sliding glass doors and headed straight for the security turnstiles. In his fashionable, charcoal gray wool suit and blue silk tie, he looked like every other high-powered corporate executive who had offices in the huge building. While on the move, he dug out Saitov's red keycard and held it ready. Then, serenely ignoring the armed guards deployed around the enormous lobby, he swiped the card and went through the machine. No alarms rang.

First step down, he thought. But it was a big one. Using the dead Raven Syndicate security chief's special access card not only got him into the building, it also enabled him to walk straight past the additional screening for explosives and weapons without stopping.

When Cooke arrived at the elevator banks, he avoided the restricted lifts that would have taken him directly to the Raven Syndicate–controlled floors. He figured there was no sense in poking his head directly into the lion's den. Instead, he summoned a regular passenger elevator, entered the car, and pushed the button for the forty-sixth floor. The doors slid closed, and the high-speed elevator ascended smoothly.

When its doors chimed open, he stepped out into a wide, elegant corridor. After a quick glance up at the nearest building security surveillance camera, he slid Saitov's key card into a gleaming recycling bin. Then, without further hesitation, he walked purposefully down the hall to the door of the apartment he wanted. It was where he'd delivered his phony package while scouting the Mercury City Tower weeks ago, the one belonging to a man named Povetkin, a wealthy private equity banker. Brusquely, he rang the bell.

The same dour-faced underling he'd met before, the banker's assistant, answered the door. He showed no sign at all that he recognized Cooke from the earlier visit. That wasn't a surprise, the Quartet Directorate agent knew. He'd been counting on it. On his first trip to this apartment, Cooke had been wearing a neon red bike helmet and a bright orange reflective vest—the standard attire of a bike messenger. And when dealing with people in uniform—police officers, waiters, store clerks, and the like—most people paid far more attention to the clothes than to the appearance of those wearing them.

Before Povetkin's assistant could say anything, Cooke flashed Saitov's stolen Raven Syndicate ID card at him, carefully keeping his forefinger over the dead man's photograph. "I need to talk to your boss," he said roughly. "Right away."

The other man swallowed hard and stepped back, allowing Cooke inside the apartment's foyer. "Yes, sir," he said faintly and hurried off to find his employer.

Cooke hid a slight smile. By this time, enough gossip about the Syndicate's unsavory activities had obviously circulated among the Mercury City Tower's other tenants to make them all wary of offending Voronin or any of his people. He set his briefcase down on an entry table and opened it.

Shortly afterward, the assistant returned with Povetkin. Both Russians stopped dead in their tracks—staring in shock at the suppressed 9mm pistol Cooke now held aimed squarely in their direction. "My apologies, gentlemen," he said coolly. "I hate like hell to bother you. But I really need to borrow your place for a little while."

It took him only moments to secure the two men. Tied up, gagged, and blindfolded, they were tucked away in the relative safety of the master bedroom. Humming to himself, Cooke began dragging furniture away from the center of the apartment's elaborately decorated living room. So far as he knew, everything in NEMESIS seemed to be running like clockwork.

MERCURY CITY TOWER
MAIN PARKING GARAGE ENTRANCE
A SHORT TIME LATER

A large black van turned off the entrance road and pulled up to the barrier. Its passenger side window rolled down, revealing a lean-faced, determined-looking officer wearing the all-black tactical uniform of the Spetsnaz's Alpha Group—the FSB's elite anti-terrorist unit. He crooked a finger at the closest building security guard on duty. "You!" His finger pointed downward at the pavement beside his window. "Here!" His mouth tightened. "Now!"

Perplexed, the guard scrambled to obey. "Sir?" he asked in confusion. "What's going on?"

"There's a situation," the Spetsnaz officer said irritably. "That's all *you* need to know." He jabbed his finger at the barrier in front of the van. "Now open this fucking gate and put me in touch with your boss. Understand?"

Hastily, the guard obeyed, stabbing the button to raise the barrier. Then he turned and trotted after the van as it drove down the ramp and into the garage. He had his hand-held radio out and could be heard excitedly asking to speak to the building's chief of security.

The big black vehicle parked directly in front of one of the elevators. The second it came to a stop, its doors slid open. Following their leader, more black-clad Alpha Group troops jumped out, loaded down with large equipment bags. They all wore ballistic helmets and had black balaclavas pulled up over their noses and mouths. That was common practice among Russia's elite law enforcement units. It was done to protect their identities from criminals or terrorists who might otherwise retaliate against them or their families.

Impatiently, their officer snatched the radio held out to him by the harried-looking security guard. "Captain Demidov?" he demanded. "This is Major Nikolai Raevsky of *Spetsgruppa* 'A.' I'm on my way up to your operations center now."

An agitated voice crackled out of the radio. "Look, Major, can you tell me just what the hell is happening and why you're—"

"I'll brief you more fully in person," the officer snapped, cutting the other man off in mid-sentence. "But right now, I will say that you're facing an extremely serious situation. At least one armed intruder—probably a terrorist—is likely to have breached your security, and there could easily be more."

THIRTY-EIGHT

MERCURY CITY TOWER SUB-LEVELS

THAT SAME TIME

Escorted by the security guard, Major Raevsky and his Spetsnaz troops crowded into the elevator car and rode it up one floor to the second basement level. This was the utilitarian section of the huge building dedicated to its vital mechanical infrastructure: electrical substations, emergency generators, water pumps and storage tanks, and the fiber optic telecommunications and internet cables that connected it to the outside world. It was also the site of the skyscraper's internal security operations center.

Under blue-tinged lights, this security station resembled a military command post. Computer consoles and wall-sized screens allowed the uniformed guards on duty to monitor feeds from the dozens of surveillance cameras positioned in and around the Mercury City Tower's seventy-five floors. Keeping track of potentially threatening activity in the building's more than one hundred and seventy thousand square meters of internal space was an enormous job—one that required a combination of dedicated specialists and sophisticated software to help winnow the flood of information being gathered to something approaching a manageable level.

Followed by his black-clad anti-terrorist commandos, Raevsky marched into the operations center. His eyes roved around the room and settled immediately on the senior man, Iosif Demidov. The security chief wore a captain's four stars on the shoulder tabs of his short-sleeved blue shirt. A jacket emblazoned with the Mercury City Tower's corporate logo was slung over the chair at his console. He looked both worried and off-balance at this sudden and wholly unexpected intrusion into what had been a perfectly ordinary morning shift.

"I'm Raevsky. And you must be Demidov," the Spetsnaz officer said sharply. "We don't have time to waste on polite bullshit. So let's consider it all said and move on to what's crucial. First, how closely do you track everyone entering or exiting through your controlled access points?"

"Very closely," Demidov assured him. "All key card swipes at the turnstiles and restricted elevators are processed and recorded by our computer system."

"That's good news," Raevsky said with a tight-lipped nod. "Then tell me: Has a man named Saitov entered this building today? Anton Sergeevich Saitov?"

Demidov darted a finger at one of his men. "Pull that information up for the major, Yuri."

The security officer's hands flashed across his keyboard. In response, a posed ID photo of Saitov appeared on his display, along with pertinent information about his status and clearance levels. He pointed to alpha-numeric lines of text at the bottom of the screen. "Saitov? Yes, his access card registered at the main lobby turnstiles about thirty-five minutes ago."

Demidov leaned closer to the screen. His eyes scanned Saitov's details. With a puzzled look, he turned back to Raevsky. "What exactly is this all about, Major? This man Saitov is a high-ranking employee of one of our most important corporate tenants, the Raven Syndicate." He shrugged. "He's got complete building access already. He can't be any kind of threat to our security."

The Spetsnaz officer grimaced. "*Saitov* certainly isn't a threat to anyone. Not anymore," he growled. He swung round to one of his men and snapped his fingers. The warrant officer handed him a tablet computer. Swiping at it, Raevsky opened a digital photo that showed Saitov's corpse half-buried in a trash dumpster. He held it out to Demidov. "As you can plainly see."

The Mercury City Tower security chief stared down at the gruesome image in astonishment.

"The Kremlin keeps close tabs on anyone affiliated with the Raven Syndicate," Raevsky explained curtly. "When one of his neighbors witnessed Saitov being attacked in his apartment building's car park earlier this morning, flares went up all over Moscow." He indicated the tablet in the other man's hand. "Which is why we were alerted the moment the police found his body."

Seeing the look of horrified realization dawning on Demidov's broad face, the Spetsnaz officer nodded grimly. "Exactly. Whoever the hell just walked right through your security checkpoint, one thing is certain: He is most definitely *not* Anton Sergeevich Saitov."

The security chief blanched. He spun back to the console. "Find out where this impostor went, Yuri," he commanded.

The officer nodded. "As long as he kept Saitov's card with him, we can track its RFID signature," he observed. Swiftly, he pulled up a number of sub-menus on his computer and entered commands. "Got him!" he said triumphantly. He jabbed a finger at his display, where a schematic of the building had flashed into existence. It showed a blinking dot appear in the lobby, cross to the elevator banks, and ascend. There it stopped. "This guy took a regular passenger elevator to the forty-sixth floor."

"Where did he go from there?" Demidov demanded.

His subordinate shook his head. "I can't tell, sir," he admitted. He pointed to the stationary blinking dot. "It looks as though he must have ditched Saitov's key card as soon as he got out of the elevator."

Watching with his arms folded, Raevsky raised an eyebrow. "I assume you have security cameras in that part of the building?"

"Yes, of course!" Demidov said. He hurried over to another of his men. "Boris, bring up the surveillance footage from the camera covering that corridor." Then he went back to the first man. "Make sure you pull Saitov's access from the computer and deactivate that card, Yuri."

"Already done," his subordinate assured him.

It took a couple more minutes to retrieve imagery from the appropriate camera and return to when the RFID signature of Saitov's key card was shown leaving the elevator. But eventually, they were all watching as a man in a business suit and tie got off the elevator and briefly scoped out the camera. Turning away, he dropped something small into the nearest recycling bin.

"There goes the key card," one of the security men commented.

Demidov stilled him with an irritated glare. They continued watching the video and saw the stranger stride quickly down the corridor, ring the bell of an apartment, and then step briskly inside. The door closed behind him. Fast-forwarding through to the present moment confirmed that he hadn't left. Whatever else was going on, the man who had murdered Anton Saitov and stolen his identity was still inside that apartment.

"Who owns that flat?" Raevsky asked, his voice taut.

Demidov quickly checked the address. He turned even paler. "Vladimir Povetkin," he said slowly. "He's a financier . . . and one of our wealthiest tenants." He turned to the Spetsnaz officer. "What does all this mean?" he asked plaintively, obviously rocked by how easily their vaunted high-tech electronic security systems had been duped.

Raevsky scowled. "At best, it means we have a nasty hostage situation on our hands." He shrugged. "At worst, this could be just one element of some major terrorist operation."

"Terrorists?"

The Spetsnaz officer nodded at the screen in front of them. "I doubt this man is working alone. And if so, we have no idea yet of how many other intruders have penetrated your so-called security—or where exactly they may have gone inside this building."

"More intruders?" Demidov stammered. "But how would they get past our checkpoints?"

Raevsky smiled unpleasantly. "Perhaps the same way this one did. Kill a tenant or someone employed in one of the businesses here and take their access card. How many people live or work in this building?"

The number was in the thousands, Demidov knew. Dire possibilities suddenly raced through his mind.

"Exactly," the Spetsnaz officer said, correctly interpreting the look of horror on the security chief's face. "Who knows how many other corpses are currently littering back alleys or buried in dumpsters?"

Demidov felt sick to his stomach. The Mercury City Tower's corporate and residential tenants paid sky-high prices because they had been promised near-total protection. Any breach of security—and absolutely one of this possible magnitude—would be disastrous for the skyscraper's investors and for him, both professionally and personally. His employers were unforgiving, but they were choir boys compared to someone like the Raven Syndicate's Pavel Voronin. If the oligarch felt threatened in any way, Demidov realized, those he deemed responsible would quickly pay a lethal price. "What can we do?" he asked uncertainly.

"You and your rent-a-cops will do nothing," Raevsky said coldly. "Leave this situation to us. We're trained for it. Your people are not." Taking command, he swiveled toward two of his helmeted and masked troops. "Vanya. Kolya. Take your chemical sniffers. Inspect the machinery spaces first. See if anyone's already planted explosive devices to take out key systems. Make sure they're clean."

They nodded, grabbed one of the equipment bags, and left the operations center.

Demidov's mouth opened and then closed in consternation. He stared at the Spetsnaz officer. "You really think someone planted bombs down here? So close to us?"

Raevsky met his stare. "It's mostly a precaution," he admitted quietly. "But do you really want to find out the hard way that we should have checked?"

Seeing his point, the security chief subsided.

Some minutes later, the two Spetsnaz soldiers returned. "Everything checks out fine," one of them reported. "We're clear down here."

Raevsky nodded. "Good. One less thing to worry about." He signaled his troops. "Okay, gear up. We're going upstairs." Moving with the speed and ease instilled by intense practice and training, the black-clad commandos unzipped equipment bags and armed up with an assortment of weapons—suppressed submachine guns, magazine-fed semi-automatic shotguns, pistols, and a variety of fragmentation and flash-bang grenades.

Finished, they slid spare magazines and other equipment into their vest and leg pouches. A couple of their bulky gear bags remained unopened.

Watching the Alpha Group soldiers get ready, Demidov couldn't help but be impressed. He'd witnessed some of Voronin's Raven Syndicate mercenaries showing off their skills as a demonstration when the oligarch insisted on his people being given a freer hand to handle security for his headquarters. They were good, but these troops were at least their equal. He glanced back at Raevsky as the Spetsnaz officer finished checking over his personal weapon, a PP-19-01 Vityaz-SN submachine gun. "What is your plan, Major?"

The other man raised an eyebrow. "My plan? We're going to the forty-sixth floor to deal with this terrorist son of a bitch," he said calmly. Then he frowned. "Which reminds me, Demidov: The second we step off that elevator, I want you to turn off every damn surveillance camera on that level. The last thing I want is footage showing our anti-terrorist tactics swirling around on YouTube or TikTok or whatever. Clear?"

Demidov nodded vigorously. "Very clear, Major. I fully understand the need for discretion in this matter." Left unsaid was his own earnest desire to make sure that none of Moscow's tabloid television shows got their hands on film that would cast the Mercury City Tower, and his own security team, for that matter, in a bad light.

"Good," Raevsky said, sounding almost pleased. Then his eyes hardened. "And one more thing. When those cameras go down, I also want you to shut down every elevator in the building. Without any exceptions! I want this skyscraper of yours locked down tight, all the way from the roof to the lowest basement level. If there are other terrorists on the loose, I want them trapped and immobilized until we've dealt with their comrade."

"Shut the elevators down?" Demidov gulped, almost gagging on a sour taste in his throat. "But the other important tenants, they'll—"

"Complain?" the Spetsnaz officer sneered. He leaned closer. "Think about it carefully, Demidov. Which would you rather deal with? Rich assholes bitching because they got stuck for a little while in an elevator or had to use the stairs? Or rich assholes turned into corpses because you decided not to inconvenience them and allowed a bunch of terrorists to roam free?"

Even paler now, the security chief nodded. "I understand, Major," he said, the words almost tripping over each other in their haste to leave his mouth. "We'll shut everything down. Nothing will move without your direct authorization," he promised.

"Very good," Raevsky told him sincerely. "My troops and I are counting on your complete cooperation. It's our best chance at handling this situation."

THIRTY-NINE

MERCURY CITY TOWER UPPER LEVELS

A SHORT TIME LATER

Major Nikolai Raevsky led his team of four Alpha Group commandos toward the nearest high-speed elevator. Summoned by the security operations center, it stood waiting for them with its doors open. They all crowded inside. Between their bulky body armor, equipment bags, and weapons, it was a tight fit. Raevsky reached out and tapped the button for the forty-sixth floor.

The doors closed with a *ping*. Immediately, the car rose at a smooth seven meters per second. Glowing floor numbers above the panel flickered, increasing as they ascended. The black-clad soldiers lowered their goggles into position and readied their weapons. No one spoke.

With a small, almost unnoticeable jolt, the elevator stopped. Raevsky exchanged a sharp look with his team. The displayed floor number was "46." When the doors slid open with a faint *whoosh*, his hand darted forward in a silent tactical signal. Moving with trained precision, they darted through the opening and fanned out across the corridor—going prone with their weapons up and ready. The elevator doors closed behind them.

For a long moment, they all lay still, sighting down the barrels of their submachine guns and shotguns. Nothing moved in their field of view. From his position in the middle of the group, one of the soldiers studied the readouts on his hand-held electromagnetic and radio frequency detector. "The surveillance cameras are down, sir," he said carefully. "Looks like that security guy Demidov did what you told him to."

"Good," Raevsky commented. "That's one hurdle down." He got back to his feet and signaled the others to do the same. "Let's move out. Time's a-wasting."

Silently, they advanced down the corridor and halted just outside the Russian financier's apartment. Raevsky lifted his gloved hand and knocked politely.

The door opened, revealing a grinning Shannon Cooke. "Whoa, Nick," he said. "You guys look scary as shit. That big bad Storm Trooper vibe works. Mind if I just surrender?"

"Maybe later," Nick Flynn, alias Major Nikolai Raevsky, replied, matching the other man's smile. "Right now, we're on sort of a tight schedule." He looked past Cooke into the living room just beyond the entrance foyer. An array of small pieces of C4 plastic explosive covered its hardwood floors in a circular pattern. They were connected by snaking lines of det cord, which were, in turn, tied into the coil of flexible, twin shock tubes Cooke held in his hands. Water-filled plastic bags were taped down over each charge of C4. The U.S. Marine Corps had pioneered this technique as a field expedient to turn ordinary plastic explosives into shaped charges. When they were detonated, the gallons of water in those bags would compress the blasts—directing most of their explosive force downward through the living room floor.

"Nice work," Flynn said appreciatively. "What about that Russian banker, Povetkin, and his assistant? Do we need to move them out?"

Cooke shook his head. "They should be fine. I've got 'em stashed in a bedroom far enough away." He shrugged. "Might be a little loud, though, I guess."

"It's going to get loud pretty much everywhere soon enough," Flynn agreed. He stepped back to let the other man out the door.

Unreeling the lengths of shock tube behind him, Cooke stepped into the corridor and shooed them all farther away from the apartment, back along the hall toward the elevator shaft. He knelt and gently laid the shock tube coil on the carpeted floor. Small particles of HMX/aluminum explosive powder filled each twin plastic tube. When ignited, they would send shockwaves flashing onward at 6,500 feet per second, triggering each det cord-rigged C4 charge.

Finished for the moment, he stood back up and looked around at the rest of the team. "I sure hope you fellas brought enough toys for everyone," he said conversationally. One hand brushed his wool suit jacket. "'Cause I'm feeling a tad underdressed here." Kossak handed him one of the unopened gear bags, and Cooke quickly doffed his suit and shrugged into his body armor, tactical gear, and other equipment.

While Cooke was getting set, Flynn turned to Laura Van Horn, who was now rapidly and gratefully shedding the under-armor padding that had disguised her as a stocky man. "How long before those charges you and Wade set go off?"

She glanced at her watch. "Just under ninety seconds." While pretending to check the Mercury City Tower's machinery spaces for terrorist bombs, she and Vucovich had actually planted their own explosive devices in the rooms containing electrical substations, the building's emergency generators, and its telecommunications hubs. None of the individual charges was very large or particularly powerful. Carefully placed to avoid collateral damage, they were unlikely to kill or injure anyone in the basement sublevel. But their combined effects should be sufficient to knock out power and wired communications across all seventy-five floors of the mammoth skyscraper.

Flynn felt his gut tighten. Between those explosives hidden deep in the roots of this building and the improvised C4-shaped charges Cooke had rigged up inside Povetkin's apartment, all hell was about to break loose. "Get set," he ordered his team quietly.

Obeying him, they dropped flat, facing down the corridor toward the open apartment door. That posture oriented their ballistic helmets toward the expected blast. Next to Flynn, Cooke slipped his fingers inside the igniter rings fixed to the ends of the twinned shock tubes, waiting for the signal.

RAVEN SYNDICATE CORPORATE HEADQUARTERS, 44TH FLOOR, MERCURY CITY TOWER
THAT SAME TIME

Pavel Voronin was reading through a long, dry, and overly technical report from Neminsky's VELES disease spore production unit when his computer screen went dark. "*Der'mo*," he muttered. "Shit." He punched the power button on its chassis to reboot the machine. Nothing happened. He noticed that the overhead lights were out as well. With an irritated frown, he picked up his desk phone to demand assistance. There was no tone, only silence.

His mouth tightened. Angrily, he grabbed the smartphone next to his keyboard and thumbed it awake from its power-saving mode. A finger press on the screen confirmed his identity. It took him only a second to verify that, as he'd half-expected, he had no contact with any network. No unassisted cell signal could reliably pierce the skyscraper's steel-framed interior or its copper-clad exterior. Nor the steel-reinforced secure door to this office, for that matter, he realized. Cell phone signal boosters carefully sited throughout the three floors occupied by the Raven Syndicate's corporate offices usually offset such problems. But those boosters were useless with the skyscraper's electricity grid off-line.

Just then, a sharp *whuummp* sound echoed from somewhere overhead. The pictures and paintings on his walls shook and rattled. A thin veil of dust swirled down from the office's acoustic ceiling tiles.

Voronin sat frozen in place for a moment, staring upward. But then his mind cleared. That had been a bomb, he understood with grim certainty. And it must have gone off not far away. Somehow, despite the intense security measures around this massive skyscraper and the Syndicate's own upper-level offices, he was again under attack.

Feeling suddenly cold, he shoved back from his desk and strode to a large wall cabinet. He pressed his palm against a biometric smart lock and swore under his breath when the cabinet remained resolutely sealed. Without power, the expensive, high-tech lock was just another useless piece of junk. Fumbling through his pockets, he produced a backup key. Aware that seconds might count, he jammed it into the mechanical lock and twisted. Bolts retracted, and he yanked the cabinet doors open—revealing an assortment of weapons and emergency equipment, including a lightweight Level IIIA armor vest capable of resisting pistol rounds and knife thrusts.

Voronin grabbed items out of the cabinet in a controlled frenzy. His teeth ground together in barely suppressed fury. At least, if the worst came to worst, he decided, his enemies would not find him cowering, unarmed and helpless.

NEMESIS FORCE
THAT SAME TIME

With his ears ringing from the simultaneous detonation of Cooke's multiple shaped charges, Flynn pushed himself up off the corridor's carpeted floor. Around him, Van Horn and the others were doing the same. The blast's pall of smoke and dust cut visibility to only yards. Unslinging his Vityaz-SN submachine gun, he trotted forward into the gray haze. Readying their own weapons, his team followed. Part of him felt oddly relieved now that they were in action. All of his lingering doubts and uncertainties were gone. From here on out, the situation they faced was relatively simple. The brutal calculus of battle was either kill or be killed.

Flynn reached the Russian banker's apartment to find the explosion had blown the door off its hinges. He peered inside and saw that their improvised demolition charges had ripped a huge, still smoldering, hole in the living room floor. A couple of scorched steel support beams were now exposed, but everything else had vanished, smashed downward by the blast. The hole opened into the 45th floor, which was the uppermost of the three levels occupied by Voronin's Raven Syndicate offices. One side of his mouth quirked upward. He'd told Fox they would find a gap in the Russian oligarch's security—or make one. Well, there it was.

A quick hand signal halted Van Horn and the others just outside the door. Then he tugged a ball-shaped Russian RGN fragmentation grenade from one of his equipment pouches, armed it, and lobbed it straight down through the hole. If he'd waited even a second longer, the grenade's primary impact fuse would have armed, meaning it would have gone off the instant it hit any surface. But with those steel support beams still partially obstructing the gap, risking an impact detonation would have been dumb. "Frag out!" he yelled and dropped prone.

The rest of the team threw themselves flat, too.

Less than four seconds later, there was a sudden flash and a sharp crack as the grenade's secondary timed fuse detonated—spewing lethal, razor-edged aluminum fragments outward from its blast point. Above the hole, acoustic tiles on the living room ceiling shattered as pieces of the grenade's casing impacted them at high velocity.

Reacting fast, the six Quartet Directorate agents scrambled upright and rushed the gap. In pairs, with Flynn and Van Horn going first, they dropped down through the hole, and landed in the blast-smashed ruins of a couple of Raven Syndicate offices. Chunks of rubble from the shattered ceiling and partition walls lay heaped across broken desks and overturned chairs and spilled out past doors that the force of the explosion had ripped away.

Flynn noticed an outstretched arm, half-buried in the debris. Another body, badly mangled, was sprawled across one of the desks. He winced briefly at the sight. No matter how this went down, he and the others on his team were going to kill a lot of people today. But then he hardened his resolve. Implicitly or explicitly, the men working for the Raven Syndicate had signed on to Voronin's plans to kill millions or tens of millions of American civilians. He was sure they would have argued they were only serving the interests of their own country, but patriotism could not justify a willingness to commit mass murder.

He regained his balance and looked across the smoking debris field at Van Horn. She hefted her submachine gun and nodded. He tucked his own automatic weapon against his shoulder and angled out through the closest blown-open door. He emerged into another corridor, narrower and far plainer than the one on the floor above them, with doors on either side. This level of the skyscraper was broken up into office space, not large luxury apartments.

Flynn turned to the right. They were at the narrower, southern end of the Mercury City Tower, which meant the nearest emergency stairwell leading down to the 44th floor should lie in this direction. Two separate staircases ran through the skyscraper's central core, one opening to the west, the other to the east. They were heading up the eastern flank of the building. Van Horn slid into place on his left. Cooke and Vucovich followed them out into the corridor.

Hynes and Kossak came last and turned the other way. Their task was to protect the rest of the team against any ambush from behind. While the Pole covered him, Hynes fished inside his equipment bag and pulled out a small, olive-green, plastic-cased device. It was rectangular and slightly concave. He knelt and carefully positioned it on twin bipod legs, angling it slightly toward where the corridor turned a corner. Satisfied with its aim, he screwed a brown cylinder into a well on the top and made sure the coiled length of electrical wire emerging from the cylinder was solidly connected. Then Hynes got to his feet, slung the equipment bag over his shoulder again, and went back into the ruined offices. Only seconds later, he came out dragging a rolling chair. Quickly, he tipped the chair on its side, right in front of the device he'd deployed. Now the olive-green rectangle was, at least, loosely concealed from anyone coming around the corner. Finished with his preparations, he picked up the coil of wire and started backing away, slowly unreeling the wire as he went.

Walking steadily backward beside Hynes, still sighting down the short barrel of his submachine gun, Kossak smiled. "Someone may be in for a very bad day," he noted.

Hynes nodded. "Surprises," he said. "I hate getting them. But I *love* giving them."

By this time, Flynn and the others had advanced farther up the corridor. Van Horn's submachine gun stuttered briefly as she dropped a Russian who'd suddenly bolted out through a doorway ahead of them. Hit two or three times, the man went down without a sound. Passing the crumpled corpse, she kicked a pistol out of his hand. Seeing it, Flynn nodded grimly to himself. They would have to treat everyone they met in this warren as an armed enemy.

On high alert, they both continued to edge forward along the smoke-filled hallway. Closed doors crashed open behind them as Cooke and Vucovich checked to make sure the rooms they'd passed were really empty. Sudden bursts of submachine gun fire and shotgun blasts showed that not all of them were. "Tango on the left down," Flynn heard Cooke report through his radio headset. "Got another on the right," Vucovich echoed.

Through the haze ahead, Flynn saw the corridor veer to the right. According to the rough floor plans they'd drawn based on Kondakov's descriptions, it widened beyond that bend into an open bay with floor-to-ceiling views of Moscow and conference tables that could be flipped on their sides to create improvised barricades. That would be a solid place for Syndicate personnel to find cover and concealment, and then hit Flynn's team from the flank as they pushed past toward the door to the emergency stairs.

He put out a hand, ordering a brief halt. Van Horn and the others went to one knee. They needed to get to those stairs and down to the next floor as fast as possible, but walking mindlessly into a potential ambush didn't fall under the heading of intelligent moves. A glance across the hall showed Van Horn miming throwing a grenade. He nodded. Her favorite tactical adage was "when in doubt, blow it up," which made excellent sense in this case. The key to winning a close-quarters battle was to leverage every advantage you had—explosives, for example—rather than slugging it out in a fair, stand-up fight.

More rapid hand signals conveyed Flynn's intent to the rest of his action team. They nodded in understanding. He went down on his stomach and wriggled forward to just short of the bend. From there, he had a partial view of the open bay, but no real line of sight to where the enemy was likely concealed. He yanked another RGN fragmentation grenade out of one of his vest pouches, twisted onto his side next to the wall, pulled the pin, and side-armed it hard and fast, rolling back onto his stomach in the same, fluid motion. "Frag out!"

The grenade flew through the air, trailing blue-gray smoke from its pyrotechnic fuse, hit the far wall, and bounced away at a shallow angle, tumbling deeper into the bay out of his sight. He buried his face against the floor.

A horrified voice yelled a warning. "*Granata!* Grenade!"

Craaack!

Dust and smoke billowed outward from the blast point. Splinters hammered the wall of the corridor opposite to the bay. Shrill, agonized shrieks and screams rang out. Even before the shattering noise of the explosion faded, Van Horn, Cooke, and Vucovich were in motion. They sprinted around the bend and opened up, swiveling through narrow, lethal arcs as they fired a hail of 9mm rounds and 12-gauge armor-piercing shotgun slugs. Flynn pushed himself back onto his feet and went forward to join them.

Their weapons fell silent. "Clear!" Van Horn reported, scanning the jumble of upended, bullet- and fragment-riddled conference tables stretched across the far end of the bay. "I count three down and dead."

"Roger that," Cooke said, still sighting down the barrel of his submachine gun. Off to his flank, Vucovich dropped out a spent twelve-round magazine from his Saiga-12 tactical shotgun and slammed in a full one.

Flynn swept his hand through an arc, gesturing to the continuation of the corridor on the other side of this more open area. Through the dust and smoke, he could barely make out a dimly lit sign in red Cyrillic lettering: Аварийная лестница. Emergency Stairs. He realized that with all the regular power off on this level, that sign must be running on a battery backup. "Keep moving, guys," he ordered. "The clock's running. We need to pile on the pressure before more of these bastards wake up and figure out where we are—and what we're planning."

Growling their assents, his team regrouped and followed him toward the entrance to the emergency stairwell, with Kossak still covering their six and Hynes carefully unreeling his coil of electrical cable.

FORTY

THAT SAME TIME

Kiril Rodin finished buckling his body armor into position and then retrieved his personal weapons from the combination safe next to his desk.
A small 9mm SR-1 Vektor pistol went into a chest rig on his tactical
vest. Next, he unfolded the stock of a compact SR-2 Veresk submachine
gun and slung the weapon over his head and shoulder. He checked the
phone one last time. It was still dead.

His jaw clenched. Because he'd judged any such attempt to be
doomed to failure, he'd never really expected Voronin's enemies to attack
the Mercury City Tower. The idea that anyone would choose to hurl
themselves into the teeth of so many sophisticated security systems and
armed guards had struck him as an act of suicidal futility—one that
would be anathema to experienced enemy intelligence agents and special operators. At best, he'd calculated that a few attackers might succeed
in breaking into the skyscraper's ground-floor lobby, but he never imagined that they could penetrate any higher.

And yet, Rodin icily reminded himself, here they were. Judging by the
powerful explosion he'd heard and felt only moments before, the enemy
operatives had made a forced entry somewhere on the 45th floor, two levels

up. He frowned. How the devil could anyone have infiltrated weapons and explosives past the building's intrusive screening and ID checks? But then he shook his head. The how's could wait. Right now, his job was to see what, if anything, could be salvaged from this unfolding catastrophe.

He spun around on his heel and left his office. Just outside the door, he ran headlong into a knot of bewildered analysts blocking the corridor. They were bleating away at each other with ever-more strident voices, demanding to know what was happening and asking frantic questions that none could answer. They were all bright enough, but most had been deskbound SVR or GRU officers without even a shred of field experience, let alone life at the sharp end where strangers might shoot at you. At the sound of another muffled explosion from somewhere overhead, they fell briefly silent before breaking out again, even louder than before. He could sense they were beginning to panic.

"Shut up!" Rodin snapped harshly. He racked the bolt on his submachine gun, chambering a round. Those around him froze and fell silent. "Stop acting like sheep."

"Sir!" a voice called from the back of the shocked crowd. He turned to see members of the Raven Syndicate's internal security unit shoving their way through the bottleneck. Like him, they were in armor and had their weapons ready. Rodin counted twelve of them, but immediately noticed who was missing. "Where's Saitov?" he demanded. "Where's your damn boss?"

The guards shrugged helplessly. "We don't know," one of them admitted. "He didn't come to work this morning."

Rodin snarled a short, thoroughly profane, litany of curses, certain that Saitov's sudden absence was not a coincidence. He found the next senior man, Anatoly Nemov, among the security guards around him. From what he remembered, Nemov had been a captain in the Spetsnaz before joining the Raven Syndicate. "Where are the rest of your men?"

"Scattered," Nemov admitted. "We have teams on all three floors and in the lobby, but I haven't been able to contact them. Everything's down, computers, phones, mobiles, everything. These are the only guys I could lay my hands on fast."

Rodin thought rapidly. Without communications or power, this situation was quickly degenerating into a complete shit show. One thing, however, was evident. Those carrying out this sudden attack had achieved complete surprise. They were already inside the Syndicate's defenses and undoubtedly now moving against their primary target—which had to be Pavel Voronin. Killing him was the obvious countermove for the Americans, now that they seemed to have awakened to the dangers they faced.

This made it his duty to try to prevent that from happening, Rodin decided. Or, more accurately, to order these other men to do so. Most of the security guards were veterans of the Spetsnaz and other elite military units. They had the necessary training and combat skills to go head-to-head with the attacking force. Personally, however, he had absolutely no intention of risking his own life for Voronin. He was too old, too canny, and too valuable to the Motherland to go charging into battle like some half-witted conscript. Besides, President Zhdanov had not given him this assignment to serve as Voronin's glorified bodyguard. Quite the opposite, in fact.

His decision made, he rounded on Nemov. "All right, I'm taking command of this situation for the moment," he snapped.

The other man nodded in relief. "Yes, sir."

"Take two-thirds of your force and get up to the forty-fourth floor," Rodin continued. "Your highest priority is to reach Mr. Voronin's private office. Join up with his bodyguards there and escort him safely downstairs to the security operations center in the subbasement. Nothing else matters. Not your lives. Nor those of anyone who gets in your way. Do you clearly understand me, Nemov?"

"I do, sir," the former Spetsnaz captain assured him.

"Then get to it!" Rodin ordered.

With a nod, the other man swung away and headed for the nearest emergency stairs, calling out names as he went. The men he'd selected turned and followed him, pushing through the crowd of intelligence analysts who'd been listening with increasing anxiety.

Rodin turned his gaze on the four remaining guards. "The rest of you! Take the other stairwell and deploy to the forty-fifth floor. That's where the enemy is attacking from. You will find, engage, and destroy these intruders."

They nodded and hurried off.

He swung back to the flock of frightened analysts. They stared back at him. "As for you lot, you're coming with me."

"Where?" one of them dared to ask.

"Down the emergency stairs to the ground floor," Rodin told them. "I'm going to shepherd you out of this clusterfuck before it gets any worse." He allowed himself a hidden cynical smile. What could be better than to play the hero while also avoiding any serious danger?

NEMESIS FORCE
THAT SAME TIME

Flynn stared in consternation at the glowing red light on the card-controlled security panel on the heavy steel door to the stairwell. This was the first point where their pre-assault intelligence had led them badly astray. They'd figured that the emergency exits would be shut down from the stairs. What they hadn't realized—and they hadn't clarified when interrogating Kondakov, he remembered to his chagrin—was that Voronin's security people were paranoid enough to insist on securing both sides of the doors, whether they were intended for emergency use or not. And also smart enough to provide battery backup power for their biometric locks.

"I can go back upstairs and grab Saitov's access card," Cooke offered. "The one I dumped near the elevator."

Flynn shook his head. "Even if we had the time, and we don't, building security already pulled Saitov's access." He turned to Vucovich. "We need to breach this door, Wade."

"On it, sir," the lanky man replied. He rapped on the door and listened intently. "That steel's way too thick to shotgun the latch, but the hinges are on this side. I should be able to blast them." He patted his Saiga-12.

"Get to it," Flynn ordered. "We'll cover you." At his signal, he and

Van Horn glided further up the corridor and went prone, ready to engage any hostiles from that direction. Cooke flattened against the wall beside the door, gripping a short, two-handled battering ram to bash the heavy door open as soon as Vucovich smashed its hinges. Flynn risked a quick glance back. The former soldier had his shotgun firmly seated against his shoulder, with its barrel angled up at the top left side of the door only six inches away.

Vucovich fired twice into the top hinge. *Blaamm-blaamm.* Hammered by two solid slugs, the hinge popped loose with a metallic *ping.* He lowered the barrel and aimed at the center hinge in a smooth motion. Two more shots tore it off. His shotgun muzzle dropped toward the bottommost hinge. Another two slugs completed the job. The heavy steel door sagged slightly, now only held up on the other side by the solid bolts of its lock mechanism. Vucovich rolled back from the stairwell entrance, giving Cooke room to slide into position and slam his battering ram against the door. *Whaam. Whaam. Whaam.* Three solid blows were enough to smash it away from the left side of the frame, creating a man-sized gap they could all fit through.

Flynn breathed out. They had their way down.

————

Kossak and Hynes were about ten yards behind the rest of the team. They were prone too—but still facing along the corridor the way they'd all just come. The Pole sighted down the barrel of his submachine gun, doggedly ignoring all the noise from where Vucovich and Cooke were breaching the stairwell door. Suddenly, he caught a tiny flicker of motion far down the haze-filled corridor. A helmeted head had poked around the corner and then, almost as swiftly, pulled back out of sight. "We have company, Cole," he murmured.

Hynes nodded. He'd seen the same movement. That had been a Raven Syndicate guard scoping out the way ahead. And where there was one, he'd bet there were others. "I got 'em." He grinned tightly. "And I bet those poor SOBs figure they're in solid cover, too."

A Russian wearing body armor rolled out from behind the corner down the corridor. He was already prepping a grenade.

"Surprise," Hynes said quietly. He toggled the switch in his hand.

Wha-WHUMMP.

The Russian-made MON-50 directional mine he'd planted in the corridor detonated. A pound and a half of plastic explosive went up in a millisecond, sending 540 steel balls sleeting outward through a fifty-four-degree arc. Walls, office partitions, and doors erupted in clouds of debris as they were struck by the hail of projectiles moving at more than twelve hundred meters per second. All four Raven Syndicate security troops ready to attack the Quartet Directorate team from the rear were knocked backward by the enormous shotgun-like blast—punched off their feet by impacts that tore through ballistic armor and flesh alike with ease. They lay crumpled, bloodied and unmoving, and already dead or dying.

One prong of the counterattack ordered by Kiril Rodin had been stopped cold.

FORTY-ONE

NEMESIS FORCE

THAT SAME TIME

With Nick Flynn in the lead, four Quartet Directorate agents entered the stairwell. Gray concrete walls and steps, bare metal railings, and the dim, battery-powered emergency lights fixed to each landing made it evident that this was not a part of the Mercury City Tower intended for everyday use by tenants or visitors. He moved down the stairs with his back to the wall and his submachine gun at the ready, swiveling to clear every new aspect of the stairwell as it came into view. Van Horn, Cooke, and Vucovich came close behind him. Cole Hynes and Tadeusz Kossak were still posted up top, acting as a rearguard until Flynn and the others opened the way to the 44th floor, which, according to the information they'd gained from Kondakov, was where Voronin had his private office and living quarters.

He reached the landing for that level and moved to examine the door there. As he'd expected, it was locked. Van Horn and Cooke scooted around him and knelt at the top of the next flight of stairs, prepared to engage any hostiles coming up from the next floor, which also belonged to the Raven Syndicate. Vucovich came over to join him.

Vucovich pursed his lips as he studied the solidly constructed exit door. "I'm gonna have to blow this one open, sir," he said. "The hinges are on the other side, and shotgun slugs won't make a dent in all that steel."

"Any chance we can batter it down?"

Vucovich shook his head. "No way. I saw a video once of a bunch of guys trying to bust through a security door like this using sledgehammers and battering rams. After fifteen minutes, they weren't much closer than when they'd started and a hell of a lot more tired."

Flynn clapped him on the shoulder. "Okay, Wade. Go ahead and rig it."

The other man turned and trotted back up the stairs and around a bend to where he could look up and see the smashed-open exit to the 45th floor. He whistled softly. "Hey, Cole!" he hissed.

Hynes's head poked around the edge of the door. "Yeah?"

"I need the static SIMON."

Hynes pulled back out of sight to rummage in his equipment bag and reappeared holding a narrow cylinder with a thin rod fixed to its nose. The whole assembly was twenty-nine inches long. "Catch," he called and lobbed it gently to Vucovich, who caught it easily in both hands. It weighed a little less than two pounds.

When he brought it back down, Flynn eyed the device with interest. Designed by an Israeli arms manufacturer, Rafael Advanced Defense Systems, the original SIMON rifle grenade was designed to be fired at doors from a distance. The U.S. Army had adopted a variant for its own use as the M-100 GREM. When fired, the weapon's sixteen-inch-long stand-off rod would strike first and immediately detonate the shaped-charge grenade that same distance from the targeted entrance—widening the area affected by its explosive shock wave and eliminating any need to aim for hinges or latches. This was a static version, without the fins needed for flight or the impact fuse at the base of that stand-off rod. Instead, it came with a powerful adhesive patch fixed to the rod's flattened tip. "GREM, I get. Grenade Rifle Entry Munition. Typical military acronym BS. But what does SIMON stand for?" he wondered aloud.

Vucovich grinned back at him. "I bet that it's sort of a joke, sir," he confided. "As in, SIMON says, 'Open the fucking door.'"

Flynn laughed. "Then let's do it, Wade."

Vucovich got to work, peeling off the adhesive patch's covering and carefully centering the stand-off rod against the door. Then he leaned in hard, pressing the tip against its steel surface. Thirty seconds later, he carefully took his hands away. The SIMON breach grenade assembly hung there, firmly affixed to the door. Next, he began gingerly attaching a length of strong fishing line to a pin at the back of the grenade itself. Pulling that pin would trigger a short time-delay fuse.

Just then, a door banged loudly from somewhere out of sight below, followed by a babble of anxious-sounding Russian voices and the rapid clatter of many feet heading down the emergency stairs in a hurry. Van Horn glanced back at Flynn with a worried look. "Sounds like we've got runaways on the move, Nick," she whispered. "If one of them is that son of a bitch Voronin, we're screwed."

Flynn nodded tightly. If their target hadn't been in his office on the 44th floor when they'd launched their attack or reacted faster than they'd planned and somehow managed to get ahead of them, he could easily be escaping. And that was not an acceptable outcome. "Chase those people down and find out," he ordered Van Horn and Cooke.

She was on the move before he finished speaking, rushing down the stairs with Cooke on her heels.

Two flights down, the two Quartet Directorate agents rounded a bend in the stairwell and spotted their quarry. Only a flight ahead of them now, a crowd of people were heading down the stairs as fast as they could go without tripping. They were all male and looked reasonably fit. If she had to bet, Van Horn thought coldly, this probably wasn't just some random group of civilians fleeing the sudden explosions and staccato rattle of small-arms fire. But they weren't wearing uniforms, and she couldn't see any obvious weapons at first glance. Which meant she wasn't entirely sure who these clowns really were. Her eyes narrowed. "Damn it," she muttered.

When it came right down to it, she couldn't risk slaughtering innocents by accident, especially without warning. She skidded to a halt right at the top of the stairs, only a few yards behind the hurrying mob. "Down! Down! Down!" she yelled. "Get your asses down on the ground and then freeze!" A multitude of sheet-white, appalled faces spun toward her voice, staring up at Van Horn in shock. "I said, 'Get down!'" she repeated loudly.

That was when she spotted a cold-eyed, gray-haired man in body armor. Since he was the one who was the farthest down the stairs, it was clear that he'd been leading the frightened group. And he wasn't frightened at all. Instead, the man whirled around toward her, bringing his weapon, an SR-2 Veresk submachine gun, to bear. Before she could react, he opened up on full auto—not caring that most of the 9mm rounds he spray-fired lashed across the crowd packed into the narrow stairwell above him, killing or wounding several. Bodies slumped in all directions.

But not all of his bullets went wild. Van Horn felt a sudden, crushing impact across her chest. Pain flared red-hot and she fell onto her knees, shocked by the blow and abruptly finding it hard to breathe. Everything went out of focus. Vaguely, as if through a layer of gauze, she caught a glimpse of Cooke as he yanked out a grenade, prepped it, and lobbed it down the steps in one fluid motion. It sailed through the air and fell into the middle of the mob. Spinning away from the flight of stairs, he threw himself at her and knocked her prone.

———

When Kiril Rodin saw the ball-shaped grenade bouncing down the steps toward him, he reacted instinctively. He let go of his submachine gun and grabbed the panic-stricken Raven Syndicate analyst closest to him. Without hesitating, he yanked the screaming man directly into the path of the grenade and then shoved him straight toward it. It exploded with a sharp, flat *craaack*.

The man he'd used as an improvised human shield was hurled backward—gutted by the blast and its cloud of jagged fragments. Those above him on the stairs were mowed down, tossed aside in a wash of blood and splintered bone. Though partly protected from the worst effects of the explosion, Rodin felt himself picked up off his feet by the shockwave. He tumbled head over heels down the steps. At the bottom of the next flight, he smacked hard into the concrete floor of the landing, stunned, barely conscious, and bleeding from several small splinter wounds in his arms, legs, and scalp.

In the sudden silence, Van Horn sat up, gasping and panting for air. Frantically, she pawed at her aching chest, expecting to find a wound pulsing blood from a punctured lung. Instead, her gloved fingers brushed across a scorching hot ring of metal. She risked glancing down and felt relieved to see only a blackened circle and the faint glint of brass where a 9mm round had buried itself deep in the layers of her armor. It hadn't penetrated all the way through.

She felt a weight across her legs. Cooke was slumped there. Gently, she patted his shoulder. "Um, Shannon? Mind getting off me?"

Blearily, he raised his head. "You okay?"

"Other than being bruised as hell, I seem fine," Van Horn assured him. When he rolled over, she pushed up cautiously and peered over the edge of the steps. A carpet of torn and bleeding bodies littered the staircase. Her eyes came back into focus enough to be sure that none of them was Pavel Voronin. She frowned. That was a damned shame. Then she shrugged her shoulders, wincing at the pain that triggered. If nothing else, she decided, they'd at least effectively sealed off this escape route. That counted for something.

While Cooke covered her, she struggled to her feet and limped back up the stairs toward Flynn and the others. She found them crouched on the flight of stairs below the 44th floor landing. Near the top, Vucovich was the only one still standing. His right hand gripped the fishing line he'd tied to the SIMON breach grenade's pin. He noticed their approach and waved both of them down. Obediently, they squatted down on the steps, keeping low.

Vucovich pulled back on the line, exerting steady pressure rather than a single, mighty yank that could have dislodged the grenade from the door. With a soft *ting*, the pin pulled free. Instantly, he dropped prone himself, curled up below the top of the steps.

A huge orange flash lit the stairwell. In its wake, a thick cloud of bluish-black smoke billowed outward from the blast point, obscuring everything.

RAVEN SYNDICATE HEADQUARTERS, 44TH FLOOR
THAT SAME TIME

Pavel Voronin heard a series of muffled thumps coming from the electronically locked door to his office. He listened intently, counting the sequence in his head. Then he nodded. That was the correct identifier code he'd established for his bodyguards. Only they knew the proper rhythm and numbers to use.

He rose from his desk with his compact, semi-automatic 9mm Poloz pistol in his hand and moved toward the door. The coded banging continued, repeating the agreed-upon cycle. He opened a panel on the wall next to it and flipped the switch to activate the door's battery-powered emergency override. Then Voronin stepped away from the wall, with his pistol leveled.

The armored door's locking bolts retracted, and it whirred open. One of his senior security men, Anatoly Nemov, entered wearing body armor. Seeing the pistol Voronin had aimed squarely at his head, the former Spetsnaz captain kept his hands off the submachine gun slung over his shoulder.

"What's the situation?" Voronin asked.

"Very bad, sir," Nemov replied. "A hostile enemy of unknown strength has penetrated our facilities. And we don't have any reliable communications with our forces." He gestured toward the large outer office visible behind him. More armed security men were there, grouped near the farther door. "That's why we're here. We need to get you downstairs to safety as quickly as possible."

Voronin nodded, slowly lowering his pistol. "Very well," he agreed. He started toward the door—

And froze as a deafening explosion echoed down the corridor beyond his outer office. Only a few seconds later, the rattle of small-arms fire erupted in the same direction. "Damn it," Voronin snarled. It was too late to make a break that way. His enemies had already arrived. Curtly, he waved his pistol at Nemov. "Get out there and do your job!" he ordered. "Kill those bastards."

"Yes, sir!" Nemov acknowledged. He spun around, pulling the submachine gun off his shoulder, and raced back out, already yelling orders to his men.

The instant the other man cleared the doorway, Voronin lunged for the emergency override switch and slapped it down. The solid, bank vault–style door closed and latched again, with an audible *ca-chunk* sound as its bolts slid back into place. Eyes narrowed in thought, Voronin cast about for new options. If his troops were able to kill the intruders, he thought coldly, that was well and good. But if they failed, and the enemy somehow managed to breach this heavily armored door, the idea of trying to fend them off on his own in this large room, with only a single desk and a couple of chairs for cover and concealment, struck him as the epitome of folly.

No, Voronin decided, if he was now the hunted prey, he needed to choose a better option—to find some hidden position that, at least, offered him a chance, however slim, at turning the tables on those who sought his life. He spun around through a slow circle, scanning his surroundings with eyes now attuned to questions of tactical advantage rather than comfort and prestige. Viewed from here, a smaller door on the shorter wall on the left side of his office opened into an ornate executive washroom. A door on the right-hand wall led into his private suite, which included a dining room, chef's kitchen, and substantial bedroom.

Behind him, the security door to his outer office shuddered, hit by stray rounds that could not penetrate its solid steel core. Aware that time was growing short, Voronin made his choice.

FORTY-TWO

NEMESIS FORCE

THAT SAME TIME

Staying low, Nick Flynn wriggled past the warped, smoldering security door. Vucovich's SIMON grenade had blown it halfway open, wedging it out into the corridor on the other side. He crawled to the far wall and peered through the swirling cloud of smoke that accompanied the blast. He sensed more than saw dim figures moving in the haze and started shooting, squeezing off single rounds in semi-automatic mode with quick, light trigger pulls. Cooke slid into place on his left and opened fire himself.

Hit by multiple 9mm armor-piercing bullets, men screamed somewhere ahead of them and went down hard. Body armor sometimes stopped pistol-caliber rounds, but not always. He saw another shape moving in the veiling bluish-black fog and fired repeatedly. The Vityaz-SN submachine gun stuttered. Blood spattered through the haze, and his target went down in a heap.

Return fire whip-cracked low overhead, gouging away chunks of wood paneling from the corridor walls. Flynn's mind seemed to go into overdrive as he considered the tactical situation. They'd caught the Raven Syndicate guards up ahead by surprise when they'd blown through the stairwell door. But now the bad guys were recovering fast. And that meant this open hallway, without a speck of cover, would become decidedly unhealthy real soon. Getting pinned down in a prolonged firefight here would be suicide.

So it was high time he changed things up, Flynn decided. He lowered his weapon and felt for another grenade, frowning deeply when he realized his vest pouch only held flash-bangs and smoke. He'd used his last frag grenade earlier. There were limits to how much ammunition and other gear any given soldier could carry, so he'd only brought two RGN fragmentation types along. And in this situation, neither the flash-bang devices nor the smoke grenades would do the job. Against a prepared enemy, the flash-bangs' stun effects were minimized. Nor would adding more smoke do much good. In such tight confines, their Russian enemies didn't need to see anything to score kills. All they had to do was keep firing rounds into this narrow corridor, and they were practically guaranteed to hit people. "Well, that sucks," he muttered.

A hand slapped his boot.

Flynn craned his head around and saw Tadeusz Kossak lying prone just behind him. The Pole slid another of the ball-shaped frag grenades forward. "Thanks," he mouthed, reaching back to take it.

"*Nie ma za co*," Kossak said. "You're welcome."

With a quick nod, Flynn prepped the grenade, held it for a second to let the impact fuse arm, and then hurled it down the hallway as hard as he could. "Frag out!" he warned as he tossed it. He felt something sear across the outside of his arm and yanked it back down. A bullet had torn through his sleeve and grazed him, ripping a bloody furrow through the skin, but doing no serious damage. Ignoring it for now, he pressed his face against the tiled floor. Cooke and Kossak did the same.

The grenade flew through the open door of a large office at the end of the corridor, smacked into a large reception desk, and exploded with a sharp, ear-splitting bang. Fragments spewed in all directions, including back along the hallway toward the Quartet Directorate team. Head still down, Flynn heard shards whine past over his helmet. They smacked into the walls and ceiling with tremendous force, raising more wood splinters and puffs of pulverized fiberboard.

In the next split-second, Flynn shoved himself back to his feet and sprinted down the corridor, bringing his submachine gun up to his shoulder and opening fire on the move. He hurdled over a couple of bodies sprawled across floor. Cooke and Kossak followed close behind him while Van Horn and the others boiled out of the stairwell in their wake. Attacking while any surviving Raven Syndicate troops were still trying to shake off the effects of that explosion was the correct tactical move.

He burst through the open door and veered to the right. Amid the churning smoke and dust, Flynn glimpsed a Russian staggering upright behind an overturned leather couch. He swiveled that way and squeezed off two rounds. The man fell backward.

Cooke slid through the door to the left, engaging half-seen targets in that direction. Kossak took the middle and vaulted over the splinter-torn reception desk. He landed on his feet on the other side and shot a third Raven Syndicate guard who'd ducked into cover to avoid the grenade blast.

Flynn spotted movement out the corner of his eye and whirled toward it, already knowing he was reacting too late. Another Russian had reared up from behind a desk at the back of the office. His blood-streaked face was set and utterly intent as he leveled his submachine gun at the American. And then he folded over, hit repeatedly in the chest and stomach by several 9mm rounds fired at close range.

Flynn half-turned and saw Van Horn lowering her own Vityaz-SN. Her hands flew across the compact weapon, dropping out its spent thirty-round magazine and inserting a full one with a couple of quick, highly efficient moves. "Looked like you could use some help," she remarked.

Not trusting himself to speak just yet, Flynn only nodded his thanks. A rapid check of the large room, which Kondakov had identified for them as Voronin's outer office and reception area, showed only corpses. Between their earlier exchange of fire, his grenade, and this swift, brutal assault, they'd accounted for around half a dozen of the Raven Syndicate troops.

"I caught sight of a couple of them high-tailing it that way," Cooke told him, pointing down another shorter corridor out of the office.

Flynn nodded. "Yeah, and they'll be back soon enough, probably with friends." He found Vucovich and pointed him toward the large steel door set in the middle of the far wall. It should be the entrance to Voronin's private office. "See about getting us through that door," he ordered.

"Roger that, sir," Vucovich agreed. He took the bag containing their remaining explosives from Hynes and moved to examine the door.

More rapid-fire orders from Flynn posted Van Horn, Cooke, and Hynes on guard in the outer office with clear fields of fire down both corridors. The three began hauling couches and chairs into position to create rough, improvised barricades across each doorway. The piled-up furniture wouldn't stop bullets, but it should impede any attempt by the Russians to force their way back inside. "You have to hold here long enough for us to breach that security door," Flynn told them. "As soon as we've got it open, Tad, Wade, and I will assault in and take out Voronin." Their heads nodded. That was how they'd planned on handling this part of the mission, assuming they'd made it this far without taking significant losses.

"Uh, sir," he heard Vucovich say hesitantly. "About that door?"

Flynn turned to him. "Yes?"

"We can't breach it," the other man told him regretfully. "Not with the demolitions gear we were able to bring with us. It's a bank vault-type. The door's made out of reinforced steel several inches thick, and it's got solid locking bars . . . the works. We could bang away on it all day without getting anywhere."

Hynes turned away from the barricade. "You owe me five bucks, Wade," he said with an undisguised note of triumph. "Told you that scumbag Voronin wouldn't cut corners when it came to protecting his own hide."

Flynn raised an eyebrow. "Should I assume that you have a solution for this problem, Cole?" he asked mildly. "Because otherwise, I'm not sure winning a five-dollar bet offsets the total failure of our mission."

"Yeah," Hynes said confidently. "We'll use the Gatecrasher on one of those places instead." He indicated the stretches of wall to either side of Voronin's armored door. "Behind all the fancy wood paneling, the wall is probably reinforced concrete. Sure, that stuff's pretty strong, but—"

"Not nearly as strong as that armored door itself," Flynn suddenly understood. The Gatecrasher was a modular, water-tamped breaching charge that blew man-sized holes through concrete and brick walls. It consisted of linear cutting charges contained in separate, cylindrical, water-filled jackets that were Velcroed onto a backing material that could then be propped up against a targeted wall section. The water surrounding each charge helped direct the force of its explosion and reduced the kinetic energy of any bits and pieces of shattered wall hurled away from the blast—making it somewhat safer for use in more confined areas. In its essentials, the Gatecrasher system was a smaller and more portable version of the improvised array of tiny C4 charges and water-filled plastic bags Cooke had used earlier to blast their way through the ceiling of the Raven Syndicate–owned 45th floor.

Hynes nodded. "You got it, sir."

"We'll need water to fill those module jackets," Flynn pointed out. "Which could be a problem, since what's left in our personal hydration packs won't cut it. And I don't want to wander these halls looking for the nearest restroom and hoping there's enough water still in the pipes." When they cut the Mercury City Tower's electrical power, they'd also knocked out the pumps used to lift water to the skyscraper's higher levels.

Hynes directed his attention to a glass-fronted case in one corner of the office. It contained dozens of bottles of the finest Russian brands of mineral water. "Well, there you go, sir. Courtesy of our host, Pavel Dumbass Voronin," he said. "Kind of ironic, huh?"

Flynn nodded. "So it is."

"Contact! Contact!" Cooke yelled suddenly from his post at the doorway to the corridor they'd come from. "I count three-plus Tangos pushing out of the stairwell." He opened fire, squeezing off single, carefully aimed shots. The counterattacking Syndicate troops shot back, punching holes in their barricade of furniture. Fragments of leather and stuffing flew away. Rounds ricocheted off steel coils, throwing sparks. Cooke burned through the rest of his magazine, dropped it out, and pulled another from his assault vest. He inserted it, but then glanced back at Flynn. "I'm just about dry," he reported calmly, meaning that he was almost out of ammunition.

Flynn checked his own equipment. He was low on ammo, too, but he still had three full magazines left. He yanked out two of them and tossed them underhanded to Cooke, who caught them and stuffed them into his vest before swiveling back to the barricaded doorway to continue the fight. In the interval, Hynes leaned in and began shooting, joining Cooke to suppress the attackers before they could try a rush.

Tight-lipped, Flynn swung toward Vucovich and Kossak. "Start prepping that demolition charge ASAP. We're short on time and long on bad guys." They nodded. Vucovich began pulling the separate components of the Gatecrasher system out of their equipment bag, while the Pole grabbed handfuls of water bottles and carried them over. Flynn hurried to join them. Readying the breaching charge in time was going to take all of them working together.

"Tangos in my sector, too!" Van Horn abruptly reported from the other doorway. Her submachine gun crackled. She ducked back as incoming fire tore away chunks from the doorframe, and then leaned back out to shoot again. "One down!" she reported triumphantly. Her weapon ran dry, and she loaded another magazine. "Nick!" she called softly.

Flynn looked up. Van Horn flashed him a hand signal indicating that she, too, was almost out of ammunition. Feeling cold, Flynn fished out his last full magazine and lobbed it over. They had burned through most of their available ammo and almost all their grenades. Sure, they could probably scavenge some additional 9mm magazines from the handful of dead Syndicate guards littering the outer office, but if this close-quarters battle went on for much longer, they would be down to fighting with pistols and knives and bare hands against enemies armed with automatic weapons. And that would be a situation with only one probable outcome—a fatal one.

Gritting his teeth, Flynn grabbed more water bottles and started twisting off caps, before handing them to Kossak to pour into the breaching charge's flattened black nylon tubes. As water filled them, the tubes began to expand, gradually taking on the shape of full cylinders. He quickened his pace. He would be damned if they went down before breaking through Voronin's last line of defense.

FORTY-THREE

OUTSIDE VORONIN'S PRIVATE OFFICE

A SHORT TIME LATER

Flynn watched Vucovich carefully set the Gatecrasher's tactical sleeve against the wall a few feet to the side of the door into Voronin's inner office. The sleeve was a thin sheet of black nylon cloth with Velcro attachment points for the two water-filled cylinders containing the device's shaped explosive cutting charges. Then, while Vucovich held the assembled breaching charge in place, Kossak slotted a metal stake into a notch at the top of the black sleeve and solidly wedged the other end against the carpeted floor. He stepped back. Satisfied that the Gatecrasher would now stay where they wanted it, Vucovich pulled his hands away, too. He knelt, fitted a detonator into a slot at the bottom of the sleeve, stood up again, and backed away toward a far corner of the large outer office, slowly unreeling the attached line of det cord as he went.

Flynn and Kossak followed him. They'd piled more office furniture into that corner to form a crude barricade against backblast from the controlled explosion Vucovich was about to set off. They waited while he finished connecting the det cord to its trigger mechanism. He looked up. "We're good to go."

Flynn nodded. His eyes sought out Cooke, Hynes, and Van Horn.

The three were crouched near the doorways they were guarding, still exchanging fire with the Raven Syndicate troops. So far, the enemy had tried a couple of rushes and been driven back with losses. More bodies now littered both corridors. "Hunker down!" he called. "Fire in the hole!" All three immediately went prone, curling up and pulling in their arms and legs to bring as much of their bodies as possible under the protection of their helmets and armor.

Flynn dropped behind their improvised barricade beside Kossak. Vucovich crouched next to them with his thumb on the trigger switch. He looked at Flynn, who nodded. "Blow it, Wade."

Vucovich squeezed the switch.

An enormous, echoing blast rocked the room. Chunks of shattered concrete and splintered wood paneling flew away from the wall—slamming into their improvised furniture barricade and smashing against the other walls and ceiling. A thick cloud of whitish-gray smoke mushroomed outward, enveloping the entire outer office in a choking fog.

Flynn shook his head to clear his ringing ears. Holy crap, he thought dazedly. That had been even louder than he'd imagined it would be. Lesson Number One, he guessed, was to try your damnedest not to detonate powerful explosive charges in enclosed spaces. Or if you had to, at least make sure you were a long, long way off when they went up. Without the tamping effect of the water surrounding the Gatecrasher's charges, he suspected they'd all have been permanently deafened—and quite possibly dead or badly injured by the backblast.

He stood up from behind the barricade. "Everybody okay?" he called loudly. Van Horn and the others yelled back, reporting they were shaken but not seriously hurt. They uncurled and rolled into position again near the doorways, on guard against the next Syndicate attempt to break in.

Flynn turned to Kossak and Vucovich. "You ready to go hunting?"

"Count me in," the Pole replied, checking over his submachine gun. "I have been looking forward to this for a long time." Vucovich nodded and hefted his Saiga tactical shotgun.

"Then let's go," Flynn said, moving toward the smoking hole they'd just blown through the wall. The jagged bottom was about a foot off the floor and the whole thing was around three feet high and three feet wide. Lengths of rebar curled inward, snapped in the middle and bent out of the way by the sheer force of the explosion. Bending low, Flynn squirmed through the gap and then immediately straightened up. He angled to the right to clear the blind spot there while staying close to the wall. The muzzle of his submachine swept from side to side as he scanned Voronin's office for targets.

Kossak followed him in and went left. Vucovich was the last one through, and he took the middle.

Flynn's eyes narrowed, taking in a scene of luxury turned upside down. A fan-shaped field of smoldering debris stretched across the palatial room. What had been an elegant mahogany desk lay partially buried under a heap of cracked and blackened concrete rubble. A desktop computer monitor had been torn loose from its cabling and tossed aside by the shockwave. Modernist paintings, most probably priceless originals, had been blown off the walls and scattered across the carpet with broken frames and ripped canvases. The enormous floor-to-ceiling windows that formed the far wall were cracked and splintered—but were, astonishingly, still intact. He nodded to himself. Kondakov had claimed the glass was strongly bullet- and impact-resistant, and the Russian had been right.

"Clear!" he snapped, confirming that Voronin's inner office itself was empty. The others echoed his call. There were two other doors, one on each of the shorter walls to the left and right. Flynn jerked his head at the one on the left. "Check that one first," he commanded.

Kossak and Vucovich nodded and moved in that direction. Flynn covered the other interior door and headed around the debris field toward Voronin's desk. The computer's monitor might be toast, but he'd bet the machine itself was intact—shielded by the desk from any fragments and the blast wave. He lowered his right hand long enough to pull a multitool out of one of his vest pouches. Besides the chance to put a bullet in Voronin, this was a golden, intelligence-gathering opportunity he didn't plan to pass up.

Over by the left-hand door, the Pole leaned over, angled his submachine gun, and put a couple of rounds through the latch. It sagged open. Vucovich kicked it all the way in, leaned around the doorjamb, and pumped 12-gauge buckshot rounds from his shotgun into the room beyond. He pulled back. "Nothing," he reported. "Just a fancy bathroom."

"Presumably inoperable now," Kossak said with a straight face.

Vucovich grinned back at him. "Afraid so," he replied, equally deadpan. "Sure hope you can hold it." Weapons up, they both headed across the office toward the right-hand door.

Over by Voronin's ruined desk, Flynn finished popping the solid state drive out of the oligarch's personal computer, bagged it, and slid it safely away into a sealed pants pocket. Through the hole they'd blown in the office wall, he could hear Cooke and the others shooting more rapidly. The Syndicate's security troops must be making another determined attack. His jaw tightened. They were running out of time fast. Galvanized into action, he rose and joined Vucovich and Kossak at the other interior door. "Hit it," he said. The Pole nodded and fired a burst into the lock. The door broke free and swung open.

Without waiting, Vucovich slammed the door with his boot, driving it inward. He pivoted through the open doorway and into what had to be a private dining room. A solid-looking white oak table occupied the center of the room, surrounded by several ornate chairs decorated with gold leaf. More paintings lined the walls, along with a couple of small abstract sculptures. Shotgun at his shoulder, Vucovich opened fire, blasting buckshot rounds into the room as he turned through an arc. Splinters flew away from the table and chairs. Paintings exploded, shredded into bits of torn canvas and smashed frames. He squeezed the trigger again and heard a *click* as the weapon fell silent. He'd expended the last of his current magazine's twelve shells. "Ah, crap," the ex-GI said conversationally. He thumbed the release lever on the shotgun and reached for a reload on his vest.

And in that exact moment, Pavel Voronin, narrow-eyed and wholly focused, leaped up from behind the cover of the massive white oak dining table. He was already shooting his compact, black polymer pistol—pulling the semi-automatic weapon's trigger as rapidly as possible to fire a lethal fusillade of 9mm bullets.

Several rounds punched into Vucovich's ballistic armor. Their impact was absorbed or deflected. But one tore through his exposed throat. Bright red blood sprayed high. Choking, Vucovich slumped against a shocked Flynn, knocking him off-balance. Momentarily locked together, the two men staggered backward.

Voronin's pistol fell silent, either jammed or out of ammunition. Snarling, his face contorted in rage, the Russian hurled it at Kossak's head before he could bring his weapon on target. The Pole ducked, and, without hesitating, Voronin lunged around the table at him with a wicked-looking combat knife held low and ready to strike upward, aiming to stab up under his ribs and deep into his heart. Desperately, Kossak whirled away, narrowly dodging the Russian's first attack. But he collided with a chair in his haste and stumbled forward, briefly losing his grip on the submachine gun slung around his neck and shoulder.

Oh my God, Flynn thought—appalled by the Russian's inhuman speed and fury. He swung the dying Vucovich aside and charged Voronin. At the last second, Flynn leaned sideways and saw the blade flicker past his face in a lightning-fast thrust. He blocked a second quick strike but took a gash on his left arm. Flynn clenched his teeth hard against the sudden agony, and then viciously slammed the barrel of his own submachine gun into the side of the Russian's face—crushing his cheekbones.

Spewing curses, Voronin reeled back against the dining room table. His face was a mask of blood, with the white of bone now showing under torn flesh. Watching his opponent closely, Flynn moved forward again, barely evading another knife strike. But this time, taking advantage of Voronin's split-second loss of balance as he lunged, Flynn hooked the other man's ankle and swept his legs out from under him. Voronin stumbled and went down. Before he could get back up, Flynn stomped hard on his right wrist—smashing the delicate bones. The Russian swore loudly.

Breathing hard, Flynn kicked the knife away and stepped back from the writhing man. He raised his submachine gun again and sighted down the barrel. His finger curled against the trigger.

"Wade's gone, Nick," he heard Kossak sigh. The Pole had his hands pressed against the other man's torn neck in a futile effort to stanch the terrible wound, but the flow of blood had stopped.

Without taking his eyes off Voronin, Flynn nodded slowly. "Yeah, I figured."

Cradling his mangled wrist, the Russian stared up at him with the cold light of fury still gleaming in his pale eyes. "Who are you?" he demanded, slurring the words through his broken and bleeding mouth.

"None of your business," Flynn replied evenly in English. "All you need to know is that you fucked with the wrong people." His finger tightened slightly on the trigger. "*Proshchay*, Pavel."

Abruptly, Voronin's mad rage seemed to vanish. The blood drained from his face and his eyes widened in sudden fear. "Wait, wait, *wait!*" he stammered. "I'm worth billions of your American dollars! I can pay you—"

"Not interested," Flynn told him flatly. He fired a short burst directly into Voronin's terrified face, riding the recoil of the Vityaz-SN to stay precisely on his chosen target. When the submachine gun fell silent, he turned away without a second glance.

FORTY-FOUR

INSIDE VORONIN'S PRIVATE OFFICE

THAT SAME TIME

Somberly, Flynn moved back to the hole blown in the wall between Voronin's outer and inner offices. He squatted down and whistled loudly. Firing on the move to keep the Raven Syndicate troops pinned down, Van Horn, Cooke, and Hynes fell back from their positions. First, Hynes stuffed the last of their equipment bags through the narrow opening, and then the three agents scrambled through, one after the other.

"Where's Wade?" Hynes asked, looking around the room.

Flynn swallowed hard. "He's dead, Cole," he said in a gentle tone, laying his hand on the other man's broad shoulder. "I'm sorry."

"Who got him?" Hynes asked. "That son of a bitch Voronin?"

Flynn nodded. "He's dead, too."

"Well, damn," Hynes said, his jaw working as he processed the news. "Somehow, I don't really call that a fair trade."

"Me neither," Flynn agreed.

After several seconds, Hynes sighed. "I always knew Wade was a damn bullet magnet. He's managed to get himself shot every op we've gone on. But you know, I never really thought he'd ever catch one bad enough to kill him." He shook his head. "Guess I was wrong about that."

Flynn looked him over carefully. "You going to be okay, Cole?"

The other man nodded with a serious expression. "Yes, sir. I know we've still got work to do—like getting our sorry asses out of this dead end we just fought our way into." He shrugged. "I'll hold it together until we're back home."

"Copy that," Flynn told him. He turned back to where Cooke and Kossak were now crouched at the blast-torn hole in the wall, ready to kill the first Russian who showed himself at either barricaded doorway in the outer office. Even after looting the bodies there for more ammo, they were down to fewer than twenty rounds apiece. Flynn passed them his submachine gun, holding up a hand with five fingers indicating the five bullets he figured he had left.

"It will suffice," Kossak told him soberly. "With so many already dead, our Russian friends have become more cautious. But they may also only be waiting for more reinforcements. I would not suggest we linger here much longer."

Flynn nodded. "Not planning on it," he assured the Pole. He grabbed the heavy equipment bag and tossed it off to the side where Van Horn was waiting. She caught the bag, placed it on the carpet, and opened the seal. Quickly, she began laying out their carefully folded wingsuits and base jump parachute packs.

Each wingsuit was crafted from layers of connected nylon. Starting a couple of decades before, skydivers had begun taking to the air wearing what were, in effect, individual flying suits. The fabric panels joining their arms and legs created an airfoil, a winglike surface that generated more lift than drag—enabling their wearers to glide downward through the air, greatly extending the duration and range of any parachute jump. Thrill-seekers also used them for high-risk jumps off cliffs and tall buildings. Tall buildings just like the Mercury City Tower, Flynn had realized when developing this part of their plan for NEMESIS.

Along with Van Horn and Hynes, he quickly stripped off his assault vest and body armor and struggled into the tight-fitting wingsuit. Once they were ready, Van Horn and Flynn took over guarding the hole while Cooke and Kossak donned their jump gear.

Meanwhile, Hynes retrieved a handful of miniaturized explosive charges Vucovich had been carrying in one of his equipment pouches. Each was about the size of a firecracker and included a tiny, quarter-inch-wide squib as a detonator. He brought them over to one of the floor-to-ceiling windows which formed the outer wall of Voronin's private office. He quickly peeled away the adhesive backing on each miniature charge and systematically placed them in a pattern across the already starred and cracked glass. When he finished, Hynes stepped back into the middle of the office, carefully adjusted the frequency on a small radio, and then pressed the transmit button on its side.

POP-POP-POP-POP-POP. Fired by the squibs responding to his radio signal, the charges went off in a rapid sequence. Shattered by the repeated succession of small explosions, the huge window fell outward—spilling seven hundred feet down the side of the bronze-tinted skyscraper in thousands of tiny, glittering shards.

Hynes swung back to Flynn. "The way's clear, sir," he called.

Flynn and Van Horn abandoned their post at the blast hole and joined the others. He touched Hynes gently on the shoulder. "I need you to handle one more task, Cole," he said quietly. "We can't just leave Wade for the bad guys to find."

Hynes nodded his comprehension. "I've got it, sir." He went over to where they'd moved Vucovich's body. Kneeling beside his dead friend, he reached inside the other man's assault vest and armed one more explosive device. With that done, he laid a hand on Vucovich's forehead. "Rest easy, brother," he murmured. Then he stood up and moved back to the group, unashamedly wiping away tears. "Everything's set," he told Flynn. "But we'd better move."

Flynn nodded. "Roger that, soldier." He swung to the others. "All right, people, saddle up. It's time to go. Now, follow me!"

He sprinted ahead and dove headfirst through the open window. Instantly, he spread his arms and legs into tapered V shapes—creating a wider surface to bite into the air now rushing up past him. Despite his grief over Vucovich's death, Flynn suddenly experienced the wild, gleeful exhilaration of completely unfettered flight, birdlike and free of artificial machinery. The rest of his Quartet Directorate team followed him, plunging through the opening one by one to avoid any risk of collision.

They were all caught by the strong winds funneled between the towering skyscrapers of Moscow's International Business Center. Blown eastward by gale-force gusts, they slanted toward the ground far below at a shallow angle—dragged earthward by gravity, but buoyed up by the wingsuits' wide surfaces as they surfed the winds.

From above and behind them came a sudden, bright orange flash, followed by a new torrent of smoke and blast-blown debris curling out of the Mercury City Tower. The powerful demolition charge Hynes had armed had gone off, further wrecking Voronin's office suite and ensuring that the Russians could not successfully identify Vucovich's body.

A few seconds after he'd jumped, Flynn judged that he'd glided several hundred feet east of the skyscraper and was getting close to the minimum safe altitude for his parachute to deploy. He reached behind him and pulled the cord on his pack. The parachute's canopy streamed out swiftly and snapped open with a tooth-rattling jolt. Tugging on its front risers to control his descent, he slid downwind over the low flat roof of Moscow's enormous Exposition Center—heading straight for the green, tree-lined expanses of the Krasnaya Presnya Park, which had once been the gardens of a wealthy Russian family. A brief glance over his shoulder showed four more canopies blossoming across the blue sky behind him.

When his boots thumped to the ground, Flynn hit the quick release button on his parachute harness and shrugged out of its straps. The billowing canopy skidded away across the grass. Van Horn and the rest of his team landed near him and ditched their own parachutes. They ignored the buzz of excitement from the mostly elderly parkgoers who were astounded by the unexpected experience of parachutists suddenly drifting down out of the air into their midst.

Flynn had just grabbed the zipper of his wingsuit when three uniformed Russian police officers broke out of the murmuring crowd with their pistols already drawn and aimed. "Halt!" one of them shouted. "Get your hands up!"

Slowly, Flynn, Van Horn, and the three others raised their hands in surrender. Caught in these awkward wingsuits while they were effectively unarmed, it was clear that any attempt to resist would be futile and almost certainly fatal. While one of the officers held them at gunpoint, the other two shackled their wrists with plastic flex cuffs and marched them to a Ford Transit van waiting along the curb just outside the park's fenced boundaries. One by one, the bound prisoners were roughly bundled into the back of the van and shoved down onto folding benches.

Two of the police officers climbed in beside them. Their companion slammed the doors shut, sealing them away from the curious eyes of the onlookers who'd gathered around the van to watch these "crazy daredevils" get their comeuppance from the law. Then he went back around to the front, slid behind the wheel, and started the engine.

The van pulled away from the curb, drove north along the park access road, and then turned left onto a wider avenue that ran west toward Moscow's elevated Third Ring Road—and, not-so-coincidentally, in the direction of the nearest district police station. On the street outside, fire trucks, ambulances, and other police vehicles screamed past with flashing lights and wailing sirens, racing toward the Mercury City Tower.

FORTY-FIVE

Inside the back of the Ford van, Nick Flynn yanked his wrists and easily snapped the pre-cut flex cuffs. He looked across the narrow aisle at the wiry, brown-haired man sitting there proud as a peacock in his neatly tailored Russian police uniform. "Nicely done, Tony."

Tony McGill, who commanded the Quartet Directorate's European action team, shrugged his shoulders. "We've had all the easy jobs in this operation." McGill and two other team members, Rytis Daukša and Einar Haugen, had been prepositioned in Moscow to support Flynn's NEMESIS force. Right now, Haugen was up front, driving the getaway van, while Daukša was squeezed into the back with the rest of them. McGill nodded at the bloodstains seeping through the arms of Flynn's wingsuit from the grazes and cuts he'd taken. "Meanwhile, it looks as though you've been in the wars, mate," the former SAS sergeant remarked. He glanced around the crowded rear compartment. "As have the rest of you lot." The corners of his mouth turned down. "Vucovich didn't make it?"

Hynes shook his head in the sudden, heavy silence.

McGill nodded sympathetically. "That's a bloody shame." His eyes clouded. The Englishman had lost comrades in past operations, so he understood how much it hurt. "Wade was a damned fine man," he said simply. "He'll be missed."

"That he will," Flynn agreed quietly. "For now, though, we have to keep moving. The timing for our next sleight of hand is a bit tight."

McGill nodded. "That it is, Nick." He reached under the folding bench he was sitting on and hauled out a large duffel bag while Daukša retrieved another one from his side of the van. "You and yours need to ditch those circus act flying suits, and it's high time my lads and I resign from the Moscow police force. I don't reckon Russian coppers fancy impostors any more than ours do."

"I don't imagine so," Flynn replied. Quickly, he stripped out of both his wingsuit and black Spetsnaz fatigues. Gritting his teeth against the pain, he wrapped gauze around the flesh wounds on his forearms. Medical care could wait until they had more time. All he needed for the moment was to stop the bleeding. With that done, Flynn put on the clothes McGill handed him—a pair of slacks, a button-down shirt, a sports jacket, and a pair of brown loafers. He made sure to retrieve the solid state drive he'd liberated from Voronin's personal computer from the Spetsnaz uniform. He carefully tucked it away in the inside pocket of his new jacket. With luck, the data it contained would give the Quartet Directorate valuable insights into the new bioweapons atrocity the now-dead Russian oligarch had been planning.

By the time Flynn finished, everyone except for Haugen had changed their own clothes, too. At a stoplight, the Norwegian doffed his police cap and shrugged out of his own uniform jacket. Now, at least when seen from a distance and through the tinted windshield, he looked pretty much like any other ordinary citizen. When the light turned green, he drove sedately past the local district police station. More patrol cars zoomed by on the other side of the avenue, undoubtedly responding to additional frantic radio calls for assistance from the units already at the increasingly confused scene around the Mercury City Tower.

Reaching the end of the avenue, Haugen turned left again—this time onto a smaller street that led directly past a massive, multi-level parking garage built parallel to the elevated Ring Road. He turned into the garage, drove up a level, and pulled directly into a parking space. Once he switched off the engine, Haugen reached up to the sun visor over his seat and triggered what looked like a simple garage door opener. The day before, McGill's team had surreptitiously fitted small electronic devices to this level's two working CCTV cameras. Responding to the signal the Norwegian had just sent, those devices shorted out, frying the cameras at the same time.

Haugen looked back over his shoulder with a satisfied smile. "All is good, Tony," he reported. "Now there will be no pictures of us abandoning this vehicle."

McGill nodded and turned to Flynn and the others. "End of the line, ladies and gents, if you please," he said in a bad Cockney accent. "Transfer here for the airport shuttles." Daukša already had the van's rear doors open. Moving quickly but calmly, the two Quartet Directorate action teams fanned across the parking garage—heading for different vehicles they had prepositioned earlier. Flynn and his team got into their dark blue Mercedes S-class sedan, while McGill and his two men slid into a white Toyota Camry. A minute later, both vehicles left the garage, turned one after the other onto the street outside, and drove sedately away, as though nothing at all unusual had happened.

BYKOVO AIRPORT, SOUTHEAST OF MOSCOW
AN HOUR LATER

Located roughly twenty-two miles from Moscow's city center, Bykovo had once been a small regional airport serving the Russian capital. It had officially closed more than a decade before, unable to compete economically with Moscow's other, larger international air hubs like Sheremetyevo, Vnukovo, and Zhukovsky. As part of the closure, its old passenger terminal and hangars had been demolished and replaced with massive warehouses and industrial buildings. Now its mile-long runway was used primarily by cargo planes ferrying in large aircraft engines, like Soloviev D-30 turbofans, for overhaul and repair at an adjoining factory. Apart from these freight airplanes, only occasional private charter flights flew into and out of Bykovo, taking advantage of its relative proximity to Moscow as well as the discretion and anonymity the nearly deserted old airport offered celebrities and businessmen who wished to avoid the public eye.

First the Mercedes and then the Camry turned onto a wide road near the end of the runway. They stopped in front of a twin-engine Hawker 4000 mid-sized business jet already in position. This aircraft was painted in the sky blue and pale green livery of Procyon Services Unlimited. The Hawker's pilot and copilot stood at the foot of their airstairs, obviously awaiting the scheduled arrival of their VIP customer and his entourage.

Once Cooke, Kossak, and Hynes had formed up around the Mercedes, surveying the scene through dark sunglasses as though they were wary personal bodyguards for a powerful and wealthy employer, Flynn and Van Horn slowly emerged from the rear of the sedan. Behind them, McGill's team climbed out of the Camry and fanned out across the tarmac.

Wearing polite, deferential expressions, the Procyon air crew came forward to greet their expected passengers. "Mr. Voronin?" the pilot asked, looking at Flynn.

He shook his head. "Unfortunately, Mr. Voronin won't be coming," he said. "I'm afraid he's had a rather serious business setback."

"A permanent one," Van Horn added.

Unable to hide his surprise and confusion, the charter pilot stared at them. "Then who the hell are you people?"

"The ones who plan on borrowing this nice Hawker jet of yours for a little while," Van Horn told him coolly.

The Procyon pilot frowned. "If this is some sort of practical joke—" He froze, as did his copilot, suddenly seeing the pistols discreetly, but quite unmistakably, aimed at them by Cooke, Kossak, and Hynes.

Cooke twitched his weapon toward the airstairs. "If you please, gentlemen," he murmured. "Let's not have any unpleasantness, shall we? Your plane's already been chartered for the day, hasn't it? So why cause a fuss about who actually makes use of it?"

Ashen-faced, the two Russians allowed themselves to be ushered back aboard the Hawker business jet accompanied by both Quartet

Directorate action teams. They closed the cabin door behind them. "You're wasting your time, you know," the copilot tried to bluster as he was being tied up and blindfolded. "Neither Yvgeny nor I will fly you criminals anywhere!"

With a kind smile, Van Horn patted him gently on the cheek. "That's okay," she said. "We don't need you. I'll take things from here." She moved into the Hawker's cockpit and took the pilot's seat. Flynn settled in beside her in the right-hand copilot's position. They both donned radio headsets and plugged in.

Van Horn picked up the clipboard by her chair and quickly flipped through it, studying the Procyon crew's flight plan and their preflight checklist. Once she was done, she checked the aircraft's battery levels and then reached up and began pushing switches on a console above them. The cockpit's five large multifunction displays came to life as the jet's generator spooled up with a shrill, keening whine. Her eyes scanned each display and the various indicator panels and lighted switches, looking for any problems. There were none. Swiftly, she ran through the checklist—calling out each item to herself as she cleared it. Then, after one final check for new caution and warning lights, Van Horn punched the starters for the Hawker's twin Pratt & Whitney Canada turbofan engines. They powered up rapidly, generating even more noise. "Sweet," she commented, after examining her engine readouts. "We're good to go. Contact Moscow ACC for me and let them know we're ready to depart."

Flynn nodded. Since both the Procyon pilots were male, they'd decided not to risk anyone in the Moscow Area Control Center suddenly questioning why they were hearing an unmistakably female voice over the radio. He keyed his mike. "Moscow ACC, this is Procyon Four-Zero-Two, requesting departure from Bykovo runway one-two, per approved flight plan."

Moments later, they heard the controller reply. "*Procyon Four-Zero-Two, Moscow ACC, you are cleared for departure Bykovo runway one-two.*" Since there was no tower here, the ACC controller rattled off a series of flight headings and altitude levels they were required to follow after takeoff to clear Moscow's airspace safely. Van Horn listened intently as

Flynn repeated those back over the radio to confirm that the controller's instructions were heard and understood. She nodded. Everything matched the flight plan the Procyon crew had drawn up. She pushed the Hawker's engine throttles forward and released the aircraft's brakes, starting her takeoff roll.

The business jet accelerated fast down the long concrete runway, bumping up and down a bit as it encountered patches where maintenance on the rarely used surface had been somewhat sketchy. At a little over one hundred knots, Van Horn pulled back slightly on the yoke. The jet broke free of the earth and climbed. At twenty thousand feet, she leveled off and banked due east—flying straight toward the chartered Hawker 4000's declared destination, Chelyabinsk, a major industrial city just east of the Ural Mountains.

OVER CENTRAL RUSSIA
SOME TIME LATER

Eighty minutes after takeoff, the Hawker 4000 was approximately one hundred and sixty nautical miles out from Chelyabinsk. Van Horn looked ahead through the cockpit window. They were starting to fly over the first forested foothills and ridges of the southern Ural Mountains. She glanced at Flynn with the flicker of a mischievous grin. "Okay, here's where this starts to get fun," she said conversationally.

He shook his head. "Remind me later that we need to have a talk about your definition of the word 'fun.'"

"I'll pencil it in," Van Horn assured him. She pulled back on the jet's throttles, allowing their airspeed to bleed off fast. Watching the numbers diminish, she nodded to Flynn. "Call in our situation."

He keyed his mike, radioing the local Area Control Center, "Orenburg ACC, this is Procyon Four-Zero-Two. We've just lost our port engine. Repeat, we're down an engine. Restart has failed. We are declaring an in-flight emergency and request permission to land immediately at the closest available airfield."

Beside him, Van Horn pushed her yoke forward, nosing down. The Hawker descended, shedding altitude fast. She glanced back through the open cockpit door. "Hang tight and buckle up, guys," she called in warning to Cooke, McGill, and the others. "This is going to get a little bumpy."

"Add your definition of 'bumpy' to our discussion list," Flynn instructed dryly. She snorted.

"*Procyon Four-Zero-Two, Orenburg ACC, copy your in-flight emergency. You are cleared to land immediately at Ufa International*," a flight controller's voice said through their headsets. "*Your vector is—*" Flynn ignored the directions. They wouldn't need them. Making an emergency landing at Ufa, central Russia's largest airport was not in their plans.

"Okay, Nick, let's hit Orenburg with our next piece of bad news," Van Horn said, watching the terrain ahead of them grow even more rugged as their aircraft dropped below twelve thousand feet.

Flynn nodded. "Orenburg ACC, this is Procyon," he radioed, allowing himself to sound more panicked. "We've just lost our starboard engine, too. Repeat, both engines are out. We're losing—" He cut his mike in mid-sentence.

Van Horn chopped both engine throttles even more and radically increased the angle of her dive. The business jet was now streaking down out of the sky, plunging toward an array of mountains and razor-backed ridges tipped with spires of upthrust rock. Flynn watched the ground rushing up toward them through the Hawker's cockpit windows and gulped.

She chuckled. "You just had us all jump headfirst off a damn skyscraper wearing nothing but *Rocky and Bullwinkle*–style flying squirrel suits, and *this* worries you?"

Flynn glanced across the cockpit. "You know you're flying a business jet, not a combat fighter, right?"

Van Horn's smile only widened. She held the Hawker in the dive, watching their altitude numbers spin down. The mountains ahead took on added shape and definition, starting to fill the entire cockpit window. Then, the instant the jet's headlong dive took them below the horizon of the closest Russian air traffic control radar, she snapped, "Kill our transponder!"

Flynn hands danced across the panel in front of him. Green lights and numbers on a display turned red. "It's off," he reported shakily. To the controllers glued to those radar screens, it would appear as though the Hawker 4000 had just crashed.

Van Horn pulled back sharply on her yoke, leveling out below the crest of a ridge, and throttled back up, accelerating to a little over three hundred knots as they raced along a valley. Wooded slopes and boulder fields flashed past on either side of their cockpit windows, climbing high above the speeding jet. By the time any search and rescue aircraft or helicopters reached their supposed crash site, her plan was to be far, far away.

The next half hour felt like a lifetime for Flynn as Van Horn twisted and turned her way through the Urals at low altitude. She cut through sheer ridge lines at water gaps, dodged small towns and villages by jinking sharply away into even narrower valleys, and practically hugged higher slopes wherever possible to stay masked from Russian radars. Flynn knew that the way she was maneuvering the twin-engine business jet was a fantastic demonstration of Van Horn's incredible flying skills and sheer guts. And despite the moments of sheer terror he felt whenever pinnacles of rock and wooded peaks seemed to leap straight at them, only to vanish astern when she banked steeply away, he couldn't help smiling inside. Off-hand, he couldn't think of anyone but Laura Van Horn who could successfully pull off this kind of wild, low-level, evasive flight in a commercial aircraft. The fact that it scared the living shit out of everyone else aboard the Hawker was probably just a bonus for her.

At last, the jet broke out of the mountains and flew back out over the vast steppes of central Asia. Van Horn immediately accelerated to more than four hundred knots, but she kept them terrifyingly low to reduce the chance of being detected. They were breaking for the border with Kazakhstan, which was now only eighty nautical miles ahead. Twelve minutes later, they flashed across the frontier—still unspotted, except possibly by wandering Kazakh shepherds—and raced onward over the almost uninhabited grasslands.

Two hundred and seventy nautical miles beyond the border, Flynn saw a long gray strip of concrete appear out of a primarily featureless countryside of grazing land, occasional fields, and meandering, mostly dry streambeds. Another huge square of concrete, now so cracked and pitted that the earth below it showed through in places, marked what had been an apron for arriving planes. They were approaching the airstrip at Arkalyk. Under the old Soviet regime, Arkalyk had been a small civilian regional airport. Now it was mostly abandoned, used only occasionally by Russia's space agency as a temporary base for helicopters recovering Soyuz capsules returning from space.

Van Horn circled low over the airfield, checking for signs of any windblown debris. It looked clear, so she brought them in and touched down—reversing thrust and braking carefully as the Hawker bounced and finally juddered to a stop near the end of the poorly maintained runway. Turning, she taxied back to where a Pilatus PC-12 sat parked just off the strip and shut down the jet's engines. As they spooled down, her mouth twitched. "Gee, I wonder how long poor Rip has been stuck here?" She gestured at the terminal building. "I bet there's not even an airport bar where he could get a drink while waiting for us."

Flynn studied the structure, whose broken windows, cracked walls, and roof open to the sky in places made its derelict status abundantly clear. "It does seem kind of quiet," he agreed thoughtfully. "Then again, Ingalls is a pretty smart guy. He probably brought along his own liquor."

"Well, then," Van Horn said with a determined air. "I hope he brought enough for everybody. Because I, for one, could use a good, stiff drink."

Flynn laughed and unbuckled his seat harness. He leaned over and kissed her. "Me, too, Laura." Then he turned and went back to open the Hawker's forward cabin door and organize their departure. As a precaution, they would leave the two Procyon pilots behind, still tied up and blindfolded inside the abandoned business jet. Fox had already arranged for trustworthy locals to release the Russians in a couple of hours. Flynn suspected the headaches involved in getting the twin-engine aircraft he and Van Horn had "borrowed" back to Russia would be enormous. But then he shrugged. Procyon Service's owners had proved willing to take what they thought was Pavel Voronin's dirty money. In the circumstances, a few headaches for them could be considered a very small price to pay.

Not long afterward, the eight surviving Quartet Directorate agents climbed aboard the waiting Pilatus PC-12 and slumped, exhausted, into their seats. The turboprop's engine coughed to life and its five-bladed propeller began spinning, slowly at first, and then faster and faster until it was nothing more than a blur. With its brakes released, the Pilatus swung onto the runway, accelerated, and lifted off into the sky over Kazakhstan—already banking to the southwest to carry Flynn and the others on the first leg of their long journey home.

EPILOGUE

SEVERAL DAYS LATER

A simple stone column rose at the heart of one of Avalon House's beautiful, carefully kept gardens. It was inspired by similar memorials erected after the Second World War by veterans of the British Special Operations Executive to honor their fallen friends and comrades. The pillar carried a short inscription—"They Gave Their Lives So That Others Might Live"—and a long list of names. Each name was that of a Quartet Directorate operative who had been killed in the line of duty while on missions organized by the American station. Additional monuments scattered in quiet places around the world recognized the dead of Four's other stations.

Under a bright morning sun and a cloudless blue sky, Nick Flynn, Laura Van Horn, Shannon Cooke, Tadeusz Kossak, and Fox stood facing Cole Hynes. Each held a glass of the finest whiskey. Their eyes were fixed on the new name added to the list: Wade Vucovich. Ordinarily, Fox would have presided over this simple, quiet ceremony, but today he had yielded that role to Hynes, who had been Vucovich's closest friend.

"Wade didn't come from much of a family," Hynes said quietly. "But he found one when it counted. And that was us." He looked around the circle. "All of us. We were his family."

Flynn and the others nodded, aware that their throats suddenly felt tight.

"Now, I know Mr. Fox here has a lot of very eloquent phrases about how the battles we fight are secret," Hynes continued. "That we're not in this for medals. Or parades. Or even thanks. And that, because we're willing to risk our lives for those of folks we won't ever meet, Four has helped preserve freedom for decades now." He shrugged. "And those words are all true. I know it. You know it. None of us would be here otherwise."

They nodded again.

Hynes smiled a little now. "But, as we all know, Wade wasn't much of a talker."

Flynn and the others smiled at that deliberate piece of understatement. With rare and memorable exceptions, Vucovich had always been the quietest one in any room—preferring actions to words whenever possible.

"Which is why I remember what he said once when I asked him if we were nuts for following the captain," Hynes indicated Flynn, "on some of these crazy-ass stunts." He shook his head. "Wade just looked me right in the eye and said, 'This job needs doing, Cole. I figure we better go ahead and do it.'"

Hynes looked down for a moment, wrestling with his emotions, and then he brought his head back up. His eyes were bright with unshed tears. He raised his glass. "Here's to Wade Vucovich," he said proudly. "He did the job."

"He did the job," Flynn agreed firmly. Van Horn and the others echoed the toast.

Then, in unison, they drained their glasses to the last drop and hurled them against the base of the stone pillar. The glasses shattered. Their glittering fragments shone brightly in the sunlight, joining those left over from other such remembrances going back decades.

Later, after the company broke up, Flynn and Van Horn strolled hand in hand down the estate's wide green lawns to the nearby lake. Fox accompanied them. They stood for a time, looking out over the gleaming water.

At length, Flynn sighed. "That list of names is getting awfully long,

Br'er Fox," he said quietly. "And more and more of those deaths are on my shoulders." He felt Van Horn's fingers tighten comfortingly around his, but she stayed silent.

Fox eyed him. "Command is a difficult and lonely road, Nick," he agreed. "But you should be wary of taking too much on yourself. Vucovich and all the others who've died were volunteers. They signed on knowing full well the risks involved in service with Four. The very same risks you run yourself," he pointed out. "By all means grieve for our friends and comrades, but don't make the mistake of seeing their sacrifices—and yours—as senseless, or without meaning."

Almost unwillingly, Flynn nodded. "Yeah, I know. And I can't deny that nailing that son of a bitch Voronin was worth doing—and maybe worth dying for."

Beside him, Van Horn stirred. "What folks used to say in the Old West is right: He needed killing," she said, without a trace of doubt in her voice.

"He did indeed," Fox concurred. "Pavel Voronin's intellect and his enormous resources and personal wealth, coupled with his utter cruelty, made him a clear and present danger to this nation and to all of our allies. Eliminating him—and in the very heart of Moscow itself—struck a powerful blow. One that Piotr Zhdanov ought to feel very deeply."

Flynn nodded, accepting the older man's assessment. But then he frowned. "Eventually Zhdanov will find a replacement for Voronin," he pointed out. "Some other Russian bastard who's just as ruthless. And maybe just as driven and tough."

"That's likely," Fox conceded.

"Then all we've accomplished is to buy ourselves some time," Flynn said, still frowning.

Fox nodded. "To be sure. But time is a precious commodity," he reminded Flynn. "And the time you and your team have bought means continued life and health for millions of Americans and other free people worldwide." His eyes met Flynn's with complete seriousness. "Nick, that's a gift beyond any conceivable price."

Van Horn stirred again, plainly deciding it was time to lighten the mood. She turned and put her arms around Flynn's shoulders. "Hear that, cowboy? Br'er Fox thinks we're pretty hot stuff." She lowered her voice to a conspiratorial whisper, easily overheard by the other man. "Maybe now's the time to ask him for a big raise."

At that, Fox raised a single, quizzical eyebrow. "A raise in pay, Laura? Should I remind you about all the damaged, destroyed, and missing aircraft you've been personally responsible for over the past few years? I believe the total runs to something on the order of several million dollars."

"Strictly as per mission requirements, Br'er Fox," Van Horn assured the older man earnestly. She glanced at Flynn. "And Nick will back me up on this, right?"

Flynn nodded, feeling a smile forcing its way onto his face. "Absolutely. I swear that we wrecked all those planes for a good cause."

Fox folded his arms. "Several. Million. Dollars."

Van Horn sighed. "So no raise, then?"

"I think not," Fox said, now not very effectively hiding a smile of his own.

"How about a couple of extra weeks of paid leave instead?" Van Horn countered, with a wink at Flynn. "Some of us may need more work on our tans."

Fox laughed. "Very well," he agreed. "You can take two weeks off from saving the world. I'll consider that a reasonable compromise."

Van Horn smiled sweetly at him. "See, that's why I tell people who call you a cruel taskmaster that they're wrong, Br'er Fox." She paused for effect. "Mostly, anyway."

MERCURY CITY TOWER, MOSCOW
THAT SAME TIME

Swathed in bandages, Kiril Rodin stepped carefully around a jagged hole in the floor of Pavel Voronin's once-impressive private office. Wooden planks stretched across the scorched and shattered cavity as a temporary patch. Plastic sheeting covering the smashed windows snapped and cracked, tugged by the winds outside. Broken shards of blackened concrete and splintered wood paneling were heaped across the torn and tattered carpet in low mounds.

"What a complete damned disaster," a furious voice growled from behind him.

Rodin turned to Piotr Zhdanov. "Yes, Mr. President," he agreed without inflection. There was no way to spin or sugarcoat this situation. Voronin and dozens of other Raven Syndicate personnel were dead—security troops and highly trained intelligence analysts alike. Naturally, Rodin had concealed his responsibility for some of those deaths. But even discounting those losses as unavoidable friendly fire casualties, the Syndicate's damage was undeniably catastrophic. Plus, the fact that such a lethal attack had been carried out under the very noses of the entire Russian national security apparatus made it even more humiliating. Adding insult to injury was Rodin's private assessment, based on all the available evidence, that this raid had been conducted by a force that numbered fewer than ten enemy agents. It was one thing to be beaten. It was quite another to be crushed, despite outnumbering the foe so heavily.

Zhdanov snorted, plainly not appeased. His face darkened further. "And VELES? What about it?"

"We have to assume that the project has been compromised, sir," Rodin admitted.

"Why is that?" the president demanded.

In answer, Rodin waved at hand at the destruction around them. "We've only found a few fragments of Voronin's personal computer," he explained. "Pieces of its case, a few broken interior electronic components, and small shreds of cable. Much remains unaccounted for."

"Including its hard drive," Zhdanov realized slowly.

Rodin nodded. "Correct, Mr. President." He shrugged. "While it is possible that the device's solid state drive was destroyed in the various explosions that gutted this office, such a favorable outcome seems highly unlikely."

"Meaning those enemy agents grabbed it before escaping," Zhdanov said.

Rodin nodded again.

The president scowled. "Wouldn't the critical information on the drive be encrypted?"

"Undoubtedly," Rodin said. He hesitated before continuing. It was delicate to point out what should have been evident to a man like Zhdanov. Russia's leader did not suffer fools gladly. Nor would he appreciate having his technological blind spots exposed. Still, it was essential to be precise. VELES was now too great a potential liability to be allowed to proceed on an overly optimistic hope. "But unfortunately, Mr. President," he continued, "Voronin's personal encryption keys would also certainly be contained on the same drive."

Zhdanov grimaced. "Very well, Rodin. I take your point," he said, biting out the words as though they tasted sour. He clasped his hands behind his back. "Stand VELES down immediately. Cancel all further tests and spore production. We can't risk going ahead with the plan if the Americans already know about it . . . or soon will."

"Should we sanitize the Kameshkovo Institute as a further precaution?" Rodin asked, choosing his words with care. "Sanitize" was the preferred black ops euphemism for killing everyone involved in the project and destroying the facility and all its records.

The president frowned. "That won't be necessary. We'll keep Neminsky's weaponized disease spores as a deterrent, in case the Americans or the Chinese try something similar against us."

"Yes, Mr. President," Rodin agreed.

Zhdanov turned away and glanced around the ravaged office. He made a sound of disgust and looked back. "I'm giving you an additional assignment," he said without preamble.

Rodin waited patiently.

"With Voronin dead, and in the aftermath of this embarrassing fiasco, I have no further use for this so-called Raven Syndicate," Zhdanov said. "It's become a waste of resources."

Rodin nodded.

"I'm putting you in charge of shutting down the Syndicate," the president said bluntly. "You will transfer the best of its surviving personnel to a new unit I want you to head. Dispose of the rest as you see fit."

"A new unit?" Rodin asked.

Zhdanov shrugged. "We'll call it the Thirteenth Bureau. Nominally, you and your people will be part of the GRU, but that's just for show. Where it counts, you will report directly to me. Your Thirteenth Bureau will be my sword and shield—a special missions force far more disciplined, focused, and controlled than anything Voronin created. I want no more private armies." He smiled thinly. "Except my own, of course."

Rodin stiffened to attention, knowing that Zhdanov appreciated such submissive gestures. "I am honored, Mr. President. I will do my best."

Zhdanov's smile remained icy. "I know you will, Rodin. You, of all men, understand the consequences for those who fail me."

Rodin nodded tersely. Anyone given responsibility by the president walked a narrow path between great authority and an ignominious death. This promotion was truly a two-edged sword. But then, deep in the private recesses of his mind, a thought occurred. Two-edged or not, the chance to form and command Zhdanov's new Thirteenth Bureau opened new vistas for him. Throughout Russia's recent history, gaining control over new organs of state security had been the path to enormous personal and political power. Why not for him as well?

Rodin had served the state from within the shadows, operating primarily as a largely anonymous, though highly efficient, assassin. Now that would change. He was about to become a servant in charge of servants. And some men in such a position, those ruthless and cunning enough to seize the opportunities they were offered, found ways to become something far more than a simple, loyal, unquestioning servant. Even Joseph Stalin, Rodin remembered with an inner smile, had grown to fear Lavrentiy Beria—his chief of state security and the architect of millions of deaths. Perhaps, he thought, Piotr Zhdanov would, someday, learn the same lesson.

ACKNOWLEDGMENT

Thanks to Patrick Larkin for his hard work and extraordinary talent.